THE DEVIL'S PLAYBACK

The wall socket behind the stereo rack pulsed with moist heat. When it reached the melting point, the white plastic plate oozed, sealing the power cord to the wall in a clot of deformed plastic.

"This record is from *all* of us," the voice said, pounding out of the speakers. "The *ultimate* bootleg."

Again, something brushed Skase, but this time it *struck* him, sending him sprawling across the floor. A pulsing charge was spitting through the air, scraping against his arms like sand. He felt the skin peeling up the back of his skull. Thin rivulets of blood stained his shirt.

"You thought you could *buy* us, didn't you? *Steal* us bit by bit—"

The bones around Skase's eyes softened, bulging from the pressure building inside his skull.

"The real fans know the truth—they've known all along. See, *we're* collectors too."

Something was tearing at Skase from the inside, slowly ripping him apart. His teeth fell from his jaw like flaking paint, rattling across the hardwood floor.

"We bootleg *souls*—and you're *next* . . ."

—from "Bootleg," by Mark Verheiden

Books Edited by Jeff Gelb

Hot Blood
  (with Lonn Friend)
Hotter Blood
  (with Michael Garrett)
Shock Rock

Published by POCKET BOOKS

SHOCK ROCK

With a Foreword by
Alice Cooper

808.
8387
38
SSS9

Edited by
Jeff Gelb

POCKET BOOKS

New York　London　Toronto　Sydney　Tokyo　Singapore

This book is a work of fiction. Names, characters, places and incidents are either products of the authors' imaginations or are used fictitiously. Any resemblance to actual events or locales or persons, living or dead, is entirely coincidental.

An *Original* Publication of POCKET BOOKS

POCKET BOOKS, a division of Simon & Schuster Inc.
1230 Avenue of the Americas, New York, NY 10020

Collection and Introduction copyright © 1992 by Jeff Gelb

ISBN: 0-671-70150-9

First Pocket Books printing January 1992

10 9 8 7 6 5 4 3 2 1

POCKE
Simon

Cover a

Printed

COPYRIGHT NOTICES

The list is lengthy, but, if not for the inspiration of these individuals and institutions, this book would not have reached fruition:

The Beach Boys
Jimi Hendrix
Janis Joplin
Led Zeppelin
Genesis
Tangerine Dream
Vangelis
Kate Bush
AC-DC
WBBF
WNCR
KPRI
KGB
Radio & Records
Mick Garris

CONTENTS

Contents

Alice Cooper

FOREWORD

For as long as I can remember, I've enjoyed being frightened by horror, because I'd be scared and then I'd laugh. Most horror films are like that: they scare you and then you laugh. Like going on a roller coaster, you jump on it and you know it's going to terrify you, but you're laughing all the way.

I've always enjoyed horror films. I still see everything that comes out, and I especially like the bad ones—I go out of my way to find them at video stores.

I've always liked horror. I had seven billion comic books as a kid—*Tales from the Crypt*, all the great ones. They didn't scare me that much, but I appreciated the imagination behind the stories. I was fascinated by the way the writers gave stories an O. Henry twist, like the television show *The Twilight Zone*. I loved that program.

Most of the songs I write have a *Twilight Zone* irony—not normal love stories, but twisted—like the way David Lynch makes movies. People love a punch line they're not expecting.

That's what I wanted to do with being Alice Cooper. When I began my musical career, everybody was a rock hero. I wanted to see someone onstage who was a combination of Dracula and the Joker—a hero with a darker side. And audiences have come to expect that; they're disappointed if they don't get to see Alice Cooper as the bad guy.

But Alice also has to be punished for his sins, which is why I still do the guillotine or some style of execution. There is a morality story happening onstage. Alice gets punished, but he always comes back, stronger than ever. In fact, I created that premise way before *Friday the 13th* or *Halloween*. I keep getting killed, and I keep coming back. The hero is the bad guy now.

When I first began writing songs, there were no Freddy Kruegers. Then Alice Cooper came out, and not only was he sexually confusing, but then he hit them with blood and guts, too. That was terrifying! I never wanted Alice to be Broadway; I wanted him to be a sideshow. There's nothing creepier than a good sideshow!

Horror is one of the dominant themes in my songwriting. With "The Ballad of Dwight Fry," "I Love the Dead," and "Sick Things," I tried to inject elements of horror into each album. The whole *Welcome to My Nightmare* record was horror-oriented. I was playing a little boy who couldn't wake up out of a nightmare.

Stephen King and Clive Barker are two of my favorite horror authors. I usually carry a couple of horror novels with me at all times. I'm even a suspect in a horror novel called *Ghoul* by Michael Slade. But I'm always surprised when a book can scare me. It's great when it happens—I'll think, Wow, they actually got me with that.

As a lyricist, I think it's even harder to scare people. I have to do it in rhyme, in very few words, and tied to music. Like any other horror writer or performer, I want to sustain the shock as long as I can. I want my audience to get a good jolt out of it, but I don't want them to go back home and kill their cats and sacrifice them to the devil.

Rock and horror make for a perfect marriage. They are both sensationalistic, unsubtle, and defiant, although some bands take it too far—the whole over-the-top satanic thing.

One morning, I woke up to find two girls sitting outside my house, dressed in black, with a box at my doorstep. I opened it up, expecting a cake or something, and it was a *heart*. It was from a road kill. These girls, who called themselves white witches, had taken this dead dog's heart out, and offered it to me to ward off evil. I told them their "gift" had nothing to do with what Alice Cooper is about.

There has to be a balance between horror and real life. I

Foreword

enjoy being Alice onstage, but I also like being able to go to a mall in my jeans sometimes. I met Elvis a few times. This guy would've done anything to just go out and shoot a game of pool with a bunch of guys, but he was trapped in his own little world. Michael Jackson is getting into a situation like that, where he's gotten so big he has no freedom. Now, that's really scary!

Jeff Gelb | INTRODUCTION

A treasured early childhood memory of mine is of lying on my bed, reading an EC comic book, listening to Bobby "Boris" Pickett doing the "Monster Mash" on the local Top 40 radio station. Heaven for a twelve-year-old. Rock music and horror were two forms of childhood entertainment that never failed me. They were exciting, unpredictable, forbidden joys—neither understood nor appreciated by parents, which made them more appealing than ever to an adolescent.

Rock and roll started turning to horror for song themes long before Michael Jackson's zombie homage "Thriller." When I was a kid, there were "Flying Purple People Eater," "I Put a Spell on You," "Haunted House," and "Ghost Riders in the Sky" (what a haunting image that conjured!). These were simple songs, often novelties—innocent tips of the hat toward the cheap horror movies of the fifties and sixties, staple drive-in fare for the lust-starved teenagers who spent their remaining allowance money on 45s.

As I grew into my twenties, horror was also growing up. A new crop of horror-fans-turned-film-directors began to make their mark on movies, with decidedly darker fare than they'd grown up watching on their local "Creature Feature" telecasts. Romero, Cronenberg, Hooper, Carpenter, and others were exploring a more serious side of horror than their predecessors had. Horror novels were emerging with a newfound sense of purpose. Richard Matheson and

Stephen King planted horror smack in the middle of suburban homes like the one in which I'd grown up.

Meanwhile, rock music was broadening its musical and thematic boundaries. I knew something was changing when the Rolling Stones, always pushing the envelope of innovation, sang "Sympathy for the Devil." The music was no longer innocent, the lyrics not inspired by adolescent humor. Horror had become a serious topic for rock music to examine.

At the same time, heavy metal music was being born. Black Sabbath was the first of a legion of bands I can recall that tried to scare their audiences. Suddenly, rock bands of all kinds were lyrically dealing with the devil; AC/DC took the "Highway to Hell," Blue Oyster Cult did "Don't Fear the Reaper," Savoy Brown had "Hellbound Train." Genesis's side-long mini-epics were manic, frighteningly intense, and surrealistic musical extravaganzas. Much of Kiss and Alice Cooper's output in the seventies was colored with horror themes.

Pink Floyd experimented with feedback and electronics to create otherworldly, science fiction–tinged sonic environments, culminating with their classic *Dark Side of the Moon*. Instrumental bands like Tangerine Dream also crafted album-length works that seemed like sound tracks for nonexistent horror films.

The eighties fostered an almost endless stream of heavy metal bands who, while shunned by radio, found their dark themes embraced by eager young audiences. While controversy surrounded the supposed intent and imagery of some of these songs, most were using horror merely as window dressing—just another way to "grab" an audience with a theme proven to hold their attention.

In the nineties, horror themes in rock music continue to flourish, yet few horror writers have attempted to combine the two elements. At last count, less than half a dozen horror novels have attempted to meld rock and horror thematically. I wondered why. As a lifelong fan of horror, and a lifelong veteran of the music industry (first in radio and then at a music industry trade publication), I grew tired of waiting for more work combining the two.

Introduction

When I began to consider editing a rock and roll horror anthology, I wondered if anyone else would understand my enthusiasm for the idea. Happily, finding writers on my wavelength was not a problem. The stories that flooded my mailbox were passionate, heartfelt excursions into horror by obvious rock music lovers. They have created a unique collection, certainly the first horror anthology that almost demands its own soundtrack. While you're reading these twenty original stories you can enhance the experience by putting on your favorite rock music.

So crank up your stereo, settle back, and read for yourself that rock and roll—and horror—are here to stay.

Jeff Gelb
January 1992

Stephen
King

YOU KNOW
THEY GOT
A HELL
OF A BAND

1

When Mary woke up, they were lost. She knew it, and Clark knew it, too, although he didn't want to admit it at first; he was wearing his I'm Pissed look, where his mouth kept getting smaller and smaller until you thought it might disappear altogether. And "lost" wasn't how Clark would sput it; Clark would say they had "taken a wrong turn somewhere," and he would grudge even that.

They'd set off from Portland the day before. Clark worked for a computer company—one of the giants—and it had been his idea that they should see something of Oregon besides the pleasant but anonymous upper-middle-class suburb of Portland that was known as Software City. "They say it's beautiful out there in the boonies," he had told her. "You want to go take a look? I've got a week, and the transfer rumors have already started. If we don't see some of the real Oregon, I think the last sixteen months are going to be nothing but a black hole in my memory."

She had agreed willingly enough (school had let out ten days before, she had no summer classes to teach, and it was just the two of them still ... although not for want of trying), enjoying the pleasantly haphazard, catch-as-catch-can feel of the trip, forgetting that spur-of-the-moment vacations often ended up just like this, with the vacationers lost along some back road that blundered its way up the overgrown poop-chute of nowhere. And at the age of thirty-two, she was a little too old to see getting lost as just another adventure. Her idea of a vacation was a motel with bathrobes on the beds and a hair-dryer in the bathroom.

Yesterday had been fine, the countryside so gorgeous that even Clark had several times been awed to an unaccustomed silence. They had spent the night at a nice country inn just west of Eugene, had made love not once but twice (something she was most definitely *not* too old to enjoy), and this morning had headed south, meaning to spend the night in Klamath Falls. They had started out on Oregon State Highway 58, and *that* was all right, but then, over lunch in the town of Oakridge, Clark had suggested they get off the main highway, which was pretty well clogged with RVs and logging trucks.

"Well, I don't know. . . ." Mary spoke with the dubiousness of a woman who has heard many such proposals from her man, and endured the consequences of a few. "I'd hate to get lost out there, Clark. It looks pretty empty." She had tapped one neatly shaped nail on a spot of green on the map marked Boulder Creek Wilderness Area. "That word is *wilderness*—as in 'no motels.'"

"Aw, come on," he said, pushing aside the remains of his chicken-fried steak. On the juke, Steve Earle and the Dukes were singing "Six Days on the Road," and outside the dirt-streaked windows, a bunch of bored-looking kids were doing turns and pop-outs on their skateboards. They looked as if they simply couldn't wait to get the hell out of Oakridge, and Mary knew exactly how they felt. "Nothing to it, babe. We take 58 a few more miles east . . . then turn south on State Road 42 . . . see it?"

"Uh-huh." She also saw that, while Highway 58 was a fat red line, State Road 42 was only a squiggle of black thread. But she was full of meat loaf and mashed potatoes, and she hadn't wanted to argue with Clark's pioneering instinct while in such a condition; what she'd wanted, in fact, was to tilt back the passenger seat of their lovely old Mercedes and take a snooze.

"Then," he pushed on, "there's this road here. It's not numbered, so it's probably only a county road, but it goes right down to Toketee Falls. And from there it's only a hop and a jump over to U.S. 97. So—what do you think?"

2

"That you'll probably get us lost," she'd said—a wise-crack she rather regretted later. "But I guess we'll be all right as long as you can find a place wide enough to turn the Princess around in."

"Sold American!" he said, beaming. He pulled his chicken-fried steak back in front of him and began to eat again, congealed gravy and all.

"Uck-a-*doo*," she said, holding one hand up in front of her face and wincing. "How can you?"

"It's good. Besides, when one is traveling, one should eat the native dishes."

"It looks like someone sneezed a mouthful of snuff onto a very old hamburger," she said.

They left Oakridge in good spirits, and at first all had gone well. Trouble hadn't set in until they turned off S.R. 42 and onto the unmarked road—the one Clark had been so sure was going to breeze them right into Toketee Falls. It hadn't seemed like trouble at first; county road or not, the new way had been a lot better than S.R. 42, which had been potholed and frost-heaved, even in summer. They had gone along famously, in fact, taking turns plugging tapes into the dashboard player. Clark was into people like Wilson Pickett, Al Green, and the Staple Singers. Mary's taste lay in entirely different directions.

"What do you see in all these white boys?" he asked as she plugged in her current favorite—Lou Reed's *New York*.

"Married one, didn't I?" she asked, and that made him laugh.

The first sign of trouble came fifteen minutes later, when they came to a fork in the road. Both forks looked equally promising.

"Holy crap," Clark said, pulling up and popping open the glove compartment so he could get at the map. He looked at it for a long time. *"That* isn't on the map."

"Oh, boy," Mary said. She had been on the edge of dozing off when Clark pulled up at the unexpected fork, and she was feeling a little irritated with him. "Want my advice?"

"No," he said, sounding a little irritated himself, "but I

3

suppose I'll get it. And I *hate* it when you roll your eyes at me that way, in case you didn't know."

"What way is that, Clark?"

"Like I was an old dog that just farted under the dinner table. Go on, tell me what you think. Lay it on me. It's your nickel."

"Go back while there's still time. That's my advice."

"Uh-huh."

He just sat there awhile longer, alternating looks through the bug-splattered windshield with a close examination of the map. They had been married for almost fifteen years, and Mary knew him well enough to know he meant to go on . . . not in spite of the unexpected fork in the road, but *because* of it.

When Clark Willingham's balls are on the line, he doesn't back down, she thought, and snorted.

He glanced at her, one eyebrow raised, and she had a sudden discomfiting thought: If she could read *him* after all this time, then maybe he could read *her* just as well. "Something?" he asked, and his voice was just a little too thin. It was at that moment—even *before* she had fallen asleep, she now realized—that his mouth had started to get smaller.

She shook her head. "Just clearing my throat."

He nodded, pushed his glasses up on his ever-expanding forehead, and brought the map up until it was almost touching the tip of his nose. "Well," he said, "it's got to be the left-hand fork, because that's the one that goes south, toward Toketee Falls. The other one heads east. It's probably a ranch road or something."

"A ranch road with a broken yellow line running down the middle of it?"

Clark's mouth grew a little smaller. "You'd be surprised how well-off some of these ranchers are," he said.

She thought of pointing out to him that the days of the scouts and pioneers were long gone, that his testicles were not *actually* on the line, but then decided she wanted a little doze in the afternoon sun a lot more than she wanted to squabble with her husband, especially after the lovely

4

double feature last night. And, after all, they were bound to
come out *somewhere*, weren't they?

With that comforting thought in her mind and Lou Reed
in her ears, singing about the last great American whale,
Mary Willingham dozed off. By the time the nifty yellow
line in the middle of the unmarked road disappeared, she
was sleeping shallowly and dreaming that they were back in
the Oakridge café where they had eaten lunch. She was
trying to put a quarter in the jukebox, but the coin slot was
plugged with something that looked like flesh.

One of the kids who had been outside in the parking lot
walked past her with his skateboard under his arm and his
Trail Blazers hat turned around on his head.

What's the matter with this thing? Mary asked him.

The kid came over, took a quick look and shrugged. *Aw,
that ain't nothing,* he said. *That's just some guy's body,
broken for you and for many. This is no rinky-dink operation
we got here; we're talking mass culture, sugar-muffin.*

Then he reached up, gave the tip of her right breast a
tweak—not a very friendly one, either—and walked away.
When she looked back at the jukebox, she saw that a fine
spray of blood had stippled the inside of the glass top.

Maybe you better give that Lou Reed album a rest, she
thought, and beyond the bloody glass a record twirled onto
the turntable—as if at her thought—and Lou began to sing
"Busload of Faith."

2

While Mary was having this steadily more unpleasant
dream, the road continued to deteriorate, the patches
spreading until it was really *all* patch. The Lou Reed
album—a long one—came to an end, and began to play
again. Clark didn't notice. The pleasant look he had started
the day with was entirely gone. His mouth had shrunk to the
size of a rosebud. If Mary had been awake, she would have
coaxed him into turning around miles back. He knew this,
just as he knew how she would look at him if she woke up

5

now and saw this narrow swatch of crumbling hot-top—a road only if one thought in the most charitable of terms—with piney woods pressing in close enough on both sides to keep the patched tar in constant shadow. They had not passed a car headed in the other direction since leaving S.R. 42.

He knew he *should* turn around—Mary *hated* it when he got into shit like this, always forgetting the many times he had found his way unerringly along strange roads to their planned destinations (Clark Willingham was one of those millions of American men who are firmly convinced they have a compass in their heads)—but he pushed on, at first convinced that they *must* come out in Toketee Falls, then just hoping. Besides, there *was* no place to turn around. If he tried to do so without at least a turnout, he would mire the Princess to her hubcaps in one of the marshy ditches that bordered this miserable excuse for a road . . . and God knew how long it would take to get a tow truck in here.

Then, at last, he *did* come to a place where he could have turned around—another fork in the road—and elected not to take it. The reason was simple: The left fork was rutted gravel with grass growing up the middle. To the right, however, the road was once again wide, well paved, and divided by a bright stroke of yellow. According to the compass in Clark's head, this fork headed dead south. He could all but *smell* Toketee Falls. Ten miles, maybe fifteen, twenty at the outside. No more than that.

He did at least *consider* turning back, however. When he told Mary so later, he saw doubt in her eyes, but it was true. He decided to go on because Mary was beginning to stir, and he was quite sure that the bumpy, potholed stretch of road he'd just driven would wake her up if he turned back . . . and then she would look at him with those wide, beautiful blue eyes of hers. Just look. That would be enough.

Besides, why should he spend an hour and a half going back when Toketee Falls was just a spin and a promise away? Look at that road, he thought. You think a road like that is going to just peter out?

He put the Princess back in gear, started down the right fork, and, sure enough, the road petered out. Over the first

6

hill, the yellow line disappeared again. Over the second, the paving gave out and they were on a rutted dirt track with the dark woods pressing even closer on either side and the sun—Clark was aware of this for the first time—now sliding down the wrong side of the sky.

The pavement ended too suddenly for Clark to brake and baby the Princess onto the new surface, and there was a hard, spring-jarring thud that woke Mary. She sat up with a jerk and looked around with wide eyes. "Where—" she began, and then, to make the afternoon utterly perfect and complete, the smoky voice of Lou Reed sped up until he was gabbling out the lyrics to "Good Evening, Mr. Waldheim" at the speed of Alvin and the Chipmunks.

"Oh!" she said, and punched the eject button. The tape belched out, followed by an ugly brown afterbirth—coils of shiny tape.

The Princess hit a nearly bottomless pothole, lurched hard to the left, and then threw herself up and out like a clipper ship corkscrewing through a storm-wave.

"Clark?"

"Don't say anything," he said grimly. "We're not lost, we just took a wrong turn somewhere. This will turn back to tar in just a minute or two—probably over the next hill. *We are not lost.*"

Still upset by her dream, even though she could not really remember what it had been, Mary held the ruined tape in her lap, mourning it. She supposed she could buy another one . . . but not out here. She looked at the brooding trees that seemed to belly right up to the road with somehow unseemly eagerness and guessed it was a long way to the nearest Tower Records.

She looked at Clark, saw that his cheeks were flushed and his mouth was smaller than ever, and decided it really would be wise to say nothing, at least not yet. Better just to sit quietly and hope he would come to his senses before this miserable excuse for a road petered out in a gravel pit or quicksand bog.

"Besides, I can't very well turn around," he said, as if she had suggested that very thing.

"I can see that," she replied neutrally.

7

He glanced at her, perhaps wanting to fight, perhaps just feeling embarrassed and hoping to see she wasn't too mad at him—at least not yet—and then looked back through the windshield. Now there were weeds growing up the center of *this* road, and if they *did* meet another car, one of them would have to back up. Nor was that the end of the fun. The ground beyond the wheel ruts looked increasingly untrustworthy; the scrubby trees seemed to be jostling each other for position in the wet ground.

There were no power poles on either side of the road. She almost pointed this out to Clark, then decided it might be smarter to hold her tongue about that, too. He drove on in silence until they came around a down-slanting curve. He was hoping against hope that they would see a change for the better on the far side, but the overgrown track only went on as it had before. It was, if anything, a little fainter and a little narrower, and had begun to remind Clark of roads in the fantasy epics he liked to read—stories by people like Terry Brooks, Stephen Donaldson, and, of course, J.R.R. Tolkien, the spiritual father of them all. In these tales, the characters (who were usually short and had hair growing out of their pointed ears) took these neglected roads in spite of their own gloomy intuitions, and usually ended up battling trolls or boggarts or mace-wielding skeletons.

"Clark—"

"I know," he said, and hammered the wheel suddenly with his left hand—a short, frustrated stroke that succeeded only in honking the horn. "I *know.*" He stopped the Mercedes, which now straddled the entire road (road? hell, *lane* was now too grand a word for it), slammed the transmission into park, and got out. Mary got out on the other side, more slowly.

The balsam smell of the trees was heavenly, and she thought there was something beautiful about the silence, unbroken as it was by the sound of any motor (even the far-off drone of an airplane) or human voice . . . but there was something creepy about it, as well. Even the sounds she *could* hear—the *tu-whit!* of a bird in the shadowy firs, the sough of the wind, the rough rumble of the Princess's diesel engine—served to emphasize the wall of quiet encircling them.

She looked across the Princess's gray roof at Clark, and it was not reproach or anger in her gaze but appeal: *Get us out of this, all right? Please?*

"Sorry, hon," he said, and the worry she saw in his face did nothing to soothe her. "Really."

She tried to speak, but at first no sound came out of her dry throat. She cleared it and tried again. "What do you think about backing up, Clark?"

He considered it for several moments—the *tu-whit* bird had time to call again and be answered from somewhere deeper in the forest—before shaking his head. "Only as a last resort. It's at least two miles back to the last fork in the road—"

"You mean there was *another* one?"

He winced a little and nodded. "Backing up . . . well, you see how narrow the road is, and how mucky the ditches are. If we went off . . ." He shook his head and sighed.

"So we go on."

"I think so. If the road goes entirely to hell, of course, I'll *have* to try it."

"But by then it'll be even farther." So far she was managing—quite well, she thought—to keep a tone of accusation from creeping into her voice, but it was getting harder and harder to do.

"Yes, but I like the odds of finding a wide place up ahead better than I like the odds of reversing for a couple of miles along this piece of crap. If it turns out we *do* have to back out, I'll take it in stages—back up for five minutes, rest for ten, back up for five more." He smiled lamely. "It'll be an adventure."

"Oh, yes," Mary said, thinking again that her definition for this sort of thing was not *adventure* but *pain in the ass.* "Are you sure you aren't pressing on because you believe in your heart that we're going to find Toketee Falls right over the next hill?"

For a moment his mouth seemed to disappear entirely and she thought he was going to explode. Then his shoulders

9

sagged and he only shook his head. In that moment, she saw
what he was going to look like thirty years from now, and
that frightened her even more. "No," he said. "I guess I've
given up on Toketee Falls. One of the great rules of travel in
America is that roads without power lines running along at
least one side of them don't go anywhere."

So he had noticed, too.

"Come on," he said, getting back in. "I'm going to try like
hell to get us out of this. And next time I'll listen to you.
Promise."

Yeah, yeah, Mary thought with a mixture of rueful
amusement and tired resentment. I've heard *that* one before. But before he could pull the transmission stick on the
console down from park to drive, she put her hand over his.
"I know you will," she said. "Your apology is accepted. Just
be careful."

"Count on it," Clark said. He gave her a small, grateful
smile that made her feel proud of her restraint and engaged
the Princess's transmission. The big gray Mercedes, looking
very out of place in these deep woods, began to creep down
the shadowed track again.

3

They drove another mile by the odometer and nothing
changed . . . except that the track grew narrower still. The
scruffy firs now seemed to crowd right up to the car, like
morbidly curious spectators at the site of a nasty accident. If
the track got any narrower, they would begin to hear the
squall of branches along the sides. The ground *under* the
trees, meanwhile, had gone from mucky to swampy; Mary
could see patches of standing water, dusty with pollen and
fallen pine needles, in some of the dips. Her heart was
beating much too fast, and twice she had caught herself
gnawing at her nails, a habit she thought she had given up
for good the year before she married Clark. She had begun
to realize that if they got stuck now, they would be spending
the night camped out in the Princess. And there were
animals in these woods—she had heard them crashing

around out there. Some of them sounded big enough to be bears. The thought of meeting a bear while they stood looking at their hopelessly mired Princess made her swallow hard.

"Clark, I think we'd better give it up and try backing. It's already past three o'clock and—"

"Look," he said, pointing ahead. "Is it a sign?"

She squinted. Ahead, the lane rose toward the crest of a deeply wooded hill. There was a bright blue oblong standing near the top. "Yes," she said, not daring to hope but hoping anyway. "I'm pretty sure that's what it is."

"Great!"

"*Maybe* it just says: IF YOU CAME THIS FAR, YOU REALLY FUCKED UP."

He shot her a complex look of amusement and irritation. "Maybe, but we're going to find out. We'll go to the top of the hill, read the sign, see what's over the crest. If we don't see anything hopeful, we'll try backing. Agreed?"

"Agreed."

He patted her leg, then drove cautiously on. The Mercedes was moving so slowly now that they could hear the soft sound of the weeds on the crown of the road whickering against the undercarriage. Mary could make out the words on the sign now, but at first she rejected them, thinking she had to be mistaken—it was just too crazy. But they drew closer still, and the words didn't change.

"Does it say what I think it does?" Clark asked her.

Mary gave a short, bewildered laugh. "I guess it does. It must be someone's idea of a joke, don't you think?"

"I don't know. But I see something else that isn't. Look, Mary!"

Twenty or thirty feet beyond the sign—just before the crest of the hill—the road widened dramatically and was once more both paved and lined. Mary felt a large weight roll off her heart.

Clark was grinning. "Isn't that *beautiful?*"

She nodded happily, grinning herself.

They reached the sign and Clark stopped. They read it again:

Welcome To
Rock and Roll Heaven, Oregon

COOKIN'EST LITTLE TOWN
IN THE PACIFIC NORTHWEST!

Jaycees Chamber of Commerce Lions Elks

"It's got to be a joke," she repeated.

"Maybe not."

"A town called Rock and Roll Heaven? Puh-*leeze*, Clark."

"Why not? There's a town in New Mexico called Truth or Consequences, one in Nevada called Dry Shark, and one in Pennsylvania called Intercourse. So why not a Rock and Roll Heaven in Oregon?"

She laughed giddily. The sense of relief was really incredible. "You made that up."

"What?"

"Intercourse, Pennsylvania."

"I didn't. Ralph Ginzburg once tried to send a magazine called *Eros* from there. For the postmark. The Feds wouldn't let him. Swear. And who knows? Maybe the town was founded by a bunch of communal back-to-the-land hippies in the sixties. They went establishment—Lions, Elks, Jaycees—but the original name stayed." He was quite taken with the idea; he found it both funny and oddly sweet. "Besides, I don't think it matters. What matters is we found some honest-to-God pavement again, honey—*pavement.*"

She nodded. "Drive on, Macduff—but be careful."

"You bet." The Princess nosed up onto the surface, which was not asphalt but a smooth composition surface without a patch or expansion joint to be seen. "Careful's my middle n—"

Then they reached the crest of the hill and the last word died in his mouth. He stamped on the brake pedal so hard that their seat belts locked, then jammed the transmission lever back into park.

"Holy wow!" Clark said.

Then the two of them just sat in the idling Mercedes, saying nothing else, looking down at the small, eerily perfect town of Rock and Roll Heaven, Oregon.

4

It was nestled in a small, shallow valley like a dimple, reminding Mary inescapably of paintings by Norman Rockwell and illustrations by Currier and Ives. She tried to tell herself it was just the geography, the way the road wound down into the valley, the way the town was surrounded by deep green-black forest—leagues of old, thick firs growing in unbroken profusion beyond the outlying fields.

But it was more than the geography, and she supposed Clark knew it as well as she did. There was something too balanced about the church steeples, for instance—one on the north end of the town common and the other on the south end. The barn-red building had to be the schoolhouse, and the big white one with the bell tower on top and the satellite dish to one side had to be the town hall. You just *knew* these things, somehow. The homes all looked impossibly neat and cozy, the sort of domiciles you saw in the house-beautiful ads of pre–World War II magazines like the *Saturday Evening Post* and *American Mercury*.

There should be smoke curling from a chimney or two, she thought, and after a little examination, she saw that there was.

"Turn around," she said abruptly. "It's wide enough here, if you're careful."

He turned slowly to look at her, and she didn't care much for the look on his face. He was eyeing her as if he thought she had gone crazy. "Honey, what are you—"

"I don't like it, that's all. It's too perfect." She could feel her face growing warm, but she pushed on in spite of the heat. "It makes me think of a whole-town version of the candy house Hansel and Gretel found when *they* got lost in the woods."

He went on giving her that patented I Just Don't Believe It stare of his, and she realized he meant to go down there—it was just another part of the same wretched closed loop of maleness that had gotten them off the main road in the first place. He wanted to *explore,* by Christ—and he wanted a

13

souvenir, of course. A T-shirt bought in the local drugstore would do, one that said something cute like I'VE BEEN TO ROCK AND ROLL HEAVEN AND YOU KNOW THEY'VE GOT A HELL OF A BAND.

"Honey—" he began in that soft, tender voice that usually meant he intended to jolly her into what he had in mind, or die trying.

"Oh, stop. If you want to do something nice for me, turn us around and drive us back to Highway 58. If you do that, you can have some more sugar tonight. Another double helping, even, if you're up to it."

He fetched a deep sigh, hands on the steering wheel, eyes straight ahead. At last, not looking at her, he said, "Look across the valley, Mary. Do you see the road going up the hill on the far side?"

"Yes, I do."

"Do you see how wide it is? How smooth? How nicely paved?"

"Clark, that is hardly—"

"Look, there's even an honest-to-God *bus* on it." He pointed at a blue bug trundling along the road toward town, its metal hide glittering hotly in the afternoon sunlight. "That's one more vehicle than we've seen on *this* side of the world."

"I still—"

He grabbed the map, which had been lying on the console, and when he turned to her with it, Mary realized with dismay that the jolly, coaxing voice had temporarily concealed the fact that he was seriously pissed at her. "Listen, Mare, and pay attention, because there may be questions later. Maybe I can turn around here and maybe I can't—it's wid*er,* but I'm not as sure as you are that it's wide enough. And the ground *still* looks pretty squelchy to me."

"Clark, please don't yell at me. I'm getting a headache."

He made an effort and moderated his voice. "If we *do* get turned around, it's twelve miles back to Highway 58, over the same shitty road we just traveled—"

"Twelve miles isn't so much." She tried to sound firm, if only to herself, but she could feel herself weakening. She hated herself for it, but that didn't change it. She had a horrid suspicion that this was how men almost *always* got

14

their way: In a more-or-less situation, it was the man who got more, and in a give-and-take situation, it was the guys who ended up taking and the dolls who ended up giving. Sooner or later all the stuff they threw at you just kind of wore you down. You gave in, and why not? It was bred in the bones of a thousand generations, daughters of Eve who said, "Yes, dear," not just because they were trained by their mothers to do so but because it was almost a goddamn genetic imperative, like blinking when somebody made as if they were going to chuck a rock or a ball at you. Everything you needed to know on the subject you could learn in the two and a half minutes it took you to listen to Tammy Wynette sing "Stand by Your Man." The only thing the song neglected to say, Mary reflected, was that you usually ended up standing beside him in a pool of deep shit.

"No, twelve miles isn't so much," he was saying in his reasonable "I Wear the Balls in This Family" voice, "but what about the fifty or so we'll have to tack on going around this patch of woods once we get back on 58?"

"You make it sound as if we had a train to catch, Clark!"

"It just pisses me off, that's all. You take one look down at a nice little town with a cute little name and say it reminds you of the candy house in 'Hansel and Gretel' and you want to go back. And that road over there"—he pointed—"heads *due south*. It's probably less than ten miles from here to Toketee Falls by that road."

"I think that's about what you said when we started off on this magic carpet ride in the first place."

He looked at her a moment longer, his mouth tucked in on itself like a cramp, then grabbed the transmission lever. "Fuck it," he snarled. "We'll go back. But if we meet one car on the way, Mary-Kate, just one, we'll end up *backing* into Rock and Roll Heaven. So—"

She put her hand over his before he could disengage the transmission for the second time that day.

"Go on," she said. "You're probably right and I'm probably being silly." Bred in the goddamn bone, she thought again. Either that, or I'm just too tired to fight.

She took her hand away, but he paused a moment longer, looking at her. "Only if you're sure," he said.

And that was really the most ludicrous thing of all, wasn't it? Winning wasn't enough for a man like Clark; the vote also had to be fucking unanimous. She had voiced that unanimity many times when she didn't feel very unanimous in her heart, but she discovered that she just wasn't capable of giving him what he needed this time.

"But I'm *not* sure," she said. "That's just what I've been telling you. *Probably* you're right and *probably* I'm being silly—I mean, we all know there's no such thing as women's intuition, we're much too enlightened to believe in such things these days—but I'm still not *sure.* So you do what you think is right, and I'll soldier along beside you, but you'll have to pardon me if I decline to put on my little cheerleader's skirt this time."

"Jesus!" he said. His face was still wearing that uncertain expression that made him look so uncharacteristically, hatefully boyish. "You're in some mood, aren't you, honeybunch?"

"I guess I am," she said, hoping he couldn't see how much this term grated on her. She was thirty-two, after all, and he was almost forty-one. She felt a little too old to be anyone's honeybunch and thought Clark was a little too old to need one.

Then the troubled look on his face cleared and the Clark she liked—the one she really believed she could spend the second half of her life with—was back. And exasperated with him or not, she found that she could offer him a genuine smile, and that was something of a relief.

5

The town had no outskirts, unless the few fields that surrounded it counted. At one moment they were driving down a gloomy, tree-shaded lane; at the next there were broad tan fields on either side of the car; at the next they were passing neat little houses.

The town was quiet but far from deserted. A few cars moved lazily back and forth on the four or five intersecting streets that made up downtown, and a handful of pedestrians strolled the sidewalks. Clark lifted a hand in salute to a bare-chested, potbellied man who was simultaneously watering his lawn and drinking a can of Olympia. The potbellied man, whose dirty hair straggled to his shoulders, watched them go by but did not raise his own hand in return.

Main Street had that same weird Norman Rockwell ambience—it was so strong that it was almost a feeling of déjà vu. The walks were shaded by well-tended oak trees, and that was somehow just right. You didn't have to see the town's only watering hole to know that it would be called the Dew Drop Inn and that there would be a lighted clock displaying the world-famous Budweiser Clydesdales over the bar. The parking spaces were the slanting type; there was a red, white, and blue barber pole turning outside the Cutting Edge; a mortar and pestle hung over the door of the local pharmacy, which was called the Tuneful Druggist. One door down was a pet shop called White Rabbit. Everything was so right you could just shit. Most right of all was the town common at the center of town. There was a sign hung on a guy wire above the giant economy-size bandshell. Mary could read it easily, although they were a hundred yards away. CONCERT TONIGHT, it said.

She suddenly realized what *really* bothered her about this town: She had seen it many times before, on late-night TV. It was just another version of the Peculiar Little Town people kept stumbling into in various episodes of *The Twilight Zone.*

She leaned toward her husband and said in a low, ominous voice, "We're traveling not through a dimension of sight and sound, Clark, but of *mind.* Look!" She pointed at nothing in particular, but a woman standing outside the Rock and Roll Heaven Western Auto saw the gesture and gave her a narrow, mistrustful glance.

"Look at what?" he asked. He sounded irritated again, and she guessed that this time it was because he knew *exactly* what she was talking about.

"There's a signpost up ahead! We're entering the Twilight—"

17

"Oh, cut it out, Mare," he said, and abruptly swung into an empty parking slot halfway down Main Street.

"*Clark!*" she nearly screamed. "What are you *doing?*"

He pointed through the windshield at an establishment with the somehow not-cute name of the Rock-a-Boogie Restaurant.

"I'm thirsty. I'm going in there and getting a great big Pepsi to go. You don't have to come. You can sit right here. Lock all the doors, if you want." So saying, he opened his door. Before he could swing his legs out, she grabbed his shoulder.

"Clark, please don't."

He looked back at her, and she saw at once that she should have canned the crack about the Twilight Zone—not because it was wrong, but because it was *right*. It was the macho thing again. He wasn't stopping because he thought it was okay to stop; he was stopping because this little town had scared him, too. Maybe a little, maybe a lot, she didn't know that, but she *did* know that he had no intention of going on until he had convinced himself he *wasn't* afraid, not one little bit.

"I just want to get a cold drink. I won't be a minute. Do you want a ginger ale or something?"

She pushed the button that unlocked her seat belt. "What I want is not to be left alone."

He gave her an indulgent I-knew-you'd-come look that made her feel like tearing out a couple of swatches of his graying hair.

"And what I *also* want is to kick your *ass* for getting us into this situation in the first place," she finished, and was pleased to see the indulgent expression turn to one of wounded surprise. She opened her own door. "Come on. Piddle on the nearest hydrant, Clark, and then we'll get out of here."

"Piddle . . . ? Mary, what in the hell are you *talking* about?"

"*Sodas!*" she nearly screamed, all the while thinking that it was really amazing, how fast a good trip with a good man could turn bad. She glanced across the street and saw a couple of long-haired young guys standing there. They were

18

also drinking Olly and looking at her and Clark. One was wearing a battered top hat. The plastic daisy stuck in its band nodded back and forth in the breeze. His companion's arms crawled with faded blue tattoos. To Mary they looked like the sort of fellows who dropped out of high school their third time through the tenth grade in order to spend more time meditating on the joys of drivetrain linkages and date rape.

Oddly enough, they also looked somehow familiar to her.

They saw her looking, and Top Hat solemnly raised his hand and waggled his fingers at her. Mary looked away hurriedly and turned to Clark. "Let's get our cold drinks and get the hell out of here."

"Sure," he said. "And you didn't need to shout at me, Mary. I mean, I was right *beside* you, and—"

"Clark, do you see those two guys across the street?"

"What two guys?"

She looked back in time to see Top Hat and Tattoos slipping through the barbershop doorway. Tattoos glanced back over his shoulder, and although Mary wasn't sure, she thought he winked at her.

"They're just going into the barbershop. See them?"

Clark looked, but only saw a closing door with the sun reflecting eye-watering shards of light from the glass. "What about them?"

"They looked familiar to me."

"Yeah?"

"Yeah. But I find it somehow hard to believe that any of the people I know moved to Rock and Roll Heaven, Oregon, to take up rewarding, high-paying jobs as street-corner hoodlums."

Clark snorted laughter. "Come on," he said, and led her into the Rock-a-Boogie Restaurant.

6

The Rock-a-Boogie went a fair distance toward allaying Mary's fears. She had expected a greasy spoon, not much different from the one in Oakridge where they'd eaten

19

lunch. They entered an airy, sunshiny lunchroom instead, an agreeable place with blue tiled walls, a tidy yellow-oak floor, and wooden paddle fans turning lazily overhead. Two waitresses in aqua rayon uniforms that reminded Mary of *American Graffiti* were standing by the stainless steel pass-through between the restaurant and the kitchen. One was young—little more than twenty—and pretty in a washed-out way. The other, a short woman with a lot of frizzy red hair, had a brassy look that struck Mary as both harsh and desperate . . . and there was something else about her, as well: For the second time in as many minutes, Mary had the strong sensation that she *knew* someone in this town.

A bell above the door tinkled as they entered, and the two waitresses glanced over. "Hi, there," the younger one said. "Be right with you."

"Naw, might take a while," the redhead disagreed. "We're awful busy. See?" She swept an arm at the room, deserted as only a small-town restaurant can be as the afternoon balances perfectly between lunch and dinner, and laughed cheerily at her own witticism. Like her voice, the laugh had a husky, splintered quality that Mary associated with scotch and cigarettes. But it's a voice I know, she thought. I'd swear it is.

She turned to Clark and saw he was staring at the waitresses, who had resumed their conversation, as if hypnotized. She had to tug his sleeve to get his attention, then tug it again when he headed for the tables grouped on the left side of the room. She wanted them to sit at the counter—to get their damned sodas and get the hell out.

"What is it?" she whispered.

"Nothing," he said. "I guess."

"You looked like you swallowed your tongue or something."

"For a second or two it felt like I had," he said, and before she could ask him to explain, he had detoured to look at the jukebox.

Mary sat down at the counter.

"Be right with you, ma'am," the younger waitress repeated, and then bent closer to hear something else her whiskey-voiced colleague was saying. Looking at her face,

20

Mary guessed the younger woman wasn't really very interested in what the older one had to say.

"Mary, this is a great juke!" Clark said, sounding delighted. "It's all fifties stuff! The Moonglows . . . the Five Satins . . . Shep and the Limelites . . . LaVern Baker! Jeez, LaVern Baker singing 'Tweedlee Dee!' I haven't heard that one since Hector was a pup!"

"Well, save your money. We're just getting takeout sodas, remember?"

"Yeah, yeah."

He walked back to the counter. Mary pulled a menu out of the bracket by the salt and pepper shakers, mostly so she wouldn't have to look at his pouty face. *Look,* it was saying. *I won our way through the wilderness while you slept, killed the buffalo, fought the Indians, brought you to this funky little place, and you won't even let me play "Tweedle Dee" on the jukebox. Bad mommy! BAAA-AAAD mommy!*

The menu, she saw, harmonized with the rayon uniforms, the fifties juke, and the general decor, which, while admirably subdued, could still only be described as Midcentury Reebop. The hot dog wasn't a hot dog; it was a Hound Dog. The cheeseburger was a Chubby Checker and the quarter-pound cheeseburger was a Big Bopper. The specialty of the house was a loaded pizza; the menu promised "Everything on It but the (Sam) Cooke!"

"Cute," she said. "Poppa-ooo-mow-mow, and all that."

"What?" Clark asked, and she shook her head.

The young waitress came over, taking her order pad out of her apron pocket. She gave them a smile, but Mary thought it was perfunctory; the woman looked both tired and unwell. There was a cold sore perched above her upper lip, and her eyes moved restlessly, touching on everything in the room, it seemed, except her customers.

"Help you folks?"

Clark moved to take the menu from Mary's hand. She held it away from him and said, "A large Coke and a large ginger ale. To go, please."

"Y'oughta try the cherry pie!" the redhead called over hoarsely. The younger woman flinched at the sound of her voice. "Rick just made it! You gonna think you died and

21

went to heaven!" She grinned at them. "Well, y'all *are* in Heaven, but you know what I mean."

"Thank you," Mary said, "but we're really in a hurry, and—"

"Sure, why not?" Clark said in a musing, distant voice. "Two pieces of cherry pie."

Mary kicked his ankle—*hard*—but Clark didn't seem to notice. He was staring at the redhead again, and his mouth was hung on a spring. The redhead was clearly aware of his gaze, but she didn't seem to mind. A little smile touched the corners of her lips.

"Two sodas to go, two pieces of pie for here," the young waitress said. She gave them another nervous smile while her restless eyes examined Mary's wedding ring, the sugar shaker, one of the overhead fans. "You want that pie à la mode?" She bent and put two napkins and two forks on the counter.

"Y—" Clark began, but Mary overrode him firmly and quickly.

"No."

The pie was under a plastic dome at the end of the counter. As soon as the waitress walked away in that direction, Mary leaned over and hissed: "Why are you doing this to me, Clark? You *know* I want to get out of here!"

"That waitress. The one standing down there. Isn't she—"

"And stop staring at her!" Mary whispered fiercely. "You look like a kid trying to peek up some girl's skirt in study hall!"

He pulled his eyes away . . . but with an effort. "Is she the spit-image of Janis Joplin, or am I crazy?"

Startled, Mary cast another glance at the redhead. She had turned away slightly to speak to the short-order cook, but Mary could still see at least two-thirds of her face, and that was enough. She felt an almost audible click in her head as she superimposed the face of the redhead over the face on record albums she still owned—vinyl albums pressed in a year when nobody owned Sony Walkmen and the concept of the compact disc would have seemed like science fiction, record albums now packed away in cardboard boxes from the neighborhood liquor mart and stowed in some dusty attic alcove, record albums with names like *Big Brother and the Holding Company, Cheap Thrills,* and *Pearl.* Her face— her sweet, homely face that had grown old and harsh and wounded too soon. Her face.

Except it was more than the face, and Mary felt fear swarm into her chest, making her heart feel suddenly light and stuttery and dangerous.

It was the *voice.*

In the ear of her memory she heard Janis's chilling, spiraling scream at the beginning of "Piece of My Heart," and she laid that bluesy shout over the redhead's scotch-and-Marlboros voice, just as she had laid one face over the other. And she knew, without any doubt at all, that if the waitress began to sing that song, her voice would be identical to the voice of the dead girl from Texas.

Because she *is* the dead girl from Texas. Congratulations, Mary—you had to wait until you were thirty-two, but you've finally made the grade; you've finally seen your first ghost.

She tried to dispute this idea, tried to point out that a combination of factors, not the least of them being the stress of getting lost, had caused her to make too much of a chance resemblance; but these rational thoughts, this rational *voice,* which ordinarily exercised a control over her life so complete it might be termed ruthless, had no chance against this new voice: She was seeing a ghost.

Life within her body underwent a strange and sudden sea-change. Her heart sped up from a beat to a sprint; it felt like a pumped-up runner bursting out of the blocks in an Olympic heat. Adrenaline dumped, simultaneously tightening her stomach and heating her diaphragm like a swallow of brandy. She could feel sweat in her armpits and moisture at her temples. Most amazing of all was the way color seemed to pour into the world, making everything—the counter, the stainless steel pass-through to the kitchen, the sprays of revolving color behind the juke's facade—seem simultaneously unreal and *too* real. She could hear the fans paddling the air overhead, a low, rhythmic sound like a hand stroking silk, and smell the aroma of old fried meat rising from the unseen grill in the kitchen. And at the same time, she suddenly felt herself on the edge of losing her balance on the stool and swooning to the floor in a dead faint.

Get hold of yourself, woman! she told herself frantically. You're having a panic attack, that's all—no ghosts, no goblins, no demons, just a good old-fashioned whole-body panic attack, you've had them before, at the start of big exams in college, at school, and that time before you had to speak to the PTA. You know what it is and you can deal with it. No one's going to do any *fainting* around here, so just get hold of yourself, do you hear me?

She crossed her toes inside her low-topped sneakers and squeezed them as hard as she could, concentrating on the sensation, using it in an effort to draw herself back to reality and away from that too-bright place she knew was the threshold of a faint.

"Honey?" Clark's voice, from far away. "You all right?"

"Yes, fine." Her voice was also coming from far away . . . but she knew it was closer than it would have been if she'd tried to speak even fifteen seconds ago. Still pressing her crossed toes tightly together, she picked up the napkin the waitress had left, wanting to feel its texture—it was another connection to the world and another way to break the panicky, irrational (it *was* irrational, wasn't it? surely it was) feeling that had gripped her so strongly. She raised it toward her face, meaning to wipe her brow with it, and saw there was something written on the underside in ghostly pencil strokes that had torn the fragile paper into little puffs. Mary read this message, printed in jagged capital letters:

GET OUT WHILE YOU STILL CAN.

"Mary? Mare? What is it?"

The waitress—the one with the cold sore and the restless, scared eyes—was coming back with their pie. Mary dropped the napkin into her lap. "Nothing," she said calmly. As the waitress set the plates in front of them, Mary forced herself to catch the girl's eyes with her own. "Thank you," she said.

"Don't mention it," the girl mumbled, looking directly at

Mary for only a moment before her eyes began to skate aimlessly around the room again.

"Changed your mind about the pie, I see," Clark the Village Idiot Husband was saying. There was an incredible complacent smile on his face. *Women!* it said. *Sometimes just leading them to the water hole ain't enough—you gotta hold their heads down to get 'em started. All part of the job. It ain't easy being a man, but we do our goldurn best.*

"Well, it looks awfully good," she said, marveling at the even tone of her voice. She smiled at him brightly, aware that the redhead who looked like Janis Joplin was keeping an eye on them.

"I can't get over how much she looks like—" Clark began, and Mary kicked his ankle as hard as she could. He drew in a hurt, hissing breath, eyes popping wide, but before he could say anything, she shoved the napkin with its penciled message into his hand.

He bent his head. Looked at it. And Mary found herself praying—really, really praying—for the first time in perhaps thirty years. *Please, God, make him see it's not a joke. Make him see it's not a joke because that woman doesn't just look like Janis Joplin, that woman is Janis Joplin, and I've got a horrible feeling about this town, a really horrible feeling.*

He raised his head and her heart sank. There was confusion on his face, and exasperation, but nothing else. He opened his mouth to speak . . . and it went right on opening until it looked as if someone had removed the pins from the places where his jaws connected.

Mary turned in the direction of his gaze. The short-order cook, dressed in immaculate whites and a little paper cap cocked over one eye, had come out of the kitchen and was leaning against the tiled wall with his arms folded across his chest. He was talking to the redhead while the younger waitress stood by, watching them with an expression of pallid fright that was almost apathy.

It *will* be apathy in another year or two, Mary thought. If she doesn't get out of here.

The cook was almost impossibly handsome—so handsome that Mary found herself unable to accurately assess his

25

age. Between twenty-five and thirty-five, probably, but that was the best she could do. Like the redhead, he looked familiar. He glanced up at them, disclosing a pair of wide-set blue eyes fringed with gorgeous, thick lashes, and smiled briefly at them before returning his attention to the redhead. He said something that made her caw raucous laughter.

"My God, that's Rick Nelson," Clark whispered. "It can't be, it's impossible, he died in a plane crash six or seven years ago—but it *is.*"

She opened her mouth to say he must be mistaken, ready to brand such an idea ludicrous even though she herself now found it impossible to believe that the redheaded waitress was anyone but the years-dead blues shouter Janis Joplin. Before she could say anything, that click—the one that turned vague resemblance into inarguable identification—came again. Clark had been able to put the name to the face first because Clark was eight years older, Clark had been listening to the radio and watching *American Bandstand* back when Rick Nelson had been Ricky Nelson and songs like "Be-Bop Baby" and "Lonesome Town" were happening hits, not just dusty artifacts restricted to the golden-oldie stations. Clark saw it first, but now that he had pointed it out to her, she could not unsee it.

What had the redheaded waitress said? *Y'oughta try the cherry pie! Rick just made it!*

There, not twenty feet away, the fatal plane crash victim was telling a joke—probably a dirty one, from the looks on their faces—to the fatal drug overdose victim.

The redhead threw back her head and bellowed her rusty laugh at the ceiling again. The cook smiled, the dimples at the corners of his full lips deepening prettily. And the younger waitress, the one with the cold sore and the haunted eyes, glanced over at Clark and Mary, as if to ask, *Are you watching this? Are you seeing this?*

Clark was still staring at the cook and the waitress with that alarming expression of dazed knowledge, his face so long and drawn that it looked like something glimpsed in a fun-house mirror.

They'll see that, if they haven't already, Mary thought, and we'll lose any chance we still have of getting out of this nightmare. I think you better take charge of this situation, kiddo, and quick. The question is, what are you going to do?

She reached for his hand, meaning to grab it and squeeze it, then decided that wouldn't do enough to alter his slack-jawed expression. She squeezed his balls instead. Squeezed them as hard as she dared. Clark jerked as if someone had zapped him with a taser and swung toward her so fast he almost fell off his stool. The look of slack amazement had become one that could have been taken for sharp-eyed interest by someone who didn't know that Clark had just gotten his chimes rung by a very heavy hand.

Trying to leave together would be a mistake—she was sure of that much. If they were going to get out of here, she had an idea they would have to con their way out . . . and she wasn't sure they could do it. If only Clark had been able to suppress that look of goggling incredulity! But it was hard to blame him for it, given the circumstances. She would just have to play it by ear, and hope for the best.

"I left my wallet in the car," she said. Her voice sounded brittle and too loud in her own ears. "Would you get it for me, Clark?"

She looked at him, lips smiling, eyes locked on his with complete concentration. She had read, probably in some shit-intensive women's magazine while waiting to get her hair done, that when you lived with the same man for ten or twenty years, you forged a telepathic link with your partner. This link, the article went on to suggest, came in mighty handy when your hubby was bringing the boss home to dinner without phoning ahead or when you wanted him to bring a bottle of amaretto from the liquor store and a carton of whipping cream from the supermarket. Now she tried— tried with all her might—to send a far more important message.

Go, Clark. Please go. I'll give you ten seconds, then come on the run. And if you're not in the driver's seat with the key in the ignition, I have a feeling we could be seriously fucked here.

And at the same time, a deeper voice—perhaps the deepest one of all—was saying timidly: This is all a dream, isn't it, Mary? I mean . . . it *is*, isn't it?

Clark was looking at her carefully, his eyes watering from the tweak she had given him . . . but at least he wasn't complaining about it. His eyes shifted to the redhead and the short-order cook for a moment, saw they were still deep in their conversation (now *she* appeared to be the one who was telling a joke), and then shifted back to her.

"It might have slid under the seat," she said in her too-loud, too-brittle voice before he could reply. "It's the red one."

After another moment of silence—one that seemed to last forever—Clark nodded slightly. "Okay," he said, and she could have blessed him for his nicely normal tone, "but no fair stealing my pie while I'm gone."

"Just get back before I finish mine and you'll be okay," she said, and tucked a forkful of cherry pie into her mouth. It had absolutely no taste at all to her. But she smiled. God, yes. Smiled like the Miss New York Apple Queen she had once been.

Clark started to get off his stool, and then, from somewhere outside, came a series of amplified guitar chops—not chords but only open strums. Clark jerked as if stung, and Mary shot out one hand to clutch his arm. Her heart, which had been slowing down, broke into that nasty, scary sprint again.

The redhead and the cook—even the younger waitress who, thankfully, didn't look like anyone famous—glanced casually toward the plate-glass windows of the Rock-a-Boogie.

"Don't let it get you, hon," the redhead said. "They're just startin' to tune up. For the concert tonight."

"That's right," the short-order cook said. He regarded Mary with his drop-dead blue eyes. "Here in Rock and Roll Heaven, we have a concert most every night."

Yes, Mary thought. Of course. Of course you do.

A voice both toneless and godlike rolled across from the town common, a voice almost loud enough to rattle the windows. Mary, who had been to her share of rock shows, was able to place it in a clear context almost at once—it called up images of bored, long-haired roadies strolling around the stage before the lights went down, picking their way with easy grace through the forests of amps and mikes, kneeling every now and then to patch two power cords together.

"Test!" this voice cried. *"Test-Test-Test!"*

Another guitar chop, still not a chord but close this time. Then a drum run. Then a fast trumpet riff lifted from the chorus of Lennon's "Instant Karma," accompanied by a light rumble of bongos. CONCERT TONIGHT, the Norman Rockwell sign over the Norman Rockwell town common had said, and Mary, who had grown up in Elmira, New York, had been to quite a few free concerts-on-the-green as a child. Those really *had* been Norman Rockwell concerts, with the band (made up of guys wearing their Volunteer Fire Department uniforms in lieu of the band uniforms they couldn't afford) tootling its way through slightly off-key Sousa marches and the local Barbershop Quartet (Plus Two) harmonizing on things like "Roll On, Shenandoah" and "I've Got a Gal in Kalamazoo."

She had an idea that the concerts in Rock and Roll Heaven might be quite different from those childhood concerts where she and her friends had run around waving sparklers as twilight drew on for night.

She had an idea that *these* concerts-on-the-green might be closer to Goya than Rockwell.

"I'll go get your wallet," he said. "Eat your pie."

"Thank you, Clark." She put another tasteless forkful of pie in her mouth and watched him head for the door. He walked in an exaggerated slow-motion saunter that struck her feverish eye as absurd and somehow horrid: *I don't have the slightest idea that I'm sharing this room with a couple of famous corpses,* Clark's ambling, sauntering stride was saying. *What, me worry?*

Hurry up, Clark! she wanted to scream. Just hurry the fuck up!

The bell jingled and the door opened just as Clark reached

for the knob, and two more dead Texans came in. The one wearing the dark glasses was Roy Orbison. The one wearing the hornrims was Buddy Holly.

All my exes come from Texas, Mary thought wildly, and waited for them to lay their hands on her husband and drag him away.

"'Scuse me, sir," the man in the dark glasses said politely, and instead of grabbing Clark, he stepped aside for him. Clark nodded without speaking—Mary was suddenly quite sure he *couldn't* speak—and stepped out into the sunshine.

Leaving her alone in here with the dead. And that thought seemed to lead naturally to another one, even more horrible: Clark was going to drive off without her. She was suddenly sure of it. Not because he wanted to, and certainly not because he was a coward—this situation went beyond questions of courage and cowardice, and she supposed that the only reason they both weren't gibbering and drooling on the floor was because it had developed so *fast*—but because he just wouldn't be able to *do* anything else. The reptile that lived on the floor of his brain, the one in charge of self-preservation, would simply slither out of its hole in the mud and take charge of things.

You've got to get out of here, Mary, the voice in her mind—the one that belonged to her own reptile—said, and the tone of that voice frightened her. It was more reasonable than it had any right to be, given the situation, and she had an idea that sweet reason might give way to shrieks of madness at any moment.

Mary took one foot off the rail under the counter and put it on the floor, trying to ready herself mentally for flight as she did so, but before she could gather herself, a narrow hand fell on her shoulder and she looked up into the smiling, knowing face of Buddy Holly.

7

He had died in 1959, a piece of trivia she remembered from that movie where Lou Diamond Phillips starred as Ritchie Valens (and if Buddy was here, the real Ritchie was probably

30

rolling around someplace, too). That was more than thirty years gone, but Buddy Holly was still a gawky twenty-three-year-old who looked seventeen, his eyes swimming behind his glasses and his Adam's apple bobbing up and down like a monkey on a stick. He was wearing an ugly plaid jacket and a string tie. The tie's clasp was a large chrome steer's head. The face and the taste of a country bumpkin, you would have said, but there was something in the set of the mouth that was too wise, somehow, too *dark,* and for a moment the hand gripped her shoulder so tightly she could feel the tough pads of callus on the ends of the fingers—guitar calluses.

"Hey there, sweet thang," he said, and she could smell sweet clove gum on his breath. There was a silvery crack, hair-thin, zigzagging across the left lens of his glasses. "Ain't seen *you* roun' these parts before."

Incredibly, she was lifting another forkful of pie toward her mouth, her hand not hesitating even when a clot of cherry filling plopped back onto her plate. More incredibly, she was slipping the fork through a small, polite smile.

"No," she said. She was somehow positive that she couldn't let this man see she had recognized him; if he did, any small chance she and Clark might still have would evaporate. "My husband and I are just . . . you know, just passing through."

And was Clark passing through even now, desperately keeping to the posted speed limit while the sweat trickled down his face and his eyes rolled back and forth from the mirror to the windshield to the mirror again? Was he?

The man in the plaid sport coat grinned, revealing teeth that were too big and much too sharp. "Well, I sure hope you and y'man can hang in for the concert tonight." Mary suddenly realized that the eye behind the cracked lens was full of blood. As Holly's grin widened, pushing the corners of his eyes into a squint, a drop of blood spilled over his lower lid and tracked down his cheek like a tear. "We put on quite a show, honey. Quite a show. Why, you wouldn't believe it."

"I'm sure I would," Mary said faintly. Yes, Clark was gone. She was sure of it. Clark had left her here with these dead ghouls, and she supposed that soon enough the frightened young girl with the cold sore would lead her into the back room, where her own rayon uniform and order pad would be waiting.

"No, sir, these shows are *special.*" The drop of blood fell from his face and pinked onto the seat of the stool Clark had so recently vacated. "Stick around. You'll be glad y'did. Right, Roy?"

The man in the dark glasses had joined the cook and the waitresses. A Maltese cross hung in the open V of his shirt. He nodded and flashed a smile of his own. "You best be believin' it, ma'am."

"I'll ask my husband," she heard herself saying, and completed the thought in her mind: If I ever see him again, that is.

"You do that, sweet thang! You just do that!" Then, incredibly, he was giving her shoulder one final squeeze and walking away, leaving her a clear path to the door. Even more incredibly, she could see the Princess's distinctive grille and Benz hood ornament still outside.

Buddy joined his friend Roy, reached behind the redheaded waitress, and goosed her. She screamed indignantly, and as she did, a flood of maggots flew from her mouth. Most splattered on the floor between her feet, but some clung to her lower lip, squirming obscenely.

The young waitress turned away with a sad, sick grimace, raising one blocking hand to her face. And for Mary Willingham, running ceased to be something she had planned and became an instinctive, horrified reaction. She was up and off the stool like a shot and sprinting for the door.

"Hey!" the redhead screamed. "Hey, you didn't pay for the pie! Or the goddam sodas, either! This ain't no Dine and Dash, you crotch! Rick! Buddy! Get her!"

Mary grabbed for the doorknob and felt it slip through her sweaty fingers. Behind her, she heard the thud of approaching feet. She grabbed the knob again, succeeded in turning it this time, and yanked the door open so hard she tore off the overhead bell. A narrow hand with hard calluses on the tips of the fingers grabbed her just above the elbow. This time the fingers were not just squeezing, but pinching;

she felt a nerve suddenly go critical, first sending a thin wire of pain from her elbow all the way up to the left side of her jaw and then numbing her arm.

She swung her right fist back like a short-handled croquet mallet, connecting with what felt like the thin shield of pelvic bone above a man's groin. There was a short, pained snort, and the hand holding her arm loosened. Mary tore free and bolted through the doorway, her hair standing out around her head in a bushy corona of fright.

She blessed Clark for staying; they would worry about how he had gotten them into this mess later—if there *was* a later. And he *had* understood, because he was sitting behind the wheel instead of groveling under the passenger seat for her wallet, and he keyed the Princess's engine the moment she came flying out of the Rock-a-Boogie.

The man in the flower-decorated top hat and his tattooed companion were standing outside the barbershop again, watching expressionlessly as Mary yanked open the passenger door. She thought she now recognized Top Hat—she had three Lynyrd Skynyrd albums, and she was pretty sure he was Ronnie Van Zant. No sooner had she realized that than she knew who his illustrated companion was: Duane Allman, killed when his motorcycle skidded beneath a tractor-trailer rig twenty years ago. He took something from the pocket of his denim jacket and bit into it. Mary saw with no surprise at all that it was a peach.

Rick Nelson burst out of the Rock-a-Boogie. Buddy Holly was right behind him, the entire left side of his face now drenched in blood.

"Get in!" Clark screamed at her. *"Get in the fucking car, Mary!"*

She threw herself into the passenger bucket headfirst and he was backing out before she could even make a try at slamming the door. The Princess's rear tires howled and sent up clouds of blue smoke. Mary was thrown forward with neck-snapping force, and her head connected with the padded dashboard. She groped behind her for the open door as Clark cursed and yanked the transmission down into drive.

Rick Nelson threw himself onto the Princess's gray hood.

His eyes blazed. His lips were parted over impossibly white teeth in a hideous grin. His cook's hat had fallen off, and his brown hair hung around his temples in oily snags and corkscrews.

"You're coming to the show!" he yelled.

"Fuck you!" Clark yelled back. He found drive and floored the accelerator. The Princess's normally sedate diesel engine gave a low scream and the car shot forward. The apparition continued to cling to the hood, snarling and grinning in at them.

"Buckle your seat belt!" Clark bellowed.

She snatched the buckle and jammed it home, watching with horrified fascination as the thing on the hood reached forward with its left hand and grabbed the windshield wiper in front of her. It began to haul itself forward. The wiper snapped off. The thing on the hood glanced at it, tossed it overboard, and reached for the wiper on Clark's side.

Before he could get it, Clark tramped on the brake with both feet. Mary was thrown forward. Her seat belt locked, biting painfully into the underside of her left breast. For a moment there was a terrible feeling of *pressure* inside her, as if her guts were being shoved up into the funnel of her throat by a ruthless hand. The thing on the hood was thrown clear and landed in the street at least twenty feet in front of the car. Mary heard a brittle crunching sound, and blood splattered the pavement in a starburst pattern around its head.

She glanced back and saw the others running toward the car. Janis was leading them, her face twisted into a haglike grimace of hate and excitement.

In front of them, the short-order cook sat up with the boneless ease of a puppet. The big grin was wider than ever.

"Clark, they're coming!" Mary screamed.

He glanced briefly into the rearview, then floored the accelerator again. The Princess leaped ahead. Mary had time to see the man sitting in the street raise one arm to shield his face, and wished that was all she'd had time to see, but there was something else, as well, something worse: Beneath the shadow of his raised arm, she thought he was *still* grinning.

34

Then the Princess, doing twenty miles an hour and still accelerating, hit him and bore him under. There were crackling sounds that reminded her of a couple of kids rolling in a pile of autumn leaves. She clapped her hands over her ears—too late, too late—and screamed.

"Don't bother," Clark said. He was looking grimly into the rearview mirror. "He's getting up. No harm, no foul."

"What?"

"Except for the tire-track across his shirt, he's—" He broke off abruptly, looking at her. "Who hit you, Mary?"

"What?"

"Your mouth is bleeding. Who hit you?"

She put a finger to the corner of her mouth, looked at the red smear on it, then tasted it. "Not blood—cherry pie," she said, and uttered a high-pitched, desperate laugh. "Get us out of here, Clark, please get us out."

"You bet," he said, and turned his attention back to Main Street, which was wide and empty. Mary noticed that, electric guitars on the common or not, there were no more power lines on this street than there had been on the sides of the road that had led them here, and there really wasn't anything strange about that, was there? If you were a rock and roll ghost, Oregon Hydroelectric would probably be the least of your worries.

The Princess was gaining speed as all diesels seem to— not fast, but with a kind of relentless strength—and spreading a dark brown cloud of exhaust behind her. Mary caught a blurred glimpse of a department store, a bookstore, and a maternity shop called Rock and Roll Lullabye. She saw a young man with shoulder-length brown curls standing outside the Rock 'Em and Sock 'Em Billiards Emporium with his arms folded across his chest and one snakeskin boot propped against the whitewashed brick. His face was handsome in a heavy, pouting way, and Mary had time to recognize him: the Lizard King himself.

"That was Jim Morrison," Clark said in a dry, emotionless voice.

"I know. I saw."

Yes—she saw, but the images were like dry paper bursting into flame under a relentless, focused light that seemed to fill

35

her mind; it was as if the intensity of her horror had turned her into a human magnifying glass, and she understood that if they got out of here, no memories of this Peculiar Little Town would remain; the memories would be just ashes blowing in the wind. That was the way these things worked, of course. A person could not retain such hellish images, such hellish *experiences,* and remain rational, so the mind turned into a blast furnace, crisping each one as soon as it was created.

And that's why most people can still afford the luxury of disbelieving such things as ghosts and haunted houses, she thought. Because when the mind is turned toward the terrifying and the irrational, like a woman who is turned and made to look upon the face of Medusa, it forgets. It *has* to forget. And, God, except for getting out of this hell, forgetting is the only thing in the world I want.

She saw a little cluster of people standing on the tarmac of a Cities Service station at an intersection near the far end of town. They wore frightened, ordinary faces above faded, ordinary clothes. A man in an oil-stained mechanic's coverall. A woman in a nurse's uniform—white once, maybe, now a dingy gray. An older couple, she in orthopedic shoes and he with a hearing aid the size of a cherry tomato in one ear, clinging to each other like children who fear they are lost in the deep, dark woods. Mary understood without needing to be told that these people, along with the younger waitress, were the *real* residents of Rock and Roll Heaven, Oregon . . . and they were prisoners.

"Please get us out of here, Clark," she said. *"Please."* Something tried to come up her throat and she clapped her hands over her mouth, sure she was going to upchuck. Instead of vomiting, she uttered a loud belch that burned her throat like fire and tasted of the pie she had eaten in the Rock-a-Boogie Restaurant.

"We'll be okay. We're almost out of town. Take it easy, Mary."

The road—she could no longer think of it as Main Street now that she could see the end of town just ahead—ran past the Rock and Roll Heaven Municipal Fire Department on the left and the school on the right (even in her heightened state of terror, there seemed something very funny about a citadel of learning called the Rock and Roll Grammar School). Three children stood in the playground adjacent to the school, watching with apathetic eyes as the Princess tore past. Up ahead, the road curved around an outcrop with a sign planted on it: YOU ARE NOW LEAVING ROCK AND ROLL HEAVEN. GOOD NIGHT, SWEETHEART, GOOD NIGHT.

Clark swung the Princess into the curve without slowing, and on the far side, there was a bus blocking the road.

It was no ordinary yellow school bus; it raved and rioted with a hundred colors and a thousand psychedelic swoops, an oversize souvenir of the Summer of Love. The windows flocked with butterfly decals and peace signs, and even as Clark screamed and brought his feet down on the brake, she read, with a fatalistic lack of surprise, the words floating up the painted side like overfilled dirigibles: THE MAGIC BUS.

Clark gave it his best, but wasn't quite able to stop. The Princess slid into the Magic Bus at ten or fifteen miles an hour, her wheels locked and her tires smoking fiercely. There was a hollow bang as the Mercedes hit the tie-dyed bus amidships. Mary was thrown forward against her safety harness again. The bus rocked on its springs a little, but that was all.

"Back up and go around!" she screamed at Clark, but she was nearly overwhelmed by a suffocating intuition that it was all over. The Princess's engine sounded choppy, and Mary could see steam escaping from around the front of her crumpled hood; it looked like the breath of a wounded dragon. When Clark dropped the transmission lever down into reverse, the car backfired twice and then died.

Behind them, they could hear an approaching siren. She wondered who the town constable would turn out to be. Not John Lennon, whose life's motto had been Question Authority, and not Morrison, who was clearly one of the town's pool-hall bad boys. Who? And did it really matter? Maybe, she thought, it'll turn out to be Jimi Hendrix. That sounded crazy, but she knew her rock and roll, probably better than Clark, and she remembered reading that Hendrix had been

STEPHEN KING

a jump-jockey in the 101st Airborne. And didn't they say that ex-service people often made the best law enforcement officials?

You're going crazy, she told herself, then nodded. Sure she was—why not? "What now?" she asked Clark dully.

He opened his door, having to put his shoulder into it because it had crimped a little in the frame. "Now we run," he said.

"What's the point?"

"You saw them; do you want to *be* them?"

That rekindled some of her fear. She released the clasp of her seat belt and opened her own door. Clark came around the Princess and took her hand. As they turned back toward the Magic Bus, his grip tightened painfully as he saw who was stepping off—a tall man in an open-throated white shirt, dark dungarees, and wraparound sunglasses. His blue-black hair was combed back from his temples in a lush and impeccable duck's-ass haircut. There was no mistaking those impossible, almost hallucinatory good looks; not even sunglasses could hide them. The full lips parted in a small, sly smile.

A blue and white police cruiser with ROCK AND ROLL HEAVEN P.D. written on the doors came around the curve and screeched to a stop inches from the Princess's back bumper. The man behind the wheel was black, but he wasn't Jimi Hendrix after all. Mary couldn't be sure, but she thought the local law was Otis Redding.

The man in the shades and black jeans was now standing directly in front of them, his thumbs hooked into his belt loops, his pale hands dangling like dead spiders. "How y'all t'day?" There was no mistaking that slow, slightly sardonic Memphis drawl, either. "Want to welcome you both to town. Hope you can stay with us for a while. Town ain't much to look at, but we're neighborly, and we take care of our own." He stuck out a hand on which three absurdly large rings glittered. "I'm the mayor 'round these parts. Name's Elvis Presley."

38

8

Dusk, of a summer night.

As they walked onto the town common, Mary was again reminded of the concerts she had attended in Elmira as a child, and she felt a pang of nostalgia and sorrow penetrate the cocoon of shock that her mind and emotions had wrapped around her. So much was the same . . . but so much was different, too. There were no children waving sparklers; the only kids present were half a dozen or so huddled together as far from the bandshell as they could get, their pale faces strained and watchful. The kids she and Clark had seen in the grammar school play-yard when they made their abortive escape attempt were among them.

And it was no quaint brass band that was going to play in fifteen minutes or half an hour, either—spread across the bandshell (which looked almost as big as the Hollywood Bowl to Mary's eyes) were the implements and accessories of what had to be the world's biggest—and loudest, judging from the amps—rock and roll band, an apocalyptic bebop combination that would, at full throttle, probably be loud enough to shatter window glass five miles away. She counted a dozen guitars on stands and stopped counting. There were four full drum sets . . . bongos . . . congas . . . a rhythm section . . . circular stage pop-ups where the backup singers would stand . . . a steel forest of mikes.

The common itself was filled with folding chairs—Mary estimated somewhere between seven hundred and a thousand—but she thought there were no more than fifty spectators actually present, and probably fewer. She saw the mechanic, now dressed in clean jeans and a Perma-Press shirt, sitting next to a woman with a careworn face who was probably his wife. The nurse was sitting all by herself in the middle of a long, empty row. Her face was turned upward and she was watching the first few glimmering stars come out. Mary looked away from the woman quickly; she felt if she looked at that sad, longing face for too long, her heart would break.

Of the town's more famous residents there was currently no sign. Of course not; their day jobs were behind them now and they would all be backstage, dressing in their sequins and checking their cues. Getting ready for tonight's show.

Clark paused about a quarter of the way down the grassy central aisle. A puff of evening breeze tousled his hair, and Mary thought it looked as dry as straw. There were lines carved into Clark's forehead and around his mouth that she had never seen before. He looked as if he had lost thirty pounds since lunch in Oakridge. That was impossible, of course, but knowing that didn't change her impression.

And just how do you think *you* look, beautiful? she told herself.

"Where do you want to sit?" Clark asked. His voice was thin and uninterested—the voice of a man who still believes he is dreaming.

Mary spotted the waitress with the cold sore. She was on the aisle about four rows down, now dressed in a light gray blouse and cotton skirt. She had thrown a sweater over her shoulders. "There," Mary said, and Clark led her in that direction without question.

She looked around at Mary and Clark, and Mary saw that her eyes had at least settled down tonight, which was something of a relief. A moment later she realized why: The girl was apocalyptically stoned. Mary looked down, not wanting to meet that dusty stare any longer—it was somehow like looking at someone whose pants have fallen down—and when she did, she saw that the waitress's left hand was wrapped in a bulky white bandage. Mary realized with dim horror that the last two fingers on the bandaged hand were gone.

"Hi," the girl said. "I'm Sissy Thomas."

"Hello, Sissy. I'm Mary Willingham. This is my husband, Clark."

"Pleased to meet you," the waitress said.

"Your hand . . ." Mary trailed off, not sure how to go on.

"Frankie did it." Sissy spoke with the deep indifference of one who is riding the pink horse down Dream Street. "Frankie Lymon. Everyone says he was the sweetest guy you'd ever want to meet while he was alive and he only turned mean when he came here. He was one of the first ones . . . the pioneers, I guess you'd say. I don't know about that. If he was sweet before, I mean. I only know he's meaner than cat-dirt now. I don't care. I just wish you'd gotten away, and I'd do it again. Besides, Crystal takes care of me."

Sissy nodded toward the nurse, who had stopped looking at the stars and was now looking at them.

"Crystal takes real good care. She'll fix you up, if you want—you don't need to lose no fingers to want to get stoned in this town."

"My wife and I don't use drugs," Clark said, sounding pompous.

Sissy regarded him without speaking for a few moments. Then she said, "You will."

"When does the show start?" Mary could feel the cocoon of shock starting to erode, and she didn't much care for the feeling.

"Soon."

"How long do these concerts go on?"

Sissy didn't answer for a long time, and Mary was getting ready to restate the question, thinking the girl either hadn't heard or hadn't understood, when she said: "A long time. I mean, the show will be over by midnight, they always are, but still . . . they go on a long time. Because time is different here. Dig me? *Different.* It might be . . . oh, I dunno . . . I think when the guys really get cooking, they sometimes go on for a year or more."

A cold gray frost began creeping up Mary's arms and back. She tried to imagine having to sit through a yearlong rock show, and couldn't do it. This is a dream and you'll wake up, she told herself, but that thought, persuasive enough as they stood listening to Elvis Presley in the sunlight by the Magic Bus, was now losing a lot of its force and believability.

"Drivin' out this road here wouldn't do you no good nohow," Elvis had told them. "It don't go noplace but Umpqua Swamp. No roads in there, just a lot of quicksand. And other things."

"Bears," the policeman who might be Otis Redding had said from behind them.

41

"Bears, yep," Elvis agreed, and then his lips had curled up in the too-knowing smile Mary remembered so well from TV and the movies. "And other things."

Mary began, "If we stay for the show . . ."

Elvis nodded emphatically. "The show! Oh, yeah, you *gotta* stay for the show! We really rock. You just see if we don't."

"Ain't nothin' but a stone fact," the policeman had added.

"If we stay for the show . . . can we go when it's over?"

Elvis and the cop had exchanged a look. "Well, you know, ma'am," the erstwhile King of Rock and Roll said at last, "we're real far out in the boonies here, and attractin' an audience is kinda slow work . . . although once they hear us, *ever*body stays around for more . . . and we was kinda hopin' you'd stick around yourselves for a while. See a few shows and kind of enjoy our hospitality." He had pushed his sunglasses up on his forehead then, for a moment revealing eye sockets that were horribly blank—the emptily thoughtful eye sockets of a skull. Then they were Elvis's dark blue eyes again, regarding them with somber interest.

"I think," he had said, "you might even decide you want to settle down."

9

There were more stars in the sky now; it was almost full dark. Over the stage, orange spots were coming on, soft as night-blooming flowers, illuminating the mike stands one by one.

"They gave us jobs," Clark said dully. *"He* gave us jobs. The mayor. The one who looks like Elvis Presley."

"He *is* Elvis," Sissy Thomas said, but Clark just went on staring at the stage. He was not prepared to even *think* this yet, let alone hear it.

"Mary is supposed to go to work in the Beauty Bar tomorrow," he went on. "She has a teacher's certificate and an English degree, but she's supposed to spend the next God-knows-how-long as a shampoo girl. Then he looked at me and he says, 'Whuh bou-*chew*, sir? Whuh-*chore* special-ty?'" Clark spoke in a vicious imitation of the mayor's Memphis drawl, and at last a genuine expression began to show in the waitress's stoned eyes. Mary thought it was fear.

"You hadn't ought to make fun," she said. "Makin' fun can get you in trouble around here . . . and you don't want to get in trouble." She slowly raised her bandage-wrapped hand. Clark stared at it, wet lips quivering, until she lowered it into her lap again, and when he spoke again, it was in a lower voice.

"I told him I was a computer software expert, and he said there weren't any computers in town . . . although they 'sho would admiah to git a Ticketron outlet or two.' Then the other guy laughed and said there was a stockboy's job open down at the superette, and—"

A bright white spotlight speared the forestage. A short man in a sport coat so wild it made Buddy Holly's look tame strode into its beam, his hands raised as if to stifle a huge comber of applause.

"Who's that?" Mary asked Sissy.

"Some old-time disc jockey who used to run a lot of these shows. His name is Alan Tweed or Alan Breed or something like that. We hardly ever see him except here. I think he drinks. He sleeps all day—that I *do* know."

And as soon as the name was out of the girl's mouth, the cocoon that had sheltered Mary disappeared and the last of her disbelief melted away. She and Clark *had* stumbled into Rock and Roll Heaven, only it was actually Rock and Roll Hell. This had not happened because they were evil people; it had only happened because it *could* happen, like car accidents and heart attacks and plane crashes and cancer. They had gotten lost, that was all; it could happen to anybody.

"Got a great show for ya tonight!" Freed was shouting enthusiastically into his mike. *"We got J. P. Richardson, the Big Bopper . . . Marc Bolan of T. Rex, just back from a sold-out gig at the Albert Hall . . . Jim Croce . . . my main man, Johnny Ace . . ."*

Mary leaned toward the girl. "How long have you been here, Sissy?"

43

"I don't know. It's easy to lose track of time. Six years at least. Or maybe it's eight. Or nine."

"Keith Moon of the Who . . . Brian Jones of the Stones . . . that cute li'l Florence Ballard of the Supremes . . ."

Articulating her worst fear, Mary asked, "How old were you when you came?"

"Cass Elliot . . . Janis Joplin . . ."

"Twenty-three."

"King Curtis . . . Johnny Burnette . . ."

"And how old are you now?"

"Slim Harpo . . . Bob 'Bear' Hite . . ."

"Twenty-three," Sissy told her, and onstage Alan Freed went on screaming names at the almost empty town common as the stars came out, first a hundred stars, then a thousand, then too many to count, stars that had come out of the blue and now glittered everywhere in the black; he tolled the names of the drug ODs, the alcohol ODs, the plane crash victims and the shooting victims, the ones who had been found in alleys and the ones who had been found in swimming pools and the ones who had been found in roadside ditches with steering columns poking out of their chests and most of their heads torn off their shoulders; he chanted the names of the young ones and the old ones, but mostly they were young ones, and as he spoke the names of Ronnie Van Zant and Steve Gaines, she heard the words of one of their songs tolling in her mind, the one that went, "Oooh, that smell, can't you smell that smell," and yes, you bet, she certainly *could* smell that smell; even out here, in the clear Oregon air, she could smell it, and when she took Clark's hand it was like taking the hand of a corpse.

"Awwwwwwlllll RIIIIIYYYYYGHT!" Alan Freed was screaming. Behind him, in the darkness, scores of shadows were trooping onto the stage, some of them lit upon their way by roadies with penlights. *"Are you ready to PAAAARTY?"*

No answer from the scattered spectators on the common, but Freed was waving his hands and laughing as if some vast audience were going crazy with assent. There was just enough light left in the sky for Mary to see the old man reach up and turn off his hearing aid.

You Know They Got a Hell of a Band

"Are you ready to BOOOOOGIE?"

This time he *was* answered—by a demonic shriek of saxophones from the shadows behind him.

"Then let's go . . . BECAUSE ROCK AND ROLL WILL NEVER DIE!"

As the show lights came up and the band swung into the first song of that night's long, long concert—"I'll Be Doggone," with Marvin Gaye doing the vocal—Mary thought: That's what I'm afraid of. That's exactly what I'm afraid of.

45

You Know They Call It a Rose

| F. Paul Wilson | BOB DYLAN, TROY JONSON, AND THE SPEED QUEEN |

Dylan walks in and I almost choke.

I've known all along it had to happen. I mean, it was inevitable. But still, finding yourself in the same room with a legend will tend to dry up your saliva no matter how well prepared you think you are.

My band's been doing weeknights at the Eighth Wonder for two months now, a Tuesday-Wednesday-Thursday gig, and I've made sure there's an electrified Dylan song in every set every night we play. Reactions have been mixed. At worst, hostile; at best, grudging acceptance. Electric music is a touchy thing here in Greenwich Village in 1964. All these folkies who think they're so hip and radical and grass-roots wise, they'll march in Selma, but they'll boo and walk out on a song by a black man named Chuck Berry. Yet if you play the same chord progression and damn near the same melody and say it's by Howlin' Wolf or Muddy Waters or Sonny Boy Williamson, they'll stay. So, although my band's electric, I've been showing my bona fides by limiting the sets to blues and an occasional protest song.

Slowly but surely, we've been building an audience of locals. That's what I want, figuring that the more people hear us, the sooner word will get around to Dylan that somebody's doing rocked-up versions of his songs. It has to. Greenwich Village is a tight, gossipy little community, and except maybe for the gays, the folkies are just about the tightest and most gossipy of the Village's various subcultures. I figured when he heard about us, he'd have to come and listen for himself. I've been luring him. It's all part of the plan.

And tonight he's taken the bait.

So here I am in the middle of Them's version of "Baby, Please Don't Go" and my voice goes hoarse and I fumble the riff when I see him, but I manage to get through the song without making a fool out of myself.

When I finish, I look up and panic for an instant because I can't find him. I search the dimness. The Eighth Wonder is your typical West Village dive, little more than a long, rectangular room with the band platform at one end, the bar right rear, and cocktail tables spread across the open floor. Then I catch his profile silhouetted against the bar lights. He's standing there talking to some gal with long, straight, dark hair who's even skinnier than he is—which isn't much of a description, because in 1964 it seems all the women in Greenwich Village are skinny with long, straight hair.

The band's ready to begin the next number on the set list, our Yardbirds-style "I'm a Man," but I turn and tell them we're doing "All I Really Want to Do." They nod and shrug. As long as they get paid, they don't give a damn what they play. They're not in on the plan.

I strap on the Rickenbacker twelve-string and start picking out Jim McGuinn's opening. I've got this choice figured to be a pretty safe one since my wire tells me that the Byrds aren't even a group yet.

Dylan's taken a table at the rear with the skinny brunette. He's slouched down. He's got no idea this is his song. Then we start to sing and I see him straighten up in his chair. When we hit the chorus with the three-part harmony, I see him put down his drink. It's not a big move. He's trying to be cool. But I'm watching for it and I catch it.

Contact.

Research told me that he liked the Byrds' version when he first heard it, so I know he's got to like our version because ours is a carbon copy of the Byrds'. And naturally, he hasn't heard theirs yet because they haven't recorded it. I'd love to play their version of "Mr. Tambourine Man," but he hasn't written it yet.

There's some decent applause from the crowd when we finish the number and I run right into a Byrds version of "The Times They Are A-changin'." I remind myself not to use anything later than *Another Side of Bob Dylan*. We finish the set strong in full harmony on "Chimes of Freedom," and I look straight at Dylan's dim form and give him a smile and a nod. I don't see him smile or nod back, but he does join in the applause.

Got him.

We play our break number and then I head for the back of the room. But by the time I get there, his table's empty. I look around but Dylan's gone.

"Shit!" I say to myself. Missed him. I wanted a chance to talk to him.

I step over to the bar for a beer, and the girl who was sitting with Dylan sidles over. She's wearing jeans and three shirts. Hardly anybody in the Village wears a coat unless it's the dead of winter. If it's cool out, you put on another shirt over the one you're already wearing. And if it's even cooler, you throw an oversize work shirt over those.

"He sorta kinda liked your stuff," she says.

"Who?"

"Bob. He was impressed."

"Really?" I stay cool as the proverbial cucumber on the outside, but inside I want to grab her shoulders and shout, "Yeah? Yeah? What did he say?" Instead I ask, "What makes you think so?"

"Oh, I don't know. Maybe it's because as he was listening to you guys, he turned to me and said, 'I am impressed.'"

I laugh to keep from cheering. "Yeah. I guess that'd be a pretty good indication."

I like her. And now that she's close up, I recognize her. She's Sally something. I'm not sure anybody knows her last name. People around the Village just call her the Speed Queen. And by that, they don't mean she does laundry.

Sally is thin and twitchy, and she's got the sniffles. She's got big, dark eyes, too, and they're staring at me.

"I was pretty impressed with your stuff, too," she says, smiling at me. "I mean, I don't dig rock and roll at all, man, what with all the bop-shoo-boppin' and the shoo-be-dooin'. I mean, that stuff's nowhere, man. But I kinda like the Beatles. I mean, a bunch of us sat around and watched them when they were on *Ed Sullivan* and, you know, they were kinda cool. I mean, they just stood there and sang. No corny little dance steps or anything like that. If they'd done anything like that, we would've turned them right off. But no. Oh, they bounced a little to the beat, maybe, but mostly they just played and sang. Almost like folkies. Looked like they were having fun. We all kinda dug that."

I hold back from telling her that she and her folkie friends were watching the death of the folk music craze.

"I dig 'em, too," I say, dropping into the folkster patois of the period. "And I predict they're gonna be the biggest thing ever to hit the music business. Ten times bigger than Elvis and Sinatra and the Kingston Trio put together, man."

She laughs. "Sure! And I'm going to marry Bobby Dylan!"

I could tell her he's actually going to marry Sara Lowndes next year, but that would be stupid. And she wouldn't believe me, anyway.

"I like to think of what I play as 'folk rock,'" I tell her.

She nods and considers this. "Folk rock . . . that's cool. But I don't know if it'll fly around here."

"It'll fly," I tell her. "It'll fly high. I guarantee it."

She's looking at me, smiling and nodding, almost giggling.

"You're okay," she says. "Why don't we get together after your last set?"

"Meet you right here," I say.

It's Wednesday morning, 3 AM, when we wind up back at my apartment on Perry Street.

"Nice pad," Sally says. "Two bedrooms. Wow."

"The second bedroom's my music room. That's where I work out all the band's material."

"Great! Can I use your bathroom?"

I show her where it is and she takes her big shoulder bag in with her. I listen for a moment and hear the clink of glass on porcelain and have a pretty good idea of what she's up to.

"You shooting up in there?" I say.

She pulls open the door. She's sitting on the edge of the tub. There's a syringe in her hand and some rubber tubing tied around her arm.

"I'm tryin' to."

"What is it?"

"Meth."

Of course. They don't call her the Speed Queen for nothing.

"Want some?"

I shake my head. "Nah. Not my brand."

She smiles. "You're pretty cool, Troy. Some guys get grossed out by needles."

"Not me."

I don't tell her that we don't even *have* needles when I come from. Of course, I knew there'd be lots of shooting up in the business I was getting into, so before coming here I programmed all its myriad permutations into my wire.

"Well, then maybe you can help me. I seem to be running out of veins here. And this is good stuff. Super-potent. Two grams per cc."

I hide my revulsion and take it from her. Such a primitive-looking thing. Even though AIDS hasn't reared its ugly head yet, I find the needle point especially terrifying. I look at the barrel of the glass syringe.

"You've got half a cc there. A gram? You're popping a whole *gram* of speed?"

"The more I use, the more I need. Check for a vein, will you?"

I rub my fingertip over the inner surface of her arm until I feel a linear swelling below the skin. My wire tells me that's the place.

I say, "I think there's one here but I can't see it."

"Feeling's better than seeing any day," she says with a smile. "Do it."

I push the needle through the skin. She doesn't even flinch.

"Pull back on the plunger a little," she says.

I do, and see a tiny red plume swirl into the chamber.

"Oh, you're beautiful!" she says. "Hit it!"

50

Bob Dylan, Troy Jonson, and the Speed Queen

I push the plunger home. As soon as the chamber is empty, the Speed Queen yanks off her tourniquet and sighs. "Oh, man! Oh, baby!"
She grabs me and pulls me to the floor.

I lie in bed utterly exhausted while Sally runs around the apartment stark naked, picking up the clutter, chattering on at Mach two. She is painfully thin, Dachau thin. It almost hurts to look at her. I close my eyes.

For the first time since my arrival, I feel relaxed. I feel at peace. I don't have to worry about VD because I've had the routine immunizations against syphilis and the clap and even hepatitis B and C and AIDS. About the worst I can get is a case of crabs. I can just lie here and feel good.

It wasn't easy getting here, and it's been even harder staying. I thought I'd prepared myself for everything, but I never figured I'd be lonely. I didn't count on the loneliness. That's been the toughest to handle.

The music got me into this. I've been a fan of the old music ever since I can remember—ever since my ears started to work, probably. And I've got a good ear. Perfect pitch. You sit me down in front of a new piece of music, and guaranteed I'll be able to play it back to you note for note in less than half an hour—usually less than ten minutes for most things. I can sing, too, imitating most voices pretty closely.

Trouble is, I don't have a creative cell in my body. I can play anything that's already been played, but I can't make up anything of my own to play. That's the tragedy of my life. I should be a major musical talent of my time, but I'm an also-ran, a nothing.

To tell you the truth, I don't care to be a major musical talent of my time. And that's not sour grapes. I loathe what passes for music in my time. Push-button music—that's what I call it. Nobody actually gets their hands on the instruments and wrings the notes from them. Nobody gets together and *cooks.* It's all so cool, so dispassionate. Leaves me cold.

So I came back here. I have a couple of relatives in the

F. PAUL WILSON

temporal sequencing lab. I gained their confidence, learned the ropes, and displaced myself to the 1960s.

Not an easy decision, I can assure you. Not only have I left behind everyone and everything I know, but I'm risking death. That's the penalty for altering the past. But I was so miserable that I figured it was worth the risk. Better to die trying to carve out a niche for myself here than to do a slow rot where I was.

Of course, there was a good chance I'd do a slow rot in the 1960s as well. I'm no fool. I had no illusions that dropping back a hundred years or so would make me any more creative than I already wasn't. I'd be an also-ran in the sixties, too.

Unless I prepared myself.

Which I did. I did my homework on the period. I studied the way they dressed, the way they spoke. I got myself wired with a wetchip encoding all the biographies and discographies of anyone who was anybody in music and the arts at this time. All I have to do is think of the name and suddenly I know all about him or her.

Too bad they can't do that with music. I had to bring the music with me. I wasn't stupid, though. I didn't bring a dot player with me. No technological anachronisms—that's a sure way to cause ripples in the time stream and tip your hand to the observation teams. Do that and a reclamation squad'll be knocking on your door. Not me. I spent a whole year hunting up these ancient vinyl discs—"LPs" they call them here. Paid antique prices for them, but it was worth it. Bought myself some antique money to spend here, too.

So here I am.

And I'm on my way. It's been hard, it's been slow, but I've only got one chance at this so I've got to do it right. I picked the other band members carefully and trained them to play what I want. They need work, so they go along with me, especially since they all think I'm a genius for writing such diverse songs as "Jumpin' Jack Flash," "Summer in the City," "Taxman," "Bad Moon Rising," "Rikki Don't Lose That Number" and so many others. People are starting to talk about me. And now Dylan has heard me. I'm hoping he'll bring John Hammond with him sometime soon. That way I've got a shot at a Columbia contract. And then Dylan will send the demo of "Mr. Tambourine Man" to *me* instead of Jim McGuinn.

After that, I won't need anyone. I'll be able to anticipate every trend in rock and I'll be at the forefront of all the ones that matter.

So far, everything's going according to plan. I've even got a naked woman running around my apartment. I'm finally beginning to feel at home.

"Where'd you get these?"

It's Sally's voice. I open my eyes and see her standing over me. I smile, then freeze.

She's holding up copies of the first two Byrds albums.

"Give me those!"

"Hey, really. Where'd—"

I leap out of bed. The expression on my face must be fierce because she jumps back. I snatch them from her.

"Don't ever touch my records!"

"Hey, sorreeeee! I just thought I'd spin something, okay? I wasn't going to steal your fucking records, man!"

I force myself to cool down. Quickly. It's my fault. I should have locked the music room. But I've been so wrapped up in getting the band going that I haven't had any company, so I've been careless about keeping my not-yet-recorded "antiques" locked away.

I laugh. "Sorry, Sally. It's just that these are rarities. I get touchy about them."

Holding the records behind me, I pull her close and give her a kiss. She kisses me back, then pulls away and tries to get another look at the records.

"I'll say they are," she says. "I never heard of these Byrds. I mean, like you'd think they were a jazz group, you know, like copping Charlie Parker or something, but the title on that blue album there is *Turn, Turn, Turn,* which I've like heard Pete Seeger sing. Are they new? I mean, they've gotta be new, but the album cover looks so old. And didn't I see 'Columbia' on the spine?"

"No," I say when I can finally get a word in. "They're imports."

"A new English group?"

"No. They're Swedish. And they're pretty bad."

"But that other album looked like it had a couple of Bobby's tunes on it."

"No chance," I say, feeling my gut coil inside me. "You need to come down."

I quickly put the albums back in the other room and lock the door.

"You're a real weird cat, Troy," she says to me.

"Why? Because I take care of my records?"

"They're only records. They're not gold." She laughs. "And besides that, you wear underwear. You must be the only guy in the Village who wears underwear."

I pull Sally back to the bed. We do it again and finally she falls asleep in my arms. But I can't sleep. I'm too shaken even to close my eyes.

I like her. I really like her. But that was too close. I've got to be real careful about who I bring back to the apartment. I can't let anything screw up the plan, especially my own carelessness. My life is at stake.

No ripples, that's the key. I've got to sink into the timeline without making any ripples. Bob Dylan will go electric on his next album, just like he did before, but it will be *my* influence that nudged him to try it. "Mr. Tambourine Man" will be a big hit next summer, just as it's destined to be, but if things go according to plan, *my* band's name will be on the label instead of the Byrds. No ripples. Everything will remain much the same except that over the next few years, Troy Jonson will insinuate himself into the music scene and become a major force there. He will make millions, he will be considered a genius, the toast of both the public and his fellow artists.

Riding that thought, I drift off to sleep.

Dylan shows up at the Eighth Wonder the very next night in the middle of my note-perfect imitation of Duane Allman on "Statesboro Blues," perfect even down to the Coricidin bottle on my slide finger. There's already a good crowd in, the biggest crowd since we started playing. Word must be getting around that we're something worth listening to.

Dylan has about half a dozen scruffy types along with him. I recognize Allen Ginsberg and Gregory Corso in the entourage. Which gives me an idea.

"This one's for the poets in the audience," I say into the mike; then we jump into Paul Simon's "Richard Corey," only I use Van Morrison's phrasing, you know, with the snicker after the bullet-through-his-head line. I spend the rest of the set being political, interspersing Dylan numbers with "originals" such as "American Tune," "Won't Get Fooled Again," "Life During Wartime," and so on.

I can tell they're impressed. *More* than impressed. Their jaws are hanging open.

I figure now's the time to play cool. At the break, instead of heading for the bar, I slip backstage to the doorless, cinder-block-walled cubicle euphemistically known as the dressing room.

Eventually someone knocks on the doorjamb. It's a bearded guy I recognize as one of Dylan's entourage tonight.

"Great set, man," he says. "Where'd you get some of those songs?"

"Stole them," I say, hardly glancing at him.

He laughs. "No, seriously, man. They were great. I really like that 'Southern Man' number. I mean, like I've been makin' the marches and that says it all, man. You write them?"

I nod. "Most of them. Not the Dylan numbers."

He laughs again. From the glitter in his eyes and his extraordinarily receptive sense of humor, I gather that he's been smoking a little weed at that rear table.

"Right! And speaking of Dylan, Bobby wants to talk to you."

I decide to act a little paranoid.

"He's not pissed, is he? I mean, I know they're his songs and all, but I thought I'd try to do them a little different, you know. I don't want him takin' me to court or—"

"Hey, it's cool," he says. "Bobby digs the way you're doing his stuff. He just wants to buy you a drink and talk to you about it, that's all."

I resist the urge to pump my fist in the air.

"Okay," I say. "I can handle that."

"Sure, man. And he wants to talk to you about some rare records he hears you've got."

Suddenly I'm ice cold.

"Records?"

"Yeah, says he heard about some foreign platters you've got with some of his songs on 'em."

I force a laugh and say, "Oh, he must've been talking to Sally! You know how Sally gets. The Speed Queen was really flying when she was going through my records. That wasn't music she saw, that was a record from Ireland of Dylan *Thomas* reading his stuff. I think ol' Sally's brains are getting scrambled."

He nods. "Yeah, it was Sally, all right. She says you treat them things like gold, man. They must be some kinda valuable. But the thing that got to Dylan was, she mentioned a song with 'tambourine' in the title, and he says he's been doodling with something like that."

"No kidding?" My voice sounds like a croak.

"Yeah. So he really wants to talk to you."

I'm sure he does. But what am I going to say?

And then I remember that I left Sally back at my apartment. She was going to hang out there for a while, then come over for the late sets.

I'm ready to panic. Even though I know I locked the music room before I left, I've got this urge to run back to my place.

"Hey, I really want to talk to him, too. But I got some business to attend to here. My manager's stopping by in a minute and it's the only chance we'll have to talk before he heads for the West Coast, so tell Mr. Dylan I'll be over right after the next set. Tell him to make the next set—it'll be worth the wait."

The guy shrugs. "Okay. I'll tell him, but I don't know how happy he's gonna be."

"Sorry, man. I've got no choice."

As soon as he's gone, I dash out the back door and run for Perry Street. I've got to get Sally out of the apartment and never let her back in. Maybe I can even make it back to the Eighth Wonder in time to have that drink with Dylan. I can easily convince him that the so-called Dylan song on my foreign record is a product of amphetamine craziness—everybody in the Village knows how out of control Sally is with the stuff.

As I ram the key into my apartment door, I hear something I don't want to hear, something I *can't* be hearing. But when I open up . . .

"Mr. Tambourine Man" is playing on the hi-fi.

I charge into the second bedroom, the music room. The door is open and Sally is dancing around the floor. She's startled to see me and goes into her little girl speedster act.

"Hiya, Troy, I found the key and I couldn't resist because I like really wanted to hear these weird records of yours and I love 'em, I really do, but I've never heard of these Byrds cats although one of them's named Crosby and he looks kinda like a singer I caught at a club last year only his hair was shorter then, and I never heard this 'Tambourine' song before, but it's definitely Dylan, although he's never sung it that I know of so I'll have to ask him about it. And I noticed something even weirder, I mean *really* weird, because I spotted some of these copyright dates on the records—you know, that little circle with the littler letter *c* inside them?—and like, man, some of them are in the *future*, man, isn't that wild? I mean, like there's circle-C 1965 on this one and a circle-C 1970 on that one over there, and it's like someone had a time machine and went into the future and brought 'em back or something. I mean, is this wild or what?"

Fury like I've never known blasts through me. It steals my voice. I want to throttle her. If she were in reach I'd do it, but lucky for her she's bouncing around the room. I stay put. I clench my fists at my sides and let my mind race over my options.

How do I get out of this? Sally had one look at a couple of my albums last night and then spent all day blabbing to the whole goddamn Village about them and how rare and unique they are. And after tonight I know exactly what she'll be talking about tomorrow: Dylan songs that haven't been written yet, groups that don't exist yet, and, worst of all, albums with copyright dates in the future!

Ripples . . . I was worried about ripples in the time

stream giving me away. Sally's mouth is going to cause *waves. Tsunamis!*

The whole scenario plays out inside my head: Talk spreads, Dylan gets more curious, Columbia Records gets worried about possible bootlegs, lawyers get involved, an article appears in the *Voice,* and then the inevitable—a reclamation squad knocks on my door in the middle of the night, I'm tranqued, brought back to my own time, and then it's bye-bye musical career. Bye-bye Troy Jonson.

Sally's got to go.

The cold-bloodedness of the thought shocks me. But it's Sally or me. That's what it comes down to. Sally or me. What else can I do?

I choose me.

"Are you mad?" she says.

I shake my head. "A little annoyed, maybe, but I guess it's okay." I smile. "It's hard to say no to you."

She jumps into my arms and gives me a hug. My hands slide up to her throat, encircle it, then slip away. Can't do it.

"Hey, like what are you doing back, man? Aren't you playing?"

"I got . . . distracted."

"Well, Troy, honey, if you're flat, you've come to the right place. I know how to fix that."

In that instant, I know how I'll do it. No blood, no pain, no mess.

"Maybe you're right. Maybe I could use a little boost."

Her eyes light. "Groovy! I had my gear all set up in the bathroom but I couldn't find a vein. Let's go."

"But I want you to have some, too. It's no fun being up alone."

"Hey, I'm flyin' already. I popped a bunch of black beauties before you came."

"Yeah, but you're coming down. I can tell."

"You think so?" Her brow wrinkles with concern, then she smiles. "Okay. A little more'll be cool—especially if it's a direct hit."

"Never too much of a good thing, right?"

"Right. You'll shoot me up like last night?"

Just the words I want to hear.

"You bet."

While Sally's adjusting her tourniquet and humming along with "Mr. Tambourine Man," I take her biggest syringe and fill it all the way with the methedrine solution. I find the vein first try. She's too whacked-out to notice the size of the syringe until I've got most of it into her.

She tries to pull her arm away. "Hey, that's ten fucking cc's!"

I'm cool. I'm more than cool. I'm stone-cold dead inside.

"Yeah, but it wasn't full. I only put one cc in it." I pull her off the toilet seat. "Come on. Let's go."

"How about you, Troy? I thought you wanted—"

"Later. I'll do it at the club. I've got to get back."

As I pack up her paraphernalia, carefully wiping my prints off the syringe and bottles, she sags against the bathroom door.

"I don't feel so good, Troy. How much did you give me?"

"Not much. Come on, let's go."

Something's going to happen—twenty thousand milligrams of methamphetamine in a single dose has to have a catastrophic effect—and whatever it is, I don't want it happening in my apartment.

I hurry her out to the street. I'm glad my place is on the first floor; I'd hate to see her try a few flights of steps right now. We go half a block and she clutches her chest.

"Shit, that hurts! Troy, I think I'm having a heart attack!"

As she starts retching and shuddering, I pull her into an alley. A cat bolts from the shadows; the alley reeks of garbage. Sally shudders and sinks to her knees.

"Get me to a hospital, Troy," she says in a weak, raspy voice. "I think I overdid it this time."

I sink down beside her and fight the urge to carry her the few blocks to St. Vincent's emergency room. Instead, I hold her in my arms. She's trembling.

"I can't breathe!"

The shudders become more violent. She convulses, almost throwing me off her; then she lies still, barely breathing. Another convulsion, more violent than the last, choking sounds tearing from her throat. She's still again, but this time she's not breathing. A final shudder, and Sally the Speed Queen comes to a final, screeching halt.

As I crouch there beside her, still holding her, I begin to sob. This isn't the way I planned it, not at all the way it was supposed to be. It was all going to be peace and love and harmony, all Woodstock and no Altamont. Music, laughs, money. This isn't in the plan.

I lurch to my feet and vomit into the garbage can. I start walking. I don't look back at her. I can't. I stumble into the street and head for the Eighth Wonder, crying all the way.

The owner, the guys in the band, they all hassle me for delaying the next set. I look out into the audience and see Dylan's gone, but I don't care. Just as well. The next three sets are a mess, the worst of my life. The rest of the night is a blur. As soon as I'm done, I'm out of there, running.

I find Perry Street full of cops and flashing red lights. I don't have to ask why. The self-loathing wells up in me until I want to be sick again. I promise myself to get those records into a safety-deposit box first thing tomorrow so that something like this can never happen again.

I don't look at anybody as I pass the alley, afraid they'll see the guilt screaming in my eyes, but I'm surprised to find my landlord, Charlie, standing on the front steps to the apartment house.

"Hey, Jonson!" he says. "Where da hell ya been? Da cops is lookin' all ova for ya!"

I freeze on the bottom step.

"I've been working—all night."

"Sheesh, whatta night. First dat broad overdoses an' dies right downa street, and now dis! Anyway, da cops is in your place. Better go talk to 'em."

As much as I want to run, I don't. I can get out of this. Somebody probably saw us together, that's all. I can get out of this.

"I don't know anything about an overdose," I say. It's a form of practice. I figure I'm going to have to say it a lot of times before the cops leave.

"Not dat!" Charlie says. "About your apartment. You was

Bob Dylan, Troy Jonson, and the Speed Queen

broken into a few hours ago. I t'ought I heard glass break so's I come downstairs to check. Dey got in t'rough your back window, but I scared 'em off afore dey got much." He grins and slaps me on the shoulder. "You owe me one, kid. How many landlords is security guards, too?"

I'm starting to relax. I force a smile as I walk up the steps past him.

"You're the best, Charlie."

"Don't I know it. Dey did manage to make off wit your hi-fi an' your records but, hey, you can replace dose wit'out too much trouble."

I turn toward Charlie. I feel the whole world, all the weight of time itself crashing down on me. I can't help it. It comes unbidden, without warning. Charlie's eyes nearly bulge out of his head as I scream a laugh in his face.

David J. Schow | ODEED

Christ on a moped, thought Nicky. He's gonna jump.

Twenty yards away, nailed by a powder-blue pin-spot, Jambone cut loose a banshee howl and leapt skyward, holding his crotch in one hand and a phallic radio mike in the other. Achtung, all dicks.

He's schizzing, thought Nicky. He's gonna do the splits.

It was debased, sensual. It *hurt* Nicky to watch Jambone land in a perfect split—it *hurt* to watch the singer's package thump off the stage boards. Nicky winced.

It *hurt* to think they'd just flushed all their insurance. Jambone had *promised,* oh, how he had promised. . . .

The hyper-clean teenies in the scalper rows were sucking it wetly up. They just said no to drugs, to sex, to everything, and the music was all they had left to fill their empty widdle brainpans.

The music was like a military cargo plane crash-landing into a football stadium. Only louder. Even counting the Stinger missiles and twice-fried fans. Nicky's strategic perch was just behind Hi Fi's amp banks. In the opposite wings he could just make out the arena manager, standing knee-deep in CO_2 mist, looking not at all amused. The solemn little dude had a *clipboard,* for God's sake. He gnawed on a pencil and sweated. Nicky knew he was wearing wax earplugs, and swore he could see the guy's hairline recede as the music pounded onward.

The clipboard was for roughing out damage estimates to the arena.

That's it, Nicky thought. Scribble away, el fucko. We're gonna have us a riot here.

The terms of their hastily negotiated backstage detente suggested that if arena management permitted the metal group Gasm to exceed its scheduled ninety-minute show and perform the encores upon which Jambone had insisted, then at dawn there would still be a building on this spot. Okay, thought Nicky. All was square. Gasm had trotted back out to applause and screaming so palpable it could blow back your hair. They cinched through "Calling All Cops" (the bit with the siren never failed to bring a crowd to its feet) and "Hard Machine" and their speed-thrash cover of "Hi-Heel Sneakers." The band had run offstage, vaulted back on, sweat drops afly, for "Chain Saw" and "Too Big to Hide."

That was it, Nicky had thought. Jambone was down to his glitter skivvies. No more jazz to throw the crowd. All that was left would be for him to slash his throat and dive into his public. That, or one more encore song.

But the paying customers could smell the wrap-up and weren't about to just let it happen. They knew how to play Jambone as well as Jambone knew how to play them. When he teased, they responded with lust. When he swore and stomped, they dumped on kerosene.

The arena manager was getting ready to cut the power. Nicky could read the man's twitch like a clause in a contract.

Everybody was up, bopping wildly, surging toward the stage in breakers, pushing forward against the barricades and bouncers, at first gently lapping, but steadily working up to some serious surf. It would be as mindless as a landslide, as single-minded as a swath of army ants.

Violence. Nicky did not *think* this, he *knew* it. More than a decade of hard touring had cellularly tuned him to know. He, too, functioned as an instrument—nonmusical, yet essential to Gasm.

Nicky watched Hi Fi spread 'em and master the bass guitar. It was a long, smooth Fender fretless as big as she was. She was trapped inside a blue leather jumpsuit that stopped short of cutting off her wind. Nicky could stare at her forever, and not only that, but she was a damned good—

Nicky snapped his head as though trying to wake up. *Screw it on!* This might just be our last show.

The deal was the band did music and Nicky did the headaches. Now he was getting a trifle steamed because he had done his part . . . and the band was about to betray his fine negotiating skills. Oh, those wacky rock 'n' rollers.

He flashed on the barrage of lawsuits that had dogged them throughout the '89 tour. Holy aroma! Tonight just could be the end. His skin was tingling, not from the music, but from a new and vaguely nauseating taste of forewarning. The PA system was ramped so the band caught the least of the onslaught. Maybe it was bounceback, thudding off the hind-curve of his skull. Bad thoughts in there, being bullied around by the music. The task of all the expensive equipment surrounding him was to grab gigantic clouds of raw air and shape it, shove it around inside the arena. Nicky usually wore headphones. If he, too, did not like it loud, he could always sell mobile home parcels.

The arena manager scratched out a figure and penciled in a new one. Oh, God.

Gasm had twisted "Killshot" into a wild jam. Nicky saw Nazi Kurt crank his Marshall stack to max. Slurpee saw it, too, from the drum riser. Sweat spattered up in a spray from his flat toms; so did splinters of drumsticks. Slurpee had a quiver of replacements near his right knee and could snatch fresh sticks without skipping a thump. Slurpee saw Nazi Kurt, then Double-Ought saw Slurpee and kicked up *his* machines, amping his lead from migraine to search-and-destroy. Lyz Ah was forced to turn up, or be lost. Archie, the player who made Gasm guitar-heavy, copied. Jambone felt the slam from the monitors.

That was everybody, thought Nicky.

Lyz Ah and Archie and Double-Ought ganged up for their infamous three-way ax-massacre pose. The crowd was not only ready for it, they expected it.

They used it as an excuse to get crazier.

The audience could easily outlast the band, Nicky knew. No lie, but no strain either. He scooted half a step to observe Rocky, a headphoned tech sitting at the console. Red and green LEDs shot full-board in time. Their power consumption was awesome. There were three crew people for each member of the band, guys 'n' gals who earned their scratch by burning and bleeding through every show. Nicky had picked them all—roadbones who might consume Camels by the carton and bimbos by the six-pack, but whose true OD was adrenaline, endorphins, the electricity of the metabolism.

Nicky blew out a breath. It was nearly force-fed back down his throat by the sheer hurricane of sound. He moved to his cue position.

Jambone and Nicky had sign language worked out for all occasions. Periodically the singer would glance stage left to see if Nicky had a request.

The arena manager glared at Nicky through blue fog and the atmospheric swim of music. When he thought he had Nicky's attention, he tapped his wristwatch.

Nicky's glands upshifted to hate. Pure, ungilt. Not for Gasm, but for the audience of vampires, for that little turd-weasel in the Sears three-piece, squinting at Nicky like a high school principal, his lips pressed whitely together. Two worms fucking, thought Nicky.

Nicky nodded exaggeratedly at the minion of authority.

In that moment, Jambone turned.

Without averting his gaze from the manager, Nicky clenched his right fist, holding it up for Jambone to see. Then he braced his wrist with his left hand.

Jambone got what he wanted.

Jambone spun high on one toe, shooting his own fist up, then down, and the entire band pivoted in midbridge to another of their big 'uns, "Never Give In." It was a precision switch guaranteed to leave change from a dime, and the audience was so stunned by the relay that there was almost no reaction through the first bars.

Then they cheered. They knew the words.

You want nihilism, anarchy? Nicky thought. You got it. He grinned.

Crescendo time for the cannibals. The bouncers felt the crush from behind the plywood barricades, sliding to defensive crouches as Double-Ought fireballed through a lunatic improv. Lyz Ah and Hi Fi went on the attack; the crowd wanted them the way a leather Harley saddle wants a warm crotch. Archie rode the lip of the stage, beckoning physical contact from the pit.

The arena manager was trying to consult a munchkin underling. He could not be heard. He was going at least as berserk as the band.

Nicky caught Rocky's eye and jerked both thumbs up. The tech acknowledged, invoked his personal grapevine, and everyone who mattered had the massage in seconds.

Play it loud. Pop fuses. Break laws. Fry brains.

Flaming money, undergarments, spikes, programs, change, cherry bombs, everything not bolted to the concrete floor rained stageward. Jambone unsocketed his skull-and-crossbones codpiece, lent it a hefty sniff, and spun it into the teeming throng. A Morrison-style bust was about the only option left.

Nicky saw a whirlpool form where the codpiece landed. A piranha feeding frenzy. The morsel was won amid eye gouging and tribal slaughter.

The concert reached for critical mass, gauged in contusions and fractures and perhaps even the ultimate inconvenience. Nicky no longer cared. The unbridled power of his decision was narcotic; the rush flooded his system. *Let cochleas explode. Let the blood flow.*

Let history be made, but now.

JFDI: Just Fucking Do It.

Jambone was the first to be hit by the echoes of Lyz Ah's just-concocted solo, bouncing back from the far end of the arena bowl. The sound returned hollow and unnatural. He gawked. The mike slithered from his grasp to clunk on the stage. There was no superamplified *clunk* to follow.

Nazi Kurt slipped and fell on his ass in astonishment.

The sudden, total silence whooshed in like a shroud to compress the eardrums. The drop-off was vertiginous; Nicky felt as if he were fighting to respirate in a vacuum.

Hi Fi and Archie were still hammering away, grimacing, posing, busting strings, until they discovered they were putting out zero sound. It took exactly two heartbeats.

Slurpee stopped drumming. The sight was so lame it was nearly comic. Double-Ought, ditto.

Odeed

The arena manager peeked out from behind the wing curtains. He stuffed his fist into his face, dropping his clipboard to the floor. It landed with a solid, flat *whack* that almost startled Archie into a power dump.

Every single preamp, power amp, power booster, contour amp, and PA speaker had overloaded, arcing across protective fuses to crisp the circuitry. The speaker elements and conduits were puddles of chrome plasma. Three of the techs were still writhing from severe electrical hotfoots. The tapes, running at 15 IPS, had flash-melted into useless Frisbees of plastic as the recording hookups had cooked down to slag.

Slurpee put his sticks down gingerly. Gently, quietly. In his time he had seen sound frequencies blast glass to smithereens, crack rubber, induce coma, roast lab animals. He cleared the sweat from his eyes with the back of his hand.

The arena was littered with fallen garments. Pimp boots, trashy lingerie, metalzoid jewelry, fatigues, jeans, punk shirts, yee-hah hats, dirty undies, halters, tubes, belts, lace, thongs. The empty cavern of space resembled a sloppy flea market . . . or Nicky's bedroom, he thought, as administered by his first wife.

Mixed liberally into the piles and wads of unoccupied garb were clinking pints of booze, smuggled dope, fake IDs, smuggled weapons, scratch cash, and several thousand ticket stubs. Somewhere in front was Jambone's pirate codpiece, nestled in the clothing of the person who had battled for it.

But no people.

Jambone cursed loudly and it bounced back to meet him. He gave a disgusted shrug and stomped offstage, past Nicky, lending him only a venomous glance that said, "We have another gig one day and four hundred miles from here and what the ratfuck are we gonna do about *this* baby-rapin' mess?"

Nobody spoke. Not even the arena manager.

They had all been cowed silent, afraid to make any sound, lest they vanish, pop, the end.

Nicky walked slowly out to center stage and sat down, right on the edge. His feet dangled where the bouncers in their yellow shirts—

Had been.

Okay. Item #1: You want fame, you just got it.

Item #2: Their gear had completely filled two forty-five-foot longbed trucks. Now it was all useless and ruined. Slowly, Nicky's head dipped to rest in his hands.

Item #3: Their audience had completely filled the arena. . . .

The arena manager had left the premises. Presumably to locate a telephone that was not melted into gooey junk.

Nicky had coveted the covers of *Rip* and *Rolling Stone,* not *Time* and *Newsweek.* He stayed as he was, sitting on the edge of the stage, until men at last came for him.

How long? Time had stopped. Who cared?

Ladies and gentlemen, Gasm has left the arena.

"Excuse us."

Nicky looked up and saw three men in suits. The arena manager was standing out of range behind them. Tattlers always stand back when the poop is about to hit the propeller. FBI? CIA? Secret police? Death squad? Exactly how did you *punish* someone for something like this?

"You *are* Nicky Powers? You manage the band Gasm?"

Nicky prepared himself mentally for the cuffs. He did not answer. The lead guy seemed anxious to get the particulars correct. He spoke hesitantly.

Nicky returned the man's frank gaze. He did not read threat. He read nervous excitement.

"These gentlemen and I represent the Defense Department of the United States."

Call it intuition, but Nicky knew in a flash that Gasm would make its next concert date, no sweat. Not drop one. He smiled his very best dealmaker's smile and stood up.

Nancy A. Collins | VARGR RULE

The night was warm and sticky—hardly unusual during the summer in New Orleans.

Varley paused to check out his reflection in one of the storefront windows. While he would not look terribly out of place in a fern bar, he was passably chic for any of the establishments catering to the progressive music trade. His jacket's shoulders were moderately padded and the lapels fashionably narrow. His Japanese silk tie swam with dozens of tiny hand-embroidered Siamese fighting fish. His pants were charcoal gray and ended in stovepipes, and he wore two-tone patent-leather roach killers.

However, there was a price to pay for fashion and Varley was paying it; sweat had already stained his shirt and the material was bunching along his back. His feet ached from the pressure placed on them by his shoes, and his carefully mussed coif was degenerating into the real thing.

At least he didn't have to suffer for long; he could hear the heavy bass thumping in the bar three blocks away. As he leaned against a parked car in order to retie one of his shoes, he caught sight of the graffiti sprayed on the wall of the bank across the street:

VARGR RULE

Arcane messages were not uncommon in that part of town, although the word "vargr" was a new one on him. It looked like it was missing a vowel or two. He dismissed it and walked on.

The bar was located in one of the older retail-commercial districts near the Tulane and Loyola university campuses. After dark the strip was empty of housewives and the street became the province of students out for a night's entertainment. The building to the right of the bar had long since been demolished, providing the neighborhood with an impromptu parking lot and graffiti gallery. The bar itself had changed names and owners several times over the past decade while remaining a live-music venue.

The evening was already well under way. A handful of Tulane students dressed in acid-washed Calvin Kleins and polo shirts eyed a gaggle of punkabilly retreads, whose elaborate pompadours bobbed in the humid night breeze as they loitered on the corner.

Varley glanced at the graffiti-encrusted wall more out of reflex than genuine interest. Twice a year the landlord whitewashed the exposed firewall under the impression that this foiled the spray-can artists, when all he was doing was providing a fresh canvas for creative vandalism.

As far as he could tell, there was nothing new in the gallery: the same old scrawled depositions of teenage love; the inevitable "class of" bullshit; the handful of local bands making use of all the free publicity they could get; the familiar Who band logo sprayed in an unsure hand; the likeness of an inanely grinning man with a pipe in his mouth . . . same old crap. Then he noticed amid the overlapping conglomeration of slogans, names, and insults the words "VARGR RULE" in paint the color of blood.

Two surly young men flanked the front door. One sported a bicycle-spoke mohawk, his bulging arms wreathed in cobras and rose thorns. He wore a battered leather jacket with sleeves that looked as if they'd been chewed by a rather large, unfriendly animal. Tattered remnants of leather and lining hung like strands of gristle from a gnawed bone.

The second punk was shorter but equally muscular, with close-cut dark hair and a forelock the color of bleached bone. His jeans were so ragged the only things holding them together were the bondage straps encircling his hips. Like the spike-haired thug, he wore a black leather jacket with demolished sleeves.

70

The shorter man reached out and thumped the flat of his palm against Varley's shoulder, halting him in midstride. Three fingers the size of vienna sausages appeared beyond the tip of Varley's nose.

"Whassamatter, Sunder?" rumbled the spike-haired giant. "This guy tryin' t'sneak in without payin' cover?"

"Naw, I don't think he got th' *cojónes* for that, Hew," replied the smaller man, his dark eyes daring Varley to challenge his assessment.

Varley flushed as he handed over a sweat-dampened five-dollar bill. Sunder grunted and transferred it to Hew, who held a welter of crumpled paper money in one tattooed fist. Hew peeled off a couple of ones from the roll and thrust them at Varley. Sunder stepped aside, allowing him passage into the club. Varley could feel their eyes following him.

The club was dark, the lighting provided by the neon beer signs at the bar and a half dozen stage lights hanging over the cramped stage like metal bats. The management claimed that the establishment was air-conditioned, although the press of bodies and the propped-open front door rendered the benefits of refrigerated air negligible.

The band was playing its first set, not that Varley cared. The throb of the bass and the drums threatened to rattle the fillings out of his teeth. His eardrums sealed themselves in self-defense.

The three musicians onstage wore the same ragged leather jackets as the brutes guarding the door. The lead guitarist was a tall, gaunt youth with short, milk-white hair and a tightly braided germ-tail that hung to his belt. The bass player was a young Latino with close-cropped hair razor-cut into a widow's peak. The drummer seemed little more than a boy, though Varley knew he had to be at least eighteen in order to play in a bar where liquor was served. His head was shaved to the skull, giving him a vulnerable, almost babyish appearance, despite the cigarette dangling from his lower lip. The bald drummer flailed at his kit with the anger of a wife-beater. On the bass drum, a wolf was depicted with an open mouth and glowing red orbs; someone had glued bicycle reflectors over the creature's eyes. Under the wolf's

71

slavering jaws was the word "VARGR" in staggered, dripping letters.

Varley felt let down. He had hoped the word was something so obtuse there would be no possibility of ever deciphering it. Instead it had turned out to be the name of just another garage band.

He headed toward the bar; all he wanted to do was get himself a beer, stake out a place at the rail, and bide his time until a suitable candidate for debauchery showed up.

The bar was crowded and it took a good deal of elbowing to get his beer. As he lifted the drink to his lips, he was jostled from behind, slopping Dixie onto his shirtfront. He turned to snarl at the person behind him and found himself looking into his own face.

The illusion was brief but distracting enough for the girl wearing mirrored sunglasses and a black leather jacket with chewed-off sleeves to slide past and breach the bar. Varley didn't care that she'd screwed him out of his place at the rail; even with the mirrored lenses obscuring her eyes, he could tell she was the most beautiful woman he'd ever seen.

Her hair was so pale a blond it seemed colorless and looked like it'd been styled with a Cuisinart. The hair at her left temple was pulled into a braided germ-tail that dangled below her bustline. For some reason Varley was reminded of Yul Brynner in *The Ten Commandments*. Her lips and fingernails were the same shade of hemorrhage. She wore a low-cut leopard-skin print T-shirt and a pair of leather fetish pants with enough zippers for a motorcycle gang. Her feet were encased in a pair of red stiletto-heel pumps that would have deformed a normal instep.

Despite these handicaps, she moved like quicksilver on a plate, not even disturbing the head on her beer as she weaved her way through the gyrating dancers.

Varley forgot his drink. He forgot his place at the bar. His world had suddenly narrowed to the girl in the leopard-skin shirt. She was the one—the target for tonight. No other woman would suffice. It had to be *her*.

Varley had screwed New Wave sluts before. Despite their cultivated decadence, they were all middle-class Catholic schoolgirls at heart.

The girl returned to a table in the corner, parking her tightly trussed rear on a battered red leather barstool. She sipped her beer and stared in the general direction of the stage without really looking at it.

Varley sidled alongside her, then leaned over to whisper in her ear. She smelled of female. He felt his penis stirring like an animal emerging from hibernation. "Hey, baby . . . how about you and me going somewhere private? I've got some primo blow . . ."

She turned to look at him, and he stared at the twinned reflections of his lusting features. Her painted mouth bowed into a smile. It was impossible for Varley to tell if she was being receptive or mocking him. The girl pursed her lips and lifted one hand to stroke his face, the tip of her forefinger resting on his jaw. Still smiling her eyeless smile, the girl tapped the cleft of his chin as if dotting the *i* on a signature. Confused, Varley lifted his hand to his face. When he drew his palm away, it was smeared with blood.

Varley leaned against the sink in the men's room, squinting at the smeared mirror as he dabbed at his chin with a wad of wet toilet paper.

Normally he would have written off any girl who drew blood as being "too weird" and set his sights on a far more predictable bimbo. But for some reason, he could not get her out of his mind. He knew he would have to make another try.

The band was still thrashing along, its amplified roar muted to a dull thunder by the bathroom door. The sink rattled in time with the music, vibrating against Varley's hips. Things were moving beyond his ability to control them. Control was his life. He found it hard to imagine a situation where things got so far out of hand he could not bring them back to the way he wanted them to be. He was confident that, given time, he would get the beauty in those mirrored shades. It was all a question of *when*. He saw himself as hunting a particularly crafty prey, and he loved it. It had been so long since any of his weekend conquests had played hard to get. He had almost forgotten what it was like to *pursue* a woman. He smiled at his smudged reflection. He would catch her. And the consummation would be the fuck to end all fucks.

It took a couple of seconds before he realized she had followed him into the men's room. At first he did not trust the reflection in the mirror; years of neglect had produced a fog of grease on its surface.

She stood at the threshold, smiling at him, her leather jacket zippered shut. Varley gripped the sink but did not turn around. She knew he saw her, and she didn't care.

A crimsoned fingernail touched the throat of her jacket, tugging on the zipper. The black leather parted, revealing white flesh. She had disposed of her leopard-print shirt. The slow, high-pitched snarl of the zipper was louder than thunder.

Her breasts were perfect, standing firm and solid. Despite their fullness, they did not sag. The nipples were round and pink, like the eyes of a white rabbit. Varley ignored the pain cramping his fingers as he clutched the porcelain. He felt as if his legs had disappeared and the only thing keeping him from falling was his hold on the sink. He ignored the muscle tremors as sweat trickled down the tensed furrow of his back.

The zipper continued downward, exposing her second set of breasts.

They were located just under the first pair, obscuring the split of her ribs. They were smaller than the first set, resembling the tits of a girl in junior high school. The nipples and areolas, however, were far larger than those found on a seventh-grader.

At first Varley thought she was wearing a pair of foam rubber "joke" breasts, like the transvestites wore on Mardi Gras, but he could not see a seam of any kind, and he could have sworn that the nipples had hardened as they were exposed to the air.

Was it possible that he'd been drugged? Had her fingernails been dipped in some weird kind of hallucinogen? That was almost as crazy as having two pairs of tits, but at least it kept him from having to accept the thing in the mirror as being real.

Despite his revulsion, Varley could not bring himself to

look away. The zipper continued its movement downward. A third and final pair of breasts was above her belt buckle.

The third set was even smaller than the second, with most of the surface area taken up by oversize nipples. Completely exposed, she stood with her hands on her hips and sneered, daring him to turn and face her. Varley clutched at the sink to keep from collapsing to the piss-stained floor.

He came to on his hands and knees; she was gone. He was relieved to discover that he'd kept from hurting himself; except for smudges on his knees, he was all right.

Except that she had six tits, dammit!

Varley shuddered at the memory. I must be drunker than I thought. She couldn't have been in here, he told himself. It sounded realistic, plausible, and soothing.

Yeah, but she still had six tits.

Varley left the john and returned to the dance floor. The punkette was still at her table. Her jacket was open and she was wearing her shirt. Although he wasn't certain if she was watching him, he could tell she was smiling.

This was getting too weird, just too goddamn weird. All he wanted was to get laid. Varley looked forward to his weekends and the chance to exert his control with silk ties and bedposts. Now that control was being threatened by a bleached-blond slut in fuck-me shoes. It didn't make sense. Varley pushed his way to the bar, desperate for something to take the edge off the memory of six nipples pointed in his direction.

Somewhere around his sixth gin and tonic, Varley realized they'd switched bands on him. The group currently onstage, while as loud as Vargr, was dressed in spandex and had longer hair. Varley looked around, searching the bar for a sign of the girl with mirrored eyes.

His shoulders slumped when he realized she was gone. There were plenty of women still hanging around, but as far as Varley was concerned, they were invisible. A tall, leggy girl who looked like she'd stepped out of a music video made her interest in him quite clear while borrowing a cigarette, yet Varley could not bring himself to respond.

Might as well pack it in for the night. He paid for his

drinks and headed for the door. The humid night air closed around him like a sweaty palm. Varley pulled at his tie, loosening the knot, and grimaced as his stomach began a series of queasy barrel rolls.

By the end of the block he was leaning against a telephone pole studded with old staples and the faded tatters of flyers advertising local bands.

Maybe I should have called a cab. . . . He shook himself, fighting the uneasiness in his guts. He'd endured stupors worse than this before. If he could hold out another three blocks, he'd be able to catch either the streetcar or a bus. *Christ, I must be getting old. Letting a slut like that get the better of me. I got over that shit back in high school.*

Three minutes later he staggered into one of the narrow alleys flanking the street and puked into an open garbage can. He stood there for a few minutes, trying to clear the taste of bile from his mouth. He felt weak. His hands trembled as he wiped at his mouth with the back of his hand.

Maybe I'm sick. The flu or something. Maybe I picked up some kind of bug at work.

He heard the growl and realized he wasn't alone in the passageway. He must have surprised one of the half-wild dogs that prowled the area at night, raiding unsecured garbage cans. Varley peered into the alley, trying to locate the animal. The last thing he needed was to trip over the damned thing in the dark.

He edged toward the street, trying not to make any sudden moves that might frighten the creature. The growl suddenly gave way to a yelp. Varley hesitated for a second. *Maybe it was hurt. . . .*

"What's wrong, boy? Whassamattah, huh?"

Something struck him at knee-level, knocking him against a garbage can. He could tell by its smell as it passed that he'd been bowled over by a dog.

"Goddamn mutt . . ." he muttered. Varley looked up, and his throat constricted into a dry tube.

There were five of them, their pelts shining greasily in the dim moonlight. At first he thought they were dogs, then he saw that they were jointed the wrong way. Two of the larger creatures restrained a German shepherd bitch while a third wrapped its taloned fingers around her muzzle. They needn't have bothered; Varley could tell the poor animal was too frightened even to move, much less bite.

One of the things stood upright on its crooked hind legs, grinning evilly at Varley. Its fur was the color of spoiled cream, the face a disturbing melange of lupine and human characteristics. The foreshortened snout allowed the creature to speak in a twisted, guttural parody of a human voice: "Ripper! Cover!"

Varley tried to get to his feet, only to be pinned by one of the pack. It was smaller than the others, but its strength was immense. Varley could feel its short, piglike bristles scraping against his skin.

Although he'd never been a horror movie buff, Varley was certain that the shaggy, crooked-legged creatures surrounding him were werewolves. But that was impossible! Maybe he was hallucinating the whole thing. The possibility that he was sprawled unconscious in a deserted alleyway suffering from severe fever seemed positively upbeat.

A long, pointed penis emerged from the furred pouch between the leader's legs. It glistened wetly in the dim light of the alley. Something resembling laughter came from the others as the monster mounted the terrified dog.

He was forced to watch as the werewolves took turns raping the German shepherd. Whenever he tried to look away, the thing perched on his back grabbed his head between its furred claws and pulled on his ears until he reopened his eyes. When they were finished, the bitch lay on her side, legs twitching. Blood seeped from her nostrils. Varley could tell that she was torn up pretty bad inside.

The werewolf with the spoiled-cream fur squatted next to the dying animal, its tongue lolling from its mouth in parody of her suffering. The thing on Varley's back giggled. The werewolf twisted the shepherd's head sharply to one side, snapping her neck.

The smaller werewolf jerked Varley to his feet, squeezing his wrist until it felt as if it was caught in a vise. When he cried out, one of the larger beasts pulled the linen handkerchief out of Varley's breast pocket and stuffed it in his mouth. The cream-colored werewolf fingered Varley's tie and grinned at him, licking its lips with a long, red tongue.

"Nice tie."

Varley was certain the thing meant to rip his throat out. He shut his eyes tightly; he didn't want the blood pumping out of his jugular to be the last thing he'd see. He felt the windsor knot loosen as the werewolf removed his tie.

"Make sure it's good and tight, Ripper."

The smaller werewolf quickly and expertly fastened Varley's wrists together. Varley knew enough about knots to realize that it would be impossible to work himself free in time to escape whatever they had in store for him.

Two of the larger werewolves were gnawing at what remained of the German shepherd. They grinned at Varley, exposing sharp, yellow teeth flecked with blood and gristle.

"Hurry up!" growled the leader, kicking the larger one's hairy shank. Although it was easily twice as heavy, the bigger werewolf yelped like a scolded dog.

Varley moaned as he was dragged down the alleyway by his captors. Sharp talons pierced his clothes, lacerating the flesh underneath. He felt himself swoon as the smaller werewolf twisted his arm again.

There was a Volkswagen minibus parked at the opposite end of the alley, its rear door hanging open. It was too dark for Varley to read the name painted on its side, but he knew what it was. He'd known ever since he saw the long, braided germ-tail dangling down the lead werewolf's back.

The cream-colored werewolf picked up Varley and tossed him into the back of the minibus like a bundle of newspapers.

"Sorry, Sis," leered the leader of the pack. "The male got away. Hope this'll tide you over."

The thing in the van moved forward, snuffling the air like a bloodhound. Varley screamed into the handkerchief. A twisted, taloned hand reached out and caressed his face. The palm was dry and hot and felt like the catcher's mitt he'd had as a boy.

The werewolf bitch eyed him, idly fondling her middle set of tits. "It'll do."

78

Vargr Rules

Varley tried to pull away from the white-furred creature crouching over him. The door slammed shut, leaving him in the dark with the werewolf bitch. The smell of female was strong in the confined space of the minibus. Varley choked on the bile rising in his throat as he felt himself stiffen inside his pants. The bitch leaned forward, her breath hot against his cheek.

"Relax, baby," she growled as she unzipped his fly. "Vargr rule."

Ronald Kelly | BLOOD SUEDE SHOES

Ruby Paquette was walking home from the big show in Baton Rouge when the headlights of a car cut through the moonless night. The lights blazed like the luminous eyes of a demon cat, casting a pale glow upon the two-lane highway and the swampy thicket to either side. She turned and regarded the approaching vehicle, squinting against the glare. The car sounded like a predator, too; its big eight-cylinder engine seemed to rumble and roar with an appetite for something more than oil and gasoline.

The crimson '58 Cadillac began to slow when the head-lights revealed her short, dumpy form walking along the gravel shoulder. Ruby turned her back to the headlights and kept going. She stared straight ahead, following her own expanding shadow and the whitewashed borderline beside the highway. As the automobile slowed to a creep and prepared to pull alongside her, Ruby chanced a quick glance over her shoulder. The illusion of a ravenous feline was compounded by the Caddy's front grillwork. It leered at her with a mouthful of polished chrome fangs.

"Hey, sugar!" called a man's voice from the convertible. "Can I give you a ride somewhere? Kinda late for a beauty like you to be out all by your lonesome."

Beauty? Ruby bristled at the word, especially when it was directed at her. She was no beauty and she knew it. She was just a homely Cajun girl, an overweight, acne-ravaged teenager with limp black hair and jelly-jar eyeglasses. How could the driver of the expensive car have made such a stupid mistake? True, he probably hadn't seen her face yet,

Blood Suede Shoes

but he didn't really need to. One glimpse of her squat, elephantine body waddling down the road should have told him that she was certainly no beauty.

"No, thanks," she called back to him. "I don't have far to go." She was aware that the Caddy was almost at a standstill now, inching its way beside her. She twisted her face toward the tangle of swamp beyond the road. *Please, God, just let him drive on. I don't want him to see how much of a dog I really am.*

"Aw, come on, darlin'," urged the driver. He was right alongside her now. "Let ol' Reb give you a ride home."

It was the dawning familiarity of the voice, as well as the mention of his name, that made Ruby's stomach clench with excitement. She looked around and, yes, it *was* him. It was Rockabilly Reb in the flesh!

"You know who I am, don't you, sugar?" grinned Reb, flashing that pearly smile that was becoming increasingly famous in the South and beyond.

"Yeah," said Ruby in bewilderment. "You're Rockabilly Reb. I saw you at the Louisiana Hayride tonight."

"And I saw you, too."

Reb winked at her—actually winked at *her*—Rumpy Ruby, as her peers in high school were cruelly fond of calling her.

"Third row, fifth girl to the left . . . right?" Reb asked.

"Right." Ruby blushed, feeling the heat of embarrassment blossom in her full cheeks. She stopped walking and stood, wondering if her encounter was actually a dream. She crossed her thick arms and pinched herself through her sweater. No, it was really happening. She was actually talking, face to face, with a genuine rockabilly singer.

"Well, how about it, sugar? Gonna let me play the Good Samaritan tonight and give you a lift home? I was heading in that direction anyway." Reb's immaculate smile hadn't faltered in the least. It seemed to be a part of his natural charm.

Ruby looked ahead toward the three miles of swamp that stretched between Baton Rouge and her bayou home, then back to the idling Cadillac and the offer of getting there in style and comfort. What was she going to say—"No, thanks,

81

but I'd rather walk?" This was the bad boy of rock and roll—the potential heir to the heartthrob throne left empty after Elvis Presley had been unexpectedly drafted into the army earlier that year. Her mother was forever drumming the rule of never riding with strangers into her mind, but to pass up such a golden chance would be pure madness. It wasn't every day that a chubby wallflower got the opportunity to cruise with a certified superstar.

"Okay," she said. Ruby opened the passenger door of the car and climbed inside. The seats were of smooth, crimson leather, as was the rest of the interior. From the rearview mirror dangled a set of fuzzy dice, jet black with bright red spots like tiny eyes peeking through the dark fur. She settled onto the seat next to the driver, feeling the coolness of the upholstery against the backs of her thighs. That, along with the thrumming vibration of the Caddy's big engine, sparked a naughty sensation deep down inside her. The same sensation of arousal that she got at night, when she lay awake in her bed and thought about Will Knox, the high school quarterback, and the time she had passed by the boys' locker room and caught a fleeting glimpse of him, completely naked, just before the door shut.

"Ready to go?" asked Rockabilly Reb.

"Sure," said Ruby. "There's a turnoff about a half mile down the highway. I live a couple of miles back in the swamp there."

Reb nodded and sent the big convertible roaring down the highway. The singer flashed a glance at his young passenger. "So you're a bobby-soxer, are you?"

Ruby's face turned beet red. She looked down at her clothes: navy blue sweater and skirt, monogrammed white blouse, white ankle socks, and sneakers. She knew the outfit looked silly, especially on a fat cow like her. "No," she blurted self-consciously, "I just dress like this when I go to a show."

Reb flashed another smile that turned her heart to jelly. "So you're just a rock and roll beauty, eh?"

Again, that twinge of bitter anger. "Why do you keep calling me that? I'm not pretty at all. Are you making fun of me or something?"

The singer shook his head. "Why, I'd never do a thing like that, darlin'. I wouldn't hurt one of my fans for anything in the world. True, you may not be a Marilyn Monroe or Jayne Mansfield, but you do have your own inner beauty. You know how a candy bar looks like a dog turd when you tear off the wrapper? It doesn't look very appetizing at all, does it? But when you bite into it, it's just as delicious as can be. That's how some girls are. They ain't so pretty on the outside, but underneath they're honest-to-goodness beauties."

Reb's simple explanation put Ruby at ease. She pushed her shyness aside for a moment and studied the man sitting next to her. He looked a little different than he did up on that stage surrounded by klieg lights and a blaring sound system. Up there he looked like a wild Adonis, clad in sparkling red, white, and blue. But here in the car, Reb seemed less glamorous and more than a little exhausted. His bleached-blond hair looked frizzled and lank, like corn silk that had withered beneath a hot August sun. His lean face seemed pale and lined with the weariness of long, sleepless miles on the road. Even his trademark costume had seen better days. Up close, the rhinestone coat with a rebel flag emblazoned on the back seemed dull and lackluster. And his red suede shoes—the opposite of Carl Perkins's famed blue ones—looked scuffed and rusty, like blood that had congealed and dried to an ugly brown crust.

Thunder rumbled in the dense clouds overhead and a few drops of rain began to hit them. "Looks like we're in for a real downpour," Reb said. He pushed a button on the Caddy's dash and the top began to unfold behind the backseat and rise slowly over them. By the time Reb fastened the clips to the top of the windshield, the bottom fell out. Great sheets of water crashed earthward, drenching southern Louisiana with their wet fury.

Reb turned off where Ruby told him to, but they had gone only a quarter of a mile into the black tangle of the swamp when the rain cut their visibility down to nothing. "I reckon we'd better park for a while and wait out the storm. Wouldn't want to make a wrong turn and end up in the swamp as some hungry gator's midnight snack."

"I reckon not." Ruby sat there, her bashfulness pushing her to the limits of the seat and pressing her against the passenger door.

"How about a little music to pass the time?" Reb turned on the AM radio. Chuck Berry's "Johnny B. Goode" was winding down and next up was Rockabilly Reb's newest single, "Rock and Roll Anatomy Lesson."

> "A little bit of heart, a little bit of soul,
> A little bit of mind, and a whole lotta rock and
>   roll . . ."

"What a coincidence!" Reb laughed.

Ruby sat listening to the monotonous drumming of rain on the roof and the haunting melody of Reb's electric guitar. After the song ended and the Everly Brothers' "Bird Dog" began, Ruby eyed the grinning rocker with wonderment. "I can't believe that I'm really here . . . sitting right next to you."

"Well, you are, Ruby." Reb's smile glowed dashboard green in the darkness.

The girl returned his smile, then frowned just as quickly. "How did you know my name was Ruby? I didn't tell you it was."

Reb shrugged. "I don't know. You just look like a Ruby, that's all." Smoothly, he changed the subject. "So, how did you like the show tonight?"

"It was great!" Ruby thought back to the three-hour Louisiana Hayride that had featured big names like gravel-voiced Johnny Cash, piano-playing Fats Domino, and, of course, Rockabilly Reb. "You were the best, though." She smiled demurely. "I think you're even better than Elvis."

Reb chuckled. "Well, that's mighty high praise, darlin'. But I reckon I must have disappointed some folks on those last couple of songs I did. My voice was kinda going out on me and my guitar-picking was a bit off."

Ruby recalled the last two numbers: "High School Honey" and "Bayou Boogie." Reb's voice had been unusually flat and his normally hot guitar licks seemed strangely off-key. She had attributed it to the rigors of being on the road too long, driving from gig to gig without time to rest up.

"Want me to sing you a song, Ruby?"

The bespectacled girl felt her heart leap with joy. "Sure!" Again, she couldn't quite believe that she was here, stranded in a violent downpour with her idol. And now he was going to sing to her!

Rockabilly Reb reached into the backseat and found his guitar. It was a sunburst Les Paul Special—a custom-made model for the left-handed player. He slipped the sparkling rhinestone strap around his neck. The sickly green glow of the dashboard light played upon the taut strings of the instrument and the glittering spangles of his gaudy jacket, illuminating the interior of the car with an eerie light.

"Sorry I can't hook up my amplifier, but we'll just have to make do the best we can. So, what would you like to hear? What's your favorite Rockabilly Reb song?"

Ruby smiled. "Forever Baby," she said without hesitation.

Reb grinned. "That's my favorite one, too. Here goes . . ." He began to strum on the unelectrified guitar, producing a series of metallic cords that could scarcely be heard above the rainstorm.

> "Ruby, Ruby, be my forever baby . . .
> Ruby, Ruby, be my forever lady . . .
> Ruby, baby, tell me you'll be mine."

The teenager was a little startled. He was using her own name in place of the customary one. Sitting there listening to him, Ruby couldn't quite remember whose name originally had embellished the lyrics. Sometimes it sounded like Lucy, sometimes like Judy or Trudy. Every time she heard the song on the radio or on the jukebox in the soda shop in town, it seemed as though Reb sang about a different girl. But that was impossible. The record company wouldn't allow him to cut alternate versions of the same hit, using a different name each time.

After he was finished, he sat back and grinned that

country-boy grin of his. "I know, I was a little off-key, but it's been a long night and I'm kinda tired."

"It was perfect," Ruby said. "You know, I always wondered how you got your start. I hadn't even heard of you until the first of the year, and now here you are a big star and all."

"It wasn't an easy row to hoe, I'll tell you that." Reb lost his smile for the first time since he'd picked her up. "Started out as a guy who was long on good looks but mighty short on talent."

"I can't believe that," she said in disbelief.

"Well, it's the God's honest truth, sugar-pie. I saw all those fellas out there making records and money by the fistfuls, and I figured to get in on the action. And I thought I had a good chance, too, but there were others who thought otherwise. I went up there to Sun Records once, and you know what old Sam Phillips told me? He said, 'You got the look, boy, and you got the moves, but you ain't got a lick of natural-born talent. You can't pick a guitar, can't tickle the ivories, and can't sing a note without sounding like a year-old calf with its privates hung up in a barbwire fence.' I must admit, it was pretty darned discouraging, that trip to Memphis."

"But he was wrong, wasn't he?"

"No, Ruby dear, that man was right on the mark. I had no talent at all, except for looking pretty and grinning like a happy jackass. I figured I'd have to just face the fact that I wasn't gonna make it in the music business. Then, when I was drowning my sorrows in a honky-tonk on Union Street, I made the acquaintance of my present manager, Colonel Darker."

"You mean Colonel *Parker*, don't you? Elvis's manager?"

"No, Darker is the complete opposite. He's an oily little rat of a fella, but he has a good head for business. He sat down at the bar and asked me what was wrong. I told him, and he made me the strangest offer I ever heard. Said he'd make me a bona fide rock and roll star if I'd sign my soul over to him. I thought it was pretty darned funny at the time. I mean, I'd heard of such corny lines before, but only on spooky radio shows and in those EC comics before they were banned. Well, since I was half drunk and I didn't figure I'd need that no-account soul of mine anyway, I agreed. I signed the contract on the spot, and then he took me out to the parking lot. He gave me the keys to this apple-red Cadillac, as well as the costume you see me wearing here and the guitar I'm holding here. He also told me what I'd have to do to get the talent to be a star. At first, I didn't want to have no part in it, but soon my hunger for money and fame got the best of me."

Ruby felt her skin crawl with a sudden shiver. "What . . . what did you have to do?" Something deep down inside her wanted to know, while another part didn't.

Rockabilly Reb smiled, and this time it possessed a disturbing quality, a quality that had been there all along, only hidden. "Tell me something, Ruby," he said in a voice that was barely a whisper. "Do you believe what all those hellfire preachers say about rock and roll? Do you believe that it's unwholesome and unclean? That it's the Devil's music?"

"No, of course not," stammered Ruby. "That's just silly talk by a bunch of holy rollers. Rock and roll is just plain fun, that's all."

"I'm afraid you're wrong about that, dumpling. Rock and roll *can* be safe and fun, but it can also be dark and dangerous. The grown-ups, they can sense something is basically dangerous about the music, but they can't quite put their finger on it. Most of the time the music is sung by decent, God-fearing boys like Elvis and Roy Orbison and Carl Perkins, to name a few. I don't know about Jerry Lee. That old boy has a mean streak a country mile long."

Ruby said nothing. She just pressed her back against the passenger door and listened to him ramble on. Inconspicuously, her chubby hand fumbled for the door handle, but, strangely enough, she couldn't find it. The inner panel of the door was smooth . . . and warm to the touch.

"I'm one of the first of the truly dangerous ones," he told her. His pale blue eyes blazed with the madness of desperation. "My talent wasn't a gift from God, but from Satan himself. Colonel Darker likes rock and roll because it reminds him of hell. All those girls screaming and hollering, well, that's just how the Bible describes purgatory—weeping and wailing and gnashing of teeth.

"The Colonel, he's given me fortune and fame . . . as well as power. And when someone gets in the way of my success, I get riled up. I went up north recently and auditioned for a winter tour that's coming up with Buddy Holly, Ritchie Valens, and the Big Bopper. But they turned me down. Said I was too much of a vulgar hillbilly to appeal to midwestern teenagers. Well, they'll learn their mistake soon enough. Me and the Colonel are gonna cook up a little surprise. Those boys are gonna climb to the top, only to fall . . . and fall mighty damned hard, too."

Ruby believed every word he said. She watched in growing horror as Reb's eyes lost their natural blueness and took on a muted crimson hue, like a smoldering coal wavering between living fire and dying ash. Behind her back, her hand continued to search for the door handle, but still she was unsuccessful in finding it.

"You know where I get my talent?" asked the rocker. "The human soul. But not from my own . . . no, the Colonel has my own damned soul under lock and key. That was stipulated in the contract. Instead, I must have the soul of an innocent, the truly beautiful essence of an unsoiled virgin to give me the power I need to rock and roll."

It was at that moment that Ruby noticed that the head of the electric guitar was not like those of other instruments. It was wickedly pointed at the end and honed to a razor sharpness. Reb gripped the neck of the guitar and began to lower it, directing it toward the center of her broad chest. She screamed and tried to push up on the movable roof of the Caddy. Her hands recoiled in repulsion. The underside of the roof was sticky with warm, wet slime.

"Let me sing you a song," Rockabilly Reb rasped.

Then the blade of the guitar was inside her, slicing through her blouse and the elastic of her bra, then past the soft flesh and the hardness of her breastbone. As her heart exploded, Ruby heard the song Rockabilly Reb had sung to her only moments before. But this time it came with a savage ferocity that originated from a realm commanded by the notorious Colonel Darker.

"RUBY, RUBY, BE MY FOREVER BABY . . . RUBY, RUBY, BE MY FOREVER LADY . . . RUBY, BABY, TELL ME YOU'LL BE MINE!"

"No!" she screamed. She watched in mounting panic as her life's blood flooded the floorboards of the car in great, sluggish pools. It was instantly absorbed by Reb's red suede shoes, which pulsed with a life of their own, bulging with dark veins as they drank in the crimson fluid. Reb's costume took on a new brilliance, sparkling with an unholy inner fire. His face lost its pallor, his skin grew tanned and robust. The head of lifeless hair grew fuller and lighter in hue, until it blazed like white-hot steel.

"TELL ME!" shrieked the singer. "TELL ME, RUBY! TELL ME YOU'LL BE MINE!"

Ruby could feel the guitar strings strumming within her body, sending sonic notes of utter agony throughout her tubby frame. She opened her mouth to scream in protest, but she no longer possessed a tongue to vent her awful terror. The vibrations from the hellish instrument racked her spine and blossomed with deadly force into the chamber of her skull. There was a moment of incredible pressure and then her ears and mouth gave explosive birth to her brain. She felt her eyes shoot from their sockets with such force that the lenses of her glasses shattered.

Rockabilly Reb's demonic song grew in intensity and her empty skull became the guitar's makeshift amplifier. Waves of trebled sound flowed from the orifices of her head, turning the inside of the Cadillac into a concert hall for the damned. Then, as the ballad came to an end, she felt her soul being siphoned from her body, channeled through the strings, into the wooden body of the Les Paul.

As unconsciousness took her into its dark and comforting folds, Ruby knew that there was no longer any use in struggling. She mouthed a single word in answer to Reb's evil chorus . . . a silent *yes*. And, although she could neither see nor hear, she knew that the rocker's voice was rising in a howl of triumph and that his grin stretched wide with a renewed power born of a spirit that was not his own.

Colonel Darker was right. It *was* like hell.

The screams, the writhing bodies, the pressing heat of the spotlights and the crowd; it filled the high school auditorium like a crazed purgatory confined within four walls. And she and Rockabilly Reb were at center stage, engulfed in the dancing flames of youthful passion.

She sensed the Colonel standing in the wings, watching the show. She loathed the man as much as she loathed her treacherous lover. She could sense his eyes upon the crowd, enjoying the thrashing of young bodies and the shrill shrieks of females torn between teenage infatuation and womanly lust. She had been among them once, but that seemed like an eternity ago. She had not been beautiful like most of these squealing girls. She had been burdened with an ugly and cumbersome body, but at least it had been one of flesh and bone, and not one constructed of gleaming steel and polished wood, like the one she now possessed.

Rockabilly Reb finished the song and stood before the microphone, letting the screams of wild adoration engulf him. He glanced at his manager and gave the man a wink. Colonel Darker nodded and, with a wolfish grin, merged with the backstage shadows.

"Thank you very much," said Reb, sending the crowd into a renewed frenzy with a flash of his smile. "Here's one of my biggest hits and one of your favorites."

He began to sing,

> "Ruby, Ruby, be my forever baby . . .
> Ruby, Ruby, be my forever lady . . .
> Ruby, baby, tell me you'll be mine."

It was her song and she had grown to despise it. During the past few weeks it had thrummed through her new body, bringing pangs of disgust and despair rather than the rapture of undying passion. The promise of eternal love was a lie. Others had shared the song before her and there would be others afterward. It was only hers until the essence of her captured soul faded like a faltering flame.

As Rockabilly Reb's nimble fingers caressed her taut strings, bringing forth the hot licks of demon rock and roll, she could restrain herself no longer. She screamed out in tortured anguish, hoping that at least one of the teenyboppers in the crowd would hear the cry and recognize it as a warning.

But her torment fell on deaf ears. It emerged as the piercing squeal of feedback, then was swallowed up by the blare of the music.

And the damned rocked on.

91

Don D'Ammassa

THE DEAD BEAT SOCIETY

J ason saw the dead boy's face during his third viewing of the rock video.

He leaned forward, staring into the television screen, but the familiar face disappeared almost immediately into the manufactured mist that obscured most of the set. He brushed the surface of the tube with one finger, and a faint electric charge made his skin tingle. Even after the flaming finale, as the last strains of the Dead Beat Society's hit single "Payback" faded away, he sat dumbly, waiting for some explanation of what he had seen, or perhaps for the inevitable recovery of his sense of proportion, or reassurance that he had fooled himself with a chance resemblance. But ten minutes later, he remained convinced that Mark Walton, or the image of Mark Walton, had been present in the video, one of the lost souls drifting through the mist of the void in which, according to the lyrics, they searched for salvation, consolation, or retribution. It was a fleeting moment, obliterated by the fiery denouement, but no less powerful for its brevity.

It was impossible, of course. Mark had been enamored of rock music to a degree that disconcerted even his teenage friends, but the closest he had ever come to interacting with a genuine rock star was helping Jason sweep out some dressing rooms at the Sheffield Concert Hall in Providence. There was certainly no possibility that he had been involved in the production of a rock video prior to his death, almost exactly one year earlier and only three weeks before the two

92

of them would have graduated from Managansett High School. That would have been a coup too marvelous to keep to himself. Neither was there any possibility that Mark had not really died, that the body recovered from the burning car on Breakneck Hill had been anyone else. Jason knew this with absolute certainty, because he had been there, had in fact been responsible for Walton's death.

"Goddamn," he whispered softly, sitting back in the overstuffed but leaking chair he had picked up from the Salvation Army thrift store while furnishing the dingy, dirty, overpriced apartment he had taken in Providence following graduation. His mother had offered to let him stay on at home, but his father's overt silence had been eloquent enough to dispel any lingering doubts he might have held about his welcome there. Besides, now that he was out of school, he needed his own place, room to stretch out and enjoy life.

This shit's more powerful than I thought, he reflected, staring down at the homemade joint that was slowly turning into ash on a plate littered with the remnants of last night's pizza. Better go easy, Jason, or you'll be seeing vampires and werewolves next. He giggled inanely, without humor.

But the incident was disturbing enough that he watched all through the evening, waiting for the discordant, atonal strains of the Dead Beat Society to return, hoping to watch more closely this time. To no avail, as it happened; the video was not shown again that evening.

The incident had almost passed from his mind before it was repeated. He was in the kitchen the following day, retrieving a cold beer from the small icebox to wash down a meatball sub, when he heard the opening guitar riff. He banged his thigh against a chair rushing into the other room, arrived as the guitars were fading back to make room for the electronic drums, an almost disturbing beat building with each recurrence of the opening theme, understated at first, then progressively louder, more complex, pulling the listener into the monotonous but compelling pattern.

He waited patiently while the instrumental section receded, not even listening to the lyrics. A few seconds into the final verse, when the fogmakers had concealed most of the set with billowing clouds, the Dead Beat Society visible above on their elevated stage, the "restless souls" appearing and disappearing in the mist below, Mark Walton stepped out into clear view, head tracking from his own left toward the center of the screen, locking onto Jason's eyes for just a split second before fading away as an animated human figure enshrouded in flames rushed out to fill the entire screen—"the hell-born vengeance" of the final refrain.

And that was even more peculiar, because Jason was quite sure that, on the first occasion, the familiar face had appeared at the opposite side of the screen, and had moved slowly from left to right. This time, "Walton" had remained relatively motionless, his features obscured only when the burning caricature rushed forward to fill the screen.

Could they have shot two different versions of the same video? It seemed unlikely.

Jason had some really good dope hidden unimaginatively in his refrigerator. (The janitorial job at the Hall normally didn't pay that well, but his uncle was the manager, and nepotism was certainly numbered among his vices, even if he didn't think of Jason with any particular familial fondness.) He'd been saving it for a special occasion, and currently his senses were distorted by nothing stronger than the single beer he'd downed immediately upon arriving home from work. So he was pretty certain that what he had seen was what had really been there.

So how had Mark Walton become part of a rock video that only appeared twelve months after his death?

Reluctantly, Jason allowed his mind to recall the night he and Mark had met for the last time.

Jason had been dealing in those days—low-grade stuff he picked up from equally unreliable suppliers, cutting it himself out in the back of his garage when his old man wasn't around, repackaging it and selling primarily to younger kids who didn't know any better. Some of the little assholes could get high on just the idea of holding, didn't have to light up at all. He figured he was doing them a favor, keeping them away from the stronger stuff.

The Dead Beat Society

His mistake had been in telling Mark what he was doing, and providing a little cosmetic enhancement of the quality of his merchandise.

"How soon can you get me some of the good stuff? I need it for this weekend."

At first, Jason hadn't understood what Walton was talking about. The two were casual friends, united primarily in their interest in rock music and disdain for the faculty, staff, and most of the students at Managansett High.

Something of his confusion must have shown, because Walton moved forward, pressing him up against the hall locker. Voice lowered, he spoke rapidly, eyes alert for potential eavesdroppers.

"I got a hot date coming up Saturday night, you know? I think I can get in this bitch's pants if I loosen her up, you know, but I need to loosen her up."

Jason blinked with realization. "Oh, sure." He made a point of glancing around conspiratorially. "Look, meet me down at the cemetery tonight, around seven. It's gonna cost you, though."

"Yeah?" Walton didn't seem distressed. "How much?"

Jason quoted a price that raised the other boy's eyebrows, but he didn't back off. "All right, but this better be some good shit."

"Oh, it is, Mark. It's the best."

It hadn't been. As a matter of fact, it wasn't even up to his own rather dismal standards. He had run through most of his supposedly uncut stock recently, and he suspected that his sources were heavily adulterating their wares even before he compounded the process. What remained would not accommodate Walton's demands and another delivery he had promised for the following day—unless he became very creative.

"What the fuck," he said aloud, "he'll be so interested in getting laid, he'll never notice. Probably never had any good shit himself, anyway."

Walton unfortunately had more experience with drugs than Jason had suspected, and had not been pleased. Sunday afternoon, the two stood next to Walton's car, parked off the

95

road in Lincoln Woods State Park. Jason was trying to smooth things over, while Walton grew angrier with every passing moment. When Walton finally struck out angrily, slapping him along the side of the head, Jason had reacted without thinking, backing away, crouching down, and picking up the first thing that came to hand, a fist-sized stone. Walton was, after all, three inches taller and thirty pounds heavier.

Perhaps confusing Jason's crouch with a cower, Walton had advanced again. "You'll never fuck me over again, you asshole!" Fury clouded Jason's vision as he rose, swinging his makeshift weapon up from the waist, aiming at Walton's jaw. But the larger boy ducked partially away and was struck instead squarely on his left eye socket. He dropped as though shot, unconscious, blood streaming from lacerated skin and what Jason realized was a burst eyeball.

Loading him back into the car wasn't so bad, nor did he feel any great remorse when he reached through the open window a minute later and shifted into drive, sending the car and its unaware passenger hurtling off the side of Breakneck Hill. To his disappointment, the vehicle did not burst into flames during its descent, and he was forced to climb down the wooded hillside and use his lighter to ignite a pool of spilled gasoline, then escape through the woods before anyone showed up to investigate.

He never did know whether Walton had survived the crash only to be burned to death. It didn't really seem to matter.

The night he first saw Walton in the video, he'd dreamed that he was attending a concert by the Dead Beat Society, and the audience had been filled with thousands of clones of Mark Walton. They had all been watching him, Jason Van Oort, instead of the performers, impaling him with their eyes. Transfixed by their stares, he was unable to react when the room erupted into flames, flames that quickly engulfed the seated figures, melting their features to reveal the naked skulls beneath the flesh.

He woke with a start, blinking, then scrambled to extinguish a small, smoldering flame in his blankets. Although he couldn't remember doing so, he must have lit a final cigarette before going to bed.

Jason didn't have a rational explanation, and wasn't ready to accept a supernatural one, but without consciously deciding to do so, he stopped watching videos. He was taking in enough money from his job now that he could afford a really good CD player and a stack of discs, and there was always the radio. Within a few days, he no longer felt the urge to flick on the television as soon as he arrived home. He even found himself enjoying "Payback," which had climbed to number one in only the second week after its release.

He'd already listened to the song dozens of times when he first heard the whispering.

It was an indistinct sound, a susurration below the level of clear audibility. At first he thought it was just surface noise, a bad recording that the radio station hadn't replaced. But by the time the song ended, its final notes rising to a crescendo and abruptly cut off, he had grown convinced that there were actually spoken words scattered within the white noise. Once, he even thought he'd heard his name.

The undertones were there the next time he heard "Payback" as well, and on every occasion thereafter. He was never quite certain what was being said, no matter how closely he listened, but with each repetition, he became more convinced than ever that it wasn't just random noise, that there was some hidden message lurking, waiting to be deciphered.

He decided to buy a copy of the CD and play it at home where he could adjust the bass and treble and try to bring some clarity to the fuzzy sound.

The Dead Beat Society's second album, *Melody Drama*, was already rising on the charts, bolstered by the popularity of the lead single. Jason had no difficulty finding a stack of them piled up in a display in the front window of Raspberry's Stereo Shop. The picture on the cover was a shot from the "Payback" video, the musicians standing at the top with arms upstretched, a half dozen wandering souls emerging from the mist below.

One of the faces was unquestionably that of Mark Walton.

"Hey, fella. You all right?"

Jason glanced toward the man at his side, disoriented. "What? What's the matter?"

His sudden companion looked to be in his mid-twenties, dressed in a low-key punk style. "You looked really bummed out. I thought maybe you were sick or something." A cigarette stuck out pugnaciously, its end glowing redly, and Jason found his eyes drawn to focus on that slowly crawling flame.

"No, shit, no." He shook himself back into something like composure. "Just got to thinking and lost myself." He turned away, cutting off the conversation. After a second, the other man shrugged and walked off.

He bought a copy of the CD, carefully avoided looking at the picture, relieved that the bags at Raspberry's weren't transparent like those at Record City.

Even with his relatively high-quality equipment, it took considerable experimentation before he was able to improve the clarity of the whisper significantly, and even then he was only able to make out a few fragments, fragments that seemed almost to be answers to the lyrics themselves.

"A song unsung, by anyone," sang the Dead Beat Society, ending the first verse, and a trailing whisper added, "A life undone." The final line of the next was, "Facing life with resignation," to which was appended, "Hello, Jason." And finally, following the concluding line, "Paybacks sometimes can be sweet," came "Soon we'll meet."

Troubled, he turned off the CD player and glanced down to the floor where he had discarded the cover.

The too-familiar face stared up out of the fog, smiling but without humor.

The next several days passed, each indistinct in Jason's memory. He tried to stay high as much as possible, but his dreams remained disturbed, filled with fiery images of accusation. Although he worked pretty much on his own at the concert hall and was not popular even with the rest of the custodial staff, several people asked if he was feeling well—including, eventually, his uncle, who insisted he take a couple of days off (with pay, of course).

Jason found that he could no longer bear to listen to the

radio; the possibility always existed that the next song to be played would be "Payback" or some other piece by the Dead Beat Society, and he didn't want to think about that whispering again. He had not removed *Melody Drama* from his CD player, but had no intention of listening to it again. Ever. He had already thrown the cover into the garbage.

After two days, he thought he should return to work. He forced himself to shower, shave, brush his hair into something approaching order, and dress as neatly as possible in his unpressed, infrequently washed clothing. But something about his expression seemed to disconcert his coworkers, though there was nothing overt that they could object to, and he was soon set to replacing the posters in the display cases out front.

That's how he learned that the Dead Beat Society was booked to play two concerts at the hall—and only three weeks off. Jason was suddenly possessed with the certainty that his answers lay there, if he could only find the right questions to ask.

The intervening period passed with dreamlike slowness, and it was with a certain degree of surprise that Jason finally awoke one Saturday afternoon to the realization that the arrival of the Dead Beat Society was only a few hours away.

Normally, the maintenance staff was expressly forbidden to enter the stage area while the performers were present, but Jason's family connections had allowed him to bend the rules from time to time, although it was tacitly assumed that he would be circumspect in the matter. Tonight, he didn't care what the consequences might be; he was going to be in the wings when the group went onstage.

He waited until he was certain the musicians were already in their dressing rooms behind the stage before working his way forward. He carried an overflowing box of trash for camouflage until he had reached his chosen waiting place, a jumble of infrequently used props, sound equipment, and other flotsam that had accumulated slightly to the rear and away from the audience. It was out of their line of sight, concealed by the curtain and the supporting structure for the light bars and other paraphernalia elevated above. When he was sure that he was unobserved, he slipped behind a rack of extension cords and crouched, waiting for his moment. Without realizing it, he nodded off, dreaming of human figures dancing through fire.

No one noticed his slumping form as final preparations were completed for the evening's performance. Nor did he notice any of them.

"You say you've waited for me, well I'm worth waiting for."

The opening line of "Cold Love" shocked Jason back to consciousness. He flailed about with both arms, disoriented, before remembering where he was and why. By the time he had recovered enough to peer out of his hiding place, the Dead Beat Society was working its way through the refrain.

"Your hot blood is no match for my . . . ice-cold love."

Already, the stage was obscured by an ankle-high layer of mist rising from the fogmakers below the stage, curling up around the feet of the musicians, spilling over the side and dissipating just before it reached the front-row seats.

Now that the moment was upon him, Jason realized he had absolutely no idea how to proceed. Something had told him that he needed to confront the Dead Beat Society concerning Mark Walton's lingering presence, but how? Rush out onstage and shout accusations of supernatural powers, or act with more diplomacy? "Excuse me, sir, but could you tell me how it happens that a dead person appears in your video?" Sure, he could do that. As the last notes of "Cold Love" faded, Jason found himself near panic. Why hadn't he planned for this moment?

"Motionless Emotion" followed, the Society's first single, a moderately successful hit that had been eclipsed within weeks by the group's first million-seller, "Paying the Dues," into which they immediately segued. The closing instrumental section continued with material not on either of their albums, perhaps spontaneous jamming, Jason thought. Like most of their music, it was dominated by the relentless, inventive percussion of the drummer, a hermaphroditic type fortuitously named John Tapper, the least reclusive of the atypically reticent rock group. The keyboards played a shrill counterpoint that wove around the beat, while the three guitarists chased one theme after another, sometimes independently, but always working their way back toward a regular, unified rise in volume that brought a small rush of inappropriate applause from the audience each time it crested. The mist became more pervasive, even penetrating into the wings. The stage manager had rigged the lights to emphasize the flowing currents, highlighting the heads and torsos of the Dead Beat Society as they swayed above the roiling, earthbound cloud.

The music crashed to an abrupt stop, and the audience exploded into shouts, screams, and the more traditional applause. The artificial fog rushed out in ever greater volume, and the stagehands in the wings retreated before it. Jason took advantage of the cover to move closer to the musicians; none of the staff looked in his direction as he advanced.

Deeper into the fog.

The uproar from beyond the stage lights died away while the members of the Dead Beat Society stood motionless, not responding to the evident adulation. They were a strange group, lacking a dynamic stage personality, but undeniably exerting a considerable degree of charismatic power over their audience. But as time passed and the silence grew, their fans grew restive, and there were impatient and puzzled whisperings from the darkness. Jason pressed forward, almost close enough to be seen from out front.

Without warning, the Dead Beat Society broke into the opening chord of "Payback."

Jason froze, left hand raised to brace himself against the hanging curtain. His knuckles clenched the tough fabric, his nails scoring its surface. Fog billowed and drifted on every side. The Society had deliberately dropped the sound level, so that the audience was forced to remain quiet, unconsciously leaning forward to hear the lyrics better.

"A song unsung, by anyone," they whispered into the darkness.

Directly behind Jason, someone whispered, "A life undone."

He closed his hand even more tightly, felt the hard edge of fingernails against his palm despite the heavy curtain. As the second verse began, he continued to watch the performers, unwilling or unable to turn to see who, or what, might be behind him.

"Facing life with resignation," breathed the Dead Beat Society.

"Hello, Jason." And this time, something touched his shoulder.

Pivoting slowly on his left foot, still refusing to relinquish his hold on the curtain, that last anchor to the physical world, Jason turned toward the barely visible figure looming behind him. The strobing lights from the stage did little to dispel the darkness, and the mist was at shoulder height now, impossibly thick and clinging. Surely something must be wrong below the stage; this was far beyond the usual effect the crew had been able to manage in the past.

"Paybacks sometimes can be sweet," came the final line of the refrain, and the unknown other stepped forward, close enough that Jason could recognize his companion.

"Again we meet," said Mark Walton, smiling.

Jason released the curtain and staggered back, out onto the main stage. The Dead Beat Society was deep into an innovative jam session, again straying from the recorded version by building one variation upon another, all playing with the original theme, but none entirely true to it. The band members seemed to pay no attention to him, nor was there any indication that his presence had been spotted from the packed house beyond.

Still smiling, Walton followed.

Jason's immobilizing terror broke and he spun away from the advancing figure, unconcerned whether he caused a scene. Almost immediately, his feet became tangled in the electrical cords leading to the gigantic amplifiers emblazoned with the stylized "DBS" that had already become a popular trademark. He threw out his hands to break his fall as his head dropped into the bank of fog.

Effectively blinded by the all-encompassing mist, Jason squirmed about on the floor, kicked free of the power cord, and scrambled back to his feet. The instrumental background continued.

He was even more disoriented now. The fog lifted on

every side generally at eye level, periodic ripples making the surface heave and subside. He had lost sight of the Dead Beat Society, although he could still hear their music. Strangely, it seemed to come from every side, as though he had stumbled right in among them, although he couldn't see their chalk-white costumes anywhere.

In fact, he couldn't see the audience, either. Or the wings. Or any other identifiable point of reference. The stage lights seemed to be diffused, decentralized, and he couldn't quite decide where they were positioned. And somewhere, concealed by all this, was Mark Walton.

Jason forced himself to keep moving, arms groping about to avoid collisions. He set one foot in front of the other, counting as he moved in a more or less straight line, convinced that if he could only find one end of the stage or some other concrete reference point, he could determine his location and escape. But long after he knew he must have walked at least twice the length of the raised stage, he remained enshrouded in the mist.

And the Dead Beat Society was still developing its impossibly prolonged jam session.

Just as he reached the point of despair, the fog began to recede. There was no clear line of demarcation, but with each forward step, the clinging wisps receded slightly, down from his shoulders, across his chest, to waist, then hip level, and then below his knees. It was still incredibly dark ahead and he could see nothing clearly, but somehow he knew instinctively that the audience was ahead, that he was finally moving toward something rather than away.

The fog was swirling around his ankles when he ran into a barrier.

It was as though he had run into a shield of plexiglass, smooth, cool to the touch, featureless, almost but not quite transparent. It spread from right to left and as high as he could reach. What's more, there was a strange, electric sensation when he touched it, something weird but familiar, something he knew he should recognize.

"Shit, no!" He jerked his hands away as though they'd been burnt. "No fucking way, man!" It was the same sensation he had felt when he reached out and touched his television screen the first time he'd spotted Mark Walton's face. Except this time he was on the same side as the mist.

"Oh, there you are, Jason. I wondered where you'd gotten to." Mark Walton emerged from concealment, one arm extended. "I have something for you, old buddy. It's payback time."

And as the Dead Beat Society broke away from the instrumental variations into the refrain of the last verse of "Payback," a tiny flame sparked in Mark Walton's fist, reminding Jason of the fiery figure whose immolation climaxed the video of this very song.

"Paybacks *can* be sweet," Walton whispered.

Graham Masterton | VOODOO CHILD

I saw Jimi ducking into S. H. Patel's, the news agent on the corner of Clarendon Road, and his face was ashy gray. I said to Dulcie, "Jesus, that's Jimi," and followed him inside, shop doorbell clanging. Mr. Patel was marking up stacks of *Evening Standard*s and said, "*New Musical Express* not in yet, Charlie," but all I could do was to shake my head.

I walked cautiously along the shelves of magazines and children's sweets and humorous birthday cards. I could hear Mrs. Patel's television playing the theme tune from *Neighbours* somewhere in the back of the shop. There was a musty smell of manila envelopes and candy shrimps and fenugreek.

I came around the corner of the shelves and Jimi was standing by the freezer cabinet, looking at me wide-eyed; not sly and funny the way he always used to, but wounded almost, defensive. His hair was just the same, frizzy, and he was wearing the same sleeveless Afghan jacket and purple velvet flares—even the same Cherokee necklace. But his skin looked all white and dusty, and he really scared me.

"Jimi?" I whispered.

At first, he didn't say anything, but there was a chilliness around him and it wasn't just the freezer cabinet with its Bird's Eye peas and Findus mixed carrots and original beefburgers.

"Jimi . . . I thought you were dead, man," I told him. I hadn't called anybody "man" for more than fifteen years. "I was really, totally convinced you were dead."

He snuffed, and cleared his throat, his eyes still wounded-looking. "Hallo, Charlie," he said. He sounded hoarse and remote and blocked-up, the same way he'd sounded that last night I saw him, September 17, 1970.

I was so scared I could scarcely speak, but at the same time Jimi was so much the same that I felt weirdly reassured —like it was still 1970 and the past twenty years just hadn't happened. I could have believed that John Lennon was still alive and that Harold Wilson was still prime minister and that it was peace and love forever.

"I've been trying to get back to the flat, man," Jimi told me.

"What? What flat?"

"Monika's flat, man, in Lansdowne Crescent. I've been trying to get back."

"What the hell do you want to go back there for? Monika doesn't live there anymore. Well, not so far as I know."

Jimi rubbed his face, and ash seemed to fall between his fingers. He looked distracted, frightened, as if he couldn't think straight. But then I'd often seen him stoned out of his skull, talking weird gibberish, all about some planet or other where things were ideal, the godlike planet of Supreme Wisdom.

"Where the hell have you *been?*" I asked him. "Listen, Dulcie's outside. You remember Dulcie? Let's go and have a drink."

"I've got to get into that flat, man," Jimi insisted.

"What for?"

He stared at me as if I were crazy. "What for? Shit! What for, for fuck's sake."

I didn't know what to do. Here was Jimi, three feet in front of me, real, talking, even though Jimi had been dead for twenty years. I never saw the actual corpse, and I never actually went to his funeral because I couldn't afford the fare, but why would the press and his family have said that he was dead if he wasn't?

Monika had found him lying on the bed, cold, his lips purple from suffocation. The doctors at St. Mary Abbot's Hospital had confirmed that he was dead on arrival. He had suffocated from breathing vomit. He had to be dead. Yet here he was, just like the old psychedelic days, "Purple Haze" and "Voodoo Chile" and "Are You Experienc-c-ced?"

The shop doorbell rang. It was Dulcie, looking for me. "Charlie?" she called. "Come on, Charlie, I'm dying for a drink."

"Why don't you come and have a drink with us?" I asked Jimi. "Maybe we can work out a way of getting you back in the flat. Maybe we can find out who the estate agent is, and talk to him. Courtney probably knows. Courtney knows everybody."

"I can't come with you, man, no way," Jimi said evasively.

"Why not? We're meeting Derek and all the rest of them down at the Bull's Head. They'd really like to see you. Hey—did you read about Mitch selling your guitar?"

"Guitar?" he asked, as if he couldn't understand me.

"Your Strat, the one you used at Woodstock. He got something like a hundred and eighty grand for it."

Jimi gave a dry, hollow sniff. "Got to get into that flat, man, that's all."

"Well, come for a drink first."

"No way, man, can't be done. I'm not supposed to see nobody. Not even you."

"Then what are you going to do?" I asked him. "Where are you staying?"

"I ain't staying nowhere, man."

"You can stay with me. I've got a house in Clarendon Road now."

Jimi shook his head. He wasn't even listening. "I've got to get into the flat, that's all. No two ways about it."

"Charlie?" protested Dulcie. "What the hell are you doing?"

I felt a cold, dusty draft, and I turned around, and the Patels' multicolored plastic curtain was swinging, but Jimi was gone. I dragged the curtain back and shouted, "Jimi!" But nobody was in the Patels' armchair-crowded sitting room except a brown, bare-bottomed baby with a runny nose and an elderly grandmother in a lime-green sari, who stared at me with eyes as hard as stones. Above the brown-tiled fireplace was a luridly colored photograph of the Bhutto family. I apologized and retreated.

"What the hell's the matter with you? I've been waiting outside for ages," Dulcie said.

"I saw Jimi," I told her.

"Jimmy who?" she demanded. She was bleached-blond, pretty, and tarty—and always intolerant. Perhaps that was why I liked her so much.

"Hendrix, Jimi Hendrix. He was here, just now."

Dulcie stopped chewing gum and stared at me with her mouth open. "Jimi Hendrix? What do you mean, Jimi Hendrix?"

"I saw him, he was here."

"What are you talking about? You're out of your fucking tree, you are!"

"Dulcie, he was here, I swear to God. I've just been talking to him. He said he had to get back into Monika's old flat. You know, the flat where he—"

"Pree-cisely," Dulcie mocked me. "The flat where he died."

"He was here, believe me. He was so damned close I could have touched him."

"You're mad," Dulcie declared. "Anyway, I'm not waiting any longer. I'm going down to the Bull's Head for a drink."

"Listen, wait," I told her. "Let's just go round to Monika's flat and see who lives there now. Maybe they know what's going on."

"I don't want to," Dulcie protested. "You're just being ridiculous. He's *dead*, Charlie. He's been dead for twenty years."

But in the end we went round to the flat and rang the doorbell. We saw the grubby net curtains twitching, but it was a long time before we heard anybody coming to the door. A cold gray wind blew round the crescent. The railings were clogged with newspaper and empty crisp bags, and the trees were scrubby and bare.

"I don't suppose they even know that Jimi Hendrix used to live here," Dulcie sniffed.

Eventually the door was opened about an inch and a woman's pale face appeared.

"Yes?"

"Oh," I said. "I'm sorry to bother you, but I know somebody who used to live here, and he was wondering if you'd mind if he sort of came back and took a look around. You know, just for old times' sake."

The woman didn't answer. I don't think she really understood what I was going on about.

"It wouldn't take long," I told her. "Just a couple of minutes. Just for old times' sake."

She closed the door without saying a word. Dulcie and I were left on the step, under a cold north London sky the color of glue.

A black woman in a shiny Marks and Spencer's raincoat pushed a huge, dilapidated pram across the street. The pram was crowded with children and shopping.

"Now what are you going to do?" asked Dulcie.

"Don't know," I told her. "Let's go and get that drink."

We drove down to the Bull's Head and sat by the window overlooking the Thames. The tide was out, so the river was little more than a dull gray ribbon in a stretch of sloping black mud.

Courtney Tulloch was there, and so were Bill Franklin, Dave Blackman, Margaret, and Jane. I suddenly realized that I'd known all of them back in 1970 when Jimi was still alive. It was a strange feeling, like being in a dream.

What had John Lennon written? "Yea though I wart through the valet of thy shadowy hut, I will feed no Norman."

I asked Courtney whether he knew who was living in Monika's old flat, but he shook his head. "All the old faces are gone now, man, long-gone. It's all changed from what it used to be. I mean, it was always run-down and seedy and all that, but everybody knew where they was, black and white, bus driver and whore. Nowadays these kids run riot. It's like the moon."

But Dave said, "I know who took that flat after Monika left. It was John Drummond."

109

"You mean *the* John Drummond?" I asked him. "John Drummond the guitarist?"

"That's right. But he was only there for a couple of months."

Dulcie said, "You're being really boring today, Charlie. Can I have another drink?"

I bought another round: snowball for Dulcie, Holsten Pils for me. Courtney was telling a joke.

I hadn't realized that John Drummond had lived in the same flat as Jimi. For my money, John had been a better guitarist than Jimi—technically, anyway. He was always more single-minded, more creative. He'd been able to make his guitar talk in the same way that Jimi did, but the voice that had come out had been less confused than Jimi's, less angry, less frustrated. And he'd never played an uneven set like Jimi did at Woodstock, or a totally disastrous one like Jimi did in Seattle the last time he ever appeared at a concert in America. John Drummond had played first with Graham Bond and then with John Mayall and then his own "supergroup," the Crash.

John Drummond had reached number one both sides of the Atlantic with "Running a Fever." But then, without warning, he'd suddenly retired, amid newspaper reports of cancer or multiple sclerosis or chronic heroin addiction. That had been the last that anybody ever saw of him. That was—what?—1973, 1974, or something like that. I didn't even know if he was dead or alive.

That night in my one-bedroom flat in Holland Park Avenue, the telephone rang. It was Jimi. His voice sounded distant and powdery.

"I can't talk for long, man. I'm in a call box in Queensway."

"I went to the flat, Jimi. The woman wouldn't let me in."

"I have to get in there, Charlie. No two ways about it."

"Jimi—I found out something. John Drummond had that flat after Monica. Maybe he could help."

"John Drummond? You mean that young guy who kept hanging around wanting to play with the Experience?"

"That's right, amazing guitarist."

"He was shit. He couldn't play for shit."

"Oh, come on, Jimi. He was great. 'Running a Fever' was a classic."

There was a long silence on the other end of the phone. I could hear traffic, and Jimi breathing. Then Jimi said, "When was that?"

"When was what?"

"That song you mentioned, 'Running a Fever,' when was that?"

"I don't know. Early seventy-four, I think."

"And he was good?"

"He was amazing."

"Was he as good as me?"

"If you want the God's honest truth, yes, he was."

"Did he sound like me?"

"Yes, he did, except not many people would admit it, because he was white."

I looked down into the street. Traffic streamed endlessly past the front of my flat, on its way to Shepherds Bush. I thought of Jimi singing "Crosstown Traffic" all those years ago.

Jimi said, "Where's this Drummond guy now? Is he still playing?"

"Nobody knows where he is. He had a number-one hit with "Fever" and then he quit. Warner Brothers couldn't even find anybody to sue."

"Charlie," urged Jimi hoarsely, "you've got to do me one favor. You've got to find this guy. Even if he's dead, and you can only find out where they buried him."

"Jimi, for Christ's sake. I wouldn't even know where to start."

"Please, Charlie. Find him for me."

He hung up. I stood by the window for a long time, feeling frightened and depressed. If Jimi didn't know that John Drummond had played so well—if he wasn't aware that John had reached number one with "Running a Fever"— then where had he been for the past twenty years? Where had he been, if not dead?

* * *

I telephoned Nik Cohn and he met me in this stuffy afternoon drinking club in Mayfair. Nik had written the definitive work on pop in the sixties, *Awopbopaloopa Alopbamboom,* and he had known just about everybody, including the Beatles, Eric Burdon, Pink Floyd in their UFO days, and Jimi, of course—and John Drummond.

He hadn't seen John for yonks, but about six years ago he had received a postcard from Littlehampton on the south coast, saying nothing much except that John was trying to get his mind and his body back together again.

"He didn't exactly explain what he meant," Nik told me. "But he was always like that. You got the feeling that he was always thinking about something else. Like trying to deal with something that was going on inside him."

Littlehampton in the middle of winter was windswept and bleak. The funfair was closed, the beach huts were closed, the Red Indian canoes were all tied together in the middle of the boating pond so that nobody could reach them. Fawn sand waved in flat horses'-tails across the promenade, and old lolly wrappers danced across the tufted sea grass.

I spent hours walking around the town center looking for John Drummond, but that first afternoon I didn't see anybody between the ages of three and sixty-five. It started to rain—a cold, persistent rain—so I rang the doorbell at one of the redbrick Edwardian villas close to the seafront and booked myself a room for the night.

It wasn't much of a place to stay, but it was warm. There was also fish and chips for supper in a small dining room I shared with two traveling salesmen, an unmarried mother with a snotty, wriggling boy in soiled dungarees, and a bristly-mustached retired colonel with leather arm-patches on his jacket and a habit of clearing his throat like a fusillade of gunshots.

Not a drum was heard, not a funeral note, as his corpse to the ramparts we hurried.

Next morning it was still raining, but I walked the silvery-gray streets all the same, looking for John Drummond. I found him totally by accident, in a pub on the corner of River Road, sitting in a corner with an untouched pint of McEwan's and a half-eaten packet of salt-and-vinegar crisps. He was smoking incessantly and staring at nothing.

He was thin, so much thinner than the last time I'd seen him, and his hair was graying and wild. He looked a bit like a geriatric Pete Townshend. He was dressed in tight black trousers and a huge black leather jacket with about fifty zippers and D-rings. He wore a lapel badge with a picture of three pairs of scampering legs on it and the motif "Running Men Tour 1986."

I parked my lager next to his and dragged up a chair. He didn't even look at me.

"John?" I said, without much confidence.

His eyes flicked across at me, and narrowed.

"John, it's Charlie. Charlie Goode. Don't you remember me?"

"Charlie Goode?" he asked dully. Then, very slowly, as if recognition were penetrating his consciousness like a pebble falling into treacle, "Cha-a-arlie Goode! That's right! Charlie Goode! How are you keeping, man? I haven't seen you since . . . when was the last time I saw you?"

"Isle of Wight."

"So it was. Isle of Wight. Fuck me."

I lifted my beer and drank some and wiped my lips with the back of my hand. "I've been looking for you since yesterday," I told him.

He sucked at the butt of his cigarette, then crushed it out. He didn't make any comment, didn't even look as if he'd heard me.

"I'm not really sure why," I said, trying to sound light-hearted about it. "The thing is, Jimi asked me."

"Jimi asked you?"

"It sounds stupid, doesn't it?" I said with a forced laugh. "But I met him in Notting Hill. He's still alive."

John took out another cigarette and lit it with a cheap plastic lighter. Now he wouldn't take his eyes off me.

I said, more seriously, "He was trying to get back into Monika's old pad. He didn't say why. The thing is, he found

113

out that you lived there for a bit, after he—well, after he
stopped being around. He said I had to find you. He said it
was crucial. Don't ask me why."

John blew out smoke. "You saw Jimi, and Jimi told you to
find me?"

"That's right. I know it sounds stupid."

"No, Charlie, it doesn't sound stupid."

I waited for him to say something else—to explain what
was going on—but he wouldn't, or couldn't. He sat there
and smoked and drank his beer and occasionally said, "Jimi
asked you, fuck me." Or else he sang a snatch from one of
Jimi's old songs.

In the end, though, he drained his glass and stood up and
said, "Come on, Charlie. You'd better see what this is all
about."

Hunched, spindly-legged, he led me through the rain. We
crossed River Road and into Arun Terrace, where a long
road of small Victorian artisans' cottages with slate roofs
and majolica-tiled porches stood. The hedges smelled of cat
pee, and wet cigarette packets were snared in the shrubbery.
John pushed open the gate of number 17, "Caledonian,"
and opened the front door with his own key. Inside, it was
gloomy and crowded with knickknacks: a miniature ship's
wheel with a barometer in it, the plaster head of a grizzled
Arab with a hawk on his shoulder, a huge ugly vase full of
pink-dyed pampas grass.

"My room's upstairs," he said, and led the way up a flight
of impossibly steep stairs, covered in red sculptured carpet.
We reached the landing and he opened the door to a small
bed-sitting room—a plain, cold British bedroom with a
candlewick bedspread and a varnished wardrobe and a Baby
Belling cooker. The only indication that this was the home
of one of the best rock guitarists since Eric Clapton was a
shiny black Fender Strat with finger marks all over it.

John pulled over a ratty basketwork chair with a collapsed
seat. "Make yourself at home," he told me. Then he sat
down himself on the end of the bed, and took out his
cigarettes again.

Cautiously, I sat down. I felt as if I were sitting down at
the bottom of a dry well. I watched John light up again and

testily smoke. He was growing more agitated by the minute, and I couldn't figure out why.

After a while, however, he started talking in a low, flat monotone. "Jimi was always talking about the time he used to tour with the Flames—years ago, before he got famous or anything, just after he left the Army Airborne. They played in some back-of-beyond town in Georgia somewhere, and Jimi got mixed up with this chick. I always remember what he said about her, 'foxy to the bone.' Anyway, he spent all night with her, even though he missed the tour bus, and even though this chick was married and kept telling him that her husband would beat her when she got home.

"He told her he wanted to be famous, and she said, sure, you can be famous. At about four o'clock in the morning, she took him to see this weird old woman, and this weird old woman gave him a voodoo. She said so long as he fed this voodoo, he'd be fine, and famous all over the world, and every wish he ever wished would come true. But the day he stopped feeding that voodoo, that voodoo would take back everything, and he'd be shit, that's all, just shit.

"But Jimi wanted fame more than anything else. He could play good guitar, but he wanted to play brilliant guitar. He wanted to be so fucking brilliant that nobody would even believe that he came from earth."

"So what happened?" I asked. The rain pattered against the window like handful of currants.

John blew smoke out of his nose and shrugged. "She gave him the voodoo and the rest is history. He played with the Isley Brothers, Little Richard, Curtis Knight. Then he was famous; then he was gone. Why do you think he wrote that song 'Voodoo Chile'? He was a voodoo child, that's all, and that was true."

"John, he's still alive," I insisted. "I saw him; I talked to him. I wouldn't be here otherwise."

But John shook his head. "He's gone, Charlie. Twenty years gone. When he became famous, he started to starve that voodoo, but in retaliation the voodoo made him weak, made him crazy. Jimi wanted to play for an audience, but the voodoo made him play music that was way beyond anything that an ordinary audience could understand. It was beyond anything that even great guitarists could understand. You remember Robin Trower, from Procol Harum? He went to see Jimi in Berlin and said that he was amazing, but the audience was out of it. Robin was one of the greatest guitarists ever, but *he* was out of it. Jimi was playing guitar that nobody would understand for about a hundred fucking years.

"So Jimi tried to get rid of the voodoo, but in the end the voodoo got rid of him. The voodoo canceled him out, man: If you don't live with me, then you don't live at all. But you don't die, either. You're nothing—you're absolutely nothing. You're a slave, and a servant, and that's the way it's going to be forever."

"Go on," I whispered.

"There was only one thing he could do, and that was to take the voodoo back to that little town in Georgia where he first got it. That meant leaving his grave in Seattle and bumming his way back to England, finding the voodoo, and taking it back, in person, to that weird old woman and making her a gift of it. Because if the person you're giving it back to doesn't accept it as a gift, it's still yours, man. Still yours, forever."

I sat in that ridiculous chair with its collapsed bottom and I couldn't believe what I was hearing. "What are you trying to tell me? That Jimi's turned into some kind of zombie? Like the walking dead?"

John smoked and looked away, didn't even try to convince me.

"I saw him," I insisted. "I *saw* him, and he talked to me on the phone. Zombies don't talk to you on the phone."

"Let me tell you something, man," John told me. "Jimi was dead from the moment he accepted that voodoo. Same way I am."

"What do you mean?"

"You want me to show you?"

I swallowed. "I don't know. Maybe, yes. All right."

He stood up awkwardly. He took off his scruffy black coat and dropped it onto the bed. Then he crossed his arms and lifted up his T-shirt.

He was white-skinned and skeletal, so thin that I could see

116

his ribs and his arteries, and his heart beating under his skin. But it was his stomach that shocked me the most. Tied tightly to his abdomen with thin ropes of braided hair was a flattish ebony figure, very African in appearance, like a small monkey. It was decorated with feathers and diseased-looking fragments of dried pelt.

Somehow, the monkey-figure had become part of John. It was impossible to tell where the figure ended and John began. His skin seemed to have grown around the ebony head and enclosed in a thin, translucent webbing the crooked ebony claws.

John let me look at it for a while; then he dropped his T-shirt and covered it.

"I found it under the floorboards in Monika's hallway. It was all wrapped up in one of Jimi's old shirts. I'm pretty sure that Monika didn't know anything about it. I knew it was dangerous and weird, but I wanted the fame, man. I wanted the money. I thought that I could handle it, just like Jimi thought that he could handle it.

"I wore it for a while, tied loose around my waist, under my shirt, and I fed it bits and pieces just like you'd feed a pet animal. In return, it kind of *sang* to me; it's hard to describe unless you've experienced it. It sang to me, and all I had to do was play what it sang.

"But then it wanted more. It clung tighter and tighter, and I needed it tighter because when it was tighter it sang such amazing music, and I got better and better. One morning I woke up and it had dug a hole in my skin, and kind of forced its mouth inside me. It was sore, but the music was even better. I didn't even have to listen to it anymore, it was right inside me. I didn't even have to feed it with scraps anymore, because whatever I ate, it sucked right out for itself.

"It was only when it was taking stuff direct from my stomach that I realized what was really happening. And by that time, I was playing music that nobody could relate to. By that time, I was so far out that there was no coming back."

He paused, coughed. "Jimi took it off before it went into his gut. But he couldn't play shit without it. It's a need, man. It's worse than any drug you've ever imagined in your whole life. He tried pills and booze and acid and everything, but until you've needed the voodoo, you don't know the meaning of the word 'need.' "

"So what are you going to do?" I asked him.

"Nothing. Go on living."

"Couldn't you give it back to Jimi?"

"What, and commit suicide? This thing's part of me, man. You might just as well tear out my heart."

I sat with John talking about the 1960s until it began to grow dark. We talked about Bondy at the Brighton Aquarium, John Mayall, Chris Farlowe and Zoot Money at the All-Nighter in Wardour Street, where you could get bashed in the face just for looking at somebody else's bird. We talked about sitting on Tooting Graveney Common on cold, sunny autumn afternoons listening to the Turtles on a Boots tranny. We talked about the Bo Street Runners and the Crazy World of Arthur Brown, the girls in the miniskirts and the white PVC boots. All gone, man. All vanished, like colorful, transparent ghosts. It had never occurred to us at the time that it could ever end.

But one gray evening in 1970 I had walked down Chancery Lane and seen the *Evening Standard* banner "Jimi Hendrix Dead," and they might just as well have announced that our youth had shut up shop.

I left John just after eight o'clock. His room was so dark that I couldn't see his face. The conversation ended and I left, that's all. He didn't even say good-bye.

I walked back to the boardinghouse. As I stepped through the front door, the bristly-mustached colonel held up the heavy black telephone receiver and announced harshly, "It's for you."

I thanked him, and he cleared his throat like a Bren-gun.

"Charlie? It's Jimi. Did you find him?"

I hesitated. Then I said, "Yes. Yes, I did."

"He's still alive?"

"In a manner of speaking, yes."

"Where is he, man? I have to know."

"I'm not sure that I ought to tell you."

"Charlie—did we used to be friends?"

"I suppose so."

"Charlie, you have to tell me where he is. You have to."

His voice sounded so panicky that I knew I had to tell him. I heard myself saying the address like a ventriloquist. I didn't dare to think of what might happen if Jimi tried to get the voodoo back. Maybe I should have minded my own business, right from the very beginning. They always say that it's dangerous to mess around with the dead. The dead have different needs from the living, different desires. The dead are more bloody desperate than we can even guess.

I went round to John's place the next morning after breakfast. I rang the doorbell, and a fussy old woman with a brindled cat on her shoulder let me in.

"Nothing but trouble, you people," she complained, hobbling away down the hall. "Nothing but noise. Nothing but loud music. Hooligans, the lot of you."

"Sorry," I said, although I don't think she heard me.

I climbed the stairs to John's room. Outside on the landing, I hesitated. I could hear John's cassette player, and a tap running. I knocked, too softly for John to hear me. Then again, louder.

There was no answer. Only the trickling of the tap and the cassette playing "Are You Experienced?"

"John?" I called. "John, it's Charlie!"

I opened the door. I knew what had happened even before I could fully understand what I was looking at. Jimi had gotten there before me.

John's torso lay on his dark-soaked bedspread, torn wide open, so that his lungs and his stomach and his liver were spread around in brightly colored profusion, interconnected with webs of fat and torn-apart skin. His head was floating in the brimful washbasin, bobbing up and down with the flow of the water. Every now and then his right eye peeped at me accusingly over the china rim. His severed legs had been pushed bloodily beneath the bed.

The voodoo was gone.

I spent a week in Littlehampton "helping the police with their inquiries." They knew I hadn't done it, but they strongly suspected that I knew who had. What could I tell them—"Of course, officer! It was Jimi Hendrix!"? They'd have had me committed to one of those seaside mental homes in Eastbourne.

I never heard from Jimi again. I don't know how the dead travel the seas, but I know for a fact that they do. Those lonely figures standing by the rails of Icelandic-registered cargo ships, staring at the foamy wake. Those silent passengers on cross-country buses.

Maybe he persuaded the old woman to take the voodoo back. Maybe he didn't. But I've pinned the album cover of *Are You Experienced?* to my kitchen wall, and sometimes I look at it and like to think that Jimi's at peace.

PAUL DALE ANDERSON

Paul Dale Anderson | RITES OF SPRING

Static electricity filled the night air and added a spectacular sense of excitement, heightening expectations. Big bass speakers began belting out familiar rhythms that brought goose bumps to Bobby's flesh.

"I can't believe they're *here*," Lorraine said, a faraway look clouding her blue eyes. "It's their first-ever tour and they could have gone *anywhere*. I feel so special, Bobby. It's almost as if they came to play just for *me*."

Everyone in town seemed to feel that way; everyone, that is, over the age of twelve and under the age of thirty. Half the county had assembled tonight to hear Rites of Spring perform at a public concert, and young bodies covered the park grounds—lining green grass, granite boulders, or leaves and pine needles amidst the trees—like scattered litter after an annual Fourth of July picnic.

"Wait until they become big-name famous," Bobby said. "They won't come anywhere near here when they're super-famous."

"Then I'll go to *them*," Lorri said, and Bobby could tell from the tone of her voice that she would, too.

Pangs of jealousy ripped his heart. Though Rites of Spring included both male and female band members, the majority were ruggedly male and super-sexy.

Did it matter that the band turned Lorri on in ways Bobby only dreamed of? Why should it?

After all, he planned to reap the real benefits of that turn-on after the concert ended. He'd take Lorri home to his

121

apartment and program the latest Rites of Spring disc on his CD to repeat indefinitely, and then he'd be able to do whatever he wanted to her supple body until they were both so sore and satiated he'd be forced to pull the plug. Just thinking about what it'd be like to manhandle Lorri's luscious body parts made his groin ache, and he suddenly wished he hadn't worn such tight-fitting jeans.

"They're coming out!" Lorri shouted as the prerecorded music crescendoed to announce the band's entrance.

Attention riveted to the moonlit clearing where a rented stage had been hastily erected earlier in the day. Behind the stage sat two immense semitrailers and a motor home, makeshift dressing rooms for the band. A single spotlight focused on the center of the stage.

Suddenly, as the beat of the music became wildly erratic, the single spotlight began to strobe on and off in syncopated cadence. Bobby turned around and tried to see how the lighting techs—obviously mounted on scaffolds hidden high in the trees, where anonymous sound mixers also performed their special brand of magic—could accomplish such a startling effect. But the bright light was too blinding to look at directly, and Bobby had to close his eyes and turn away.

A cheer went up from the crowd as the band bounded out onstage. Bobby was still blinking motes from his eyes and missed most of what he imagined was a grand entrance. By the time he could see again, the entire audience was standing, shouting, jumping up and down, and otherwise blocking his view.

Then he heard their opening number.

Waves of emotion flooded every inch of his body. Unlike recorded sounds on a CD, this live music shook his very soul. Paroxysms of frenzy infused his physical form and nearly drove him mad.

And he wasn't alone.

Rocking and rolling in the true sense of those words— looking like fundamentalist religious fanatics experiencing rebirth at a revival meeting—people all around him jerked and danced like drunken marionettes tied to invisible strings. In the eerie light of the oscillating strobe, bodies in one position when the spot blinked out appeared in completely different poses when the strobe flashed on again.

What the fuck is happening? the little that was left of his conscious mind demanded to know. Had commie infiltrators finally managed to slip acid into the town's water supply, as J. Edgar Hoover had once feared?

Try as he might, Bobby couldn't control his body. Nothing scared him more than losing his cool—losing control—a fact he'd only recently, after reading Freud for a psychology class in college, attributed to guilt feelings fostered by an overly zealous mother during early toilet training.

Thank God his bladder and sphincter still functioned!

But the rest of his body wouldn't respond to conscious commands. Though he could see and hear, he could neither close his eyes nor cover his ears.

He felt trapped inside a body that wasn't his anymore.

The music owned him now, made him do things he didn't want to do. His hand reached out and touched one of the women dancing next to him. It wasn't Lorri, he instantly noticed—*where the fuck was Lorri, anyway?*—and his thumb and fingers closed around the top button of the woman's pristine white blouse. As if with a mind of their own, his fingers unbuttoned the button.

Stop! he ordered. Please, stop!

But the fingers continued, as if unable to hear the sound of his tiny inner voice above the blare of bass amps. When he finished unbuttoning the blouse, his fingers removed the material from her lily-white shoulders and began on her bra.

Her hands, meanwhile, were busily working on the buckle of Bobby's belt.

Other people, too, Bobby noticed as the strobe continued to flash, were removing clothes left and right. Men undressed women, and women undressed men—delicately, as if they were being uncharacteristically careful not to tear any of the garments. Bare flesh appeared, disappeared, then reappeared as the single spotlight blinked on and off.

The young woman—whom Bobby now recognized as Sally Hogan, a girl from his high school graduating class—opened Bobby's fly and reached inside. She seemed thoroughly delighted when her hand discovered he wasn't wearing underpants.

He tried to fight off an erection, but his efforts proved useless. As if in sync with the pounding beat of the music and bright flashes of strobe light, he began to feel light-headed. Hot blood flooded penile sinuses, and his engorged tool popped free when Sally suddenly shoved Bobby's tight jeans down to his knees, then to his ankles.

He'd never before had a hard-on half as big. It stuck straight out and the skin was stretched so taut he thought for a moment he'd burst like an overcooked sausage.

While Sally paused to remove her own tastefully tailored skirt and pull off panties and panty hose with a single motion, Bobby stepped out of his jeans. Socks and shoes went next.

Both naked as the day they were born, Bobby faced a woman he didn't know well enough to greet with a passing hello should they happen to meet on the street. If she felt as embarrassed as he did, he certainly couldn't tell from looking at her.

He knew what was bound to happen next.

And it did.

She was already well lubricated when he entered her without foreplay, and they rammed together, slamming together to the beat of the music.

Seconds later, the music escalated, and he felt her series of violent convulsions match his own. He'd never experienced anything quite as intense in his entire life, and he lost consciousness as the first spurts of hot seminal fluid shot out the tip of his penis. . . .

Only to awake with a different woman straddling his lap like a cowgirl barebacking a bucking bronco.

He didn't remember anything after that.

Until the music stopped.

"Hope you had as much fun tonight as we did," the lead singer said over the sound system. "We'll be back to visit you again next spring, same time, same place. Plan to make it a tradition around here."

The single spot that was focused on center stage dimmed, faded, flashed out. Bobby quickly blinked.

But the singer was gone.

So was the stage.

And the two semitrailers.

And the motor home.

Subdued applause filled the wooded glen. Then, singly and in pairs, the audience started to leave.

Lorri, fully dressed—as was everyone else, Bobby discovered, including himself—came out of the crowd and walked toward him, moving slowly and limping slightly as if it hurt to walk.

"Wasn't that a great concert?" she asked.

"Where were you?" Bobby demanded. "Where did you go?"

"I don't remember. I guess I got so caught up in the music, I must have . . ."

"What? Must have what?"

"Must have danced." She shook her head and shrugged. "You know how carried away I get when I hear Rites of Spring. I can't help myself; I have to dance. That's why my muscles feel sore, I suppose. I must have danced up a storm."

"You don't remember, do you?" Bobby said. "What's the last thing you remember?"

"I remember the band coming out," she said, "stepping into the spotlight. Then . . ."

"Then?"

"The music. I remember the music."

"And?"

"What else is there? I remember the music, and the music is everything. Isn't it?"

"Yeah," Bobby agreed.

"I'm tired," she said, reinforcing the thought with a yawn. "I think I should go straight home."

"Aren't you coming over to my place? I thought we could talk, maybe have a drink. . . ."

"Not tonight, Bobby. I'm too tired."

Bobby was disappointed, but he had to admit he was tired, too. For months now he'd planned on getting into Lorri's pants after the concert. He'd wined her and dined her and sweet-talked her into going with him alone—rather than attending with more than a dozen of their friends—to pave the way for this moment.

But tonight he was too tired and too sore to push for more, though it might have been nice to talk things out—if only to try to learn what really had happened here tonight. Maybe tomorrow night. For now, it was enough just to feel he was back in control of his own body.

For the life of him, though, he couldn't remember why it had seemed so important to be in control.

Overhead, gathering storm clouds obscured the first full moon of spring. As the clouds passed, bright moonlight once again illumined every abandoned blade of grass in the tiny clearing at the edge of the woods.

A rapid succession of rain clouds followed almost immediately.

And frail moonbeams streaming through the tall trees blinked on and off, on and off, on and off.

On and off.

Until the rains came.

Michael Garrett

DEDICATED TO THE ONE I LOATHE

Lieutenant Burt Bevins carefully guided his police cruiser along the rain-slicked surface of a rural North Carolina highway, his partner, Sergeant Mack Isbell, at his side. The light mist in the air was scraped off the windshield at twenty-second intervals. It was midmorning on an October Wednesday, the dead leaves of autumn drifting to the ground. Isbell slowly shook his head and turned to Bevins.

"We should've checked the fuckin' weather forecast before we drove out here. We could've waited for the storm to pass."

Bevins exhaled. "I don't know. I can think more clearly out here, where it all took place."

Isbell nodded. "Me, too, I guess. You think the connection with the radio station is solid, though, huh?" he asked, unconvinced.

Bevins glared through the fogged windshield. Not another car was in sight on the lonely, ribbonlike stretch of highway. "We've got to check it out," he answered. "It's the only lead we got."

Isbell pulled a clipboard pad from beneath the front passenger's seat and reviewed his notes. "All right," he began. "We got two separate homicides, apparently committed by the same perp. First, we got the two kids. One male Caucasian, age seventeen, one female Caucasian, age sixteen. Found on the side of the road just a few miles from here. Both of 'em with .38 slugs in the back of the head. The engine was still runnin' and the boy had this 45 rpm record

127

in his lap, 'Last Kiss' by J. Frank Wilson, an oldie from back in the sixties."

Bevins nodded. "You remember when that song was popular?"

Isbell lit a cigarette and grunted.

"It's funny," Bevins continued. "We get down on the kids today about lyrics in the songs they like, but we listened to some pretty morbid stuff ourselves when we were teenagers."

Isbell laughed. "Yeah, when you think about it, how did that song ever get so fuckin' popular? I mean, it was about a couple of kids on a date and the girl gets snuffed in an accident, for Christ's sake. How could we have ever liked shit like that?"

"Hell if I know," Bevins answered as he scratched the five-o'clock shadow on his cheek. "But our killer didn't exactly follow the lyrics. I mean, these kids didn't die in no accident. And both of 'em were killed, not just the girl, the way it was in the song."

"Well, sure," Isbell said with a smirk. "The killer couldn't afford to leave no witnesses."

Bevins ignored his partner's sarcasm. "No fingerprints on the record—shit, there was no hard evidence left at all. Everything wiped clean, and it was probably over in a matter of seconds."

"Yeah, and no sign of funny business on the girl," Isbell added.

Bevins nodded, then wrenched the steering wheel to the left as a small deer darted in front of the car and bounded down the steep slope to the right of the highway. He exhaled. "What were those kids doing on a deserted stretch of highway like this anyway?" he asked, more to himself than to his partner.

"Parking, asshole!" Isbell blurted. "What the fuck did you do when you was a kid?"

Bevins took his eyes off the road just long enough to shoot his partner a menacing stare. "I never endangered a date's life by taking her out in the wilderness to park."

Isbell laughed. "Yeah. You only endangered her when you unzipped your pants."

Dedicated to the One I Loathe

The patrol car rounded a curve and the officers found themselves at the first murder site, one of the few areas along the road wide enough to pull over and park. "Any need to stop here?" Isbell asked.

Bevins shook his head. "We've been over this spot more times than I can count. Let's go to the next one."

Isbell flipped over a couple of sheets of paper and reviewed his notes about the second murder. "Okay, next time we got a male Caucasian, age twenty-three, found dead at the base of a telephone pole. Same stretch of highway, just a few miles farther. Again, he's got a .38 slug in his head that matches the slugs in the other two. Same weapon. His motorcycle is about twenty feet or so down a steep embankment, lying on its side, but its engine was off. Damage to the bike looks like it was pushed over the edge and slid down on its side. In the guy's lap is another record, this one covered with blood and guts, and it's "The Leader of the Pack" by the Shangri-Las, another tasteful oldie from our generation."

Bevins nodded. "Another teenage death song. And again, it was no accident, like it was in the song."

Isbell belched without excusing himself. "I guess it'd be kinda difficult to convince a guy to wrap his Harley around a telephone pole."

"You know what I mean." Bevins groaned. "The killer is no perfectionist—otherwise, he'd make the crime fit the song better—or at least try to stage it more accurately."

Finally, another automobile approached from the opposite direction, its headlights glaring through a thin layer of fog. "The guy was ridin' a Harley," Isbell snorted. "Would've had more punch if he'd been on a Honda—you know, like in the Beach Boys song?"

Bevins groaned again. "Give it a rest, Isbell."

Isbell stretched his short legs to the floorboard and reached beneath his seat again, this time pulling out a dual-speaker portable radio/cassette player. "I borrowed this from my daughter. Thought we might listen to that morning oldies show on K-99. Might give us something to think about."

"Good idea," Bevins agreed. "Anything beats the squawk

of this fuckin' thing." He stared at the police radio hanging from beneath the dash. Isbell held the portable radio in his lap and extended its aluminum antenna, twisting it until the reception was almost clear. "Gimme Some Lovin'" by the Spencer Davis Group was playing.

"The signal will probably fade between these mountains," he said.

"We can live with that," Bevins answered. "If we're lucky, our killer is still connected with that radio station. The lab confirmed that the grooves on those 45s were cut by a broadcast-quality turntable. And the lab boys say that K-99's logo was scratched off the labels of the records. That's where the 45s came from."

"Yeah, but it's still a long shot," Isbell argued. "Like the jock told us, too many people have access to their stash of old records. Somebody from the maintenance service could've even ripped them off. And you know what kind of turnover they have at maintenance services."

"So, what else can we do?" Bevins countered. "This is our only hope. There's a definite connection with K-99. That's at least a starting point."

"I understand," Isbell said, "but you gotta admit, it's a long shot. They haven't inventoried their records in years. There's no way of knowing when these particular oldies disappeared."

Bevins exhaled deeply and ignored the last comment.

Isbell finally shrugged and stared ahead. "This is where the biker bit the dust," he said, pointing to a telephone pole just ahead. "Wanna stop?"

Bevins turned the windshield wiper to a faster speed. "I intended to, but it's rainin' too fuckin' hard. Let's grab a cup of coffee at the service station at the top of the mountain, then stop on our way back if the rain slacks."

"Here Comes the Night" by Them was playing now. Isbell hummed along while Bevins was deep in thought. Finally Bevins said, "If the killer is still linked with K-99, he'll back off if he's got any brains at all."

"Yeah, but you're assuming that the guy's sane. Whoever did this is totally out of it, if you ask me."

The radio announcer blurted something about the big

K-99 cash giveaway and its yellow Toyota cruiser handing out money to motorists. Bevins straightened his neck and noticed Isbell clenching his teeth, apparently sharing the same thought. "Nobody at the radio station mentioned this promotional gimmick," Bevins mumbled, "about cruising around and stopping motorists to give money away."

Isbell looked back at him in silence, then said, "Nobody would be suspicious of a canary yellow Toyota with K-99 plastered all over it. Most folks would stop in a flash, even if they didn't know the station was giving away money. Most folks would trust a radio station's publicity car."

Bevins hit the brakes a bit too quickly, and the squad car fishtailed on the rain-slick pavement. "Son of a bitch!" he barked. "Our link just might have gotten stronger." He reached over to shake his partner's hand as he slowly pressed the accelerator. "Got to find a place to turn around."

Isbell gazed out the side window at the increasing distance between himself and the valley far below. "Too dangerous to turn around here. The shoulder ain't wide enough, and the road's too crooked. Might cause an accident from oncoming traffic."

Bevins nodded, beaming from ear to ear. "Now all we gotta do is find out who at the radio station has access to the yellow—" He stopped in midsentence as his gaze became affixed to the rearview mirror. "Well, maybe we don't have much more to figure out after all," he said.

Isbell twisted around in his seat and looked out the back window. A bright yellow Toyota was gaining on them from behind. "A fuckin' basket case!" he said. "What does this idiot plan to do? Is he gonna stop us and give us money? Taunt us like a big-time serial killer? The guy's an idiot!"

The Toyota quickly closed the gap as Isbell continued to stare. "I can't tell if we talked to this guy at the station. The windshield's fucked up and I can't see his face."

"Must've gotten the word from his buddies," Bevins said, still glancing repeatedly at the rearview mirror. "I suppose we better wait until he does something before we stop him. So far we've got nothing concrete on him. We don't even know who the fuck he is."

Isbell cleared his throat. "Looks like he's talking on his mobile telephone now," he said. "He probably thinks he's tough shit."

Bevins shrugged. "Not for long."

"Laugh, Laugh" by the Beau Brummels faded out on the portable radio as the deejay announced a report from the K-99 Kash Kar. "Turn it up!" Bevins blurted. "The son of a bitch is on the air!"

"I've got lots of money to give away, and you could be next. Just keep an eye out for the K-99 Kash Kar and pull over when its emergency lights flash. Then just wait till you see what I've got in my pocket for you! I'll be making my next cash donation in just a few minutes, but first I've got a special oldie dedication for a couple of friends of mine who are getting a little too close. If they're listening, they know who they are—and if they're not, they're gonna miss a great blast from the past."

Bevins swallowed hard when the Toyota roared ahead and rammed the squad car from behind. "What the fuck?" he muttered.

Isbell held tightly to the seat. "The bastard's gonna kill himself, too," he gasped.

Sweat beaded across Bevins's brow. "Maybe that's the idea."

The Toyota veered onto the wrong side of the road as if to pass. "Hit the brakes!" Isbell blurted. "Hit the brakes and let the asshole go ahead!"

"Hell, I can't do that!" Bevins said. "The fuckin' road's too slick. We could slide off the mountain!"

Isbell knew the road well. The twists and turns grew more treacherous just a short distance ahead. He glanced out the side window again. A hazy fog hung over the valley below. It was a long, rocky way down.

Suddenly the Toyota rammed the side of the patrol car. Bevins struggled to maintain control, praying that an eighteen-wheeler would appear from around the next bend and smash the Toyota to hell.

The big red K-99 emblazoned on the side of the Toyota was clearly visible now as the radio car drew almost even with the police. "Shoot him!" Bevins screamed. "Shoot the son of a bitch!"

Isbell drew his revolver. The K-99 driver extended his middle finger and shook his head as Isbell took aim. With a sudden wrench of the steering wheel, the crazed driver slammed the Toyota directly into the side of the patrol car, nudging it to the road's uneven shoulder. The patrol car clipped a yellow sign indicating a backward *S* for the snakelike road ahead. The right front tire splashed into a puddle of standing water, sending a dark muddy wave over the mountainside. Steam hissed from the car's broken radiator, damaged by the collision with the signpost.

Bevins gripped the steering wheel tighter, wrenching the car back onto the pavement. The yellow car was just ahead of them now.

The highway curved sharply ahead. Bevins speeded up and rammed the Toyota from behind just as it entered the turn. The driver lost control and the K-99 car slid sideways on the wet asphalt, finally careening off a rocky bluff. Bevins gasped, and felt his stomach turn as he watched the car disappear over the edge. There was a deadly silence for several seconds until the car crashed and the sound of twisting metal erupted far down the steep slope.

Bevins hit the brakes and gripped the steering wheel as the patrol car slid into a large, protruding rock on the side of the road. As Isbell's body tested the seat belt from the impact, the portable radio jarred from his grasp and clattered to the floor.

Jan and Dean were singing "Dead Man's Curve."

Brian Hodge | REQUIEM

When the larger-than-life are no longer around to fuel the fires of their own lives, that's when mystique surrounding them solidifies into mythology. Or so my thoughts were drifting when Doug and I had to rappel down our second hundred-foot cliff face in as many hours.

Our waists were strapped within Swiss harnesses. Firm rope was secured at the cliff top and fed through the break-bar descenders locked to our harnesses. All around us—God's country. Because if anyone but the Almighty was keeping an eye on us, I didn't know who it could be. The Colorado Rockies were desolate even in August and as chilly as October at lower altitudes. When we'd left Fort Collins that morning, flannel shirts and jackets had seemed laughable. Not so now, spiderwalking down granite in fifty-degree breezes.

At the bottom of the cliff, we landed with gentle thuds of hiking boots, Doug's landing a bit more wobbly than my own. I had taken to the rigors of rappelling more readily, and wondered how he felt, bested by a woman nearly twenty years his junior. Finesse only, though. Results were the same. Both down, both intact.

We readjusted our packs. The two of us were toting some seventy pounds and four grand worth of recording equipment and accessories. Sometimes I tried to look at this rationally, instead of as some wistfully hopeful idealist, and each time, I felt like calling off the expedition before we both felt like grand fools. Instead, we stripped off and repacked our harnesses. And hiked onward, north, across a vast rolling plateau covered with whispering pines.

Chasing phantoms.

"You ever think what we're doing up here? Really *doing?*" I'd wanted to say this for hours. Weeks, actually, ever since Doug had gotten the idea and had us begin training: hiking and rappelling. "We're staking this whole thing on the word of some hermit who probably got cabin fever his first winter up here and never got better."

Doug nodded; the tiny ruby in his earlobe glittered. He smiled that tight smile that made him look like some punkish version of the Marlboro Man. "If we'd stayed home, by tomorrow you'd be ready to slash your wrists because we didn't at least come to see for ourselves."

Wrist-slitting might have been a bit extreme, but in my heart I knew he was right. *I had to know.* Still, play the pragmatist. I'd feel a little less foolish, maybe, when all tonight showed us was a spectacular sunset and a billion stars.

"You know what it probably was that guy heard?" I said. "Probably some die-hard fan comes up here every year to commemorate the occasion with a ghetto blaster."

"And a hologram?"

I had to concede him that one.

We each had our reasons for being here in the mountains. Mine was soulful, Doug's monetary. I thought of him as a flower child who had come of age in the late sixties without necessarily adapting to its sentiments. He was well suited for the eighties and beyond. Tall and rangy in a pioneer sort of way, with a roguishly lined and handsome face, he had a mind that never stopped calculating gross, net, and percentages. A self-styled musicians' agent, a club concert promoter around the Denver area. And bootlegger extraordinaire.

Wherever there was a buck to be made from the illegal taping or unauthorized sale of performances, Doug tried to be there. Smuggling microgear into concert halls to record from an acoustically balanced spot. Bribing a soundman to plug him directly into the mixing board. Selling illegal dupes of unused master tapes out of studios from L.A. to London.

Doug Reece: thief of performance, dealer to dozens of covert bootleg album and compact disc manufacturers all across the U.S. and as far away as Australia.

I knew he was diametrically opposed to almost everything I held sacred—which made rationalizing his status as occasional employer and sometime lover one of the more difficult snow jobs I had to pull on myself. But hey, didn't *everybody* sell their soul for rock and roll, eventually?

He was loyal to his friends, I told myself. And Doug *had* busted his rump to get me and my Ovation acoustic bookings all around Denver, Boulder, Fort Collins. It didn't matter that sometimes I looked at myself in barroom mirrors and saw a twenty-four-year-old cliché—this tall, willowy girl with long hair, a neo-folkie playing songs of bitter angst and childlike hope. At least it was honest.

More so than being an accomplice to a bootlegger. But it's no surprise which pays better. Something to consider if your eventual goal is Los Angeles, to bravely butt heads against a predominantly metal scene. Seed money. This wouldn't last forever.

We all sell our souls. We just don't all have the stones to believe it.

Doug and I trouped along with our burdens, dwarfed and made insignificant by the distant peaks, gray rock capped with snow that never melted. Carved and sculpted by glaciers when wind and beasts were the only music the earth knew, no two refrains quite the same. For eons. I envied that long-lost purity.

By late afternoon, we had found our destination. It was a sort of natural amphitheater, a vast niche cut into a slope in rough horseshoe shape. Tiers of striated granite rose up until they melted into the parent rock. All around, towering pines and firs gave silent testament to the fact that, yes, this idyllic spot was the site of a holocaust. This was where the music, for me, had died. You could see it in the scars along a particular gauntlet of trees, knotted bark at the same height on each trunk, where once upon a time, all had been sheared off—by a blade the exact size and shape of an airplane's wing.

136

Names tolled in memory, a litany of the dead. Terence Dobbins. Dylan Pryce. Ian Smyth-Taylor. Jon Wakefield. Geniuses, one and all. I missed them like brothers, like lovers, like fathers, like friends linked at the soul. They had been all those to me, and more.

Grendel, I thought. Rest in peace.

Doug had shed his pack atop a rock the size of a half-buried Volkswagen. Out of the corner of my eye, I saw him looking at me, watching me take it all in, still as a statue and silent as the rocks that had watched the millennia pass. He came up behind me, like a father dealing with a lazy child, and slipped my own backpack off. He flipped up the hair at the nape of my neck and, in a completely unexpected show of tenderness, kissed me there.

I needed it. But oh, would that it had been Terence. Or Dylan. Or Ian, or Jon. Some residual trace of their spirits, drawn out of rock and trees and earth by the arrival of one whose life they had so deeply touched nearly a decade ago. Who still grieved whenever she played their albums.

But . . . it was Doug. Only Doug.

"Can you feel it?" I whispered. "I can almost believe that a part of them is still here."

Doug looked up from his rock, his recording gear now half strewn out of the packs. "You're not gonna cry on me, are you?"

So much for tenderness.

I left him to assemble his components and wandered along the path that their chartered private jet had taken down toward destiny, until I stood in the midst of what surely had been ground zero.

I looked to the sky and saw a circling hawk. Saw the peaks near and far, carpeted with snow and foliage. Pastoral calm, Disney calm. It wasn't easy to imagine this as the site of the fireball that had snuffed out the lives of the band called Grendel.

Underfoot were pine needles, old leaves, pebbles, and soil—the mulch of a million years. The wreckage was long-gone, but I wondered if all their bodies had been recovered, every precious fragment. Wondered if I was treading an unmarked mass grave. Wondered if it would be a sacrilege to tug off my jeans and try to make love to the very earth where they might have been absorbed.

Grendel was named for the beast killed by Beowulf. It had arisen in London in the late seventies, a phoenix from the ashes of the British art-rock scene. Such timing was a blessing and a curse. Like prophets respected everywhere but in their own land, they found precious few fans at home. Instead, they found cult acceptance across the Atlantic with intellectual rock fans and imaginative middle-class kids who couldn't identify with the nihilistic punk sneer and its minimalist approach, which had taken London by blitz-krieg.

Grendel was signed by L.A.'s Toreador Records, and I could still remember unearthing their first album in 1980: *Here There Be Dragons.* That forbidding phrase of antiquity was used on maps to indicate the end of all that was known, the beginning of all that was mysterious. The album cover itself resembled an old-world map on ancient parchment. And within? The music of Olympian gods.

In addition to the latest guitar and synth technology, they freely used mandolin, harpsichord, church organ, panpipes, lute, harp . . . the diversity was stunning. Their focus was toward things medieval, ominous minor keys derived from Dark Age modalities and Gregorian chants. Precursors of gothic rock, they were either far ahead of their time or woefully late by a thousand years. A millennium ago, they would surely have been branded sorcerers for their music and condemned to the stake. Either way, they burned, I suppose.

Their second album, *Sympathy for the Beast,* was released in 1981. It was a retelling of the Beowulf story from Grendel's point of view. Next came *Odyssey,* tales of the travels of Leif Eriksson. And lastly came their most ambitious project, *Scourge,* in 1983. Their musical impressions of Vlad, the Impaler, whose bloodthirsty legacy gave birth to the legend of Dracula, came complete with one of the most intricate stage shows ever to tour. I still have the *Rolling Stone* review of the kickoff concert on their Scourge Across

America Tour, the paper laminated in plastic: Madison Square Garden, July 17, 1983.

The tour raged through the States for the next several weeks, their most successful ever. That extravagant show was the one thing, I think, if need be, I would've sold body and soul to see. Grendel and its fanciful flights of imagination had sustained me through the adolescent purgatory called high school. I was a cliché even then—couldn't even hone my nonconformity into something original. I was the slim, small-chested girl whose face wore a somber mask from contemplating the painful mysteries of life and love; who carried stained notebooks filled with poems as bleak as November rain and set them to music; who often dressed in black and didn't date; who read the books and listened to the music no one else cared about.

And Grendel got me through it, my solace when imagination was the only escape. At least, until the start of my senior year.

For the grieving fans, truth eluded us in a jungle of rumor. Senseless tragedies breed their own myths. But what seemed persistently likely was this: Grendel was embroiled in a haggle over royalties with Toreador at the time of the tour, and tempers were flaring on both sides. The label had booked them one night in Seattle, two nights later in Denver. More than 1,300 miles to cover by bus, plus teardown and setup. It wouldn't have given time for an adequate sound check. And for a band that prided itself on flawless polish, this was anathema. When they complained and asked the label to spring for a chartered jet, Toreador refused. Teach them a lesson, how dare they question the hand that fed them.

So they chartered a small jet out of their own bank accounts. But over the Rockies, they ran into a sudden storm that had veered off expected course. And late that night, Grendel joined the ranks of Buddy Holly, Ritchie Valens, Lynyrd Skynyrd, Randy Rhoads and Stevie Ray Vaughan. One last great blinding light show. August 25, 1983.

August 25—the same date as our day of mountain

trekking. The darkest of anniversaries, when I mourned the deaths of my musical saviors.

I knelt, laid a flat hand against the sparse grass. Maybe they *were* here, waiting for the annual cycle to click once more, to turn their spirits loose for a time. I wanted to believe it. Needed to believe it, with the frightened passion of a girl still waiting for that first kiss.

I rose then, wandered back along the path of the crash, beneath the boughs of trees that had rebuilt themselves season after season. Doug had his equipment set up, and was now double-checking all the cable connections.

"If it's true," I said, "how are you going to explain the tape?"

He smiled, a Rhett Butler born of the Me Decade. "I'll take the master and add some crowd noise into the mix. Swell the applause after the songs, you know how it sounds. Grendel, live in concert. Who gives a damn when and where it was taped?"

I do, I thought. And everybody else who loved them.

At first, a few weeks ago, it had sounded like psychotic babble. Doug had caught wind of it from a friend who frequented a rustic diner and coffee shop on Fort Collins's western edge, in the foothills where Route 14 leads into the mountains and where the world's best cinnamon rolls can be found. There'd been a former Vietnam vet who hadn't readjusted well and, a decade after coming home, had decided he belonged in the mountains—only to return to Fort Collins years later with tales of survival and of spirits.

Toward the end of every August, he'd said. Every year since he'd been up there, the mountains had quaked and the trees shaken. The hills were alive with the sound of music. Grendel, dead and in concert, came back to play its final show.

Post-traumatic stress syndrome ravings perhaps. But it was an opportunity neither Doug nor I could forgive ourselves for ignoring.

We spoke little as we waited. We ate some trail mix and dehydrated fruit, hikers' staples. With another couple whose relationship was less parasitic, the solitude and surroundings might have been ample inducement to shed clothes and make love. But not us. Our encounters seemed limited to sweaty bedrooms and soiled sheets, locked into love-hate banging in a miasma of smoke and fear of the future. There would be no mountaintop raptures for us, ever.

Afternoon died, evening struggled. The sun settled behind the western peaks, the snowcaps devolving between the pinks and blues of newborn babies, until the sky blackened and the snow was once again white, but ghostly in the moonlight.

Even if Grendel never showed, the night would not be a loss.

But when they came—as they had to, as I *knew* they would—the night became a treasure.

Doug and I were leaning against the largest of a scattering of rocks when the sound began, so low and subaudible that it had sneaked up on us. But my ears weren't fooled for long. This was no wind, no trick of mountain acoustics.

The chant arose from the ground and rock, cyclical and overlapping. I recognized it from *Here There Be Dragons* . . . a brooding funereal cadence. Sung in Latin over droning synthesizers, their voices overdubbed until there were dozens of voices, a hundred. A requiem to herald the passing of kings.

It swelled into the night, rebounding from cliffs and peaks, a triumphant cyclone that rippled goose bumps over every inch of flesh. By the time the amphitheater erupted into an unearthly netherlight more dynamic than any concert stage had ever seen, I was already crying for joy.

I looked over at Doug. His eyes were wide, his jaw dropped at the spectacle. But his hands were sure as they glided over rotary pots, switches, and sliders. He was sucking it all up into a reel-to-reel driven by battery packs and voltage converters. Microphones had been set up in a perimeter aimed at the amphitheater. Once he had slapped on his headphones, I could tell that he'd never heard sound like *this*.

I stumbled a few steps away, then fell to my knees. There was no intrusion of traitor thoughts, denials, explanations of hallucinations. No. This seemed natural; it seemed *right*.

It was like stepping into the *Rolling Stone* review's

accompanying photo. I'd memorized every trapping, every piece of stage gear, great and small. The entire amphitheater and surrounding grounds had been appropriated for reconstruction.

Grendel's "Scourge Across America" stage depicted a countryside in ruin. Stone walls had crumbled; thatched roofs burned continually, lit by the torches of Vlad the Impaler's army. Silhouetted horses and riders stampeded across a backdrop. Decimation Boulevard. And branching away on either side of where the band played, a growing row of grisly poles that had given Vlad his nickname. As the music played, a horde of fur-clad barbarians set about their task with unhurried efficiency . . . affixing animatronically writhing bodies to sharp stakes, then erecting them like flagpoles. Where they squirmed, where they dripped stage blood. It had all been very real-looking then as well as now.

I left Doug's side, rushing for the amphitheater, a stage stampede of one. Their music was dark majesty, and they never even seemed to notice I was there: Terence Dobbins, a twentieth-century Paganini on guitar; Dylan Pryce, bass guitar and lead vocal; Ian Smyth-Taylor, wizard on keyboards new and antiquated; Jon Wakefield, master percussionist.

Colors pulsed, slid one into another, vibrant and eerie. The band members were shadowed silhouettes against red backlighting, then each played from within his own pyramid of swirling blue . . . on and on.

I fixated on Dylan Pryce, singing of what lay beyond the edge of the earth. His legs were spread wide, his black mane brushing his shoulders. Wearing a shirt with rawhide lacing over his chest, he was poster-perfect, every bit the pubescent fantasy I'd found him ten years ago. His throat pealed with the voice of a sullied angel.

The songs flowed on, scarcely a break between them. The flames scorched the ruined stage-village. And the ranks of bleeding bodies steadily increased, the giant stakes tilted at odd angles to one another, their rough-hewn wood dark and stained.

Requiem

Forty minutes in, they did a song I'd never heard. Slumped before the amphitheater, I listened closely to the lyrics over the sound of baroque trumpets conjured up from the keyboards. Arthurian lyrics, something about Mordred. Behind me, I barely heard Doug give a whoop of joy. *Unreleased tracks.* The cash register in his head was chiming even higher totals. It had to be music from the unrecorded fifth album, rumored to be about King Arthur and the knights of the Round Table.

Lucky, lucky Doug. Here to profit with his boundless enthusiasm and his reels of magnetic oxide.

Seventy minutes in, the power rock was forsaken in favor of a usual feature of Grendel's concerts. Terence's electric guitar was traded for an acoustic twelve-string, Dylan's bass relinquished for mandolin and harp. Ian joined in on harpsichord, and Jon emerged from behind his drums to sit in with a flute. The raging flames atop the walls and thatched roofs dwindled into warm, friendly flickers. The gauntlets of the impaled dead were halted, the barbaric army disappearing into shadows.

The music held sway over theater. Delicate, lively, and gentle. Intricate lines weaving together in sonata form. Apart from their dress, it would be easy to imagine Grendel entertaining dancers at a Renaissance ball.

They had been playing for no more than a minute when this flawless performance developed its first hitch. Hunched intently over his twelve-string, Terence Dobbins's fingers stumbled. He straightened, and in the lights I saw drops of blood seeping from his nose to patter onto the guitar. Moments later, the affliction had stricken them all. Blood, weeping from eyes, ears, nostrils, fingertips, mouths. It dribbled onto clothes, spotted the ivory keys of the harpsichord, slicked Jon's flute.

They faltered, each and every one, winced like men in pain.

And bravely attempted to continue.

From where he was seated on a low stool, Dylan Pryce lifted his head, shifting his gaze from the mandolin whose fretboard he'd smeared with blood. And for the first time

since this night's concert began, he looked at me. Not with
the random chance of looking in my direction. But *at me.*

Once upon a time, had he beckoned, I'd have followed
him backstage, around the country, across the globe. I
would not follow him beyond the grave, but he wasn't
beckoning for that. I could tell in a glance what he was
feeling.

I knew that look of pain. Had seen it reflected in my own
eyes many a time when I'd been fourteen, fifteen, sixteen
and seventeen. When the aspects of my life that made it
unique served only as fodder for ridicule; when my soul
shrieked, "These are what I have and these are what I am, so
please leave them alone!"

Dead superstar, budding hopeful. We had more in common than I would have thought. Whatever its source, pain is
universal.

My idol, my savior. Now it was time to finally repay the
favor. That understanding passed between us, just in time.
For Dylan's eyes were then blinded by blood.

I went running back from the amphitheater to where
Doug lorded over his reel-to-reel deck and digital gauges.
The ecstatic face he had worn earlier had soured into
frustration.

"What the hell's wrong with them?" he said, too far away
to see the blood clearly. "They sound like shit!"

"Shut the tape off, Doug." I reached for the power switch,
and he swatted my hand aside. When I tried it again, he gave
me a shove that sent me sprawling.

"Doug, *please,* just shut it off, you're killing them." I had
gotten up as far as my knees, and hated to beg.

"Killing them?" He laughed incredulously. "They're already dead!"

"But not *all* of them, not the part that made the music.
The music came out of their souls, not their bodies. The
music's all they have left now. You steal that, you take away
the only thing they have anymore. You're bleeding them
dry!"

Doug shook his head and rolled his eyes, but when I made
one more lunge for the switch, those eyes turned vicious. He

turned against me. He knocked me to the ground with a backhand that crunched over my eye socket. It would swell badly—that was a given.

I ran a few yards in the direction of the amphitheater, to the nearest of the unidirectional mikes he'd set up. It was mounted on a small metal stand, aimed at the band, and I ripped the microphone free. Yanked the stand and its round base up like a club.

And I charged. Unsteady. But, oh, such determination.

Doug ran between me and his ever-rolling tape deck, a rock in hand. I could tell by his eyes that if he could not dissuade me, he would not hesitate to stop me. But I couldn't let it go on, not when petty greed over their royalties had killed them in the first place. And so, beneath the towering branches of ageless trees, we clashed like two beasts fighting for territorial dominion.

I swung, Doug threw. We each took the brunt in the head. It might even have been funny, in a Buster Keaton film. His stone knocked me in the forehead a half second before I felt the mike stand connect with his temple. And down we tumbled.

While the tape kept rolling.

I moaned, rolled from side to side, helpless as a half-dead child. My head roared thunder, the great white-hot flash of the blow lingering in my skull. The one eye was blinded from swelling and blood. But the other worked fine, and so did my ears.

All through the concert, I had been wondering one single thing: *Could I touch them? Were they solid?*

Regarding the band, I'll never know. But the barbarian army? They were real enough. For this night, they were solid.

Solid enough, at least, to emerge from behind the trees and lift a half-conscious Doug aloft, and carry him toward the amphitheater. I watched with one blurring eye, with traitor limbs that would not move the way I told them to.

While the tape kept rolling.

Tonight's acoustic set was cut short. But that was okay. And during a slight intermission that I could no longer face,

I thought I saw Dylan Pryce standing over me, smiling down, mopping himself with a sodden red towel. But he sweated no more blood.

And then he was gone.

Consciousness was nearly ready to shut down, and I had no choice in the matter. But just before it happened, I heard the screaming begin. Vlad's army on maneuvers.

And that's when the *real* power rock began.

Dawn comes early in the mountains, cold and bright.

I came to, shivering, left cheek stiff beneath a crust of blood. I rose, wobbly, and the world swam before settling into focus. At least I had only one eye to confuse, for the time being.

The air was still. Where once guitars and keyboards had rung out now only birds and breezes sang.

Several more discoveries remained. The tape deck and microphones, pulverized into fragments against rocks. After finding this, I hobbled toward the amphitheater. Gone, all gone, the glorious stage set. The burning village, the instruments and their masters. The rows of poles, top-heavy with victims.

All, that is, except for one.

Doug had always operated behind the scenes. Now? Center stage.

He hung eight feet in the air, body rigid and contorted, his limbs curled, two feet of stake protruding up through his abdomen. I felt no joy at his passing, but no real remorse, either. Maybe because, while death is as natural as life, its aftermath seems so unreal.

Or perhaps it was because Doug himself seemed so unreal. Scarcely recognizable. A withered bag of loose flesh and bones. How much of the human body is liquid? Whatever the percentage, Doug had been drained of most of his.

It was only after staring at his wrinkled, dehydrated form that I let my gaze wander down along the stake, to the ground beneath him. To the two things resting there.

First, the reels of tape, boxed and intact. Waiting. A gift? I saw it no other way. A gift, to be played without profit motives getting in the way of enjoyment.

And the second . . . a simple slip of paper, stained with three stray spatters of dark red. Doug's, I had no doubt of that. Just the blood, and a few words penned by a firm, sure hand.

Royalties: Paid in Full

R. Patrick Gates | HEAVY METAL

(With apologies to Edgar Allan Poe)

TRUE!—nervous—very, very, dreadfully nervous I had been and am; but why *will* you say that I am mad? The incident has sharpened my senses, not destroyed, not dulled them. Above all was the sense of hearing acute. I heard all things in the heavens and in the earth. I heard many things in Hell, like the music coming from that infernal—but I get ahead of myself. Listen and observe how healthily, how calmly I can tell you the whole story.

When this whole thing started, I was a simple artist, a sculptor, toiling away in my Village loft. I had started out working with clay but found my fingers too indelicate for molding the unwieldy stuff. It was with metal that I found my forte—hammering, riveting, soldering; I was battling the metal to make it bend to my creative will.

Though I was far from achieving financial success with my art, I had received some critical acclaim with a small show I did last year in a Soho gallery. Perhaps some of you saw it?

Perhaps not.

No matter. A small inheritance left me by my mother was allowing me to spend two years devoting myself full-time to my art, if I lived frugally, that is. Two years to make it was all I had, so you can see why I was so nervous and why any interruption was costly and upsetting.

I was working on a particularly difficult piece—a mesh of copper and iron that I was trying to make soar to some vague expression of my imagination that I couldn't quite fully grasp. All I knew was that I wanted the metal to transcend its mass, leave its base weight behind, and become a symbol of spiritual metamorphosis.

I was working at my anvil—a genuine blacksmith's anvil weighing four hundred pounds, which I picked up for a song at a dingy little antique shop in Jersey—when the miraculous happened. I was hammering some scrap copper tubing into flat, ribbony lengths when I began to have a revelation about the piece. Suddenly it all started to come together. Like a pyramid under construction, the idea for the sculpture began to rise in my mind.

It was *fantastic!*

It was *beautiful!*

It was going to be the best thing I'd ever done!

Truly, to be immodest, it was going to be the best work of art *anyone* had ever done. It would make me famous. It would make me rich. It . . .

Was suddenly gone, replaced by a blaring, jarring cacophony of screaming guitars, demonic singing and the whining feedback of electric amplifiers. My greatest idea was driven right out of my head and replaced by a piercing, horrible noise that surely was the Muzak of Hell itself.

I threw my hammer down, copper ribbons spilling everywhere, and furtively searched for the source of the sound. It was coming from outside. I rushed to the window, looked down, and there it was, the destroyer of ideas, the bane of my creativity.

It was the size of a suitcase and shone with chrome and black plastic in the hot, summer city sun. Its knobs glistened malevolently and its volume gauge danced spastically to the din pouring from its speakers. It was the biggest boom box I had ever seen and, with the horrible auditory torture it produced, it surely was the ugliest.

A madman would have screamed at the young, long-haired youth to whom this Ghetto Blaster from Hell belonged. And I certainly had good reason to, since his infernal machine had just wiped out perhaps the greatest idea in all the long history of art. A crazy person would have run down the stairs and accosted the youth, screaming for

149

the police, threatening the boy with wild words and even wilder deeds.

That is what a madman would have done. But as I said, I was not insane; I *am not* insane.

I never blamed the boy. He was the product of a poor home—his mother was a drunkard, his father nonexistent. I didn't begrudge him the futile escape he sought in the wretched tunes of the loud and crude heavy metal bands that he listened to. He had never wronged me. He had never given me insult.

It was the boom box I hated. From that moment on the mere sound of it, no matter how muffled by closed windows and background noise, made my blood run cold.

I calmly closed the window, though the temperature in my loft was reaching the high nineties, and acted as if all were well. But deep down there was nothing I desired more than to see that screeching box of noise, that destroyer of fame, lying smashed in a heap of plastic and metal, transistors and wires, all over the front steps of my building.

I lay awake nearly all night that first night, and for every night after, listening to the thumping of the boom box's heavy metal vibrating up through the floor and the very walls themselves. The boy's mother passed out from her drink like clockwork every night by ten and a nuclear explosion would not have woken her. Until the wee hours of the morning that dreadful noise some call music thudded up to me. AC/DC banged on the walls; Poison pounded the floors; Iron Maiden shook my bed. Each night, I didn't sleep until the music stopped, usually shortly before dawn, and I was awake again in a couple of hours, trying to work before the cacophony returned as the youth took up his perch on the front steps again to while away another day.

Night after night this went on, and night after night I lay staring at the ceiling, my very bones vibrating. Those nights were not wasted, though. I did not toss and turn, cursing the noise, banging on the floor for a respite from its torture. I did not call the police and have the youth arrested for disturbing the peace.

No.

Instead, I planned.

Now, this is the point. You fancy me mad. But madmen know nothing. You should have seen *me*. You should have seen how wisely I proceeded—with what great caution—with what extreme foresight—with what huge dissimulation did I go to work. I was never kinder to the boy. When I went out, I smiled at him and said hello, all the time eyeing the accursed box as it blared at me, seeming to mock me with its ear-shattering volume.

But I would have the last laugh. I would see the thing destroyed, and to this end I spent my insomniac nights and all my creative energies trying to devise a suitable revenge against the monster music-maker.

Curiously enough, it was while watching television one day that the perfect plan came to me. I often put the TV on while I work, but rarely look at it, enjoying rather its unobtrusive background noise. However, one day, sluggish from lack of sleep and with the hellish noise from outside still accosting my ears, I found myself staring at the TV quite frequently.

A cartoon was on, and as I watched it, the idea hit me like a hot blast of subway train air. It was a vintage Road Runner cartoon. Wile E. Coyote was atop a cliff; the ribbon of highway that the Road Runner sped along was far below. Wile E. was unpacking one of his infamous Acme do-it-yourself kits. I watched with fascination as he set up his trap, then had it go all wrong as it always did, backfiring on him. But that didn't matter. I had found the perfect revenge, and unlike the comic, bungling coyote, I would not fail.

Now, tell me truly, is that crazy?

I spent all night readying for D Day. In the depths of darkness I crept down to the step, tape measure, notepad and calculator handy. I measured. I estimated. I calculated. I did it all with an acute precision that madmen are incapable of. By the time the youth resumed his perch on the steps the next morning, Guns n' Roses screaming from the boom box, I was ready.

I had taken a long, smooth board and propped it between a small stepladder and the windowsill at just the right slant, nailing the outer edge to the sill. Several times during the early morning hours, I rolled quarters off the board, making minor adjustments until the trajectory was just right. A thick coating of axle grease on the board's surface, and several strenuous moments spent lugging my anvil to the top of the ladder, and *bombs away!* I would show that blasted sound machine what *heavy metal* really was and the evil boom box would boom no more!

Can you still say that I am mad? Could a madman have planned so meticulously, so thoroughly, so ingeniously?

But the plan failed, you say?

Yes, it did, but through no fault of mine. My measurements were exact, perfect, genius. Was it my fault that the youth chose D Day to set his boom box on a different spot than usual and to occupy its former space himself? And is it any wonder that after I dropped the anvil out of the window, yet still heard that torturous noise go on unabated, mocking me more than ever, that I flew down to the steps in a fit of rage and smashed the thing with my bare hands as I slipped in the splattered remains of the youth's head?

Was that crazy?

Was it?

Was it?

| **BUNKY**

W hoooooaaaaa, Jenny, Jenny!" Mitch Ryder boppin'
out along the quadruplexing Z-band—oh, man, ain't *no-body* ever could do it bad as Mitch Ryder, am I right or
what? Jenny got her blue dress on. Jenny take a ride. Shit,
Jim, that fucker's cookin' like a bandit, and I pop for the
mike.

"Whoa, Joan! Hold the phone! This is *rad*, 'n' bad to the
bone!"

Segue the straight a cappella and into a spot cluster? No
way, Doctor Jay. I kill the spots and blast right back into the
past. You're a bitch, Mitch, but wham-bam, Sam, Jimi show
ya how to jam. Profundity and ideational lightning bolts.
It's the night of the living-dead rockers. Finger boogie-rama.

"Get some Morrison," I tell the gainrider. Do I love it
here or what? X-ROQ. Big time, Hoss. X-Rock. Clear
channel on the Z-band, 250,000 powerhertz outta Villanue-
va, Mexico. "Hold it one, dude, I gotta get my log down."

I look up and see DAYPARTS SUB-MENU/ HOT
CLOCK B and I holler over the box to Doctor Jay. "Hey,
bro, you got me on the fuckin' Dayparts thing, dickhead,
and we're on Hot Clock 'D,' not 'B,' I hate to tell ya. Other
than that, we're stone perfect." He laughs and corrects the
screen.

"Was that 'B' as in buttface, or 'D' as in dorkbrain?" he
asks me, his voice metallic on the intercom box.

"D" . . . dufus, as in a dick submarine up your Love
Canal. Awright, now, lemme see. Seg outta Hendrix into

153

Bumpers, Spot One, Bridges, Spot Two, me, then Chuck Berry."

Doctor punches it up and I see:

```
PURPLE HAZE
BUMPERS (:01)
SPOT ONE (:29)
BRIDGES (:02)
SPOT TWO (:29)
ANNCR
MAYBELLINE
```

"Aw, fork you, mortar flogger," I mumble into the box, adding up the cluster in front of me. "That's sixty-one seconds! Kill the spot-breaker, go right into music."

"We'll miss you terribly," he snarls. Goes dah, dah, dah, on a keyboard and the screen changes to:

```
PURPLE HAZE
BUMPERS (:01)
SPOT ONE (:29)
SPOT TWO (:29)
BUMPERS (:01)
MAYBELLINE
```

Damn thing corrected me. Amazing! I love it. It's one of those dynamite new IMPAC programmers. You feed in the hot clocks and cluster-busters 'n' stuff, tell it how to program, it corrects to the nearest parameter maximums, and you can go to lunch. It knew to jam in a jingle before the music.

The format is ultra-complex. Sort of a hybrid mutation between postmodern rock and old-time Top 40 boss. It's called "rad." Top of the hour, we go outta spots and into maximum rad, which is a solid rockin' gold format. But the nuances and the pacing components get very tricky. That's why anything that helps sand off the rough edges is good. IMPAC's got alternate pace routing, remote programmability—hell, it's even got fail-safe fallback geared to the cue-tones.

You really need it in Dayparts, with a heavy log, but I like it on this shift because it keeps me honest with the numbers. Helps you pace your act, too. We had the old MacKenzies at Q-92, and it could get very hairy. Rad is a demanding format, but the sound is worth it—dig?

A year ago I didn't know a parametric EQ from a parachute, and a few months later I'm doin' drive time on Q-92. Fuckin' amazing! Then Ed Bowman calls. National PD for Am-West. Completely restaffing at X-Rock. Would I have a tape? Sheeeiiiitttt! Would I have a tape? Do Harvey got a wallbanger? Rest is history.

"Hold it a second. We're coming to a setup."

"I got Morrison." He shows me the screen.

"That's right. Boogie till you puke," I tell him, killing the studio monitor. The mind is a precision instrument. A year ago, I was in fuckin' jail. The big boys come to me with this wild-ass scheme. I get sent to jock school, I take an all-night gig playin' rock and actin' weird. When the thing winds down, they cut me loose, I get a "time-served" waiver and twenty thousand cash.

They lay this paper on me. A thick contract with my real name, the company's cover name. Looks legit down to the witnesseths. No details. It's strictly need-to-know spook-stuff. Do I want to make the scene or not? Shit! Do bunnies fuck? I'm outta there.

This guy across from me—he's got one of them honkie names like Chuck Lipshitz or something, which I know from git-go street ain't his name, anyway. He's in his suit. And he's got the little razorcut and all that WASP, whitey shit down, and I just half-listen to this crap.

". . . sending you and several other penetration teams in . . . combo operations . . . station contracts within the Dye chain . . . midnight show . . . hard rock . . . complete secrecy . . ." And then he starts with the threats. "You ever open your yap, you're back in the slams." That sorta shit.

Hell, I tell him, I never ratted out anybody.

He knows that, he says. They "factored that in," he says. They really talk like that.

What it is, is this: This Howard Hughes–type recluse with a lotta bucks is named Donald Dye or Dickie Dye or something. He's done very bad things. He's butt-fucked the government. Put the ol' sperm machine to Uncle. Done some kinda deal with the Libyans or the Iranians—whatever. He's gotta go bye-bye. I tell 'em from square one I ain't no heavy hitter. They got the wrong maniac. No, they say. I don't gotta whack nobody. The idea is, I'm supposed to grease the way in for the guy who does the deed. He goes in as my engineer. I just keep that mutha' on the air while the hit goes down.

Say what? I tell them. What kinda grab-ass deal is this, anyway? They lay it out for me. Show me a picture of the dude I'm supposed to work with, and it all comes together. Jeezus freakin' mondo bongo! It's fucking' Bunky! I ain't seen that crazy animal for a hundred years. We did a little time together when I was a kid, doin' a pound at Algoa. I won't even tell you the goony, bogus flim flam I was in there on. I wouldn't insult your intelligence. All you need to know is I was innocent. Shit! *Bunky!*

He looks just the same—five hundred pounds, eight feet tall. Little cold black eyes starin' out this face like a pan fulla pizza dough. Balls-all killer. Some people said the fucker had whacked out a human being for every pound of his weight. He did three people *inside* that I personally can guarantee, man. That ain't no jive. Stone death dealer.

"You expect me to believe Bunky gonna do some kinda engineer gig? That's pure bullshit, Jack. Forget about that shit right now."

But they say he's behind this. Bunky's got this thing about animals. Fact is, that's how we got tight. I saved this little cat from being throwed off of D-tier in the bull tank, but how a cat got in there is a whole 'nother thing.

Bunky likes to kill *people*, but he loves animals. They told him how Don Dye fucks up all these dolphins and shit, and it got my man all crazy to ice him down. The deal is this: You can't just walk up to the Dye dude and do him, see, because he's like a hermit. He never goes anywhere like, you know, out. Nobody sees him. He does his business by phone.

They tell Bunky about Dye's big milling company. They own canneries. They buy from the people's putting out these nets 'n' crap, killing all the dolphins, rippin' their asses up and throwin' 'em back in, tossin' the babies in without their mamas 'n' shit—and fuckin' Bunky, he goes wild. Man, he wants to rip Dye's guts out and *eat* 'em, Jim. 'Cause that's his scene. He takes *hearts,* you know?

Dye has one weakness—he likes to fuck with his radio stations. They're his toys, dig? The only time anybody ever sees him, he'll come in with his big Jap bodyguard on the night shift and he'll be fuckin' around in the production room, or you'll see him on the all-night trick—just a shadow going through the sales office. Whatever. He's a fuckin' *buff*—you know, like a radio nut. It's in the fucker's blood.

The big boys are putting in "penetration teams," a combo team of engineer and jock, at every one of his radio operations. When Dye shows up—if he shows—he goes.

Ain't nothing to getting the teams in. Once they can boogie big-time on the air, all they do is offer the men or women in place more bucks, and you know Uncle. He's got nothing but. Then—soon as the people give notice—the team is on the scene with resume and tape in hand. These are union ops, some of 'em, but that's cool, too. Uncle don't gotta sweat that, either.

First I gotta go to jock school. Then me and Bunky work together till we get the act down. Then we go in. Twenty thou, man. And I can *walk* when it's over. Shit. Why not?

'Course, I wasn't born yesterday, man. I mean—I didn't just fall off a fuckin' turnip truck. All that shit about a recluse, and Uncle Sam, and dolphins. That's just somebody's wet dream. One of them Langley jack-offs had him another masturbation fantasy. You get to fuckin' with them spooks, why, you be finding out they lie like sons of bitches. Lies ain't lies to them fuckers, they're *tradecraft,* you dig?

I know whatever it is, I ain't ever gonna know the truth of it, and whatever it is—it's super baaad. And whatever it is beats what I was doin', which was sitting in the joint, scared shitless, hoping I wouldn't make the wrong move and come outta there with an asshole the size of a wastebasket. Anything beats that shit. I say, yo, bro, go with the flow.

157

The big boys send me to jock school. It's Johnny Hitt's school, man. Ever heard of Johnny? I heard of that cat since God was a pup. He was one of them Stone Age fuckers back when Top 40 was first invented. He used to bring R & B and early rock acts into the Coliseum, and he was kind of a cross between Alan Freed and that cat who booked people into the Fillmore. An entre-pre-neur—dig?

Hitt's an old dude. Wears a Yankees cap alla time and talks out of the corner of his mouth.

First thing I say is, "Hey, my main man, the legendary Johnny Hitt!" Or some such crap.

And he goes, "That's the first thing." Already busting my balls, ya know? Not even saying hello. "That's the number-one thing—cut out all the jive talk. No jivey stuff. It's bullshit. And I only got a few weeks to bring you up to speed. Speak regular English. Speak in complete sentences. Forget the slang. Understand?"

"Yeah." I ain't deaf. But he just looks at me like he wants to fry my nuts for breakfast. "I understand," I say.

The second thing don't have zip to do with being a rock jock. He starts me out on all these moves. Head signals. Vocal signals. Hand movements. It's good I don't know anything, he says, so he can teach me from scratch.

"In radio, you cue an engineer like so." He points. "You don't ever cue *your* engineer like that."

I can be with that, Jim. Nobody goes stickin' a finger out in Bunky's face. Not if they don't want him to snap it off and eat that shit. So I learn the signals.

Hitt plays like my engineer. By the end of the first day, we got the signals down and we're running some semblance of what I later come to find out is called a "tight board." I got a tight board and a tight asshole.

"Your man has absolutely no feel for radio. I'm not sure you do, either, frankly. But you can pick up sufficient technique to fake it. Half the people in radio don't have a feel for it, so that's no prerequisite. Thing is, he is faster than any engineer I ever worked with. He manages, without anticipating the cue and stepping on anything, to react quicker to a visual sign than I'd have imagined. It's like running your own board, his responses are that quick." Of course, I have no fucking idea from "Jumpin' Jack Flash" what this happy shit is all about.

"He'll never have to clean heads, jerk a busted stylus, check a dirty spot on a pot, or kick an auxiliary transmitter on. We've got him backstopped on all of that. He simply has to look like an engineer and be able to follow the cues, ride gain, and run the board. You'll be working the graveyard trick, so no worries about spotload. Your job, in addition to sounding like a pro, is learning the format.

"The operation where you two will be inserted is dead easy. Maximum music. Plenty of segues, where the tunes go back to back. And the format is loose enough you won't have to have much musical knowledge."

The second day, I still don't do any jocking. I get a crash course in trial-and-error engineering. Simple replacement of solid state snap-in/snap-out stuff, but they dig right away it's wasted on me. If something breaks down, we call a dude who comes right in and fixes it. The rest of the day I get prepped on the proper way to "interface."

The third day is the hardest. Hitt really takes me to school on how to do it. I never open my mouth. I just soak up the theory:

"Ever see a famous radio deejay on TV?" he asks me. "Some big-time jock gets on the television and invariably he sucks. What goes over on radio and what goes over on the tube are two different things. You react to a live audience one way, react to a target audience in your head in another. A lot of jocks work to their engineer, or they work to somebody sitting in the newsroom, and it doesn't play on the air. You will not work to your engineer, ever. You work to a target in your mind. She is twenty-two. Has a boyfriend. Likes to go places. Enjoys rock." He starts describing this chick, this mythical bitch I'm supposed to work to in my head. It's all I can do not to ask him if she has big milk machines.

On the fourth day, he has me talk for the first time. I'm sweatin', sittin' in front of a microphone, and he has me read something. Some bullshit about the next record I'm gonna play, the wreck of the Ella Fitzgerald, or Gladys and the Pimps, or whatever the shit is—and I open my yap and he says cool it.

"The tone is wrong. Let me explain the sound. You seat your voice in rockabilly." He says that like he's giving me the answer to the mystery of the ages.

I don't know rockabilly from Rock fuckin' Hudson, but I keep listening.

"The voice itself is warm. Forget that shit you were just doin'. It's called 'puker,' that tone, and we don't want that."

I try again, trying to sound like an announcer.

He says, "No. Too far the other way. That's old-time broadcasting stuff. You're not going to be a staff announcer, you're going to be a rock jock. Get the voice natural, the tone warm, work closer, softer."

It goes on like this. Be softer, closer, taller, whiter. Sheeeeeeiiiiitttt!

The fifth day, he has me ad-libbing song intros. Gettin' into "Brown Sugar" by the Stones. Alice's "Eighteen." Bobby Day. Elvis. Black Sabbath. All kinds of mainstream pop rock. "No" is a word he says a lot, this Hitt.

"You seat your *voice* in rockabilly . . . your *words* in soul . . . but your *tone* is in jazz. Dig?"

"No," I tell him. I don't dig. He explains it seventeen different ways. Shows and tells. Finally I begin to get the drift. The pitch or timber or sound of the voice itself is like the rockabilly jocks. Warm, resonant, deep if it's not forced, a pleasant, straight-ahead thing. What you *say*—that's soulful. A little black, he calls it. And the *way* you say it, the tone of the voice, that's in jazzy rhythms and hip cadences. Jockspeak. Eventually I start to get with it.

By the end of the week, he says my sound is better. I am doing okay. Not great, but okay. We spend the weekend listening to airchecks of other jocks: Rockin' Rob Rocket, C. Bruce Badfinger, Lar Boggs and Sweet William Trace. Gary Shapiro out on the coast. The biggies.

Monday is the first day it feels serious. Serious as fucking cancer. Hitt has me work a little in the morning, and then a couple of suits come in and unfold a big folded sheet of paper that looks like a blueprint.

"This is a diagram of the second floor of the station where you'll be going," one of them says. "Beneath this studio are the front offices. You'll work in this room. Your engineer will work here." He points a manicured index finger, and I think of Bunky, wondering how he's gonna get behind all this shit. "Double glass wall here. Music library here. Access to the lobby. Stairwell. Elevator. Production room—where you'll most likely see Don Dye if he ever shows up during your shift."

"What exactly do I do then?"

"That's the easy part. You don't do a thing," he promises me.

The suits go on about the floor plan. The alarm systems. All kinds of crap. Then he tells me about another feature of the station.

"You have to assume you will be under surveillance at all times. We know there is select audio surveillance that is directed through equipment in the station manager's office. But we think they probably have some cameras in the building as well. Assume you're being watched and listened to at all times." Even in the bathroom? I want to ask.

"The maid and custodial service is always done with tight security, and no visitors are allowed on the all-night shifts. Nothing you do or say, no gesture or syllable, must ever tip that you're anything but a jock and engineer."

I haven't felt like this since me and Home Tyrell broke into Pine's Jewelry Store and the cops were waitin' for us. It's like playin' football in the empty lot and that screen pass lands you right smack in the shitter; there's the first-string quarterback under eleven hundred pounds of enraged apes, and strawberry Jell-o where he used to have a right knee.

That night, I dream I love my work, goin' to the desert on a horse with no name, virgins headin' for the coasts, Jeremiah was a fuckin' bullfrog, the pump don't work, but you get what you need. It all comes to sit on my head. I'm really goin' in on some spook thing with fuckin' Bunky! Man, if that won't put a stutter-step in your Valentine, what will?

I'd be seeing him soon, Hitt promised. Threatened. We'd be getting our act together. One day I was walkin' past an open door and saw his "mission shirts," custom-made XXXL shirts as big as flags, custom-built with panels of Kevlar body armor sewn in. I imagined him as he must look by now, even bigger, tougher, and meaner—if that was possible—battle-hardened in Nam, I heard.

Again, I dreamed. This one was realistic. I was in a studio I'd never been in, and Bunky, the way he looked back in the old days, he was running my board. We see a pair of shadows—humongous, scary blurs of shadow playing on the control room wall. There's light and movement in production, and before I can blink, Bunky is gone, moving.

In the vivid center of the dream, I can recall trying to get out a door, but it's locked. I think of throwing the fire extinguisher through the window, but I'm on the second floor, and the noise might anger Bunky, who would then kill me.

What is going on down the hall in production? I cannot look. I have to pee. My music is running out. Oddly, a detail of the dream nails itself to my memory: We were playing Archie Bell and the Drells when Don Dye and his body-guard appeared out of the night. "Tighten Up" rocks out of the monitor, loud and proud, so that I cannot hear the screams.

The music cue-light flashes as bright as a small shaped charge going off above me. I have dived down under the announcer console. There is an old turntable well above me, with an emergency table in it. Wires and cables everywhere. I tremble in the dust.

But the station does not go to dead air. I hear the a cappella jingle, another irritating dream detail, as the tape segues from cartridge to standby. I had forgotten the state of the technology.

An eternity later, I hear movement in the room. I freeze, willing my heart to cease beating—just for a minute or two. The soft creak of leather. The gliding presence of great weight moving across the floor. Turntable oil drips on me.

My breath sounds so loud inside my ears. I curse my lungs. Two gigantic 15EEEEE bata boots hove into view, covered in blood. Then I see the dripping blade of the fighting Bowie and the monstrous hand that holds it, and my heart almost does what I asked. I squint my eyes tightly shut in prayer.

The next sound I hear is one I remember from many years ago. That barking, coughing noise that approximates the starting of a chain saw. It is the closest sound to a human laugh Bunky the beast ever makes.

Twenty-one days into the Johnny Hitt course, I report to the studio and Hitt is not there. A man I have never seen before gives me an envelope and leaves. It contains a cashier's check for twenty thousand dollars and the lamest bullshit imaginable about this only being "a preparedness test" for types of "emergency security operations," and so forth. Like I'm suddenly to believe this was just a training exercise.

There's a phone number and a name. I call it, and we jack off back and forth, and I get the message: Consider yourself lucky. You got what they call in the radio biz "a pay-to-play." A payoff for not working. Beat that shit?

I am reminded how if I ever breathe a word of this fiasco, my balls will be fed into a meat grinder, and what is left of me will rot in some lonely solitary box, and blah-blah national security, and kiss my ass.

I can take a hint. I'm outta there like a roadrunner in the cartoons, man. Cashing that mutha 'fore the ink can dry, dig? And hell, I'm a trained personality jock now, baby. I get some tapes made and, fuck me Roy, a couple months later I'm working drive on Q-92! Don't it tie your shorts in a knot?

"Hold the phone, Joan! This is rad! Stone bad to the bone!"

Hell, I almost forgot the most important part. Five, six days after I got my money, I'm thumbing through a news magazine and I see under "deaths": Dye, Donald Fornier. Financier, pioneer broadcaster, blah-blah. At the end of the obit, it reads, "of a heart attack."

I whispered one word under my breath, and I don't have to tell you what that word was, do I?

Bill Mumy
and
Peter David

THE
BLACK '59

Their bare arms were glistening with sweat, and their shirts were pasted to their chests. In addition, Neil Kalmick's long brown hair was matted, as if he were playing in a sauna, while his fingers flew up and down his guitar.

And nobody cared.

"Up to the Wire" was the last song in the set, and Neil ended it with a searing thirty-two-bar guitar solo. Chuck and Gary Wilkes, the black rhythm section, played like they were one musician.

And nobody cared.

There, onstage at the Chestnut Club, their opening set had been a glorious fusion of traditional blues, heavy metal, and hard rock—all and none at the same time. They had played hard, and tight, and good. Damned good.

And nobody cared.

The crowd was waiting for Zip, the headliners. A glam-rock band, all theatrics and no chops. But they were the ones with the record deal and the hot video running five times a day on MTV.

Applause for the opening act, the Neil Kalmick Band, was polite, if sporadic. Certainly not long enough to tease them into thinking they *might* get an encore. Just long enough not to be rude. Ah, Hollywood.

"Thanks for taking care of the business end, babe," Neil said for what was probably the hundredth time in his life.

Pam Sullivan smiled briefly, one lean leg half-cocked against Neil's heavy Marshall amplifier that was, in turn, leaning against the wall of the ratty dressing room. Calling it a dressing room was like calling a coffin a bungalow. A filthy, torn, stained, burnt couch sat on an equally disgusting rug. The cramped room also featured a luxurious, cracked, dirty, full-length mirror, and years of rock and roll graffiti on the yellowing walls.

As Pam gave Chuck his sixty-six dollars—his share of the night's earnings—brother Gary, who'd already been paid, added the Neil Kalmick Bank logo to the tattooed wall with a felt-tip marker. He tossed a ragged grin at Neil as he did so.

"Thanks, Pam," said Chuck, and he turned to Neil. "And thanks, man," he said, holding up the money. "Look, Neil—you're the songwriter, the singer, the soloist, and the front man. You're always splitting with us even-steven, though. If you're at all strapped, just—"

Neil waved it off. "That's the kind of guy I am," he said with light sarcasm. When they left, they closed the door quickly so that the semitalented pounding of Zip from the stage would be at least marginally less irritating.

Pam stepped up behind him and dug her fingers into his shoulders as he started to tighten a loose tuning key on his guitar. "You were great tonight, lover," she told him. Her long blond hair fell around him and tangled with his. "And your time's gonna come. You'll see."

"Bitch," he murmured.

Her fingers stopped. "What did you call me?"

"What?" He looked up at her, his eyes focusing as if for the first time. "Oh . . . sorry, hon. I wasn't talking to you. Talking about this," and he tapped his finger against the chrome gear. "My B string kept slipping, plus I'm not getting enough sustain."

"Here's something to sustain you," she said teasingly. "Unlimited Travel Agency wants me to make copies of some antique Dutch cabinets for their new offices. I should clear enough for us to fly to Hawaii for a week when I'm done."

"That's great, Pam!" he said with as much enthusiasm as he could muster. "At least one of us is hitting it big."

"Oh, Neil," and she blew out an impatient breath. "I didn't want you to—"

He waved it off. "Look, I'm happy for you. Really. How about if I come over later, okay? That okay?"

"Sure." She shrugged. She knew better than to try to jolly him out of anything when he was acting this down.

Moments after Pam had left, there was a knock at the door. Neil turned, and his eyes widened in surprise.

"John Hemly," he breathed.

Hemly stood there, as seedy and nasty-looking as ever. He spread his arms wide as if to hug Neil, but stayed where he was. In one ratty hand was a guitar case. When he spoke, it was as if he was expelling foul air. "Neil," he said. "It's been . . . what, years since we played together? And you still sound great, man."

Neil turned back to the mirror, and then frowned. Hemly's reflection seemed to shimmer. Neil's head snapped around, but Hemly was still there, big as life.

Hemly stepped into the cramped dressing room and spoke in that odd, singsong voice he sometimes used. "This place sucks, dude. You deserve better than this shit." He clucked disapprovingly. "Our group was never the same without you, Neil. You were the glue, man. After you left, it all fell apart."

"Yeah, well . . . I did what I had to do, Johnny," said Neil, placing his guitar in its beat-up case. "I had to go solo. It was time."

"I was your partner, man," said Hemly with a sort of strange urgency. "That meant something to me. Something big."

"It meant something to me, too," Neil shot back. It meant I had to put up with your goddamned drug-dealing bullshit, and I didn't want to be part of that energy anymore. "It meant something to me, too. Was time, that's all. You know that."

Hemly came slowly toward him, and again there was that damned, brief moment in the mirror where it seemed as if he weren't quite there. "It's cool, Neil." He lit up a Marlboro. "Fuck it. You were the only one in the band with any real talent, Neilo. The rest of us were just rippin' off licks from old records. You're an original. And shit, man, don't worry about me! I'm in fat city now. I'm probably making ten times what you're pulling in, and I don't have to haul amps anymore."

"Yeah? What're you doing?" asked Neil.

John Hemly smiled thinly with those parched, eerie lips of his. "What do you think, man? Supply and demand." He brought his right index finger up to his nostrils and gave them a tap while he made a little snort.

Neil stared at him through narrowed eyes. That feeling of creepiness he used to get whenever he was around Hemly returned full force. Neil said nothing. He started to close the locks on his guitar case.

"I got some serious clients now, man," Hemly continued. "Remember Vernon Stampede?"

Neil didn't laugh. "Good trick, Johnny, selling blow to Vernon Stampede. Vernon fucking Stampede. The guy *Billboard* voted 'Rocker Most Likely to Take a Life.' The guy *Rolling Stone* called 'both halves of an evil twin.' Real good trick, Johnny, considering Psycho Stampede killed himself riding a motorcycle into a school bus more than a year ago. Autopsy showed he had more drugs in him than a pharmacy."

Hemly rested a hand on Neil's shoulder, crunching the leather of his jacket. The words hissed from the corner of his mouth. "Vernon Stampede was the fucking best guitar player in the fucking world, Neilo. Fucking best. His old lady knew he was ripped, but she sent him on a munchie run anyway, and he never came back. Fucked her head up real good, man. Major guilt trip. And it just so happens that his old lady is now a customer of mine. 'Cept she burned through the money he left her and now she's really into basing big-time. I just came from her place. You should've seen her, quivering and shit. She would've done anything for a few grams, man. Fuckin' anything."

"Yeah, well, this is really charming, Johnny, but—"

Hemly held out the guitar case he'd been holding. "Vernon Stampede's ax, man. His black '59 Gibson Les Paul Custom. Three P.A.F. Humbuckers. 'The fretless wonder.'

She swapped it for half an ounce of shitty blow, cut six times. It's yours, Neilo. I want you to have it. It's important to me. To show there's no hard feelings."

Neil stared into Hemly's icy gray eyes for what seemed an hour. Finally, Hemly put the case on the couch and gestured for Neil to open it, which he did. Reverently.

"Whoa," was all Neil could manage. The ultimate instrument stared back at him in ebony silence.

"Remember the solo on "Hellbound Howl," man? Or the live Stampede *Uncontrollable* album?" He slapped Neil on the shoulder and it made the musician twitch with nervousness. "Vernon Stampede would want a great player like you to have this, Neilo. Nobody else. All those great riffs, all those monster songs. They're in there, man. They're fucking in there!"

Neil finally found the strength to pick up the black '59. It was indeed a wonder to hold. "Not heavy, like the new ones," he murmured distantly. "What a neck! And the sustain I could get . . ."

"Will get. It's a done deal, brother. Give me a special thanks on your greatest hits album."

"Johnny . . . look, I—"

"I gotta go, dude," said Hemly with abrupt finality.

When Hemly walked out, there seemed to be an additional spring in his step. Just before the door closed, Neil glanced in the mirror. And Hemly's reflection was fine. None of that buggy flickering. Johnny's mirror image was perfectly okay, and Neil was writing it off as a trick of light, except . . .

Hemly gave the strangest little laugh just as he swung the door shut behind him.

"Honey, I've never heard you play better! You're right, the tone is incredible," Pam said as Neil blazed on the black '59. "Even at such low volume, it sounds fantastic! But, Neil, it's after three in the morning. Why don't you come to bed, honey? Why don't you play me for a while?" she added teasingly.

Neil tore himself away from the guitar long enough to

notice two things: His fingers were bleeding because he'd been playing so hard; and Pam was standing in the doorway to her bedroom wearing only a tan. Her golden hair which she had worn in a ponytail all night, was now set free and fell wildly around her ample breasts. Her nipples stood at attention.

Neil put the guitar in its case.

The sex was as incredible as the playing, but fueled by a violent urgency that had never been there before. Pam almost asked him to stop. Almost.

Neil bruised her, and when it was over, they didn't cuddle and talk like they usually did. Neil apologized for hurting her, then quickly got up and left the room. When the sun came up, he was still playing the black '59, oblivious to time.

Backstage was as packed as the outside of the theater, where hundreds of kids hoped to scalp tickets to the sold-out show.

Not since Elton John became an "overnight success" at Doug Weston's Troubador in 1970 had there been such a buzz in the music industry. A mere eleven weeks after being a two-bit opening act for Zip, the Neil Kalmick Band had signed a major recording contract and was headlining at the Wiltern, an old, prestigious theater in midtown Los Angeles.

The audience was packed with celebrities and Hollywood hotshots of all kinds, anxiously squirming in their seats, awaiting Tinseltown's newest star on the chopping block. It was the kind of audience that couldn't wait to tell you that you were the best thing they'd ever seen, and then rip you to pieces the minute your back was turned. The type of crowd that gets up from a show every ten minutes to check their answering machines; a group that wants to appear too busy to stay for the entire event.

The noncelebs in the audience—the ones who'd scraped together money for scalped tickets, or were seated in the cheap seats—displayed their lack of chic by gawking at the TV cameras being set up and waving like dorks at the mobile cam unit coming through the crowd. They thought they were going to be on the TV news. What they were actually supposed to be on was the video package being prepared for the Neil Kalmick Band live album that was also being taped that night.

Backstage, Neil was in his dressing room, which resembled the pit at the Chestnut Club only in that they both bore the term "dressing room." Gary and Chuck Wilkes paced nervously across the plush, deep red velvet rug, past baskets of fresh fruit and telegrams from assorted sycophants. Neil was stretched out, casually leafing through a pile of telegrams, looking totally at ease. Around his neck, as always, hung the black '59 Gibson guitar.

Chuck looked at his watch yet again. "Neil! We were supposed to be on twenty minutes ago!"

"Waiting makes 'em want it more." He strummed an unamplified riff. "They'll love me."

"Love *us*, babe," reminded Chuck.

"Sure. Us. You guys go onstage, check your gear. I'll be right out."

Neil pulled on a red satin cowboy shirt as they walked out, and leaned into the mirror to get a closer look at himself. Taped to the mirror was a telegram from John Hemly. It read simply, "You'll kill 'em."

"You're on, lover!" came a voice from behind, startling him.

He spun on Pam. "Shit! Don't sneak up on me like that!"

"Well!" she said in surprise, teasingly biting his right earlobe. "You nervous?"

He pushed her away roughly. "I'm not nervous! I don't need . . ." His voice trailed off, and then he giggled a little laugh that sounded odd. Very odd, even to him. More like John Hemly's bizarre chuckle than his own. "Guess I am a little nervous. Showtime, huh?"

"Break a leg, handsome." She gave him a kiss for luck. It wasn't needed.

Onstage, Neil's solos soared with a frightening dark passion. The black '59 with its three gold pickups glistened under the stage lights like Excalibur. And it seemed to wield the same power as that mythic blade, cutting through the theater.

The crowd of Hollywood hotshots applauded, screamed, and stamped their feet for eleven minutes before Neil Kalmick returned for the second encore.

"Thanks. Thanks for listening," Neil spoke into the microphone. "We're gonna do one for you that I didn't write. It's an old Vernon Stampede song. . . ." And with that, he cranked up his volume to earsplitting level, and ripped into the incredibly difficult slide guitar riff from "Hellbound Howl."

The house went crazy. And no one in the audience knew that Neil Kalmick had never played slide guitar before.

Except Gary and Chuck. They also knew that the band had never even rehearsed "Hellbound Howl." And as Neil continued to drive the audience wild with Stampede's classic slide guitar riffs, it blew their minds.

Pam watched from the wings. She watched as Neil moved and played and sang differently than he ever had before. And it frightened her.

When Neil was a boy, he had gone to see *Fantasia*. The part that had had the greatest impact had been "Night on Bald Mountain." For weeks afterward, in his waking hours and in his sleep, he'd been haunted by the image of the demon of the mountain, unfolding its crimson wings, gesturing with satanic command and summoning the souls of the damned to dance and writhe in its palm.

That's how it was now. There was something in the music pouring from his guitar, something deep and low and laughing, always that damned laughing, running up and down the fingerboard, blazing and howling as fast as Neil's fingers could move. And for a moment, they didn't even feel like his fingers. They felt longer, faster, more confident, like there wasn't any stretch they couldn't reach.

The audience responded. The music reached out and caressed something hidden in them, the chords of the guitar striking resonating chords within the souls of the fans.

Neil felt the power that the demon must have had. It caused a bizarre giddiness, a natural high, a feeling of strength and invincibility that just flowed, just kept on coming and coming and coming. They were dancing in his palm and their lives were his to squeeze from existence or consign to the pits of hell, the flames rising up to lick the skin from their flailing bodies.

No one could have, or would have, been able to put their finger precisely on what it was. When the police arrived within the hour to try to restore order, when the ambulances arrived to cart away the thirty-nine people who were seriously injured and the one who had died—no one knew what had caused it.

No one could figure out why people had started ripping out chairs and tossing them around, or why men had turned on their dates, shoving and beating them. No one could figure out why people were howling and shrieking with unearthly voices, long after the music was over.

The only thing that anyone knew for sure was that there hadn't been chaos like this since the last Vernon Stampede concert.

Oddly, the punks in the cheap seats got their wish. Footage from the roving cameras would up on the evening news.

It also went straight into the video package, promoting the debut album, *Neil Kalmick Band Live: No Restraint.* The record company shipped more than a million copies before one track from the album was played on the radio.

Pam stood in the doorway of Neil's Hollywood apartment, the pounding waves of Vernon Stampede's last album washing over her like polluted water. Neil sat crouched on the floor, eyes closed, listening to the dead rocker's music. It was turned up so loud they could probably hear every word all the way in Malibu.

His long brown hair was stringy and unwashed. He was unshaven, and he looked like he hadn't bathed in weeks. When Pam stepped in front of him, getting his reluctant attention, he stood and instinctively reached for the black guitar.

"I thought you were in New York," she said.

He pulled off the headphones, seeming displeased at her presence. "Just got back," he said sullenly.

"You look exhausted." She reached out for him, but he

pulled away in a series of quick, jerky movements, like a bug.

"Working. Just . . . you know, working. New song."

She put her hands on her hips. "What, I'm not even worth complete sentences anymore?" she said, trying to use some of that old teasing tone.

It seemed out of place. He simply glowered at her.

"Fine," she said with a shrug. "Work." She turned on her heel and walked out.

Neil stared at the closed door for a moment, and a slow, roiling anger swirled in his stomach. "Bitches," he murmured. This time it wasn't in reference to a guitar key.

He swung the black '59 around and stood in front of a full-length mirror. A hand swung down, struck a chord, and he reveled in it, and didn't notice his reflection . . .

You could see the Hollywood sign very clearly from Christine Stampede's bedroom window. Nestled high up in Beechwood Canyon, you could see lots of things.

Christine Stampede, carrying the weight of being the widow of a dead rocker, and the buzz from some shitty cocaine—coke that was cut as badly as her ratty red hair—lay sprawled on the couch and couldn't see a fucking thing.

There was a sound just outside. The cat's fur bristled when the sound of boot heels on Mexican tile was heard. Seconds later, the doorbell rang.

Wrapped up in her world, Christine ignored it. She didn't want to see anyone, or deal with anyone. She just wanted to be left alone with her pipe and her torch and her shitty cocaine. She'd had the best pure Peruvian flake money could buy in her time, and this shit didn't hold a candle to it. But it was hers. All hers. And it was her world.

The doorbell rang again, over and over, alternating with knocking. Christine lost count. "Get the fuck out of here, okay?" came a withered, ghostly voice that bore only passing resemblance to hers. She ran her tongue across her bottom teeth and noticed absently that her bottom molars were loose.

The ringing stopped, and then there was a noise at the bottom of her door. Something being slid underneath.

Her tired eyes widened. It was green, the color of money. It *was* money. It was folded in half, but the numbers one, zero, zero were clearly visible.

"Lots more where that came from," came a male voice that sounded familiar somehow. "Bet you could use it, huh, Christine?"

Her mouth opened for a moment, to tell whoever this bozo was to get the hell away. There was something about his voice that made her stomach churn, that caused the warning birds in her head to take flight.

But there was the money.

If it was legit, it would solve her problems. Even if it wasn't legit, who cared?

"Okay," came the voice from the other side, after one final knock. "You want to play games? That's fine. I'm gone, sweetheart."

That knock. Opportunity knocking. The money on the ground.

She crossed the room quickly and unlatched the dead bolt.

Within two minutes, the bolt wouldn't be the only dead thing in the room.

He swept in with the look of a crazed stallion, and even in Christine's drug-induced haze, she smelled a stench like rotting meat, or maybe rotting souls. He didn't seem to enter the room so much as envelop it.

"Honey . . . I'm home."

There was a laugh like a rusty hinge, and before she could even get out, "Who are you?" she felt something snap out around her neck.

"G string," came a voice from deep within the wave of darkness. "Dean Markley unwound .18-gauge G string, to be exact."

She slammed against him, struggling, thrashing, and felt a warmth dribbling down her throat. And a voice sounded in her ear, hot and intense: "You fuckin' bitch. You stupid fuckin' bitch! All any of you ever want is to take, and take, and take . . . fuck you! Take this! Fuckin' bitch. . . ."

She clawed at the hands, big hands, with long, powerful fingers like no one in this world, and there was a faint outline on the back of the right hand, a black ax. . . .

She tried to whisper, "Oh, my God," but she couldn't, and even if she had, God wouldn't have done a damned thing except perhaps chide her about opening doors to strangers.

Except it was no stranger. And then the blackness of the ax enveloped her, and the warmth pouring down her throat and down the front of her dress swept her away. . . .

John Hemly didn't open his door.

His was kicked in.

He rolled out of bed and looked up, and the darkness rolled over him.

"You were right," hissed the darkness. "Your soul was shittier, but he's the better musician. More to work with there. Any soul can be trashed, but the right musician— that's not always easy to find. You helped me find him. You gave me to him. That was so damned nice of you. I'm gonna fuckin' thank you."

John started to stand, tried to find the words. A second later he couldn't even find his brains, as the guitar swung around, and the ax, and blood and skull flew.

When Neil awoke the next morning, with fog in his head and stiffness in his back, MTV was blaring at him. He lay there in a hazed stupor, not even recalling when he'd put it on.

Then the rock news came on, with the report about Vernon Stampede's widow and her brutal rape and murder.

Neil sat up, taking only a distant interest—and then he saw the blood on his hands. . . .

His hands . . .

Hands that seemed larger than they usually did. He'd chalked it up to, what . . . he didn't know. Exercise, or something equally ridiculous that had seemed a reasonable explanation at the time. . . .

And there was the tattoo. A black ax, with blood tinging it.

It was there. On his hand, and in the back of his mind was . . .

He hurried to the closet where he kept his record collection. He fumbled through a large stack of LPs, mumbling to himself. He noticed for the first time how much his breath stank, and his body, and then he found the record in the pile of vinyl, because the bootleg hadn't been released on CD yet. . . .

The Vernon Stampede album, *Burnin'*, with Vernon bending a string way up on the neck of the black '59 Gibson Les Paul Custom. Both hands in sharp focus, and on fire, and there was the tattoo on the back of his hand.

He spun, records flying, and grabbed up the guitar. It glistened, showing no signs of stains, but in his mind's eye he could see gore across the bottom of it. And the G string—God, there was blood on the G string.

Hands that didn't feel like his slammed across the strings, and there was a sound that filled the apartment, an unamped sound that nonetheless crashed deafeningly. Sound. Sounds. The sound of a woman screaming, and the sound of a man who sounded vaguely like John Hemly, giving off a panicked howl, crying to be let out, all mixed together in a hideous cacophony, and over it all, a deep, bass chord of a laugh, a hideous laugh providing the backbeat.

Neil screamed as he ran toward the fireplace. As he passed the mirror he didn't look, because he didn't want to chance seeing a reflection other than his own. He pushed the button igniting the gas burners, and threw the black guitar into the flames.

It would not burn.

The neck stuck out at him, but flames surrounded the hard body and it wouldn't fucking *burn*, man. And when he yanked it from the fire, the damned thing was ice-cold.

Neil lifted it high over his head and smashed it against the wall, against the floor. It wouldn't break, even when he raced outside and ran over the neck with his Jeep.

Throwing the instrument in his car, Neil drove the dark blue Jeep like mad to the top of Mulholland Drive. Rushing from the vehicle with the guitar in his hands, he stood at the top of the cliff, looking down into the rocky canyon hundreds of feet below, like Satan surveying the pits of hell about to throw a morsel down to the damned. The guitar was over his head—

And suddenly, Neil Kalmick was gone, and Vernon Stampede was cradling the black '59 and howling at the sky. He slammed his fingers, *his* fingers, down across the strings and reveled in the wailing that rose from them.

The wailing of three voices. . . .

Vernon leaped into the Jeep and peeled out, the spinning wheels leaving treadmarks and the stench of burning rubber. He angled down the hill, taking the turns at dizzying speeds. He cut down through a side street, hit a curve, sped up and kept going.

Just ahead of him, he saw a toddler, a little girl with red hair who had escaped from under the watchful eye of her mother. Plump arms waving, she had strolled into the middle of the narrow street.

Vernon floored it, howling as the Jeep roared forward, bearing down on her, to wipe her out, to turn her into a small smear of red before she could grow up and be one of those bitches, those castrating bitches who—

Then there came a woman's scream, and the child's mother leaped from nowhere, and she scooped up the child like a football and lunged for the far side of the road. She crashed into a hedge, her face and arms cut by the branches, her now-wailing daughter clutched desperately to her breast.

The Jeep roared past a split instant after they were clear, gone before she could even get the license plate. But the laughter—that, she would never forget.

In her garage workshop, Pam Sullivan, cabinet maker extraordinaire, stepped back from the standing circular saw. She held up the piece of wood and, lifting off her goggles, examined it closely with a trained eye to make sure it was straight.

She sensed, rather than saw, that someone was behind her. She spun.

He smiled down at her, picking out a blues riff on his black '59.

She started to sigh in relief, but the sigh caught in her throat. "Neil?" she said. "Neil, are you okay?"

"Neil's fretting away somewhere," said Vernon. He took a step toward her, and reflexively she stepped back.

Her voice low and concerned, she demanded, "Neil, something's wrong. What's the matter with you?"

"Bitches," growled Vernon. "Always asking what's wrong. Always wanting to help." His hands began to squeeze, as if in anticipation.

She backed up faster, unconsciously holding up the newly sawed plank between them. "Get out of here, Neil," she ordered.

He circled around toward her. "Bitches always giving orders. Bitches always leeching off you, coming between me and my music!" He slammed a hand down on a workbench, and Pam saw the ax on a hand that was too large to be Neil's. "They just want to drag you down! They just want to cut your nuts off and feed them to you, to show you that they can!"

The words "You're scaring me" died in her throat, because that was clearly his intention. The door was on the far side of the workshop. Pam hurled the board at him and dashed for it.

Stampede knocked the board aside and lunged around the workbench toward her. He leaped, tackling Pam around the knees and sending her to the ground. She squirmed. She howled. He loved it when they howled.

He flipped her over on her back because he wanted her to see it, man, he wanted her to fuckin' see it coming.

She was tough for a bitch, he would give her that. She wanted to be as tough as a man. That's all they ever wanted, to show they could be as tough as men. He'd show them. He'd show every damned bitch in the world what was what.

His thumbs worked their way down into the folds of her neck just under her jaw. She struggled, but he had one knee firmly down across her thighs, and as for her hands beating on his arms, well, hell, he just ignored those. His filthy fingernails edged into her skin and he laughed that hideous, godawful laugh.

She was choking, making those wild "aww-huk, aww-huk" sounds that Christine had made, that they would all make, because Vernon Stampede was back, dammit, he was back and he was lean and mean and . . .

Her eyes started to roll back in her head. Those eyes, the eyes that had looked at Neil once in adoration. The eyes that held love and forgiveness, light and beauty.

He tried to banish the thought, but here it came again. And those hands that had pulled and thrust at him, the hands that had once caressed him, that had given him pleasure. The hair, now filled with sawdust, that had hung down in his face as she moved languidly atop him. The—

He let out a shriek that was part his voice, part another. The guitar, the black '59, slammed against his back, straining against the strap. It was throbbing with heat and power, and Neil staggered across the workshop, howling with Stampede's voice. His hands were strangling air, the ax on his hand as black as night and the blood on the tattoo now tinged with reality.

Pam was sucking in air greedily, her hand at her throat, coughing and wheezing as she inhaled sawdust.

"I want her!" howled Stampede.

"I won't let you have her!" Neil screamed.

"She's mine! They're all mine! *You're* mine!" Stampede told him. "And your ass is mine, boy, your ass is mine, and I'm gonna *cook* ya, and *eat* ya, 'cause you can't stop me!" Stampede's hands thrust up in front of Neil's face. "More talent than you'll ever have in these hands, boy! More knowledge! More *everything!* Do her! You know you *want* to! Do her! *Do her!*"

And Neil knew he wanted to, God help him, it was bubbling to the surface, and there it was, hatred stoked by Vernon Stampede, throbbing and pulsing with life, and there would be her throat beneath his hands, *his* hands, already turning back to reach for her again. . . .

Neil lunged toward the whirring circular saw.

It took Stampede a second to figure out what was about to happen. Even as Neil leaped, Stampede didn't believe it.

Neil passed his left wrist across the saw. The blade sliced through without the slightest hesitation, blood and gore splattering across the flat surface. Stampede howled. Neil did not. He was beyond screaming, beyond pain. His left hand flopped to the ground, a useless slab of meat, and Neil kept going, brought his right hand around like a karate chop. The blade cut through bone and muscle and gristle, and his right hand plopped down, inches away from the first one.

The black '59 on his back began to sizzle and fry. Neil wriggled, bending forward, ignoring the blood fountaining onto his boots. The guitar slid down and over his head, clattering to the floor. The cold surface of the guitar had heated up, the paint blistering away. The strings snapped with a succession of twangs, staccato, like machine-gun fire. The black '59 flopped about on the floor, next to the hands that were shriveling and blackening, and they were trying to fucking get back to the guitar, trying to reach for it, to touch it, to stroke the strings, to reconnect to it.

Neil staggered, the world spinning, but Pam saw it and she lunged forward, hook-sliding as if she were sailing into home with the winning run. Her foot hit the black '59, kicking the instrument away. It slammed against a wall and shattered, with an explosion of burning air that scalded Neil's skin. The hands, out of reach, clenched and unclenched spasmodically, and then blackened and shriveled with the stench of burning meat. Within seconds, they had withered away, resembling nothing so much as small, overcooked hunks of beef.

He heard a screaming, from somewhere inside and outside his head. A high, undulating scream of *"Bitches!"* as something dark and loathsome was pulled away, sucked down and into a distant blackness that receded further and further until it was gone from his mind's eye.

He turned toward Pam, shoving his stumps into his armpits and immediately becoming soaked with blood, and then he fell forward and landed heavily on the floor of the workshop. The sawdust grew dark red.

Although Pam wheeled Neil out the back entrance of the hospital, it did no good. The newshounds descended on them, all shouting questions at the same time, all demanding to know about the mysterious "accident" (which tabloids were already announcing as being part of an aborted mutual suicide pact), about the alleged miniseries on his life, the movie deals, the book deals, about what in hell a musician who could no longer play could possibly do.

"Your career is over, Neil!" shouted a TV reporter. "How do you feel?"

Neil tried to think of something to say, but Pam stepped to the mike and said firmly, "His career is far from over. If Beethoven could make music when he was deaf, Neil can make music without his hands. I have lots of ideas—"

"You?" said Neil, looking up.

She smiled. *"We* have lots of ideas," she said, running her fingers through Neil's clean, short hair. "And *we* are going to have a lot of impact on the music world still. We're looking at a lifelong partnership here." She looked down at him.

He looked up at her, and it was all there in her eyes. They hadn't discussed any of it, but they hadn't needed to. She had figured it all out. All of it. But she was saying nothing, not to him, not to any associates, and not to the police. It was understood. It was all understood.

"Lifelong partnership," she repeated. "Isn't it, love?"

He regarded her with the correct expression of tenderness, with the correct look of sincerity and happiness that said they would be together forever and ever. . . .

His wrist stumps throbbed.

And somewhere . . .

Deep, deep in the darkest reaches of him, there was a small voice, and it whispered, *Bitches* . . .

But he wasn't listening.

Yet.

Richard
Christian
Matheson

GROUPIES

Digital counter: 000. Fast forward. Smeared VHS images; face fringed. 024. Stop.

Fourteen. Staring.

Makeup, a snowy death mask. Jewelry, provocative. Hair, shoe-black.

Q: Why are you here?

A: Next question.

A maneuvering giggle. A denying glance.

A: I deserve it, I guess. Right. Is that the answer?

Fast forward. 046. Stop. Graveyard eyes stab, loathe. A cigarette. Tongue tip circling, luring.

A: Why are you so hung up on this?

Q: I'm here to help.

A: People don't help other people.

Fast forward. 057. Stop. Lips curving softly, sexual predation. Rewind. 055. Stop. Smoke lingering in a ghoul grin.

A: Yeah, he got off. He got off during, and I guess if you wanna talk legal, he got off after.

Q: He may go to jail. It's not over yet. So, you were a fan.

A: Him mostly. The group. The albums. Him mostly.

Q: He's a hell of a singer.

A: He's got a hell of a cock.

Dirty silence. Dimples kniving cheeks.

Q: That why you gave him what he wanted?

A: He didn't ask me. He asked . . . you know.

Q: What did he say? What did she say?

A: I didn't hear him . . . what he told her. But . . . she told me in the bathroom and we were totally fucked up and I told her she was crazy.

Q: But you went for it. Finally.

A: Obviously.

The floor without carpet. Her eyes circling nothing. Fingers strolling over hair, earrings; layers.

A: I was gone. Fucking gone. It just sort of started.

Q: Were you afraid?

A: I've gotten insane with guys. Whatever. You earn the right to be around them.

Face lost in ravaged glory, confessional.

A: I've been tied up. Gang-whatevered. This one Australian guy, his group was touring with Inxs, he was a fucking party with a view. Tied me down with guitar wire. My wrists and ankles. . . . Made me suck him and his band off.

A candid shrug.

A: They just left me. I couldn't move. I was just left, to die. I almost got gangrene. The band is very heavy—I'd tell you who it is, but they'd be pissed. They got a new video on MTV.

A Lolita yawn.

A: So, what do you think? You like that story? You like imagining me with no clothes on doing nasty stuff?

A thought. A look. The T-shirt lifted to show no bra. Perfect breasts. Scars—drunken hieroglyphs covering stomach and chest. One nipple cleaved by healed, bitten skin. Burn marks.

A: I'm kind of in love with all these scars of men I've fucked. It's my scrapbook. Maybe you'd like to leave your picture?

Q: You never minded the pain?

A: I wanted to be with guys.

Q: The good groupies don't mind the pain.

A: The good groupies dig it.

Fast forward. 135. Stop.

Q: So, how did it start?

A: I didn't even know what I was doing. It just . . . what do you mean?

Q: Describe what happened.

A: What did I do?

Q: Yeah.

A: We had sex after they played. Sucked him off. Ate him. Let him watch us. Camcord. Whatever.

Q: Right.

A: Then, he wanted something else. So, he's sitting there doing lines and crystal and whatever the fuck. And he's playing with his dick and . . . so he wanted us to do something different. So, I slapped her on the tits while I was going down on her. Real hard.

Q: How hard?

A: They were red, small welts . . . and the nipples were hard. He loved it.

Q: Did she cry . . . scream?

A: You getting off on this? Your dick getting hard?

Q: No.

A: The things I could do to your body, you couldn't pay enough to find some cunt to do that. You like your dick in a pretty girl's pretty mouth. I'm only fourteen. Did you know that?

Q: Yes.

Microscope eyes.

A: So, what do you want to know?

Q: You tied her down.

A: Yeah. She liked it. So did he.

Q: Then what?

A: I don't know.

Silence. Burial still.

Q: You cut her. What did you use?

A: Razor.

Q: Where?

A barricaded glance.

A: Tits. Face. Stomach.

Q: Were you scared?

A: It was a mess. But I wasn't scared. He loved it.

Q: And you loved him, so that made it okay.

A: I told you, it was her idea. I met her in his room. I didn't know her. I never met her. She was there to get fucked. She got fucked.

Q: Why are you angry?

A: You act like it was my idea. I was just trying to help him get off. I never met her.

Q: No guilt?

A: She was a fucking groupie. We all gotta please somebody.

Q: One last question.

A: Now what?

Q: When you were . . . doing that to her, he actually enjoyed it? It didn't bother him?

A: Guys on the road. They see it all. They lose interest. They need something new. That's what it's about. Keeping them interested. And proving you were there. Getting—something.

Q: A piece of them.

A: Yeah.

Q: Even a scar?

A: It's the ultimate autograph.

Through a connection at the D.A.'s office, who wanted tickets to see Jagger smirk at Madison Square, I got a copy of the murder tape and took it home.

I was done with the article and ready to turn it in. Only thing left was my editor at *Time* wanted a sidebar essay on the corrosion of empathy as modern plague, or some equally crippled moralistic overlay. I said I'd take a crack, sculpt the utopian debris. But I didn't want to do it.

I'd had a bad year. Writing about wars for different magazines. Traveling to where blood, pain, and bodies gathered—chips in death-squad casinos.

Interviewing kids who'd gunned down their veins in dying cities with names like where you live.

Watching my own father die in a hospital.

I was drinking too much. Feeling too little.

This murder was so thick with cynicism, its cruel shapes and colors only numbed me more.

I hadn't wanted to write the article to begin with, come anywhere near it. But like she'd said, we all have to please somebody. I was her voyeur. The readers were mine.

We all wanted to feel pain that wasn't ours.

I sat in my apartment with a pipe of smoldering hash and

watched the interview tape, again. Her child's face, the traumatizing calm of it.

Then I put on the murder tape.

I watched it, stunned.

The other girl was tied to the hotel bed, lost on dunes of crack and Huerredura, writhing as she was sliced apart and the guy with a ponytail horsing down his spine masturbated. The camcorder light described it all—autopsy-bleak.

My skin got cold as I watched it, again.

It was a snuff film, minus the obscure, Latin trappings and scraped reproduction. The camera remained stationary, and every few minutes, the girl I'd interviewed turned to seduce the lens with pouty smiles and lascivious eyes as she cut the other girl up, again and again, creating hideous scrimshaw.

I ran the tape again, trying to understand what got the guy off about a bleeding girl, tied to a bed, screaming. I ran it over and over, trying to comprehend. Trying to find the point.

I must've watched it a hundred times, by now.

Michael Newton | REUNION

Standing on the grassy berm of Highway 65, in Yuba County, Freebie Franklin turned his collar up against the drizzling rain. It wasn't cold, but there was nowhere he could find shelter unless he ran back to the trees, and that meant giving up the road and his prospects for a ride.

So, fuck it. Half a dozen northbound cars had passed him by since it began to rain, but he would give the highway one more chance. Another fifteen minutes, give or take, before he doubled back to Marysville to liberate some wheels.

He heard the van before he saw it, rubber singing on the rain-slick pavement, and he had his thumb out when the old VW breadbox rattled into view. At first, he thought the rain and light were playing tricks, but then he recognized the handiwork of kindred souls. A peace sign painted on the cover of the van's front-mounted spare, with faded stick-on flowers plastered on the sides.

And Freebie knew the van would stop before the driver even noticed him. It was a lock: the van decelerating, veering toward the shoulder where he stood; his smile in place before the cargo door slid open.

"Paradise?"

"That's me," he said, and crawled inside the time machine.

"I'm Rachel." Slim, brunette with flecks of gray he pretended not to notice. "This is Sherry. Jeff and Rick, up front."

It took him back, the hair and beads and handworked leather, with the smell of grass erasing seven thousand yesterdays. He caught himself in time, before "Boone Franklin" passed his lips.

"I'm Freebie."

"Beautiful."

"Hey, thanks for stopping."

"Are you kidding?" Jeff or Rick, behind the wheel, could not believe his ears. "The children stick together, man."

"Right on," from Rick or Jeff, beside him in the shotgun seat.

"You want a joint?"

He smiled at Rachel, getting into it. "Why not?"

It made the rounds, some fair Colombian, and he was working on a mellow mood when Sherry asked, "It's not your first time, is it?"

"Hmm?"

"The Child, I mean."

He shook his head. "I heard them twice, when they were on the road."

"I love their sound. Were you at Paradise before?"

Boone took another drag and closed his eyes, retreating. "I was there."

Hell, *everyone* was there. They came from far and wide that August weekend, flocking into Paradise like pilgrims homing on the Grail. It wasn't Woodstock—nothing was, or ever would be—but it was the best they had that summer, with their time already running out. Aquarius descending, all in flames.

The Age of Peace and Understanding had degenerated into Manson madness, days of rage, and bombs on campus. Love grass giving way to speed and savage violence as the gangs tuned in, turned on, and finally took over. Star Child was a bridge between two worlds, perhaps the first transition band. Their power chords anticipated heavy metal, while their lyrics tried to bring a drifting generation back to earth, demanding confrontation with the grim realities of here and now. With songs like "Flowers," "Stone Cold Dreams," and "Blue Steel Lullaby," they spoke to children who had grown up on the streets and kept themselves anesthetized against the cold.

Reese Stamper on lead guitar and Billy Teague on rhythm, switching off on lyrics till they found the proper cutting edge. Dale Clark on keyboards, Jerry Knox on bass, and spacey Eric Gates on drums. They came from nowhere in the spring of '69 and put three heavy singles on the Top 10 chart within a year, reminding everybody that the world was fucked and something had to change.

Boone Franklin loved them, twenty years ago.

The end, for all intents and purposes, had come in Paradise. It was supposed to be a "people's concert," kicking off a tour for Star Child that would put them up there with Jefferson Airplane and the Doors. Instead of having cops around to queer the act, a crew of outlaw bikers was employed to keep the peace. They worked for beer and grass, plus any teenage gash the band could spare, and they were cool about kids getting stoned and dancing in the aisles.

Bad medicine.

Somehow, the animals were "in" that year, before they started building meth labs in the desert, mowing one another down with automatic weapons in an endless war for turf. They were the last free spirits in America, quoth Dr. Gonzo, and if anybody questioned the mystique, they would be pleased to kick his fucking teeth in, thank you very much. Still, they had covered other concerts—some of them for Star Child—and the only casualties had been a couple of photographers who tried to slip backstage in Bakersfield. Some said they would have pulled it off okay in Paradise, if not for Axel Grubb.

He came from San Mateo, the obituaries said, and Boone had taken time to verify the point. Five-nine, a hundred sixty pounds of dead meat on the hoof, with pitted cheeks and stringy hair, a pair of granny glasses balanced on his nose. The morgue team found a wallet on his body, with a standard-issue snapshot of a smiling actress and an SDS card, two years out of date.

Illusions.

No one could decide why Axel rushed the stage that night, with Teague and Stamper belting their duet on "Wings of Fire," but when the bikers shoved him back, the poor dumb bastard pulled a gun. At that point, nothing could have saved him—twenty, thirty goons, and only six rounds in the cylinder—but Axel never even tried. Instead, he turned and ran, a critical mistake when facing hungry predators, and they were on him in a flash.

By sheer coincidence, Boone saw it all. The bikers wading in with boots and chains and sawed-off pool cues, taking turns, a ragged effigy the focus of their rage. Grubb broke the circle once, before he lost the gun, and stumbled into Boone, his blood on Freebie's face and paisley shirt before the hunters dragged him back to finish it.

The rest was anticlimax. Uniforms and badges. Editorials and endless questions, leading to a fruitless call for hearings by the California legislature. Star Child was going nowhere, as auditoriums began to cancel out. The tour closed as a one-night stand. They hung together for another eighteen months before the cracks began to show, with Billy Teague the first to split. By autumn, Richard Nixon was a shoo-in for a second term, and Star Child was a memory.

Sometimes, it seemed like yesterday.

The anniversary gig had been a natural, inspired by Woodstock and the whole nostalgia binge that turned the sixties into something they had never been. A new, improved regurgitation of the good old days. Promotors worked for seven months convincing Paradise that people change, that they had a chance to get it right this time. Too late for Eric Gates—a boozy suicide in '81—and Billy Teague had fallen off the earth somewhere, but Stamper, Knox, and Clark had all signed on. It was supposed to be a one-time thing, a couple new kids on the drums and backup vocals, but you never knew where lightning might touch down.

This time, Boone told himself, we do it right.

They left the rain behind in Oroville, and Paradise had scattered clouds with blue sky showing through. A perfect day for starting fresh. The city fathers had a constable directing concert traffic toward the outskirts, west of town, where scaffolding and lights had been erected on the fairgrounds, screened by bleachers and a chain-link fence.

Another time, the locals might have rallied there to watch a rodeo or demolition derby, but tonight belonged to rock and roll.

They weren't the first, by any means. From the appearance of the parking lot, some pilgrims had been camping out to guarantee themselves a place inside when Star Child took the stage. Boone was surprised by all the vintage junkers—vans and bugs, an ancient psychedelic bus with curtains in the windows—sharing space with newer yuppie wagons. Shiny Volvos broke the grip of déjà vu.

Until he saw the choppers.

Three of them together, leaning on their kickstands, painted in a rainbow of metallic shades, with long chrome forks in front and sissy bars behind. No riders visible as Jeff or Rick drove past and found the van a berth some fifty yards away.

Coincidence, Boone told himself. No fucking way the Mongols would have nerve enough to show up after all this time.

Not after Axel Grubb.

"How long?"

The question came from Rachel, sitting close beside him with her right hand on his knee. He glanced at Rick and Jeff, to see if either one of them was watching, but they had their heads together, working on another joint. Boone's Timex told him it was half past five.

"Say ninety minutes till they open, then you wait an hour for the show."

"Too long. I need the ladies'." Rachel poked at Sherry with her foot. "You coming?"

Sherry blinked and took a moment to decode the question. "Unh-uh."

Rachel shrugged, turned back to Boone, her hand a little higher on his leg. "You want to keep me company?" He shot another glance at Rick and Jeff before she smiled and said, "It's not like that."

"Okay."

Outside the van, he stretched his legs and followed her across the parking lot, admiring how her buttocks moved inside their faded denim skin. There was a line outside the rest room, and he dawdled past the choppers while she waited, still no bikers visible, but bad vibrations coming off the three machines and burrowing beneath his scalp.

"All done." He jumped as Rachel tapped his shoulder, time resuming its arrested flow. "A penny for your thoughts?"

"You wouldn't get your money's worth."

"Nice bikes."

"I guess."

"You ride?"

Boone shook his head. "No sense of balance."

"You should try it. It's a rush, the wind and all that power, right between your legs."

He smiled, his engine turning over.

"Can you feel it?" she asked.

"I'm beginning to."

"Let's go."

She took his hand and started for the van, Boone standing fast.

"What's wrong?"

"Your friends." Not telling her the rest of it, the way the choppers made him feel.

"I told you, it's not like that."

"Still."

"You're shy? I'll have them take a walk."

A glance back at the motorcycles, as he shrugged the feeling off. "Okay, I'm in."

She laughed and slipped an arm around him. "Hold that thought."

The opener was new, a younger metal band with black lace and mascara covering for inexperience, but Boone was not discouraged. They had managed two more joints in spite of uniforms positioned at strategic points around the stage —no swastikas and chains, this time—and killer munchies had descended on him by the time the rockers hit their second number.

"Snack bar," he told Rachel, shouting to be heard above the din.

"Come back?"

He kissed her lightly on the cheek and left her giggling as he turned away. It wasn't far, in terms of yardage, but the crush of bodies and a pair of rubber legs slowed Freebie down. He would have made it, even so, if chance or something else had not commanded him to glance in the direction of the rest rooms.

Just in time to see the bikers going in.

Black leather under sleeveless denim, in defiance of the muggy August night. Long hair in ponytails, and heavy, steel-toed boots. The grinning skulls in stylized Viking helmets blazoned on their backs, surmounted by the title of their club, its home base named below.

Boone saw them clearly: MONGOLS—SAN JOSE.

Impulsively and quite against his will, he followed them inside, prepared to turn and run if they so much as glanced in his direction. He was instantly relieved to find two aging flower children at the urinals, another running water in the sink. A pair of sandals visible beneath the short partition of the nearest toilet stall.

No Mongols.

Boone checked out the other stalls—both empty—and retreated in a daze. A mind fuck. Too much grass on top of ugly memories. At least the munchies had retreated, overpowered by a sick sensation in his gut. The growling music only *sounded* like a pack of motorcycles revving in the parking lot, beyond the flimsy chain-link fence.

Boone rushed outside, in need of air, colliding with a figure in his path.

"Hey, sorry, man."

"No sweat," said Axel Grubb.

Boone tried to speak—if nothing else, to say "I know you"—but he could not find his voice as Axel turned away and vanished in the crowd. His mind was spinning in a dizzy whirl, for which the grass was not responsible. No tricks, this time. No mind-fuck games.

I know you.

And he should have, after all, this man whose blood had flecked his cheeks and stained his clothing on this very night, two decades past. A taste of Axel on his lips before the

193

jackals pulled him down. This *dead* man, who had been reduced to something like a slab of meat before Boone's eyes.

In twenty years, a day had not gone by without the face of Axel Grubb intruding on his conscious thoughts or secret dreams. Before-and-after shots of Axel, though *before* had come from blurry photos in the papers, and they only knew each other *after*. Too damned late to really know, at all.

He had researched the life of Axel Grubb compulsively, collecting bits of trivia from every source available, as if by understanding Axel he could somehow understand himself, the wasted years that lay ahead. In San Mateo, he had badgered friends and relatives for their impressions of the man and came back hopelessly confused. The *Barb* had cheerfully advanced him fifty dollars for an "inside" article on Axel's final night in Paradise—the check a validation of his own obsession with a stranger—but he had to give it back when he fell six months behind deadline, then a year, and all without a word on paper.

There was simply nothing he could say.

Not then, not now.

But he could follow Axel's scent. That much, at least, was still within his power.

Shoving through the crowd, Boone reached the nearest aisle as Star Child came onstage. The audience was on its feet and cheering, chanting, "Rock and roll!" Hands clapping overhead like fundamentalists at a revival meeting, as their heroes started warming up in front of open microphones.

A glimpse of Axel in the crush, his profile unmistakable despite the flashing strobes that made Boone feel like an escapee from a 1920s silent film. Beyond him, barely visible, the deputies down front had been replaced by shaggy, barrel-chested watchdogs sporting greasy Levis and tattoos.

Reese Stamper opened up with "Hell on Wheels," in tribute to the bikers standing guard, and while Boone knew the backup vocal wasn't Billy Teague, it *sounded* like him, Jesus, plain as day.

This time, we do it right.

He started after Axel, down the aisle, with dancers in his way until he elbowed them aside. Too stoned to notice, some of them, and others shouting, "Easy, brother," as he jostled them in passing.

Axel heading for the stage, with bikers in the way. Intent upon a mission no one had deciphered in the span of twenty years. Boone could not have explained it, but he *knew*, this time, that Axel had the gun in hand before he made his move.

A wise man learns from his mistakes.

A couple of the bikers saw him coming, saw the gun, and they were grinning as they moved to intercept. The others closing in behind them, instinct taking over at the moment of the kill. Grubb's pistol tracking on a point beyond the rough defensive line, in the direction of the band.

Boone lunged for Axel, one arm circling his neck, the other clutching at his gun, to drag it down. His first shot muffled by the music, wasted in the air.

Somehow, the wiry figure twisted in his grasp, and they were face to face, their bodies pressed together, struggling like partners in an epileptic waltz. There was a flash of something—recognition? understanding?—in Axel's eyes, before the gun went off a second time. Boone saw the love and hatred there, all jumbled into something new and deadly, as the bullet burned across his stomach, drawing blood.

No time to scream, before the nearest Mongol struck at Axel with his loaded pool cue, winding up like Wade Boggs at the plate. They fell together, Boone beneath and Axel plunging into him, then *through* him, with a strangled, fading cry that sounded almost sexual in its release.

Alone. No sign of Axel as his eyes snapped open and he saw the Mongols all around him, staring down at him with glassy, sunken eyes. One of them grinning with a mouth that seemed to stretch from ear to ear, the whole pack smelling worse than any bikers ever had in life.

Boone tried to reach the pistol, knowing it was useless, and a heavy boot heel crushed his hand. The pain was bright and fragile, a preliminary to the main event. A blade ripped

into him, somewhere below the waist, and he had time to
scream before the others went to work with cue sticks, bats,
and chains.

"I know you!"

Glimpsing Rachel in the gap between a biker's denim legs,
with Axel at her side—and yet, not Axel somehow.
Changed.

I know you all.

He screamed again, and Star Child played him on his way.

Mark Verheiden | BOOTLEG

The sun was already low as Larry Skase stepped over an overflowing box of empty Coke cans and old donuts, making his way to the stairs that led to the lower level of the swap meet. The record dealers had been segregated on the service deck of the campus, behind the echoing concrete of the school's tennis courts. The organizers wanted them kept a discreet distance from the old ladies with their hand-carved towel dispensers and the anxious scavengers hawking cracked Kmart "antiques."

Technically, the open-air college bazaar came to a close at 4 PM, but the scattered vendors, hot-dog peddlers, and would-be entrepreneurs always waited for the shadows before packing up their wares. The shadows meant nothing to Skase. It was a *different* world behind the courts—*his* world. He'd come to find bootlegs.

He wandered down the steps overlooking the record show, zipping up his light blue Members Only jacket and wishing he had a cigarette. On a good day you might have called Larry handsome, but the good days were few and far between lately. He worked his day job, spent his evenings alone, and on the weekends indulged his sole passion.

In the past, Skase had haunted the swap meets and flea markets for legitimate collectibles—alternate pressings, imports, radio station promos, anything that deviated from the standard record-store fare. In time, however, the thrill of those "discoveries" had faded. Even the pricey record company promos were authorized, homogenized, and readi-

197

ly available. Like a junkie searching for that next, better high, Larry Skase wanted something new.

His hobby had become a frustration, and that frustration festered into anger. Larry grew bitter toward his favorite performers for not appeasing his ravenous desires. They were selfish bastards, the lot of them—taking his money and his time and his love, but never giving anything *special* in return. He had invested so much of his life in their music; he *deserved* something back.

Bootlegs gave him that. Collecting them was a way of leveling the psychic debt, clipping off a little piece of superstar soul and staring deep inside. Stolen outtakes, discarded remixes, long-forgotten live shows—he bought them all, devoured them, *reveled* in them. The bootlegs brought him closer to his musical gods.

Many of the bootleg dealers had gone into hiding following a well-publicized bust in the Midwest, but a few were trickling back, like rusty water from a broken faucet. There was something desperate about the dealers, something small and pathetic. They hovered ratlike over their precious boxes, backs hunched as they sorted and sniffed, eyeing would-be customers with a queasy combination of greed and fear. Somehow they seemed more at home in the dimming afternoon light.

Larry passed a line of dirty cardboard boxes packed with cracking legit vinyl, his nose wrinkling with exaggerated disdain. As his collection grew and his tastes stratified, Skase eschewed vinyl boots almost entirely for "imported," illegal compact discs. He wanted his collection of stolen dreams to last forever, permanently, with no scratches, pops, or nicks.

A fat man in a Raiders sweatshirt was hawking a few boxes of assorted vinyl wedged into the trunk of his old blue Chevy. Major name groups vied for space between a bald spare and six empty cans of motor oil. There hadn't been much new at the meet, so Skase condescended to flip through the man's meager bootlegs, checking labels for song titles and running times.

Skase was starting through the second box when he

glanced at the van parked two spaces over. That's when he saw the eyes.

They were staring at him from a faded photocopy, half hidden under a stack of brittle newspaper clippings. Skase moved away from the Chevy, fixated on the image.

"You're a *collector?*" a man with black teeth asked, stepping out of the moist shade of his battered VW van. He was thin, all elbows and knees, like a gangly puppet that had lost its stuffing. "Anything *particular* you're looking for?"

Skase couldn't help but stare at those gray eyes. "Depends," he said, uncomfortable even talking to the man. "I've got most of the studio stuff. I'm looking for rare takes—you know, live and—"

"You're looking for *bootlegs.*" Skase was surprised by the casual admission; most of the dealers described their material with euphemisms like "rare imports" or "special live tracks." "I've seen you here *before,* looking for your Beatles and your Stones and your Roses." He spat out the names as if they were beneath contempt.

Skase had seen Blackteeth before, always in the same spot. He'd spread his wares across a faded pink and orange blanket that spilled over the pavement like some deranged magic carpet. Skase usually ignored him and his worthless promos, but this time was somehow different.

"Don't have any of that record-company shit," Blackteeth continued, "but I've got something else that might interest a collector like you." He brushed away the dusty papers covering those gray eyes.

"Jesus," Skase said, recoiling. The eyes were dead, propped open with wire. It was an autopsy photo of recent vintage, with a gleaming background of hot chrome and steel. The man's head had been severed from his body at the neck, skin peeled back like a ripe orange. The corded facial muscles and wet sinews were plainly visible, even in this blurry copy. The photograph had been pasted to a plain white record jacket, then shrink-wrapped with a thin sheen of cellophane, giving the dead eyes a slick, wet luminosity.

"You said you were looking for something *special,*" Blackteeth said.

"I—I'm not interested in vinyl," Skase said, looking for a reason, *any* reason to get away from there. Without thinking, he flipped the cover over to check for a title and song list. The back of the jacket was completely blank save for a single word, scrawled in brown/red ink.

"Ritual?" Skase read. "Who's this by? Metallica? Roses?"

Blackteeth drifted into the shade of the old van. "Does it matter?"

Skase's eyes narrowed. He wasn't into playing "mystery disc," and besides, there was something *wrong* about the thin little man. "How much," he asked, hoping the price would be too high and he could get the hell away from there.

All he could see of Blackteeth was a sparkle of light reflecting off his wet lips. "For you?" he said. "It's free. If you like it, come back next month and pay me what you think it's worth."

Skase slid the record under his arm, looking at Blackteeth skeptically. "And what if I don't come back?"

Blackteeth laughed—a rattling, raspy noise rising from the base of his chest. "I trust you," he said as Skase hurried away.

Skase tossed the record on the passenger seat of his car and backed out of the parking garage at reckless speed. The dead man's face stared up at him, mouth locked open, a bloody, toothless jaw jutting out in defiance. As Skase drove, he couldn't help looking at the face, feeling almost compelled to study the grisly image again and again.

Maybe that's when he noticed it. Or maybe he'd seen it all along. The soft flesh of the head was almost gone, but what remained of the man's lips had curled not into a scream, but into a grotesque, frozen smile.

Skase turned the record facedown and kept driving.

He lived in a typical third-floor apartment in a typically sunny southern California suburb, all palm trees and hot asphalt. The building had seen better days, but Skase wasn't one to notice such niceties. He slammed the door of his apartment, tossed his jacket over the back of the green Goodwill couch in the living room, and went straight for the stereo.

He slit the plastic shrink wrap of *Ritual* with his thumbnail, puffing the sleeve open against his stomach. The cardboard smell was old and damp. He slipped the record out, careful to hold it by its edges. The black vinyl shimmered in the flickering fluorescent light.

The labels were blank white and the inside run-off groove was clean—no matrix code numbers, not even an "A" or "B" to mark the sides. Skase slid the record over the spindle of his turntable, watching it catch hesitantly on the worn rubber mat, then swiped an antistatic brush over the plastic. The hair on his forearm prickled from the static electricity.

That's when he felt something dark and cold—*there*—in the room, standing right beside him. He turned sharply, half expecting to find someone watching him.

The refrigerator clicked on with a soft hum. The room was empty and dark.

Skase's eyes followed the line of the record as it rotated on the turntable. The grooves formed black-on-black concentric circles, spinning down, down, always down. Skase dropped the tone arm into the run-on groove, stepping back as a burst of plastic crackle rumbled through the speakers. God, he *hated* that sound. "Goddamn vinyl," he muttered, kneeling in front of the equalizer.

That's when he heard the voice. "Welcome to *my* world, *collector.*"

Skase jumped, reaching out reflexively to bang the needle off the record, but something—*stopped* him. Tendrils of black plastic, wispy as a spider's web, rose up from the center of the record and wrapped around the cartridge, pulling the needle deep into the vinyl groove. Thin twirls of burning plastic danced off the disc, cut by the grinding cartridge, drizzling over the edge of the turntable like hot curls from a metal lathe.

The wall socket behind the stereo rack pulsed with moist heat, turning soft and malleable. When it reached the melting point, the white plastic plate oozed around the steel teeth of the record player power cord, sealing it to the wall in a clot of deformed plastic.

"This record is from *all* of us," the voice said, pounding out of the speakers like thudding concrete blocks. "The ultimate fucking bootleg."

Something brushed Skase, the same feeling as before, but this time it *struck* him, sending him sprawling across the floor. He could feel a pulsing charge spitting through the air, like sand scraping against his skin. He stared up at the brass hinges of the stereo cabinet as they began to warp and shimmer. The entire room was suddenly awash in thick, desert heat.

"They say rock is the devil's music," the voice continued. "We're always so fucking *glib* and *rational* when we defend ourselves to our fans—to our 'public'—but who's to say they're all *wrong?"*

Skase felt the skin peeling up the back of his skull, like cupboard paper curling on a humid day. Thin rivulets of blood stained the collar of his shirt, turning purple as it mixed with the blue dye.

"You thought you could *buy* us, didn't you? *Steal* us bit by bit—"

The bones around Skase's eyes softened, distorting and bulging as they stretched from the pressure building inside his skull. His vision blurred to soft focus. At first he thought the room was changing, and then he started to scream.

The room wasn't any different. *He* was.

Writhing in terrible pain, Skase rolled toward the stereo cabinet and stared at the gray album cover—the skinless, peeled face, teeth bare and bloody and pulled back in hideous pain. After a moment, the light shifted, and suddenly he saw his *own* face reflected in the sticky remnants of the shrink wrap. They were beginning to look surprisingly alike.

"The *real* fans know the truth—they've known all along. See, *we're* collectors, too."

Something was tearing at Skase from the inside, slowly ripping him apart. His teeth fell from his jaw like flaking paint, rattling across the hardwood floor. As he reached out to catch them, the tips of his fingers swelled to twice their normal size, blotching purple and red. His fingernails sloughed off like dripping wax, leaving wet tendrils of red dangling from his hands.

"We bootleg *souls*, asshole. And you're *next.*"

Doubled over in pain, Skase threw himself into the stereo cabinet, shattering the glass doors. The voice stopped, replaced by a throbbing, painfully low tone. Even in his agony, Skase could feel the tone rumble through his stomach, across his chest, into his throat.

It was the sound of pure, coarse evil. And it was inside him.

He convulsed spasmodically, slipping in the blood spilling from his mouth and hands. The skin on his chest began to separate, cracking open like red molten rock. As his ribs began to spread, tearing cartilage and flesh apart, he saw a rush of white light—and then that voice, one last time.

"You're going to die—*chik*—die—*chik*—die—*chik*—"

"*Scratch*" Skase said, blood spitting from his lips.

With his last strength, he pushed the stereo cabinet sideways, dumping it to the floor with a crash. The phonograph cartridge remained securely attached to the record, but the amplifier split open like a ripe cantaloupe.

Skase lay there in his own blood, trying to understand what had happened. He touched his cheek gingerly, feeling around the distended, splintered bone. His face was a swollen mask, a maze of broken capillaries and torn flesh. For some reason the pain had stopped—at least for now.

He rolled over and stared at the blank record, still spindled on the overturned record player. He reached out with trembling, bloody fingers and touched the shiny vinyl —trembling not with fear, but *anticipation*.

He was filled with a crazy kind of satisfaction. He had seen the black heart of his obsession—better, he had almost *joined* with it. His fingers traced the concentric vinyl grooves, finding the deep scratch that had broken the spell. He had come so close to the truth. He took a breath, the pain of his cracked ribs bringing a twisted, gasping smile to his lips.

"I wonder if I can find this—on CD."

Ray Garton | WEIRD GIG

Bill Wyatt stood up suddenly behind his desk when Travis Block walked into his office unannounced. Wyatt's quick smile faded when only two other members of the band sauntered in behind him.

"Where's Elmo?" Wyatt asked with urgency in his voice as the three men seated themselves before his expensive cherrywood desk.

J.J. White spoke in his usual slow, quiet drawl. "Across town. He's doin' one of them antidrug TV spots."

"Son of a *bitch!*" Wyatt snapped, pounding a fist on his desk as he dropped back into his chair. "That means he'll be coked out of his fucking mind by the time he gets here, and I wanted to make a good impression on this guy."

"What guy?" Travis asked.

"The guy I called you here to meet. When is Elmo gonna be through over there?"

Buddy Flatt shrugged. "You know what happens when he gets together with those antidrug guys. Party-party-party."

"Shit. Okay, here's the deal." Wyatt stood, walked around his desk, and leaned back on the edge. "There's this guy, Leverett—um, uuhhh, *Malcolm* Leverett, yeah—called me a couple days ago and said he was interested in hiring you guys for a gig. Private. I mean, you can't buy tickets, okay? This isn't like a regular concert or anything. He has a client—clients, actually, a bunch of people—who want—"

The door opened and Elmo Carr hurried in, grinning broadly and tossing his bushy brown hair. He hopped into a chair and fidgeted for a moment before saying, "Hi, guys, how's it hangin'? Sorry I'm late, but we ended up doin', oh shit, I don't know *how* many takes, and then the—"

"Are you fucked up, Elmo?" Wyatt asked.

"Fucked up?" He laughed nervously, bouncing in the chair. "I'm not fucked up, hell, no. I'm not fucked up, shit, we spent the whole day doin' one take after another and then we—"

"Shut up, Elmo," Wyatt said firmly. "I want you to just shut up, sit still, and try to make a good impression."

"Good impression, a good impression on who—who'm I s'posed to be makin' a—"

"Just *listen*, dammit. This guy, Malcolm Leverett. He's got these clients, some big group of—I don't know—maybe a club or something. He didn't tell me. Anyway, they want you for a private concert. You. Understand? He said they aren't even *interested* in anybody else."

"Aw, c'mon, man," Travis sneered. "What, are we back to playing dances now? What *is* this? After fourteen albums and about a dozen hits, we're doing some fuckin' convention?"

Wyatt held up his hands. "Just listen. This guy says—are you listening?—he says money is no object. *No object.*" He folded his arms and cocked a brow confidently. "So I kind of think this is more than just some fuckin' *convention*, okay?"

"Where is it?" Buddy asked.

"I don't know yet."

"Who are these people?" Travis asked.

"Look, I don't know *anything* yet, okay? Leverett wanted to meet with you guys. Personally."

The four musicians exchanged glances.

Still bouncing in his chair, his fingers dancing over an invisible keyboard on his lap, like a graying, hyperactive teenager, Elmo rattled, "Well, shit, man, it sounds good to me 'cause, y'know, it's not like we're booked up to our asses these days and I mean, y'know, we've gotta—"

"Sounds like some kinda bullshit to me," J.J. drawled, pulling a handful of pills from his pocket. He picked out a few, popped them into his mouth, and put the rest back as he walked slowly to Wyatt's liquor cabinet, filled a glass with Jack Daniels, and drank them down, finishing the glass in three big gulps.

Wyatt glared at him for a moment, then shouted, "Now, dammit, J.J., if you do that while he's here, I swear I'll kick your ass up around your shoulders and you'll walk outta here on your fuckin' *hands!* And you!" He stabbed a finger at Elmo. "If you don't stop crawling all over that chair like a fucking circus monkey, you'll get the *same!*"

Travis leaned forward, frowning. "Correct me if I'm wrong, Billy, but . . . don't you work for *us?*"

Wyatt closed his eyes and rubbed them, nodding.

"Then how come *you're* doing the yelling here?"

"Okay, okay. You're right. I'm sorry for yelling. I *do* work for you. For almost twenty years. We've been through a lot of shit together, right? You think I'd be with you that long, after all we've been through, if I didn't really *love* you guys? Huh? I'm asking you. No, I wouldn't. I'd be out spending all my time digging up new bands, *hot* bands. You're right, Travis," he said, pacing, "Jagged Edge *did* cut fourteen albums and you *did* have a dozen hits and you *were* hot shit on a silver platter for a lotta years. But you notice something about what I just said?" He stopped and faced them. "It's all in the past tense. Now, I know your slump began when Johnny OD'd, that's a given, because we all know that Johnny was everybody's favorite. Sexy Johnny, sensual Johnny, the kids loved him, the press loved him, *everybody* loved him. But when Johnny died . . ." He shrugged and shook his head. "Then all those kids overdosed at that concert, and six months later a bunch of them were crushed to death against the stage at another. And what about that kid who blew his dad away with a shotgun because his dad was taking away his Jagged Edge albums, huh?"

"C'mon, Billy," Travis said, "we didn't have anything to do with—"

"I know, I know, you guys didn't do it, but the media had a heyday with it because the kid was a rabid fan of yours and his mother claimed he'd been going down the shitter since he started listening to your music and when he finally did his dad in, he was so full of drugs the cops needed a prescription to question him. And, of course, you guys were always getting arrested. Hell, I was bailing you out every time I turned around. You were making the papers twice a month, maybe more. And pretty soon . . . nobody cared anymore."

Wyatt seated himself behind his desk and rubbed his eyes again. "Yeah, I work for you guys because I love you and I want you to come back. I want the old days back. When you guys couldn't take a crap without all of America wanting to know how big the turd was. But you know what? They're not coming back, those days. Things are different now. Look around you, watch the news for a change. Listen to that man in the White House. There *is* a new breeze blowing and it's blowin' you guys away! Why do you think I keep telling you to write new songs? I mean, different songs! Last year, *Time* magazine called you 'the band that killed a generation.' Drugs, man. That's all you were back then and that was fine. You read *Us* last week? Your *Wild Horse* album was number three on the list of top ten all-time favorite rock albums, guys. You know that? But that was back then. This is *now* and you haven't changed. You keep writing about drugs and singing about drugs and doing drugs and—"

"Hey, man," Elmo said, a little angered, "you know what I just *did,* man, I just did a fuckin' antidrug statement on national fuckin' television, and I'm not gonna sit here and—"

"You doing an antidrug statement is like a Christian going on TV and saying Jesus Christ was a clown, Elmo. You *had* to do it because you got busted three months ago, so don't give me *that* song and dance. It's the third one you've done and you're still bouncing around here like a fucking Ping-Pong ball. And you—" He pointed at J.J. "You're a fuckin' *zombie,* popping downers like they were breath mints. And you two guys probably have livers harder than your dicks'll *ever* get. Hell, we're all about the same age, but you guys look ten or fifteen years older than me. But none of you stop. And you're poison out there now, do you hear me? *Poison.*" He scrubbed his face and groaned hopelessly.

"Look, Billy," Travis said, standing, "if we have to sit here and listen to a sermon about—"

"Don't you see I'm trying to save your asses?" he shouted. "I'm your agent and manager, not your mother, but if I can't save your lives, maybe I can at least breathe a little life back into your career. Now, you've got a guy here who says money is no object. You know what that means? How long has it been since you've done a gig? I mean, a really big one, not some dive in a bad part of town, but a real gig! And how long has it been since you've gotten any positive press? Something without the word 'arrested' in the headline? This could do it. This could make people notice you again. This could—"

The intercom on Wyatt's desk buzzed, and he punched the button. "Yeah?"

"A Mr. Leverett is here to see you, Mr. Wyatt," his secretary said.

Wyatt licked his dry lips and whispered, "Please, guys. Just . . . shape up for a few minutes here and give me a chance to put you back on the map. Okay?"

More glances were exchanged; then Travis nodded.

Malcolm Leverett looked like a giant, shaved hedgehog. He was round, slightly hunched, had no neck, and looked rather sweaty. His eyes were magnified by the thick lenses of the round, rimless spectacles that rested on his shiny, pointed nose. With his briefcase tucked under one arm, he introduced himself in a pleasant but very quiet, tremulous voice, then took a seat and folded his puffy hands delicately on the briefcase on his lap. There was a smell about him: faint, rather sweet, moist, and slightly unpleasant.

"As I'm sure Mr. Wyatt has explained to you, gentlemen," he said in his feathery voice, his words sounding rehearsed, "I have a client who wishes to enlist your talents in a private performance. My client represents a large group of people who have unanimously chosen Jagged Edge for their entertainment. They have no interest whatsoever in any other performers and have authorized me to approve of whatever fee you wish."

He cleared his throat again, wriggled his interlocked fingers, and twitched his nose as he sniffed. His brows rose high above his magnified eyes, and he waited.

"Who's your client?" Travis asked, looking unimpressed.

"It is my policy to maintain the anonymity of all of my clients."

"And what do your clients hire you to do? What are you, a lawyer? An agent? What?"

Wyatt stiffened behind his desk and took a deep breath, closing his eyes.

Leverett removed a card from his breast pocket, leaned forward, and handed it to Travis. It read, simply:

MALCOLM LEVERETT
Intermediary

"It is my job," Leverett said, "to intermediate between two or more parties attempting to reach an agreement or make a deal. And I assure you that this deal is entirely legitimate." He blinked slowly, tilted his head back, and pursed his lips for just an instant. "All you need do is name your price."

Elmo was making an effort to remain still and calm in his chair, but some part of him was always twitching—his feet, his hands, his shoulders or legs—and he stuttered when he spoke. "You muh-m-mean we can ask fuh-for . . . any-anything?"

"I have been instructed to meet your fee, gentlemen, whatever it might be."

"Where's this private concert going to be?" Travis asked.

"The Chase Coliseum."

"Huh-hey," Elmo said excitedly, "we played there once, yeah, we played there."

"Burned down," J.J. said sleepily.

"Yes. But it has been restored."

"I didn't hear anything about the Chase being restored," Travis said suspiciously.

"The restoration was completed very recently and took place over a very short period of time. My client, uh . . . financed it."

Travis leaned forward in his chair, inspecting the odd man through narrow eyes. Turning to Wyatt, he said quietly, "I'd like to talk to you in private for a second."

Wyatt stood and went to the front of his desk, grinning. "Oh, no, Travis, I don't think there's any need for that. I think we ought to—"

"No, wait a sec, here, Billy. Something's not right about this. I don't want to go into anything blind, know what I mean?" Then he turned to Leverett: "What *is* this group? Are they political? Are they a club? A lodge? What?"

"As I said before, it is my policy to main—"

"Well, it's *our* policy to find out what we're getting into before we—"

"Tra-vis," Wyatt interrupted firmly, "Mr. Leverett is just trying to make us an offer and I think you're being—"

"No, no, Mr. Wyatt," Leverett said, almost whispering, never taking his eyes off Travis. "I understand Mr. Block's feelings. I think it is very wise to know all there is to know about a transaction before becoming involved. But you must understand my position, Mr. Block. I simply cannot reveal the identity of my client. I can, however, assure you that this group is neither political nor officially organized. It is nothing more than a great number of people who admire your work tremendously and have missed your presence in the limelight. They wish to express their admiration by offering you whatever sum of money you ask to perform for them. I myself have followed your work over the years—not to the extent that these people have, I must admit—and I am aware of the problems you've had. The deaths, the bad publicity, your association with drugs, and the subsequent arrests. The difficulty in maintaining your audience."

"Hey," Travis said, sounding angry, "don't come in here telling us—"

"Please." Leverett held up a sweaty palm. "I do not mean that as an insult. I simply mean to say that, considering the path of your career over these past several years, I would think this offer—this opportunity—would be difficult to turn down. You are being offered the chance to perform for a large audience of devoted, adoring fans for whatever fee you choose." He folded his hands on the briefcase again, paused, then added, "There will be a down payment, of course. In cash." He patted the briefcase daintily.

"I think the problem the guys are having with this," Wyatt said soothingly, tossing a warning glance at Travis, "is that it usually doesn't work this way, see what I'm saying? I mean, it's not customary for someone to come up and say, 'We'll pay you whatever you want.' It's a little . . . startling, if you know what I mean."

"Ah. I see. Well, perhaps a suggestion would help. Would, say . . ." He pursed his lips and stared at the ceiling for a moment. ". . . two million dollars be an appropriate start?"

All five men in the room turned to Leverett and stared silently. Even J.J. cocked one brow over a heavy-lidded eye. After a long silence, Wyatt said, "We'll take it."

Their footsteps resonated as they walked across the expansive stage of the Chase Coliseum.

Their instruments were set up, microphones were ready, the stage lights were on, but there were no seats down on the darkened floor.

"I'm tellin' ya, man," Elmo said, bouncing to a silent beat, "this is, like, I mean, y'know, this is fuckin' bizarre, y'know what I'm sayin'? This place is like new and I didn't hear *shit* about—"

"Yeah, I know," Travis said. "Something's not right about this." He pulled a flask from his back pocket and took a healthy swallow of whiskey, then turned to Wyatt. "Billy. There's something you're not telling us. Who are these people that they can restore a whole auditorium—I mean, the fuckin' *Chase*—without it even getting in the paper?"

"I'm telling you, Travis, I don't know. And frankly, I don't care."

"And these are ours," Travis said, waving at the instruments. "How did—"

Wyatt said, "Mr. Leverett wanted to have everything ready for you when you arrived, so I took the liberty of—"

"You what? This is—I don't even know if—"

Footsteps sounded down on the floor. As they grew

louder, Mr. Leverett materialized slowly from the darkness, his pudgy hands joined together before him.

"I'm assuming," Leverett said, "you'll want to . . . well, to do whatever it is you do before a performance."

"Weird gig, man," J.J. drawled quietly, shaking his head.

Travis simply stared at Wyatt for a moment, his eyes burning.

Wyatt shrugged.

To Leverett, Travis said, "Look, we got here at the time you told us to be here, right? We don't even know when this thing's supposed to start because you won't tell us shit, and I don't—"

"The concert will begin whenever you're ready," Leverett said calmly.

Buddy gawked at Elmo. Travis's jaw was slack as he stared at Wyatt. J.J. shook his head and muttered, "Weird gig, man, weird fuckin' gig."

"There aren't even any seats!" Travis snapped at Leverett. "Are these people in fuckin' wheelchairs, or what?"

"They do not wish to be seated," Leverett said. "I believe they plan to do a good deal of dancing."

Elmo said, laughing, "So where, I mean, like, when're they-um, where *are* they, man?"

"When you play, they will come."

Travis's bitter laughter rang through the auditorium as he whipped the flask from his back pocket again and drank more than a swallow. Then he turned to Wyatt and said, *Field of Dreams*, right? I saw that. Can't fool me. Tell you what, Billy, why don't you and the penguin down there entertain the Shriners. I'm outta here."

Wyatt stepped in front of him and grabbed his arms. "C'mon, Travis, don't do this, don't—"

"I assure you, Mr. Block, they *will* come," Leverett said, raising his voice. "But not until you begin to play."

Elmo jumped in front of Travis, poked him in the ribs, and jittered from side to side as he rasped, "What the hell, man, you know what I'm sayin'? I mean, you know, like . . . if they wanna pay us a couple million to play for, like, y'know, dustballs, then . . . what the hell?"

"Weird fuckin' gig," J.J. said, picking up his guitar. He

sent a grumbling bass riff into the darkness. "Sounds good, though," he said to Travis over his shoulder.

"But there's—" Travis turned to Leverett again. "Where's the crew, the sound—"

"Everything is taken care of, Mr. Block. All you need do is play."

Travis shook his head, glared at Wyatt, then picked up his guitar, saying, "We end up on *Totally Hidden Video*, I don't want to hear any bitching from you guys, because I *warned* you." He bounced a few riffs off the walls as Buddy went to the drums and Elmo ran his fingers over the keyboards.

"Okay," Travis said, "let's try, um . . . 'Snakeskin.'"

They went into the song and Wyatt's shoulders sagged with relief as he sighed. He gave the okay sign to Mr. Leverett, who nodded stiffly.

Halfway through the song, Travis stopped singing and turned to the others, waving an arm vigorously. "Whoa, hey, *hey!*"

They stopped.

Travis said, "Dammit, Elmo, you're dragging behind on the—"

Applause broke out in the darkness. What sounded like a small group of people cheered and whistled.

Shocked, Travis spun around so fast that the neck of his guitar hit the microphone stand, making it wobble back and forth, and the sound thunked through the darkness.

The *empty* darkness.

The band stared silently out at the floor, but saw no one behind Mr. Leverett.

"I *told* you," Leverett said quietly, then turned to his left and began to walk away. He stopped and said, "Well? Continue." In a moment, he was out of sight.

Elmo muttered, "But we were just, like, y'know, rehearsing."

"I don't see nobody out there," Buddy said, squinting under the shade of one hand.

"C'mon, guys," Travis said, "let's give 'em 'Needles and Whims.'"

J.J. said, *"Weird* fuckin' gig, man."

The song began with a single chord, then a long shrieked

213

note from Travis, whose raspy voice tore into the darkness like a barrage of rusty fishhooks.

Wyatt backed away from the band quickly, out of sight of the audience . . . although he still couldn't see the audience. Their voices sounded young and their number seemed to grow gradually as the song—which Wyatt had always thought their ugliest, although it was one of their biggest hits—played out.

Then they began to appear slowly. Then disappear . . . then reappear . . . dancing in and out of the darkness almost beyond the reach of his vision. He caught glimpses of lanky arms snaking upward and jerking to the beat, of legs kicking and feet stomping the floor as they came closer. But he couldn't see a whole person. Not yet.

The song ended and the crowd, now much larger out there in the dark, went wild. Wyatt watched the band soak up the applause, saw them swell with the praise. Travis tossed him a glance that, for the first time in a lot of years, was not darkened by anger, bitterness, or pain. He actually looked, for that moment, happy . . . still wrinkled and ravaged by his own addictions and excesses, but happy.

They waited for the cheering applause to die down, but it didn't. It grew as the audience grew. The movement in the darkness became more dense, and Wyatt squinted from the wing but still had no idea what kind of people made up the audience.

Travis spun on the band, shouted something, and they broke into "Purple Streak in a Night Sky."

The audience grew out of the darkness, their arms vines that led them to the stage, their faces pale blossoms, mouths opening and closing, shouting, singing . . .

Young people, mostly, it seemed. High school students, maybe? College students? Some appeared to be adults, but it was difficult to tell; they were still very hazy. Overall, they seemed to be the same kind of audience the band used to get back in those long-ago days before MTV and talk radio.

They continued to come forward into the light that bled from the stage and their voices grew even louder, so much louder that Wyatt looked up in the direction of the tiered balconies. He couldn't see them, but he knew they were loaded. And they'd filled up suddenly.

No echoing voices from the lobby . . .

No footsteps pounding in on the concrete floor . . .

Just instant audience.

The song ended. The auditorium trembled with the cheers and applause, which let up only a bit as Travis raised his arms above his head and screamed, "It's great to be here!"

The roar was deafening.

Travis grabbed the mike and screamed something else into it, but Wyatt couldn't understand the words. The band went into its cover of "Baba O'Riley."

The crowd was too loud, and it bothered Wyatt. He looked around for Leverett, hoping to ask him where they had all come from so quickly, who they were, but the old man had disappeared.

He looked down at them again as they reached up toward Travis, as if they could pull him down from the stage, and Wyatt frowned. The more he looked at the crowd, the more he realized that it was *exactly* the kind of audience they used to get. He saw a lot of long, stringy hair out there, even some beads dangling around necks and wrapped around heads. There were ratty blue jeans with bell-bottoms and patches sewn onto the denim: peace symbols, flowers, ankhs and the word *love* with the "LO" on top of the "VE". And was that long-haired kid wearing a . . . it looked like . . . yes, it was—

"Nah," Wyatt grumbled doubtfully to himself—

A nehru jacket.

As the band played, the voice of the crowd began to unify into a pulsating chant. Wyatt tried to make it out, but couldn't. Not yet.

Travis was having the time of his life—all *four* of them were—and it showed in every movement, every note. They were stars again, not has-beens, not black-and-white faces in a where-are-they-now article or in some magazine's disdainful look back at the drug culture. They were on top once more.

But Wyatt didn't feel good about it. Something wasn't

right, something more than just the mystery that surrounded Leverett—and where the hell *was* he, anyway?—no, something wasn't right about this crowd.

He looked for Leverett again, jogging into the murkiness off the stage and shouting the man's name. No response.

The chant was clearer now. The crowd was shouting, "'Wild Horse'! 'Wild Horse'!"

Wyatt hurried back to where he'd stood and saw something happening down on the floor. The crowd was splitting down the middle. Opening right up like the Red Sea in that old Chuck Heston movie. A narrow path was forming down the center of the auditorium, disappearing into the solid darkness as the chant continued.

"'Wild Horse'! 'Wild Horse'!"

It was their biggest hit, the title cut of their biggest album, and the song for which they would always be remembered . . . a song the media now referred to as a "drug anthem" or a "love song to mind-altering substances." And this crowd was determined to hear it.

"'Wild Horse'! 'Wild Horse'!"

"Baba O'Riley" was nearing its close. The chant was growing steadily louder. And Wyatt was feeling tense. A corkscrew was working its way through his guts and his tense fists were hitting his thighs nervously. He spun around, walked a few yards into the darkness, and shouted, "Dammit, Leverett, where the hell *are* you, you son of a bitch!" then told himself to knock it off because they were, after all, making two million dollars and the man had arranged it. . . .

But Wyatt couldn't shake the feeling that something was coming, something bad, something—

The song ended.

Travis shouted to the band, "Let's give 'em what they want!"

They did "Wild Horse." Wyatt felt the crowd's voice in his bones. He turned to them again and his eyes followed the path that had opened in the center of the mass and saw that a figure was making its way out of the darkness and toward the stage, moving without hurry, arms dangling loosely in a familiar way. Wyatt felt like he was about to vomit and his neck and shoulders were aching from tension and his heart was pounding faster and faster against his ribs and the figure drew closer and all heads in the crowd turned to follow it to the stage.

Travis moved like the kid he used to be, and saliva sprayed from his mouth as he sang and made sweeping motions with both arms, beckoning for the figure to come down and join in the dancing and singing.

Without knowing why, Wyatt whispered, "No Travis, no don't do that Travis," and he spun around, sucking in a breath to scream for Leverett.

But Leverett stood just two feet away from him, hands joined in front, face calm and expressionless. Wyatt rushed him, pressed his face close to Leverett's, and said, "What's going on?"

"A concert."

"No, I mean *out there.* Who are those people? Where did they come from? So quickly? Why are they dressed like that? And why are they all stepping out of the way for that—that—for whoever that is?"

"I don't know them, Mr. Wyatt. I'm just a mediator."

Frustrated, Wyatt turned back to the crowd as the figure began to move into the light.

Tall and thin and shirtless, long black hair that fell in thick curls around the bare shoulders, tight black jeans.

"Oh, God," Wyatt breathed, shaking his head, confused.

Elmo hit a sour note on the keyboard, stopped playing, and stared.

Travis's voice cracked; he stopped playing his guitar and J.J. and Buddy followed.

Their mouths hung open as they gawked down at the floor.

Wyatt spun, clutched Leverett's lapels and shook him, spitting, "What the fuck is this, a joke? Some sick fucking joke?"

"Take your hands off me." Leverett's voice was surprisingly loud in the sudden silence.

Wyatt lowered his hands slowly, then jerked around when he heard Travis's dry, ragged scream.

"Johnny?"

"Hey, Travis. Long time, huh?"

It was Johnny's voice, his movements, his face and body. . . .

217

Wyatt rushed to Travis's side and said, "C'mon, guys, let's go, we're outta here, this is fucked, this is bullshit, we're gonna—"

"Hey, Billy."

Wyatt froze and stared down at the impostor.

The last time he'd heard his name spoken by that voice, it had come from a dying man.

The man smiled, spread his arms expansively, and said, "Some crowd, huh?"

The crowd stared at him from the dead silence.

Wyatt said, "C'mon—all you guys—we're leaving."

Travis stared at the man beneath them dumbly, the way he sometimes stared when he'd had too much of everything.

"But you haven't finished the song yet," the man said.

Wyatt thought, It's not Johnny, it's not, it's—

"That's our favorite song."

No, it can't be Johnny, he's gone, he's—

"It's why we wanted you to come."

Dead, he's dead, I saw his body. I saw it!

"So we could hear our favorite song."

"Johnny," Travis groaned, "God, Johnny, Johnny, what're you—you're supposed to—I thought—"

Wyatt grabbed Travis, groaning, "Let's get outta here, this is just some kind of—"

Travis pushed Wyatt away and tried to take off his guitar but tangled his hands in the strap, dropped it, and hit the microphone stand, knocking it over. Feedback whined through the auditorium. Travis got on his knees to get closer to the man as Buddy, Elmo, and J.J. stared from behind their instruments, frozen, stunned, and confused.

"Who are you?" Travis rasped.

"C'mon, man, I'm Johnny."

"What is this? Who *are* all these people?" He waved at the darkness.

Johnny laughed. "Your fans. *Our* fans. The people who bought our albums, came to our concerts. The people who followed us all over the country from one gig to another, man, our . . . they're our followers. They followed me. But, hey, what'm I alone, huh? I need a band, man. That's why you guys're here."

Travis's eyes swept over the faces, young and gaunt, with their long hair and beads. He slapped Wyatt's shin and hissed, "Houselights, turn up the fuckin'—"

"No, Trav, you don't wanna do that yet," Johnny said soothingly, the way he used to talk to the groupies who came backstage as he ran a long narrow finger along the curve of a breast. "Why don't you just play s'more. You want, I'll come join you."

Travis laughed, but it was cold and tremulous and edgy. His features looked stretched to their limit as he looked up at Wyatt, then clamored to his feet, screaming, "Fuckin' lights, man, turn on the fuckin' lights!"

He brushed by Wyatt and ran off the stage, where Leverett stepped before him and said, "Mr. Block, you might want to—"

Travis pushed him aside, shouting, "Outta my way, you fuckin' maggot!" He found a bank of levers and began throwing them at random.

Leverett rushed over to Wyatt and said, "May I have a word with you outside?"

"What the hell's going on here, what's—"

Leverett grabbed Wyatt's elbow and squeezed hard. "Outside, Mr. Wyatt."

Light began to fill the auditorium, first in a far corner, then just over the stage, then in the center.

Buddy's voice rose in a shrill, laughing shriek and his stool toppled; a cymbal crashed as he kicked it going down.

Elmo staggered in circles, crying, "Get me outta here, I wanna get outta here. How the fuck d'ya get outta here?"

J.J. simply stared.

Wyatt jerked his arm away from Leverett and looked out at the audience. As the lights came up, endless faces appeared, all staring up at the stage. As the light grew brighter, the features of those faces changed.

Skin whitened and some of it disappeared. Lidless eyeballs stared out of deep sockets. Hair gave way to peeling scalps. Necks thinned. Lips frayed.

And they were everywhere. Below the stage and above it.

Johnny smiled up at Wyatt, skin a bluish white, shiny black hair gone, toothless and gaunt.

"Oh, God!" Travis screamed. "Oh, Jesus! God, oh God!"

Johnny spread his arms as he looked over at Travis and said, "Play for us!"

The crowd raised its hands, and long narrow bones tore through fleshy sheaves as the fingers curled into fists and the skeletal arms began to pump, pounding the air as the crowd chanted again: "'Wild Horse'! 'Wild Horse'! 'Wild Horse'!"

Wyatt's stomach was roiling and whatever was in there would be coming out soon, as the auditorium was filling with an awful stench, a thick, throat-closing stench that made Wyatt think of fat, buzzing flies.

Leverett grabbed his arm again and, with surprising strength, pulled him off the stage, past Travis, who was crawling on his hands and knees, face wet with tears as he stared out at the ocean of corpses calling for another song.

Wyatt was led forcibly down narrow concrete stairs, at the bottom of which was a metal door with an exit sign over it. His mouth had been hanging open in wordless shock, but now he turned to Leverett to demand some explanation, but instead—

Wyatt cried out in horror.

Half of Leverett's skull was gone. The left side of his face was raw meat. Only one eye was left in the white, puffy face.

Wyatt blubbered, "Whuh-what—I don't, I-I don't—how did you—"

The good half of Leverett's mouth smiled and he said, "My son did it. With a shotgun. When I tried to take away his Jagged Edge albums."

Leverett turned Wyatt around and threw the door open. "There's no place for you here, Mr. Wyatt."

Wyatt felt a foot on his ass and was kicked hard into the night. His face landed in dry, cool dirt.

He heard traffic.

A plane went by overhead.

The door didn't slam behind him . . . and yet he couldn't hear the chanting voices.

Wyatt stood. He turned.

He stared for a long time at the charred and skeletal remains of the old burned-down Chase Coliseum.

John L.
Byrne

HIDE
IN PLAIN
SIGHT

It was Jax's idea that they call themselves the Werewolves, his idea of a joke. A smarmy, sarcastic, even dangerous thing to do, but then, that was Jax.

They'd been playing the clubs for five years—a long time for any band. With their harsh, undisciplined sound they should have broken out, or faded away within the first year. Rise and fall was usually meteoric, but for the Werewolves, neither. Instead, a day-to-day drudge, town to town, club to club, making just enough to pay for lodgings, keep their equipment in shape—they'd abandoned the smashed guitar riff after the first three months; too expensive—feed themselves, with money left over for recreation. For Jax Ryker, that meant as much coke as he could push up his nose and, as he put it, all the groupies his tongue could handle.

Jax was lead singer, a shrill-throated shrieker commanding enough decibels to make ears bleed, with or without the massive amps the group hauled with them. He was proud of that fingernails-on-chalkboard voice that gave the Werewolves their sound. Not distinctive enough to propel them out of the lower arcs of the club circuit, but enough that they hung on where others fell by the wayside.

They were experiencing something of a revival, if a group that had never made it big-time could make a comeback. The werewolf killings did it; morbid interest in the group rose with the grizzly murders plaguing Los Angeles for months now. Fifteen were dead so far, so little intact it was impossible to tell the gender. Papers and TV newscasts were full of it. The press loved a good, juicy, bloody, serial killer;

this one was out to make Ted Bundy look like a Sunday school teacher.

They were not called werewolf killings out of sheer hyperbole. Real lycanthropy was not as broadly known in North America as in Europe and parts of Asia, but there was little doubt in anyone's mind that the perpetrator of these ghastly slayings was, as the big brains on TV liked to put it, *lycanthropus veritas,* a true werewolf.

So, even though the last reported werewolf killing in the continental United States had been forty years before the Werewolves picked that name for their group, they were riding high—relatively—on the public's resurgence of interest in such things. Jax Ryker had no problem with that, or with anything that increased their club dates and, therefore, his exposure to little girls.

He called them that no matter what their age—although many of them *were* legally minors. Jax didn't care. He'd gotten over delicacy about such things three years earlier, accosted backstage by a thirteen-year-old harpy demanding to blow him, there and then, in the dark, cold, concrete corridor, or she would start screaming rape. The worst four and a half minutes of Jax's nineteen years—or the worst minute and a half, maybe. Once she got going, she was very, very good; Misterogers was up and ready within seconds of that talented mouth setting to work. Since then, Jax was less concerned about the chronological age of his playthings; groupies were all thirty-six, birth certificates notwithstanding.

Like the one in front, that night.

They were playing an after-hours club, a low-ceilinged, cinder-block horror box with zero acoustics, zero air. Wide, deep, thick with smoke and sweating, lurching teenage bodies. Not as full as it might have been without the werewolf killings—one of the disadvantages was people staying home at night, parents careful that wandering progeny were in bed when they were supposed to be. Slim pickings tonight, but Jax scoped out a few likely candidates, firm little asses and jiggly titties bouncing to pounding rhythms.

Then he saw her.

She was alone. Jax kept an eye on her, saw no male attached to her. Several put the moves on, while Jax watched—she was a babe and a half by anyone's scale—but she put them off, kept standing there, three feet from the edge of the band's riser, staring at Jax. Twice he made eye contact, felt electricity jump between them. Yeah, she was a *tasty* one.

Jax assessed her as he sang. She was tall, lean, long-legged, big-bosomed. Black leather slacks tight enough to tell her religion, black T-shirt taut across breasts, nipples big as the tip of Jax's finger. Eyes big and dark in a broad, high-cheekboned face. Jet black hair glistened in the strobes. Lipstick crimson, lips full. Once in a while the tip of her tongue came out to touch those dark lips. Misterogers barked.

She was still there when they finished their first set. Jax tossed the microphone to Jimmy Fish, the drummer, jumped off the riser, crossed to her. Teenyboppers pressed in. Jax told them to fuck off; he was looking for meat a little more ripe tonight. He planted himself before the dark angel.

"Hey, beautiful," he said, summoning the sneer that experience told him made the girls crazy for him. "Your old man know you're out all on your lonesome?"

She smiled, teeth bright. "You don't look like the kind of man who'd be bothered by details like that."

A heavy metal record howled from the club's audio system, filling dead air while the Werewolves were on break; Jax could hear the woman as if she were whispering into his ear. Her voice was low and husky; up close, her skin was smooth as polished marble.

"I'm not," Jax said, sneer twisting his narrow face. He shook his head, making the long auburn ringlets bounce about his bare shoulders; he'd torn off his T-shirt, tossed it into the audience during the third number. His pale chest gleamed with sweat, catching colors from the strobes.

She put out a hand, ran a long finger down the inner curve of his right pectoral, felt the tiny prickles where he'd shaved his copious chest hair. She lifted the finger to her mouth, licked the sweat away, took the digit in to the second joint. Misterogers bounced against Jax's jeans.

223

"How much longer do you have to be here?" she asked.

Jax glanced at the neon Miller Hi-Life clock over the bar away to his right: 3 A.M. They were supposed to play for another hour, but he said, "I can leave anytime you like, sweets. Somewhere you want to go?"

"I could use an escort home," she said. Something in her voice now, maybe fear, Jax thought. She was afraid to walk home alone, with the werewolf killer out there.

"Nobody to take care of you?" The sneer was in his voice now as well as his face.

She shrugged. "I had a fight with my boyfriend earlier tonight. By now he's gone back to his ex-wife. That's where he always goes when we have a fight. And she always takes him back, stupid bitch."

"Hey, I didn't ask for your life story, okay? You want me to take you home, maybe I want to make sure there's a reason I should make like the good little Boy Scout."

She smiled, lids half lowered over huge, dark eyes. The kind of eyes you should put fences around, Jax would have said, so people don't fall into 'em. "Oh, I'm sure there'll be a reason to do your good deed," she said. "Milk and cookies for the Boy Scout." She licked her lips again.

Jax grinned. She was not being subtle; that was the way he liked it. He much preferred to begin any conversation with the opposite sex with a simple "Wanna fuck?" than with all the bullshit verbal fencing. That was why he liked eager little groupies. He dropped his pants; they dropped to their knees.

"Lemme tell the group I'm cuttin' out," he said. Her face changed.

"Oh, I thought you were *in charge.*" Enough contempt in those last two words, Jax thought, to fill a senator's wife's report on the rock industry.

"Screw 'em, then," Jax said, putting the sneer back in his face and voice, grabbing her bare arm. "When I don't turn up, they'll figure out I'm gone."

They waded through dancing teenagers, found the exit, went out and up onto the street. The night was just cold enough to raise gooseflesh on Jax's bare chest. He regretted not stopping to grab his coat, that hot leather jacket with the band's name and snarling emblem etched in tiny metal studs across the back. The woman didn't seem to feel the cold; Jax wasn't about to complain. If this went as planned, he'd be plenty warm enough later.

"Where do you live, sweets?" He shifted his hand from her arm to her opposite shoulder, drawing her close. The curve of her breast pressed against his flank, firm and high. Too good to be nature's own, Jax thought, but he had no problem with silicone.

"Three blocks down, two over," she said.

"No problem." He raised a hand to hail a cab, but she caught his wrist.

"Can't we walk? I feel like some air."

Jax frowned. Her body was a long, soft warmth against him. Misterogers was aching in his confinement. But . . . what the hell. He could play her game for now. She'd pay the price later, with interest.

They walked, the avenue blackness punctuated by pools of flickering yellow from the streetlamps. Now and then a vehicle passed; once a police car cruised by them, slowly, driver peering out. Jax sneered; the cop moved on.

"Looking for the werewolf," the woman said. She had no name yet, not that Jax cared much. As long as she had the proper working parts, it didn't matter what she called herself.

"You think that's for real, huh?" Jax said, sounding dismissive of the whole business. Of course, she believed the stories—the legends were long, the facts incontrovertible— but he was the big hero tonight, walking the little lady home through the dark canyons of L.A. He'd play the part to the hilt, until he got bored. Then . . . he smiled, licked his lips in unconscious imitation of her.

"Oh, yes, I think it's real. My grandfather was from Europe. He told me all the stories, when I was a kid. About the werewolves. The *loups-garous,* he called them."

"What's that, like, Italian?"

"French. My family is French." She turned her head, eyes bright in the artificial light. "My name is Antoinette Mercier. Tony to my friends."

Jax nodded. He didn't offer his own name; she knew.

They walked from one pool of light to the next.

"Gran'père told me all kinds of stories, about how the werewolves came down from the forests in the full moon, carrying away young men and women, children. For weeks after that, the people would find bodies, scattered over the fields around the villages, torn apart, drained of blood, until each one was accounted for. Then the next full moon would come, and it would start again. And the worst part . . . they weren't wolfmen, like in the movies. They were more human-looking. Sometimes hard to tell from a regular human being, except for their body hair, and the eyebrows. But even that was subtle. The full moon didn't *change* them; it just made them *powerful.*"

As they cleared the pool of light, Jax looked up. In the thick city sky, haze magnified the moon, a blurred copper shield just above the skyline. Last day of the full moon, they said on TV. Jax was almost counting the minutes. Tomorrow would bring an end to the fear, for another twenty-eight days.

Tony shivered. Jax pulled her closer, playing the hero. He shifted his hand from her shoulder to her side, tracing the curve of her breast with his fingertips.

"That's the way Gran'père told it," Tony said. "We turn here."

Narrow residential street. Jax had seen pictures of old L.A., when these little row houses were the edge of the city, coral pink faces bright in the clear, blue-sky sunlight, tall palms growing on immaculately manicured lawns. The lawns were gone now, street-widening projects devouring grass and trees, stucco faces grimed by the fumes and dirt of the roads they now crowded close against. No lights in any of the windows they passed. Streetlights spread wider apart, the pools of light they shed becoming more precious. Tony pressed in close to him.

Sounds of traffic dwindled, nothing moving on this side street but them. Jax was aware of their isolation. Each house butted up against the sidewalk, a gate set into the wall, access to the door on the side of the house. Some of those openings had barriers, wrought-iron gates, doors. Others were dark mouths, deep-shadowed, perfect for hiding—who knew what? Jax smirked in the darkness. Nothing *he* need fear, anyway.

They crossed an intersection. Not much moonlight now. Half a block farther down she said, "Here we are."

A small, stucco box distinguished from the others only by its number. She pulled a long, flat key from her pocket—no purse or bag, Jax registered—unlocked the tall, metal, barred gate of her side passage. Jax followed her through. There was a light fixture over the door, bulb gone.

"Sorry about the dark," Tony said. "Bulb's been out since I moved in five months ago."

"Moved in from where?" Jax asked, filling dark silence, not really caring.

"Midwest," Tony said. "Chicago." The same key opened the door. She stepped aside, let Jax enter.

Through the door, Jax found a narrow hall decorated with pale green wallpaper. A few pictures were in what looked to him to be antique frames on the left wall, either side of a single door. Two other doors stood to the right.

Tony stepped in, closed the door. The house was warm, dry. There was a faint smell carrying dim memories. Potpourri, Jax thought, grimacing at the nostalgia.

"You want something?" Tony asked. "I don't have any, you know"—a quick sniffing sound, tossing her head back—"but I've got wine, beer, coffee."

Jax decided he might like to be good and sober if he was to take full advantage of the next few hours. "Coffee."

"Living room is through there," Tony said, nodding to the first door on the right. "Make yourself at home while I get it going."

She vanished through the opposite door. Jax glimpsed a small, bright kitchen as she turned on the light passing through; the door swung closed behind her. He opened the door to the living room—a sliding pocket door, it took a moment of ineffectual tugging to discover—and went in.

Dark, but in the light from the hall he saw a standing floor lamp to his right, and he pulled the dangling chain. Yellow light flooded out of the shallow, broad shade, painting the room with warm tones, chocolate shadows.

A friendly enough sort of room, Jax thought, surprised by what he considered its middle-class ordinariness. A couch on the left-hand wall, low and deep, chair on the far wall by a small table covered with books. A fireplace behind the table, obviously never used, the mantel likewise the repository of cloth- and hardbound volumes of all shapes, sizes, colors. On either side of the fireplace, two narrow bookcases rose to the ceiling, also filled. On the floor, a dark oriental rug displayed cross-eyed dragons; thick, brown drapes bracketed the only window, to the right. Jax closed them, after a glance at the street.

He crossed to the fireplace, leaning over the low table to inspect the titles of the books. Various subjects, unrelated. Dry, philosophical tomes that didn't match the image he was building in his mind of Tony Mercier. Novels he'd never heard of, years out of print. The overall effect was of the kind of books he'd heard you could buy by the yard, to fill space.

"No, I haven't really read any of them."

Jax turned. Tony was in the doorway, hands raised above her head to lie flat on either side of the jamb, hips cocked right, head left.

"Huh?"

"I haven't really read them," Tony repeated. "That's the first thing everybody asks, when they see my books: 'Have you read all of them?' I haven't. I've just sort of, I don't know, *collected* them over the years."

She crossed to the couch, sat, patting the cushion next to her. "Coffee should be ready in a couple of minutes. Come, sit."

Jax dropped down almost on top of her.

She smiled. "Aren't you afraid I'll bite you?"

Jax barked a laugh and said with absolute confidence, "No. You're not the werewolf killer."

"And neither are you, whatever you call your band." She leaned closer. She had to bring her arms together to support her upper body. The curve of her shoulders made her V-necked T-shirt bow open. Jax fixed his eyes on pale hemispheres hiding in subtle shadows.

Tony leaned in close. Jax caught her strong perfume,

mingling with coffee aroma wafting from the kitchen. Tony draped her left arm across the couch behind Jax.

"Does it make you nervous to be alone with me?" Tony asked.

"No," Jax said. "Well, yeah. A little." He was not sure why. It was not Jax Ryker who had anything to fear.

She laughed, but it was not a mocking sound. Jax would have punched her in the mouth if it had been. Punched her senseless and finished their evening as he damn well pleased. Not so satisfying without her reacting, screaming—he especially liked it when they screamed—but better than nothing.

"I like you, Jax I'm very glad you walked me home." She pressed her lips against his, for a moment. A dozen tastes and sensations exploded across Jax's sensibilities.

Tony leaned back to sit on the edge of the couch. Her shirt had ridden up a little, showing him her smooth, flat belly. Jax reached out, ran the back of his knuckles across her skin, hooked his fingers in her belt.

"I'll go see about that coffee," she said.

"Tony . . ."

She settled back on the edge of the couch. "That's the first time you've used my name since I introduced myself, Jax," she said. Her tone indicated pleasure at the small event.

"About that boyfriend of yours," Jax said. He'd pinpointed the source of his uneasiness. He was in no mood to be interrupted. "If he comes back tonight . . ."

"I don't have a boyfriend, Jax."

Something cold reached out a thin, moist finger, ran it down the last half dozen vertebrae of Jax Ryker's back. "You . . . ?"

"I made that up. I'm sorry. I didn't really mean to deceive you, but I had to be sure. The name of your group, your style. I wanted to know for certain you were . . ."

"A Boy Scout." The sneer came back to his lips.

"Not a rapist, or a werewolf." She laughed again. "Let me get the coffee."

Jax sat back on the couch, arms along the back, knees wide apart. He smiled into the empty space between his long thighs, imagining Tony kneeling there, head bobbing. Imagining the feel of her hair in his hands when he grabbed her, pushed her head down. Women hated head-grabbers; that was why he liked being one.

"Jax . . ."

He turned toward the sound of her voice, toward the door. She stood as she'd stood before, hands upraised, hips cocked, head tipped.

Naked.

Jax tried to swallow; there was no moisture in his mouth. "Holy shit . . ." Her body was more spectacular than he'd let himself imagine.

She moved to his side on the couch. Her eyes shone into his, pinning him. "You want me, don't you, Jax?" It was a plea, as if this astonishingly beautiful woman—she really did seem more and more beautiful with every thud of Jax's heart—was not confident of her own sensuality.

"Yeah," he said, the word small and stupid, insufficient to the emotion it represented. He felt out of his depth, strangely virginal before her shimmering sexuality.

Her body was long, lithe; curves caught the soft ocher light, shaped it into subtle arcs, shadows. Her breasts were large, firm, and high; nipples dark turrets. Her belly sloped away as she leaned forward, drawing down into the dark V of close-curled hairs the same ebony as the rich mass on her head.

"And you can have me, Jax. I want you to have me," she said, leaning over him, almost on top of him, without the support of her arms. Then her hands were at his belt, loosening it, unfastening his jeans, pulling down the zipper.

Her lips came down on his, butterfly wings brushing sensitive flesh. Once, twice, a third time, before her mouth closed on his, her tongue pushed through, coiling with his own.

Jax was transported. Strength flowed out of him. He wanted to lift his arms, seize her, crush her. Most of all he wanted to get his hands on those amazing tits. Feel the pressure of hard, dark nipples against his palms. Roll the engorged flesh between thumb and fingers.

She kissed him, fingers splayed across his bare chest. She slid her mouth away, to the flesh of his throat, licking and kissing along the curve of his neck, the hollow above the collarbone.

"Say you want this, Jax." She looked into his eyes; Jax felt the last ounce of his strength fade away. It took every effort to speak.

"I want this. I want you."

Her face went down again, teeth nipping his nipples.

She straightened, lifting her right breast, guiding the nipple to his mouth. Huge! Jax felt himself an infant again, suckling at his mother's breast. All the imprinting of those seminal moments flooded back. He sucked hard, drawing supple flesh past his teeth, releasing it to slide over the sharp edges of his incisors.

"You want it all, don't you, Jax?" Her voice was different. Jax looked up into her face. Distortion in her mouth? As if she'd pushed her tongue behind her upper lip. But she couldn't speak if she'd done that, and she did speak. "You want everything I have to give you, don't you?" She spoke without parting her lips.

Jax let the beautiful breast slip out of his mouth. "Oh, yeah," he said. "Oh, yeah . . . please." Foolish to phrase it so, but he was not in control anymore. He was a little boy longing for the special treats this strange, pale woman offered.

She tore at his clothes, ripping away slacks, underwear. She left his boots on, dark oblong shapes drifting in and out of focus at the edge of his vision. Her mouth went back to his chest, licking, kissing, moving down, down, across the plane of his belly. When she reached the junction of his legs, there was little work for her. Misterogers was fully aroused, blood from Jax's pounding heart hardening his flesh.

Tony bent low between his thighs, drawing her tongue along the big, fat vein standing out in hard, sharp relief.

"It was so nice of you to walk me home," she said. "So nice of you to protect me from the werewolf." Again her voice sounded odd. He thought it was because she did not pause between the licking and the words, somehow doing both at once, teasing and tickling him, making him jump, shivers running through him. Speaking at the same time. *What was she saying?*

"A pity there *aren't* any werewolves. Not really." Using her lips now, taking him deep inside her. Cool. He would have expected her mouth to be hot, but it was cool. Almost cold.

"No werewolves, but the ones we sometimes make ourselves," she said. Jax was not following her words; the universe collapsed into the motion of her mouth, her hands moving up and down his bare flanks, cool, caressing. So cool. Not just in contrast with his own heat. His skin burned, but hers was ice.

"Once people know there are vampires," she said, "it's easy enough to convince them of something else. Something more fearsome, to a primitive mind. A man who transforms into a wild, savage wolf."

Jax was at the edge. He could not guess how long she had been manipulating him, kneeling on the oriental rug, breasts against the insides of his spread thighs, mouth working, speaking, working, tongue, lips, teeth.

Teeth. Wrong. Curled around him.

He tried to lift his head. No strength.

"Make people believe in werewolves," Tony said, from a long way away, "and they will be on the lookout for werewolves, hunt werewolves. They kill poor fools who have too much hair, eyebrows that grow together. Like yours, Jax."

Jax could not think, concentrate. Building orgasm pushed everything else out, out to the boundaries of creation and beyond, until his back arched and the surge came up as he had never felt it before. As he stiffened in ecstasy, he felt Tony's teeth sink deep into his blood-glutted flesh.

"Jesus Christ," he shouted. From somewhere came the strength to jerk his head up, to look down the wobbling length of his body into Tony's eyes.

Not dark anymore. Bright red—the red he saw bubbling and gushing from twin punctures on either side of his subsiding shaft. Tony opened her mouth, pink froth around her teeth, semen and blood mixed. Blood trickled out, two slender droplets, one from each corner of her mouth, drawing dark lines, turning her face into a grotesque caricature of a ventriloquist's dummy.

"There never have been werewolves." The distortion of her mouth was caused by the enlargement of her canines. They were an inch long, gleaming bright white in the yellow light. "We made them up. Made them up so we could prowl and prey unmolested. People don't look for vampires when the bodies are torn apart as if a wild animal had been at them. They see the signs, the old signs we planted in their brains, and they think 'werewolf.'"

"Please . . . don't . . ." Jax could not find strength enough to speak the rest.

Tony smiled her horrible fanged smile, crawled up the length of him—how long her arms and legs! How skeletal! She kissed him. Jax tasted mingled blood and semen. His blood. His semen.

"You said you wanted it all," Tony said. She placed her hand flat on his belly, pushed the long nails up under the arch of his sternum. She drove her fingers deep, wrapping them around his pounding heart, twisting.

This time there *was* mockery in her laugh.

| Thomas Tessier | ADDICTED TO LOVE |

This man I work for, he is very, very powerful," Mr. Garcia explained solemnly in his deliberate English. "Cali cartel."

"I understand, but—"

"You know of Cali cartel? Good. So if I return to Colombia, bang, I am dead man. Bang, bang, bang, bang, my wife and also my children are dead." Mr. Garcia now dared to rest an elbow on the desk, as if physically consolidating his imaginary gains. "So we must stay here."

Neil Jensen said nothing for a moment. He felt as if a huge rock had settled on him. It was that time of the afternoon, when the day's work caught up with him and his mind began to turn numb with quiet despair. Neil's eyes vacantly scanned the large room. It was filled with identical government-issue desks, and at every one of them similar minidramas were being played out.

Too long, too long. Neil felt he was going stale, drying up from the outside in. He had started working for the Immigration and Naturalization Service nearly six years ago. At first he saw it as a temporary position, something to do after college to earn a living while he sought a better job in the private sector. But then he'd found that he rather enjoyed this kind of work. It was a challenge, meeting people from all over the world, trying to help them solve their problems.

Over the years, however, Neil had gone through the emotional cycle from concern to weary indifference. There were simply too many people, and they all had tragic or terrifying tales to tell. But there was little Neil could do for them. Half of his job was processing paperwork, while the other half consisted of formulaic explanations of why they couldn't stay—why, after all their appeals had been exhausted, they would have to go back home, regardless of where that might be.

You didn't really meet these people; you merely listened to them, and then you turned them down. Neil had been forced to say no to almost every nationality and occupation, including teachers from Tanzania, electricians from Ireland, bakers from Jordan, and nurses from Guyana. Now he would do the same to a nervous little accountant from Colombia.

"Colombia is a functioning democracy," Neil said. "What you are basing your claim on is not political oppression but a threat of criminal persecution, which, I'm afraid, does not fall within U.S. guidelines for discretionary consideration."

Mr. Garcia had expected this. He was not alarmed, although a line of sweat did appear at the top of his forehead. He argued politely, as they always did at first. Neil listened and tried to appear sympathetic, but pain and inevitability crowded his brain. He shuffled the first few pages of the open file on his desk, so that the plaintive photographs of Mr. Garcia's handsome wife and sturdy children were no longer staring up at him.

Neil's apartment was a converted attic in an old brick house on the Lower East Side. He had taken a chance on it a few years ago, when the immediate neighborhood was a no-go battle zone with drugs and gang violence on every corner. But new money had begun to infiltrate the area, and things were no longer quite as bad as they had been.

Neil had redecorated the kitchen, bathroom, and living room himself, at his own pace and as money allowed. His bedroom would follow in due course, and then the small second bedroom, bare now but for a few storage cartons and suitcases.

The real centerpiece of Neil's home life was his living room. He had refinished it with one thing in mind: music, specifically rock and roll. The furniture Neil chose was neither too angular nor too cushiony, and there wasn't much of it. The wallpaper was carefully selected to enhance the room's acoustic properties, and the lines of the gleaming hardwood floor were disrupted only by a single Turkish rug that wasn't very large. The stereo components and speakers were at one end of the rectangle, the chairs arrayed at the other.

Neil's collection numbered between seven and eight hundred albums and about two hundred compact discs. He also had several dozen cassettes, but they were mostly bootlegs unavailable in any other form. Neil considered tape to be an inferior medium, so he limited his purchases of it to essential items.

In spite of its size, his collection covered a narrow range. Neil believed that 90 percent of worthwhile rock and roll was British, and the music on his shelves reflected that. He was not sure why it should be so—Neil was from a fairly quiet suburban town on the outer fringe of Westchester County, after all—but it was undeniably true that British groups sang to him, spoke to him, and reached him in so many ways that relatively few American bands did. London, Liverpool, Manchester, and Newcastle were holy cities in a desolate landscape to Neil.

Because rock was *the* thing in his life. While other people went home every day to husbands or wives or lovers or families, he came back to his music. It never let him down. Crank it up, and it would blast away the scaly encrustations of anguish and anger that had grown over him during the day. It would dissolve all his calluses and vent the poisonous depression that clouded his mind. Music *was* his life away from work. It was, increasingly, Neil's only life. Once, a few years back, he had seen Pete Townshend on TV, talking about how people kept telling him he couldn't simply stop, that he had to keep writing songs and releasing new albums, because so many people needed and depended on the Who. Listen to them, Pete, Neil thought at the time, because they're right. I'm one of those people. If you couldn't come home to another person, a lover, say, then music was a pretty good alternative.

It was not that Neil hadn't tried to install *someone* in the inner precincts of his life. Any number of women had been to his apartment over the years, and most of them had even spent an hour or two in his bedroom. But then they left, they always left, and Neil was saddened—if not truly sorry. Women were such strange creatures! Their minds seemed to run in just a few deep ruts and little else got through to them. They were concerned about their jobs, their careers, their bodies, and their futures. Well, sure, who wasn't?

Most of them liked rock and roll, but their interest in it usually never went beyond the superficial. They couldn't discuss the Dickensian range of the Kinks, or the subtle use of rhythm by New Order, or Irish motifs in the music of Thin Lizzy, and he had yet to meet a woman who could identify T.V. Smith. Maybe it was just Neil's bad luck. He wanted nothing more than to meet a girl he could love, who loved him and who shared his deep response to music. He would even settle for someone willing to learn.

Neil had mixed feelings about the Bombsite Boys. They were from Coventry, and the English rock press had reported excitedly about them. Neil picked up their first album on import, *Crossed Nails,* and he found definite signs of talent in their ability to create melodic lines and to write pungent lyrics. They had not yet achieved breakthrough commercial success, but in Neil's mind that was good. Too much too soon was usually a recipe for quick burnout, and the English were notorious for pronouncing a band's obsolescence when it had barely gotten off the ground. He liked the Bombsite Boys just enough to keep an occasional eye on their progress, and when the group made its first New York appearance, at the Marquee West, Neil was there.

It had been a rough day at work, so he was not in the best state of mind. To make matters worse, the Bombsite Boys came up short in live performance. The vocals were submerged and there were too many neopsychedelic instrumental digressions that went nowhere. During the break, Neil nursed a beer on the fringe of the bar crowd, wondering if he should stick around for the second set or go home early. That was when he saw Cheryl.

"Like the band?" Neil asked.

"They suck."

"He's not worth it."

"Who?"

"The guy you're mad at."

"How would you know?"

"Just looking at you, he can't be."

Neil had learned that in the land of the oblique and evasive, anything like a direct compliment was often received as a welcome surprise. Cheryl glanced at him for the first time, and Neil saw signs that she was beginning to relax a little.

"Do you like English groups?" Neil asked.

"Some."

"Like who?"

She shrugged. "Public Image. The The."

Neil felt a tremor of excitement. If she could appreciate groups like those, she had to have some musical intelligence. He bought her a drink, reminding himself not to get his hopes up too high. He had been disappointed before, every time. Her body was as slender as a boy's, but she displayed lovely long legs beneath an incredibly tight microskirt. Cheryl also had a rather pretty face, and her dark hair was fashionably disheveled. Neil led her to a less crowded corner of the club. She still looked angry and bitter as her eyes restlessly scanned the scene, and she acted as if she were doing Neil a favor by talking to him, but he remained moderately optimistic.

"Ever hear of T. V. Smith?" he finally dared to ask.

"Sure. The Adverts. *Crossing the Red Sea.*"

Neil's face lit up with a broad smile.

"I don't know why I'm doing this," Cheryl complained.

"He's not worth thinking about."

Neil, a step behind her as they climbed the narrow staircase to his apartment, kept his eyes fixed on the wonderful movements of her snug little fanny.

"Not him," she corrected. "I mean you."

Neil chose not to respond to this somewhat deflating remark. They reached the third floor, which was vacant and gutted pending eventual reconstruction. The unknown owner apparently could not get the money together at this time. The longer it took him, the better, as far as Neil was concerned. It meant he could play his music as loud as he wanted without disturbing anyone. "The next floor is mine," he told Cheryl as they turned on the landing.

"What I mean is, you remind me of my older brother."

"Nothing wrong with that," Neil said, thinking that it added a little Freudian spice to the situation.

"But I don't like my older brother. He's a creep and I hate him," Cheryl said.

"Well, I'm not him."

They came to Neil's apartment and he fished the key out of his pants pocket. Cheryl seemed surprised.

"You live in New York and you only have this one little lock on your door?"

"It's not little, and it's the best," Neil explained. "And the way I had this steel door set in place, anybody who wants to break in will have to dismantle the whole wall."

"Wow."

She said that again a moment later, when they entered Neil's living room. She slipped off her shoes, dropped her handbag, and approached his music collection reverently.

"What do you want to drink?"

"Got any vodka?"

"Sure."

"Skip the glasses," Cheryl said. "Let's swig it out of the bottle, back and forth."

That wasn't exactly Neil's style, but he thought it might be fun as he headed toward the liquor cabinet in the kitchen. There was an unopened bottle of Stoli. When Neil brought it into the living room, he found Cheryl sitting back in the leather armchair, her legs dangling delightfully in the air. Well, they were her best feature, and she was obviously proud of them, and Neil was not one to avoid an attractive view. Cheryl snatched the bottle from his hand and took a healthy gulp, smacking her lips.

"Play something," she said.

Neil took a cautious belt of the vodka and placed the bottle on a small table. He saw her reaching for it again while he looked over the rows of albums.

"Do you like Joy Division?"

"When I need a downer."

Neil interpreted that as a no. "How about Morrissey?"

"He's an even bigger mope."

"The Nipple Erectors ... the Snivelling Shits ... 999 ..."

Neil continued to recite names, waiting for Cheryl to choose one she wanted to hear. But she ignored him. Her attention just now was on the vodka bottle. He was pleased to notice, however, that she had moved from the armchair to the sofa.

"Horslips ... Siouxsie ... A Guy Called Gerald ..." God, he was roaming all over the musical landscape, and yet Cheryl failed to respond. "Or maybe you'd prefer Dusty Springfield."

The crack went right by her.

"Got any Cure?"

"Everything."

"They'll do," Cheryl said, adding needlessly, "Loud."

Glad you didn't want a downer, Neil thought as he loaded one disc. Then he reminded himself to avoid sarcasm—it never went over well with women, for some unknown reason. He slid onto the couch beside Cheryl as the music began to fill the room. She put her head on his shoulder and stretched her legs out.

"Great sound."

"Thanks."

Cheryl offered him the bottle and Neil tilted it carefully to his lips. She was definitely buzzed, no doubt about that, and nothing wrong with it either, but he intended to go slow with the vodka. Experience had taught him that there was nothing quite as bleak as getting blitzed with a stranger, passing out, and waking later in the early morning, a couple of sick dogs who didn't even know each other. No sex, no contact, no future, nothing, just an elusive aching sensation. Neil stroked Cheryl's hair lightly, but she didn't react at all.

"One thing about this group, their—"

"Hey!" she interrupted, bolting from the couch. "You've got a set of earphones."

"Headphones," Neil corrected. "Yes."

Cheryl crossed the room quickly and took the headphones from their hook by the stereo rack.

"They look expensive."

"They are."

About two hundred dollars' worth, Neil recalled. A touch of extravagance, since he seldom used them. But there were times or moods when the only thing that would do was to get the damn music pumped straight into his brain.

"Can I try them?"

"Sure. It's plugged in."

"Wow, it's got a long wire."

"Yeah, I bought a twenty-five-foot extension cord for it, so it reaches anywhere in this room and the kitchen."

"I love earphones."

"They can be fun," Neil admitted.

Cheryl unwound the coil of cord behind her as she came back to the couch. She sat down, slipped the headphones on, and smiled blissfully as she sank back. In somewhat of an afterthought, she draped her legs across Neil's lap. Abruptly, she pushed herself up far enough to reach the bottle of vodka, took a hit, and then settled back, still clutching the liquor. Cheryl was on a solid buzz now, and lost in the music.

Neil smiled, trying to convince himself that she really was worth a little indulgence. He put one hand on her leg, caressed her thigh tentatively. Cheryl did not seem to notice, so he slid his hand higher. So much leg—gorgeous. But she still did not react to his touch. Neil moved so that he could stroke her cheek and neck, and then her eyes opened briefly. She flashed a smile at him, but he thought he saw something of a smirk in it, too, and then she drifted away again. Neil felt sad. He brought his hand down and searched for her breast. There it was, firm but small, with a tiny, worn-down eraser nub of a nipple.

It had never been this bad before. Never when he had anyone in to visit had he felt so lonely. They were listening to music, but not precisely together. It was as if they were two different people in two different worlds, connected only by the same stereo system. It shouldn't be this way. Touching her body like this, intimately, should be a pleasure and a joy, and at the same time she ought to be touching him. This way, Neil felt uncomfortable, as if he were groping someone who was vibrating in a coma.

Cheryl startled him again, jumping up suddenly. She pulled off the headphones and smiled at Neil beseechingly. He found it offensive and transparently manipulative, even before he learned what she wanted.

"You know what I'd really, really love to hear?"

"What?"

"Do you have 'Addicted to Love'?"

Neil sighed. "Yes."

"Oh, please, please, play it for me."

"All right," Neil said wearily.

"God, I love that song."

He hated that song, and he could hardly believe that Cheryl wanted to hear it. Robert Palmer didn't speak to him, or sing to him, not at all. The only reason Neil even owned a copy of the *Riptide* disc, which contained that song, was because his mother had given it to him as a gift. It was flying high in the charts back then, and some clerk had convinced Mrs. Jensen that it was the perfect choice. Neil had listened to it once, out of a sense of duty, and to confirm his dislike. Now he loaded it, checked the track listing, and tapped the number-three button on the front of the player. Only that song, he thought, and only once.

"Not with the—"

But as Neil turned around he saw that Cheryl already had the headphones on again. She was sitting on the floor, in the middle of the Turkish rug, eyes closed, body rocking to the music. Even worse, she had the remote in her hand, which could only mean that she intended to repeat the song . . . again and again.

Neil stomped past her. He sat down on the couch and drank a large measure of Stoli. Anybody who liked this song couldn't possibly understand Public Image Ltd. That was for sure. He had to suffer it, though, because she was his guest. And because he was unlucky enough to own it in the first place.

When Cheryl's hand flicked out with the remote, Neil decided that *he* was not obliged to hear the song a second time, so he got up and strode back across the room to the amp. He turned off the speaker switch, so the hated song could only be heard through the headphones. The sudden silence was wonderful, but by the time he had the bottle in his hand again he realized that Robert Palmer's voice had been replaced by Cheryl's.

She was singing along with the music. Like most people who are fooled by headphones, Cheryl emitted a bizarre sound, a thin, restrained, high-pitched whine. It was in the same county as the original tune, but that was all that could be said for it. Neil sipped the vodka while Cheryl rocked on in her own little heaven. Then he went and put the bottle in her free hand. It worked, and the hideous, strangulated droning was interrupted long enough for Cheryl to chug a generous mouthful. But then it resumed, and she also kept the vodka.

Neil knelt down behind her on the rug. He kissed her neck and put his arms around her, letting his hands come up just under her breasts. It would be nice if she leaned back against him and purred contentedly—but Cheryl didn't acknowledge his presence. Her body continued to rock and shake with the music, bumping Neil in the face with her shoulder and the headphones. He backed off, went into the kitchen, and poured a glass of bourbon.

He was very disappointed. She had all but lied to him about her taste in music. Then she had tuned him out completely, going into a trance with Robert Palmer. He could yank the plug on the headphones, or he could simply change the disc, but that would be rude. It would surely annoy her, and then she would leave. Neil knew that he'd be even more miserable if she left. He felt angry just thinking about it. They always left.

When Neil finished his bourbon, he went back into the living room. The only thing that had changed was the level of vodka in the bottle Cheryl held. Music is for sharing, Neil thought as he walked toward her. That's all he wanted to do, share some of his music with her. It was right that she was there, but everything else had gone wrong.

He was annoyed. Neil took up some of the slack in the cord. If he yanked it out at this distance, he might pull over the whole rack. That would get through to her, but in the end he would only hurt himself and his equipment. How many times had she listened to that goddamn song now? Four? Five? Six? Amazing. He felt so alone. It was outrageous—especially since, aside from her brain and her breasts, she offered a pleasant enough package; her legs in particular were the best he'd seen in a long time.

Neil looped the cord over Cheryl's head and pulled it tight around her neck. She squawked and jumped, dropped the bottle, and tried to hit him. Neil held on fiercely. The headphones slipped off and the tiny sound of that song wobbled in the air. Cheryl's legs kicked frantically—God, they looked so good, the way they jerked and thrashed. Neil couldn't take his eyes off them.

It was so good to come home and find her there. Waiting for him on the couch, her head resting back in one corner as if she were dozing and her legs stretched out, parted, her skirt hiked up daringly, she was definitely someone to come home to. A tough day, a string of difficult Haitians, disappeared behind Neil when he closed the door and saw her. He played the Smiths, repeating "Girlfriend in a Coma" three times. Well, it was kind of a funny song at that.

On the first day, Neil removed her patterned tights, and her legs looked even better. On the second day, he took off Cheryl's skirt. By the third day, she'd been through rigor and it was not hard to rearrange her any way he wanted on the couch. Neil gave it some thought. He bent one leg at the knee and propped it up, but it didn't look as nice as he had expected. He ripped off her flimsy panties and adjusted her so that one of her legs stretched along the seat while the other one splayed up onto the top of the couch. Now, that was a saucy pose! Later, Neil placed the girl's hand firmly in her crotch.

By the time he got home on the fourth day, she had lost some of her charm and was showing signs of ripeness. He knew it would be impossible to get her off the premises. He went downstairs to examine the ceiling on the vacant third floor. It was cement, he noted with satisfaction. This place must have been a mill in the old days, something like that. Perfect.

Back upstairs, he stood in the doorway of the spare bedroom. He knew he would have to do something to keep her from ballooning up and becoming unbearably offensive. Messy, but not a problem, thanks to the garbage disposal unit in the kitchen. And the wide floorboards would come up easily.

It was sad. Neil had enjoyed her company, her so-decorative presence. She had a much better attitude toward Joy Division now. But the worst part was that once she was safely tucked away, the old loneliness would begin to creep back into Neil's life. There was no question of this crime happening again. It could not; it simply could not. But for the sake of order, at least, when Neil took the pry bar into the spare bedroom, he began his work in the farthest corner.

John Shirley | FLAMING TELEPATHS

He saw them, that first time, because they were invisible.
Spaced noticed holes in the crowd. Places, in the packed
nightclub, where no one seemed to be standing—yet people
moved around those places as if someone were there.
Something on the floor no one wanted to step on, maybe. He
could imagine that, all right. But there seemed to be a lot of
those empty spaces. And they were weirdly . . .
symmetrical. So he pushed his way over to check it out. That
was Spaced: He was an investigator. A questioner. A looker
as much as a participator. That's what set him apart from
the rest of the scene—and what endeared him to the others.

Saturday night had packed the Black Glass. The place was
dimly lit, walls glittering with a constellation of chrome,
covered with studded black leather (they'd spent all their
money on that, which was why they had only one functional
bathroom; just one of many flagrant violations of city
codes). As gum-chewing roadies put the guitars in place on
their racks by the Marshall stacks and laid out the cables,
getting the medium-small stage ready for the first band, the
deejay spun a cut from Motorhead's *Orgasmatron,* speed-
metal shaking the floor, walls, and ceiling like the monstrous
amplification of a steel foundry, the sounds of some sinister
and sentient factory aglow with molten metal.

A cauldron spouting sparks—Incandescent arcs—went
the lyric Spaced made up in his head. He wrote lyrics for
people, but made his paltry living writing rock reviews and
performance art crit for *Ear Spear* magazine. He wasn't a
musician himself; he didn't like being onstage. He didn't

246

like anyone to look at him that closely. "The shamans of the rock stage act out our psychodramas for us, exorcising our demons," he'd written the previous week. And Velcro Cunt, reading that, had said, "Spaced, you're too intellectual about it to enjoy it. Or maybe, like, you're—I mean, no offense, but—maybe you're like too old to really get into it. The scene."

Thirty-one? Too old? "I get into it, my way."

"You're too . . . I dunno . . . too *Warhol*, man."

"No, uh-uh, Warhol was a drone. You wanta come home with me, I'll prove I'm not a fuckin' drone."

"One of these days I'm gonna take you up on it and you'll be scared shitless."

That was last week. This week, it was a hot September in Los Angeles—hot in the Black Glass, too, because it was crowded. The Iron-Ons were headlining, with a Texas band called the Strokers opening. The Iron-Ons had a following that was almost bloodthirsty in the intensity of its devotion. Working his way across the room, Spaced sniffed the air, sifted impressions, getting the tone of the scene tonight. Like a coyote sniffing the air at a water hole. Tonight was a screwed-down steel spring, tensility precariously in check. The air was heavy with tobacco smoke and dusted pot; you had to be careful where you breathed if you didn't want a PCP buzz. Spaced stood well out of the way as a bouncer rousted an ice smoker, shoving him ahead by the collar, the guy dropping his glass pipe to shatter on the floor as he tottered out the door, his eyes jumping like riffled cards—buzzed on ice, smokable methedrine. That and crack weren't tolerated here. Acid was back, though, and Spaced picked up LSD and MDA vibes in the giddy animation of the faces around the edge of the crowd, the kinetic excess of the dancers moving on the dance floor. He watched a tall, anorexic girl in a neoprene bikini moving like the hand of a Wild West show performer trying to get some serious snap into a bullwhip.

But most of the crowd was simply drunk, or trying to get there.

And there was, as ever, the C and S crowd. Clean and Sober. Over by the open exit door where the freshest air was, dancing together. A growing contingent, the C and S—like Spaced and like Velcro Cunt, Gigger, and Benny—they took no drugs, nor drank. Their rock trancing was inwardly induced.

More than once Spaced had found himself wondering how he could thrive so in this hot, dark, and claustrophobic miasma of posturing. And he'd answered himself: It was like asking how you could enjoy being in a woman's vagina, a place that was also hot, moist, and swollen with self-declaration.

He edged on through the crowd, and got to one of the holes, the place where no one had been, where everyone stepped around—and there *was* someone there. Twenty feet away you couldn't see the guy, though he wasn't particularly short. Up close, he was suddenly *there*. The first of them. Conspicuous for his lack of movement, like a concrete piling in a surging sea.

He was a pasty-faced man with thin hair. The hair was pattern-balding in an odd way; like shrubbery on a veldt, it wisped here and there. For some reason, the odd hair really struck Spaced, though the club was a showplace for odd hairstyles. *This* hair just grew like that. It was like the guy had a disease. And then the pasty guy looked over at Spaced—looked from his fixed niche in the crowd like an oppossum Spaced had once seen in the park, watching him from inside an overturned garbage can. The dude's eyes bugged a little; his lips were slightly too red. He wore a suit.

The suit, in itself, wasn't so strange. You might find any sartorial style at the Black Glass. There was punk—now in the form of thrash and speed-metal, Metallica modalities—and there were head-bangers and there were neopsychedelics and there were people who affected the austere look that might fit into a really anal, severe sort of suit—the Eurotechni look.

But this guy's dull white suit fitted him badly, and not the kind of David Byrne bad fit that was deliberate. So Spaced thought: Must be from the Liquor Control Commission, maybe watching to see if they serve underage here. I oughta warn Alfredo.

The deejay was playing The Pixies' "Wave of Mutilation" as Spaced went to find the Black Glass's owner and warn him that some sort of bureaucratic dweeb was going to hassle him. But then, thirty elbow jabs and grunting pushes later, he came on another hole in the crowd. With a woman in it, a woman with a scarf on her head, who could have been the twin sister of the first dweeb. And moving between a couple of bodyguards, pushing through to join her, Spaced saw the Reverend Carlyle.

No, really. Reverend Carlyle, king of Channel 47.

Carlyle was scarier than Swaggart, scarier than Jim Bakker, because he was smarter and slicker and didn't make mistakes. He wore the same kind of vaguely western three-piece suits the usual televangelists wore, the requisite slick of oil pulling back his widow's peak, the sparkling smile and those deep-set eyes that gave out reassurance like a key pumping beer. He had, too, the slight southern accent, a folksy way about him, a big gold Rolex, and a wife who had hair as fixed and calcified as a snail's shell. He had that televangelist's avuncular earnestness; he had the televangelist's Pentecostal strut when he was working the stage. He had all of it. But he *didn't fuck up*. He was never caught buggering choirboys, or skimming money. Every investigative reporter in the state had tried to dig up some dirt on him, and aside from the conspicuous consumption of his lifestyle—which seemed to be a necessary part of his image, a sign that God was rewarding His Beloved—they came up with zilch. Even the IRS sheepishly admitted Carlyle was legally clean.

And here he was right smack in the middle of the Black Glass. Like a crucifix laid in a vampire's coffin.

"Van Helsing was a fucking killjoy," Spaced muttered, staring at Carlyle, forgetting about warning Alfredo, the owner.

That's when the first band started. The Strokers were flailing out a southern boogie with a hard metal edge, fueled by speed and Jack Daniels. It was hard and fast enough; it went over okay.

Spaced watched Carlyle, who watched the band and the

crowd. After a while, Spaced felt someone watching *him*. He looked around and saw the hairless dweebs, their eyes fixed on him. A smell like rotting dog food gusted through his head—and a pain that was like a sentient migraine, coming in waves from two directions.

He staggered away and shoved toward stage right. The music was so loud here near the speakers he felt like he was pushing through the amplified sonic medium as well as through people. And then he was backstage, behind the stacks. Gary, one of the skinhead bouncers, glared, then relaxed when he recognized him. He waved Spaced on through, and went back to doing a homemade tattoo on his arm with a small knife, a bottle of ink, and a bottle of alcohol. Puncturing in the pattern, some kind of crude zombie face; dabbing the ink onto the stipples in his skin; wiping with the alcohol.

Spaced felt his head clear as he moved through the warren backstage, past the stammering scribbles of graffitied press-board walls, thinking, What the fuck was that? That thing I felt out there . . . Drug flashback? He'd been clean for years. . . .

He found Velcro Cunt, Benny, and Alfredo sitting around with the drummer of the Iron-Ons in the cramped dressing room; the drummer and Alfredo, on the couch, were nursing bottles of Dos Equis from a Styrofoam cooler. The room smelled of stale beer, sweat, old smoke, and pee, much of the stench from the slumped, legless, and colorless couch that barely fit between the walls. A broken, much spray-painted mirror leaned against one wall. A naked light bulb, spray-painted pink and blue, on the ceiling, gave the air a carnival tinge. Benny and Velcro were, of course, drinking mineral water. Spaced accepted one gratefully and squatted on the floor next to them. The Strokers throbbed in the walls like a poltergeist presence, but it took only a little shouting to be heard in here. "You won't fucking believe who's out there!" Spaced said. "Did you see him? Carlyle?"

Alfredo squinted at him as if that would help him hear better. He was a tubby Hispanic dude about forty, with flat-topped black hair and little designs shaven into the sides of his head over his ears—guns crossed with dollar signs. "Whatchoosay? Who?"

"The fucking Reverend Carlyle! From TV!"

"Shit!" Velcro Cunt let her mouth drop open and stay that way. "Bullshit!"

"No way bullshit. It's the man."

She shook her head. She was a white girl, but she had her hair cornrowed, each row a different color. Her face was made up livid, lips black, her clothing more or less like Minnie Pearl's. She lacked only the hat with the tag. And she had big, battered motorcycle boots which looked oversize on her long, skinny legs. She'd met Spaced at a meeting— Narcotics Anonymous—and got him into the Black Glass scene because of the sizable contingent of Clean and Sobers here. They insulated one another from the drugs and booze.

But they believed in rock and roll.

"Carlyle from TV?" she asked, incredulous. "You mean rock-'n'-roll-is-the-Devil's-drillbit Carlyle? You mean every-performer-in-every-rock-band-is-a-living-demon-disguised-as-a-man Carlyle? *Here?*"

"You got it."

The drummer was drunk and skinny, his pimply chest bare; he had two mohawks that were grown extra long at the front to droop over his face, clear down to his chin—moth antennae. He giggled and shouted, "All right! Fucking Carlyle! I'll give him some fuckin' Devil's music, ma-a-an!"

Alfredo groaned. "Oh God, no. It's not a joke. He's picked us for some reason—he'll have parents picketing us, police in here, narcs—" He said some more in morose Spanish.

Benny frowned thoughtfully. Everyone waited to see what he would say. Whatever Benny said mattered. Benny had waist-length hair, half dead white, the other half jet black. A beard bifurcated in the same colors. Weathered cheeks from working at the docks. Sleeveless black leather jacket, rotting Levi's, and disintegrating tennis shoes. Fading biker tattoos. He also had a master of fine arts from Stanford.

"Motherfucker," he muttered. "Carlyle. It's funny, but it's not. Alfredo's right. He's gonna fuck with us. And some of us are going to die."

He said it in that weird, offhand way of his. Like he wasn't guessing. Like he'd seen it, somehow. Now and then he said something like that, and it always came true.

That's when Gary burst in. "They got TV cameras out there!"

The doormen hadn't recognized Carlyle, had naturally assumed that Alfredo would be happy with any TV publicity. And Carlyle's crew was already set up. Nerdy, mustachioed camera- and soundmen wearing earphones and carrying portable cameras. Expensive ones.

Carlyle had a mild-mannered but immovable-looking quartet of bodyguards standing around him, big beefy guys with sweet smiles and T-shirts that said, GOD LOVES YOU AND THE DEVIL HATES YOU. TAKE YOUR PICK! —REV. CARLYLE

Spaced and Velcro stood to one side, staring, as Alfredo argued with Carlyle over the shoulders of a wall of beef. They couldn't hear a lot of the argument through the heavy sonic weather generated by the band, but Spaced could make out that Alfredo was saying he had the legal right to oust anybody he liked, and Carlyle replied, "If you've got nothing to hide, why forbid the cameras?"

Alfredo returned to his friends, looking defeated. "No matter what I do, he'll make it look bad. Let 'em see, fuck it. Let 'em take their pictures. Let 'em see it's just dancing and a little drinking. Mostly." He turned to Gary, who'd stayed at his elbow. "Check the dressing room, make sure nobody starts fucking back there. No one gives head in the bathrooms. And no drugs anywhere. Have the bartenders check everybody's ID, even if they got gray hair and no teeth."

"I know some eighteen-year-old ice-smokers fit that description anyway," Velcro said.

Spaced was watching Carlyle and his crew. The cameramen were getting shots here and there, but only in a token, sporadic way, and Spaced had a sense that Carlyle was waiting for something specific to come down. What did they think was going to happen? The days of slam-dance riots had passed. Mostly. The crowd was too polyglot for that now. The scene in the early nineties was a confluence of countercultures. All of it lumped into alternative music, alternative performance. You could see an Irish radical folk band opening for a CountryWestern–punk band opening for a speed-metal group. Mope rockers opening for rap. There were some clubs on the Strip that specialized in pure head-banger heavy metal, with all the trappings of comic-bookish diabolism—so why had Carlyle chosen the Black Glass?

Must be the Iron-Ons. The lead singer had told a newspaper recently that he thought Carlyle was the reincarnation of Adolf Hitler. And the guitar player had said the band was paganist, worshiped "The Goddess." Which was a *white* magic thing, but not to Carlyle. . . .

All of this flashing like rock-video shots through Spaced's head as he watched the televangelist. Carlyle was taking notes, smiling with celestial smugness, charged even now with the charisma that had made him God's Sole Rep for this planetary franchise—for, anyway, millions of viewers. He was cornball to look at, but gave off something appealing, Spaced decided. Like some Disney hero playing Daniel Boone. And maybe something more. A translucent numinosity. . . .

They watched each other from their two camps. Alfredo's contingent and Carlyle's. There was some mugging for the cameras, of course. First among those was, naturally, Bulb.

He called himself Bulb, but Velcro and Spaced called him Dimbulb. A gaunt, heavy-metal rocker with a flaking Motley Crüe T-shirt and ancient black leather pants beginning to rip at the seams, long, desiccated black hair with a white lightning-bolt streak, six earrings on each ear, a skull nose-stud, and teeth that should have been growing at the base of some swamp cypress. His tattoos Carlyle was certain to take an interest in. Dimbulb lived next door to the club and had decided it was his true home. He had spurts of intelligence and long, dry wastes of vacuity. Lately, he had attached himself to Spaced and Velcro Cunt.

"Hi, Cunt!" he said, jogging up from the dance floor, reeking of sweat and various smokes. "Got a butt?" He was completely oblivious to the annoying congruity in his use of "cunt" and "butt."

"Only the one I sit on," she said. "And don't call me

'Cunt.' I told you. It's Velcro Cunt, or Velcro. Show some respect."

"Oh yeah, yeah, sorry. You don't smoke either, huh, Spaced? No. Hey, what you think of this moron Carlyle shit, huh, you guys?"

Velcro shrugged. Spaced stared at Dimbulb, sadly, thinking about cliques, and belonging, and not belonging. Theoretically, Spaced deplored cliques—and yet he had drifted into one. And true to cliquishness, he really didn't want Dimbulb in on it. The guy was a social abscess. He was the kind of guy who'd adopted head-banger rock, easy heavy metal form, with its charge of adolescent symbolism, as a replacement for having a genuine self-image, a sort of oily, toxic repellent against the swarming mosquitoes of self-dislike.

On the other hand, the Black Glass was a place for outsiders to come in from the cold. Even Dimbulb. And when there was a band bringing down something they could all connect with, Dimbulb, dancing in the melee, would briefly be on the same wavelength as Spaced and Benny and Velcro. . . .

Velcro, now. Velcro was a painter, with a ramshackle loft on the ragged edges of downtown L.A.; she knew who she was, and her gear, her look, were an amusement for her, and nothing more. And the music was a way to get into the trance, the true high that the Clean and Sobers talked about. She was a complex person, with an intricate mesh of light and dark places in her, all interlaced with humor. Quietly, Spaced adored her.

"Look," Spaced said, pointing, talking quietly to Velcro. "You see the hole in the crowd? Go check out who's in there."

"Somebody sitting on the floor? Or a midget? A punk leprechaun?"

Spaced laughed at the idea of a punk leprechaun. He attempted a brogue. "Faith, and the IRA'll bring anarchy to the U.K. on this fine spring marnin'!" They laughed and Dimbulb did, too, blinking in confusion. Spaced went on, "No, really—check it out."

She went. And came back. "Who was *that?* It's like if you

254

looked up 'dweeb' in the dictionary and they had a picture —it'd be that guy! He looked at me so weird! God! I felt kind of sick, too . . ."

"Yeah, did you get a feeling like—"

But just then Carlyle started his own show. The band had just finished its encore—a strained encore that they'd done on the provocation of only a smattering of applause—and the deejay'd put on some John Hiatt folk rock to give the ears a rest when Carlyle took his opportunity to do some kind of broadcasting preamble.

The makeup lady was dabbing at his face, but he waved her away and pointed at the camera. The smile came on like someone had thrown a switch. "Thanks, Joey," he said into his hand-mike, gazing benevolently into the camera.

"Huh?" Velcro began. "Joey?"

Spaced figured it out. "They're going to tape a big intro for him later, someone saying, 'And here he is, the Salvation of the Nation—the Reverend Jimmy Carlyle! Live from a remote location at . . . blah-blah-blah.'"

"At a 'den of satanic worshipers,'" Velcro said.

"Yeah, all *riiiiiight!*" Dimbulb crowed. "Satanic wor—" The rest was lost when Alfredo came up from behind and clapped his hand over Dimbulb's mouth.

"Shut up, *cabrón.* Things are bad enough."

Not that Dimbulb would know real satanic worship if it bit him in the ass. . . .

Carlyle was saying something about his show, *God's Country,* coming to you remote from a nightclub in a very, very dark corner of Los Angeles. "It's funny how things as they will be in the next world," Carlyle said gravely, his sad, we're-talking-about-lost-souls expression drooping on his face, "are sometimes foreshadowed in this world. Look around me at this nightclub. The red lights, the darkness of the place, the faces painted to look like creatures out of nightmare—friends, have you ever seen anything that looked more like Hell?"

Groans, jeers, catcalls from the listening crowd. Some applause. Velcro yelled, "Yeah, Alabama, man! Now, *that's* Hell!" More laughter: Alabama was Carlyle's home state.

He went on, looking around at them pityingly. "The truth

is painful, and they cry out against it, in their own way. This is a rock and roll club—that's right, the Reverend Jimmy Carlyle has gone to a rock and roll club! God brought me here tonight to witness. I have had a vision, a dream—like something out of Ezekiel, it came to me. God, my friends, is going to show Himself to us tonight, as He showed Himself at Sodom; as He showed Himself to the Romans when he struck down their empire. I know this as surely as I know that I will and must pray for every soul in this . . . well, they call this place the Black Glass. Very appropriate. Black glass, like the blindness of sin. . . ." He began to pace between his bodyguards, back and forth, loosening his tie, working himself up a little. "I don't know what the sign will be . . . but it comes tonight, friends, and it comes here . . . and it comes to signal a new epoch, a new era. Brothers and sisters, if you have someone you care about who may not be watching tonight, call them up, cry out to them that a miracle is readying itself, is about to be shown to everyone who chooses to tune in to Channel 47. . . . Get them in front of that TV, because what they are going to see tonight will change their lives—and confirm their faith!"

Alfredo was flat-out gaping at Carlyle. "What the fuck is this man babbling about?"

Carlyle was reading from the Bible now. From Timothy 4:1. " '. . . in the latter times some shall depart from the faith, giving heed to seducing spirits—' " He paused to look meaningfully at a girl in a leather miniskirt and extravagantly cleavaged chain-mail halter top. " '—And doctrines of devils. . . .' " And he looked up from the Bible, raising a hand as if to exorcise demons, showboating onward, churning up a mighty wake as he told his well-worn tales of rock 'n' roll debauchery and debasement. He cited teenagers who'd killed themselves while listening to heavy metal rock 'n' roll. He referred to heavy metal bands with diabolic symbols on their album covers. He spoke, without a trace of humor, about playing records backward to hear satanic messages subliminally imprinted. He mentioned so-called sociological studies from Christian universities linking rock and roll to rape, pornography, teenage pregnancy, and drugs.

He explained simply and clearly that rock and roll was a favorite tool employed by Satan's demons.

Dimbulb could hardly contain his glee; Alfredo was about to have Dimbulb thrown out.

And then Benny walked up to Alfredo, and the little group of people—Alfredo, Velcro, Spaced, and Dimbulb—turned to listen. Benny brought people into alignment like iron filings on a magnet.

"There's violence in the air here," Benny said.

Alfredo looked around. "A riot? I don't think anybody's taking the guy seriously, they're all making fun of him—"

"No. I meant *literally* in the air. You'd better stop the show, close the place down. There are—"

He was drowned out by a slow-motion explosion: a single earthshaking chord struck by the lead guitarist of the Iron-Ons. They were a white band except for the black lead singer, who was shooting for a place in the new black/white hard-rock crossover niche "Living Colour" had carved out. But with a harder edge, a Bad Brains vibe. They had their share of black leather; they draped long black silk scarves from their wrists. Just because Carlyle was out there, the lead singer had mockingly painted diabolic makeup on his face. And just because Carlyle was out there, the crowd, mocking Carlyle's down-home mythology, now erupted into their best imitation of damned souls dancing in Hell. Carlyle smirked with secret knowledge, and his cameramen grinned, getting it all.

Alfredo slapped his forehead and groaned.

The tune steamrolled right into another, even fiercer rocker, the lead singer shrieking that he was going to butt-fuck each and every member of Congress personally because that's what they'd been doing to the rest of the country for years . . . Carlyle's soundmen getting all this tinder for Moral Majority outrage. . . .

Benny was looking around with fierce concentration. At those holes in the crowd.

That's when Dimbulb jumped up onto the stage, in rock frenzy's own spontaneous audience participation, bounding awkwardly around up there, ignored by the band, dodging the roadies, making the . . . oh, shit . . . making the sign of

257

the Devil with his hands . . . looking like a rock 'n' roll
Richard Ramirez. . . .

Fuck! Spaced thought.

The camera pushing through to get a better shot of
Dimbulb. Bulb leaping off the stage at the camera. The
crowd laughing, opening up around him, giving him room to
dance, as the band did a cover of the old Iggy tune "TV
Eye."

And there was a TV monitor Carlyle's crew was using, to
one side, Dimbulb babbling in fake-demonic tongues and
leering and shoving his face right up the camera lens,
looking like a real jackass, playing right into Carlyle's hands;
another camera zooming in for a closeup of Bulb's biceps
tattoo of the down-pointed pentagram with the Devil's
head.

And over it all, Carlyle shouting a reading from Revelation: ". . . And the beast was taken . . . and them that had
received the mark of the beast, and them that worshiped his
image. These both were cast alive into a lake of fire burning
with brimstone . . ."

There was something in the air . . . something more than
dope smoke and tobacco and sweat steam . . .

A pressure. A certain suppression, a distancing of sound.
A transparent weight. A sentient and minatory heaviness.
The thunder of the band became impossibly muffled by the
sheer denseness of this presence. Until it focused . . . on
Dimbulb. Closing in on him like an invisible spotlight.

And he burst into flames.

As Carlyle read from Revelation: "'. . . and fire came
down from God out of heaven and devoured them . . .'"

There were screams. The band stopped playing. Spaced
pushed through to Dimbulb, who was writhing in the flame,
clawing himself on the floor, enveloped in blue and red fire.

Spaced's first thought was that someone, some agent of
Carlyle's, had doused Dimbulb with gas. But there was no
gas or kerosene smell, and anyway . . .

Anyway, the burning was coming from within Dimbulb's
flesh. He was burning *around* his clothes, at first, his skin
giving out little tongues of flame like the holes on a gas-stove
burner, his own flesh consuming itself—reddening, black-

ening, bubbling, breaking into tarry flakes edged in oozing red, the Devil's-head tattoo distinctly marked out with lines of red flame. . . .

A cameraman shoved in close to suck all this into his thirsty lens.

People ran for the doors, screaming, while others tried to douse the flame with pitchers of water. Alfredo grabbed a coat and threw it over Dimbulb.

Dimbulb's eyes . . . Walter's eyes . . . That was his real name, Spaced knew—Walter. Dimbulb was Walter Duffe. Walter Duffe was looking out from eyes that were about to boil out of his skull. Just one look of bone-deep imploring escaped from those eyes, and then—they boiled over.

Nothing would put out the fire. It came from inside him—it had, anyway, been seeded inside him—and there was no escaping it. It consumed him like an ant under a magnifying glass's concentrated sunlight, in less than a minute.

The lead singer shrieking into the mike, accusing Carlyle of having set Dimbulb on fire, yelling to the crowd to get Carlyle, hold him down, throw his ass in jail, send him to the fucking gas chamber—

And then the lead singer of the Iron-Ons burst into flames.

Fell screaming onto the stage. The other members of the band threw down their instruments—the guitars and bass making an amplified clangor and thrum and whine, as if the instruments were wailing out an inarticulate electronic fear—took off their coats and ran to the singer. And when they extended their hands to put the coats on him, to try to smother the flame, their hands under the coats burst into flames. A chorus of screaming that could have been rehearsed . . .

They drew back—and the flames in their hands went out. They stood there with red, blistered claws, shaking and gagging and staring helplessly at the lead singer, who burned from within. He seemed to be trying to crawl away from the flames in some way—as if they were concentrated in his lower half, and his upper half was writhing to escape them. No one could get close enough to help him.

The pockets in the crowd that held the dweebs from Hell

259

had bellied outward, everyone pressed back from the two . . . forced back by a growing intensity of the same psychic pressure that had pervaded the room just before the attack. . . .

Oh, for sure: Spaced knew it was an attack. Knew where it was coming from. And when panic spread through the crowd, driving them toward the exits, leaving the dance floor empty but for Carlyle and crew and the wasted chiaroscuro of Dimbulb who was now just more of the dance-floor litter—Dimbulb lying there, shriveled charman glimmering with receding flames amid the beer bottles and cracked plastic cups and suspect puddles—Spaced was not at all surprised to see the dweebs remaining also, near the walls, staring at the stage. Symmetrical to one another, as if at two of the points of a pentagram. With Carlyle and crew in the middle of the dance floor—in the center of the huge, unseen pentagram. What unseen presences stood at the other points?

The makeup lady and the bodyguards had fled, too. Out of primal terror, Spaced supposed. They hadn't signed up for this. And maybe they were afraid God would look into their souls and see a certain damning hypocrisy. . . . The cameramen stayed. As if held by some will beyond their own, a telltale glaze on their eyes. . . .

The lead singer was clawing at himself on the stage; his movements became weaker. Burning out, in an accelerated parody of what rockers were supposed to do anyway. Exuding suffering like a scream of guitar feedback.

Alfredo and Velcro were somewhere in the background, shrieking at bartenders to get fire extinguishers and ambulances, and the bartenders were yelling back that the phones weren't working . . .

Benny was stepping up onto the stage.

The cameramen working feverishly to record it all, God's punishment of sinners through his Chosen One, the Reverend Carlyle . . .

Until Carlyle saw Benny. "Turn off the cameras," Carlyle said softly.

Benny knelt beside the lead singer. Put his hand through

the flames. The flames sucked away, back into the singer—
were gone. He stopped writhing, relaxed. Relieved, freed.
"I'm sorry I didn't quite wake to myself until you were
gone," Benny said to the dying man. "But you will be well
received. I've asked Jimi to receive you. Go, then. . . ."

A rasp from the guitar player. "Hey . . . my man . . ."
Recognition in his voice. And then he was dead.

Benny stood, and went to the musicians. Touched them
one by one. They gaped at their hands—which became
whole. Healed. Then Benny turned, strode to the microphone. Carlyle looking at him white-faced, his mouth
working soundlessly.

"Cease your invocations, Devil," Benny told him. Not the
usual way Benny talked.

What the hell do we know about Benny, anyway? Spaced
thought. Supposedly an ex-biker, rode in from New Orleans
with some biker club. But Alfredo had asked the prez of that
MC about it once, and the guy had refused to talk about
Benny. Would say nothing, nothing at all. Just turned
around and walked away, like he was trying not to look
scared.

And Benny just hung around, made soft jokes, drank only
the occasional glass of wine, jammed on bass and drums
with people sometimes . . .

And gave advice. People just found themselves asking for
his advice, and it always came out all right if you took his
advice, too. Spaced remembered a time he—

Whoa. Wait-a-minnut.

The dweebs were pointing their hands, extended before
them, at Benny. Benny was smiling distantly, his deep-set
eyes unseen except for the occasional glimpse of two evanes-
cent points of light needling from far back within the
sockets.

The cameramen, working under the direction of an
entirely different will now, had begun filming again. The
soundmen had begun recording.

Moving like sleepwalkers, the band, the surviving Iron-
Ons, picked up their instruments and began to play an R &
B thing in four-four.

Spaced recognized it. From an early ZZ Top album.

And Benny began to sing, with understated, bluesy authority.

The lyrics were something about how Jesus just left Chicago; he goes to New Orleans, turning the Mississippi into wine—and then he heads for California. The next line was blotted out as another sound erupted from another part of the room. The dweebs. Their mouths opened wider than any human being could open them, repudiating, with howls sirening from them, their heads spinning on their necks as if on turntables. . . .

Not howling inarticulately. It was a word. One word: *"Down!"*

As in—hold it down. Keep them down. As in suppression.

"DOOOWWNNNNNN!"

A black-light radiance issued from their pointing arms, the variety of energy that manifests itself as intrusion and rape and the hammer of repression, translated into its essence—

Striking at the stage.

Flames licked up around the stage. The stage caught fire—

The bass player screamed—

But, in a trance, kept on playing—

Velcro ran up behind Spaced, grabbed his arm and shouted, "Run! Run! Let's get outta here!" But he couldn't, and she clung to him, and they watched the fire growing—

But Benny was dancing. That was all. Dancing, a perfect living manifestation of the sound from the speakers as the band played on. Benny invoking something himself, and a gust of fresh, spring-laden air rolled outward from the stage—instantly snuffing the flames.

The wind pushed on, blowing outward, making Spaced and Velcro stagger. . . .

Blowing on to snuff, also, the illusion that enclosed the dweebs and Carlyle. The wind blowing their camouflage away like smoke. And they were exposed, revealed: The dweebs were repugnant things that fused man and worm, the slick gray boa-sized worms in them slithering greasily in and out of great holes in the manform, their forebrains exposed and protuberant, pulsing.

Carlyle, too, was exposed: He was a hideous creature weirdly contorted in on itself, like a scrambled semihuman Ouroborous—his body protracted and bent, defying bone, stretching down from the upper torso so that the head was *literally* thrust up his ass, pushing up through his body and emerging from a wound under his armpit. It was a snarling, demonic face that Spaced thought he had seen when he'd visited Paris—on one of the gargoyles adorning Notre Dame.

The thing that was once Carlyle shrieked in pain and fear and drew its head back inside its own body like a snail into a shell.

The band ceased playing and Benny spoke into the mike, looking into the cameras, pointing at Carlyle. And Benny recited from the Bible: "'And if any man shall say to you, Lo, here is Christ or lo, he is there, believe him not: for False Christs and False prophets shall rise and shall shew signs and wonders, to seduce . . .'" A verse from the book of Mark, Spaced remembered, quoting Jesus.

Then the dweebs, the flaming telepaths, ran and slithered to the creature that had been Carlyle, frightened children scurrying to their parent—leaving nasty wormtrails on the ground behind them—and Carlyle and the dweebs embraced, began to claw into one another . . . tearing into each other, as if tunneling to escape in one another . . .

Until Benny made a gesture, and spoke a Name, and Carlyle and his minions imploded in flame. Flame that looked like a film of a fire running backward, sucking in on itself, vanishing, taking Carlyle and the dweebs with it. Imploding them. A flash of light, and they were gone—vanished but for a black grease-spot on the floor.

Benny turned to a camera. Looking into it gravely, he said, "The Devil—the true Devil—hates rock 'n' roll. Strives to suppress it through his false prophets. The Devil hates rock 'n' roll because the Devil hates freedom, and freedom of expression and anything that unifies men. And

God . . . God loves music. All kinds of music. God thinks with music. And when God chooses . . ." He paused—then grinned, and shouted: *"God knows how to rock 'n' roll!"*

Acting on some inner prompting, a divine instinct, tears streaming from their eyes, the band suddenly thundered into a rock 'n' roll tune of its own construction, improvised and immaculate: an immaculate conception.

Some hidden fog machine billowed silvery smoke from backstage. The smoke rose up into a cloud around the band, hiding them for a moment, cloaking Benny—and then it receded . . . the band left glistening, still playing . . .

And Benny was gone.

Of course, there never was a fog machine backstage at the Black Glass.

All the courage that Spaced never knew he'd lacked was suddenly there when Velcro gave him a ride home in her old Dodge Dart. So he asked her what he'd always wanted to ask her.

And she said, "Goddammit, Spaced, I thought you'd never ask. I've been waiting two years, man."

"I asked lots of times."

"No. It wasn't the same. You never asked like you cared about me before. It was a jokey come-on, before. Let's go to my place. Your bed's too small."

She swerved the car into a U-turn.

And on the car radio, with the synchronicity that was never quite really accidental, came a song by the Call. It was called "Let the Day Begin." It was a song about love, about God and about hope. And it had a rock-steady beat.

CONTRIBUTOR BIOGRAPHIES

PAUL DALE ANDERSON

Anderson, a past vice president of the Horror Writers of America, is the author of *Claw Hammer* and *Daddy's Home,* two single-author collections, and numerous short stories for the horror press. He lives in Illinois where he has taught creative writing at the University of Illinois.

JOHN L. BYRNE

Byrne is the author of the horror novel *Fearbook* and a veteran comic-book writer and artist. His credits include *X-Men, The Fantastic Four,* and the recent revitalization of *Superman.* He lives in Connecticut.

NANCY A. COLLINS

Collins's first novel, *Sunglasses after Dark,* won a Horror Writers of America Bram Stoker award. A second, *Tempter,* appeared in 1990, and a third in the series is imminent. Collins, who lives in New Orleans, says her favorite bands are the Residents and Throbbing Gristle, and she claims to be the founder of the "dreaded antimusic girl group Vaginal Blood Fart."

Contributor Biographies

ALICE COOPER

Debuting in 1970, Cooper's makeup, dark-themed songs, and outrageous stage show made him an instant success. Songs like "I Love the Dead," "Prince of Darkness," and "Teenage Frankenstein" demonstrate Cooper's lifelong interest in horror. Cooper has recorded twenty-one albums in twenty years; his 1991 release, *Stoopid*, was his latest in a long line of platinum albums.

PETER DAVID

Best known as a comic-book writer of such series as *The Hulk* and *Star Trek*, David is also a prolific novelist, including a best-selling *Star Trek* novel and more than a dozen others. He works in New York.

DON D'AMMASSA

Rhode Island's D'Ammassa has been reading and reviewing science fiction and horror for more than thirty years, most recently for *Science Fiction Chronicle* and *Mystery Scene*. His first novel, *Blood Beast*, appeared in 1988, and his short fiction has appeared in several horror magazines and anthologies.

MICHAEL GARRETT

Garrett is the co-editor of the *Hot Blood* anthology series for Pocket Books, and the author of *Keeper*. He conducts regional writing seminars from his home state of Alabama.

RAY GARTON

Garton is a popular Californian author of cutting-edge horror novels including *Live Girls*, *Crucifax Autumn*, and *Trade Secrets*. His latest books are *Lot Lizards* and *Dark Channel*.

Contributor Biographies

R. PATRICK GATES

Gates, a native of Massachusetts, is the author of *Fear* and *Grimm Memorials* and several short horror stories. His third novel, *Tunnelvision,* is due out shortly.

JEFF GELB

Gelb has spent his entire working life in the music industry, first in radio and currently at the music trade publication *Radio & Records.* He is the author of *Specters* and the co-editor of the *Hot Blood* anthologies. Gelb lives in southern California.

BRIAN HODGE

Hodge is the author of *Oasis, Dark Advent,* and *Nightlife* and a frequent contributor to the top horror anthologies. The Illinois writer plays keyboards well enough to wish he "could steal the soul of Keith Emerson."

RONALD KELLY

Tennessee resident Kelly's novels include *Hindsight, Pitfall,* and *Something Out There.* He also enjoys writing fiction for the horror small press as well as major anthologies.

STEPHEN KING

King lives with his wife, the novelist Tabitha King, in Bangor, Maine.

GRAHAM MASTERTON

Before becoming a horror writer, England's Masterton was a rock journalist who indeed had the pleasure of interviewing Jimi Hendrix. Masterton says "Voodoo Child" is "not only a regretful tribute, but an imaginary obituary based on a real encounter." Masterton is the editor of the successful *Scare Care* anthology and has written more than a dozen novels of horror and suspense, including *Walkers* and *The Burning*.

RICHARD CHRISTIAN MATHESON

Born into an unparalleled writing environment, Matheson has been a professional writer for more than twenty years. The southern California resident has written for more than half a dozen TV series, scripted several films, and penned more than fifty short stories. His first novel, *Created By,* was published in 1991.

REX MILLER

Missouri's Miller recently concluded the Jack Eichord sextet of serial killer thrillers and the Vietnam novel *Profane Men* and is hard at work on a suspense novel and a police procedural. Once a popular Chicago deejay, Miller was rated one of "America's Top Ten Air Personalities" in the sixties.

BILL MUMY

Mumy is a lifelong actor who is well remembered as a cast regular on the sixties science fiction TV series *Lost in Space*. The California resident is also half of the recording duo Barnes and Barnes, of "Fish Heads" fame, and is a touring guitarist and songwriter with America and David Cassidy, among others. "The Black '59," cowritten with Peter David, is Mumy's first published short story.

MICHAEL NEWTON

The ultra-prolific Newton has seventy-nine books published, thirteen completed and awaiting release, and nine in progress . . . as of last Tuesday! A chief scribe of the Mack